The Complete
Master of Hounds
Collection

Other books by R. A. Steffan

The Complete Horse Mistress Collection
The Complete Lion Mistress Collection
The Complete Dragon Mistress Collection

Circle of Blood: Books 1-3
Circle of Blood: Books 4-6
(with Jaelynn Woolf)

The Last Vampire: Books 1-3
The Last Vampire: Books 4-6
(with Jaelynn Woolf)

Vampire Bound: Complete Series, Books 1-4

Forsaken Fae: The Complete Series, Books 1-3

Antidote: Love and War, Book 1
Antigen: Love and War, Book 2
Antibody: Love and War, Book 3
Anthelion: Love and War, Book 4
Antagonist: Love and War, Book 5

Diamond Bar Apha Ranch
Diamond Bar Alpha 2: Angel & Vic
(with Jaelynn Woolf)

The Complete
Master of Hounds
Collection

R. A. Steffan

Author's Note

This book contains descriptions of graphic sex and violence. It is intended for a mature audience.

TABLE OF CONTENTS

Master of Hounds: Book 1

ONE

"Throw him to the dogs."

Princep Kaeto, the emperor's son, waved a careless hand toward two guards holding a bound prisoner between them. The pair dragged the unfortunate man forward to the entrance of the royal kennels, where sounds of growling and scrabbling could be heard coming from within.

Caius Oppita, once a respected Legatus of the Alyrion Imperial Guard, stood at parade rest as the order was given, his eyes fixed impassively ahead. Gossip had been rampant in recent weeks concerning the steady parade of prisoners arriving at the royal compound, only to meet inventive and grisly ends on the direct order of the princep. The lithe young man with bound hands and a bag tied over his head was only the latest to confront such an unpleasant fate.

One of the guards addressed the master of hounds, who stood next to the kennel doors, his head bowed in groveling subservience. "Have the beasts been starved for a full week, as His Highness requested?" he asked formally.

The houndsman's shoulders hunched a bit further inward. "Yes—it is as my imperial lord has commanded. They are near-mad with hunger."

The guard nodded. "Then lead the way and hold them off while we toss this piece of garbage into the cage with them."

With a deep breath, the houndsman straightened his spine. He clutched the handle of the whip coiled at his side with a white-knuckled grip, as he entered the low building to complete his unpleasant task. The guards pulled their captive along, following him into the kennel's dark interior. Inside, the ominous growls erupted into full-throated baying, growing in pitch and intensity until the sounds filtering out to Caius and the other observers standing in the courtyard became positively frantic.

Caius fought down a wave of queasiness, not allowing it to show in either his face or his bearing. He'd been a soldier for twenty-nine of his forty-six years… had seen men hacked apart by swords, trampled under the hooves of warhorses, and dying of dysentery in the battle camps. Yet something about this casual cruelty still sickened him. If the talk making the rounds of the palace was accurate—and he had every reason to believe it was—then the only crime committed by the men being executed under Kaeto's hand involved their conception. The wrong seed had reached the wrong womb, resulting in the birth of another inconvenient bastard son.

A few moments later, the guards re-emerged from the kennel. The one who had spoken to the houndsman approached Kaeto and bowed low.

"The master of hounds will stay to watch until the beasts calm enough for whatever remains of the prisoner to be removed," he said, speaking over the din of howling and snarling. "I don't expect they'll leave much behind."

Kaeto made a dismissive gesture. "Let the creatures crack the bones and suck the marrow, for all I care. Leave the filthy whore-son to rot in the manure pile after they shit him out."

Caius continued to stare straight ahead, his expression granite. Stoicism was not enough to prevent him from becoming the next focus of the princep's attention, however.

"You disapprove of my words, Legatus?" Kaeto's voice held amusement, which was somehow even more galling than anger would have been.

I disapprove of your actions, Caius thought. *Not just your words.*

Aloud, he only said, "I prefer witnessing honorable death in battle to death by execution, Your Highness."

The dogs were still in an uproar, though he'd heard no sounds of human screaming. They must've gotten the sad bastard by the throat quickly. At least that would have shortened his suffering, if nothing else.

"Still a soldier to the core, eh?" Kaeto replied. His tone changed, becoming pointed. "Well, if not for certain limitations, of course…" He trailed off, flicking his fingers in the general direction of Caius' twisted left shoulder, where a blow from a battleaxe had mangled the muscles on his dominant side some years ago. "At any rate, Legatus, it's all for the best. I'm certain you've heard the rumors. We can't leave men like that walking around free, now can we?"

"Indeed, Your Highness," he said tonelessly.

Thankfully, Kaeto appeared to lose interest in the exchange when Caius failed to rise to the bait.

"Now," said the princep, turning to address his entourage. "I believe that's quite enough of *that* unpleasantness. Come. Let us return to the palace and see about procuring a meal—preferably one with less gristle than what the dogs are currently enjoying."

Polite titters greeted the tasteless joke.

Kaeto shot Caius a haughty glance. "You. Stay behind. Report to me when the thing is done and the remains disposed of—since that seems to be important to you. One *does* like to have someone they can trust keeping an eye on events."

Caius felt a muscle in his jaw twitch. "As you wish, Your Highness," he replied in a monotone, thinking that from the sound of it, the 'thing' had been done less than a minute after the cage door had slammed closed.

He stood stiffly as the princep, the guards, and the group of fawning courtiers removed themselves from the courtyard, presumably in search of less bloody entertainments. A short time later, he found himself alone except for the houndsman's apprentice—a boy of perhaps twelve or thirteen years of age, with a mop of brown hair and wide gray eyes.

Flies buzzed through air heavy with humidity and the musky smell of animals. With no one but the boy left to see, Caius closed his eyes, feeling the familiar pull of the skin around an old scar bisecting his left eyebrow. The barking inside the kennel had already died down to occasional whines and yips.

His eyes flew open when it unexpectedly erupted again, the sound of baying and growling followed closely by a man's high-pitched shrieks, growing in desperation only to be cut off abruptly. The fine hair on the back of Caius' neck prickled.

What in Deimok's name?

"Go see what's happening," he ordered the boy. It seemed decidedly unlikely that the prisoner could have survived the first round of canine frenzy, but apparently he had. Whatever the case, it sounded as though the unlucky man's time was finally up.

The apprentice gulped nervously and disappeared into the building, only to erupt from the kennel's doorway a few moments later like a cork shot from a bottle of sparkling wine. His face was pale as a sheet as he ran full-pelt across the cobbled yard.

"Sir, come quickly, *please!*" he begged. "It's my master, he's... he's—"

The words choked to a standstill, lodging in his skinny throat. Caius followed with a frown as the boy grasped his sleeve and tugged him in the direction of the cacophony coming from inside the structure. Unsure what he would find, he slipped his ceremonial sword from its sheath right-handed—aware on some level that the weapon would not be enough to fend off an entire pack of crazed hounds, should such a thing become necessary.

Cool shadows enveloped him as he slipped through the door after the boy. Caius blinked rapidly in the kennel's dimly lit interior, straining to see in any detail beyond the mass of dark, milling shapes behind a wall of metal bars. That was something, at least—the cage door was closed, and none of the dogs appeared to be loose. Beside him, the pale apprentice still clutched at Caius' left sleeve, but now the boy's frightened panting had descended into poorly stifled sobs.

Caius tugged his arm free, moving cautiously closer to the bars. As his vision adapted to the low light, he could make out a limp form being jerked to and fro in the middle of the snarling melee. It was vaguely human-shaped… but becoming less so by the second. Again, the feeling of nausea assailed him at the idea of executing someone in such a manner.

He started to turn to the boy, ready to growl at him to explain himself. That was when he noticed two of the hounds fighting over a braided rawhide whip, like pups playing tug-of-war with a length of chewed rope. His brows drew together, and he gave the large area beyond the bars a longer, searching look.

Where was the houndsman?

Now that his eyes had grown accustomed to the dimness, he could make out a second figure hunched in the far corner; back turned to the carnage. It… wasn't the master of hounds.

Dusky skin stretched across lean muscles. The figure appeared to be completely naked. His fingers twined through wild spirals and mats of dark hair, clutching at his own head as though that was the only way he could hold up its weight.

Twisted scars from a long-ago flogging crisscrossed his back.

Caius stood frozen for several moments, attempting to force the tableau into some sort of context. The hounds had left the prisoner untouched—at least beyond ripping away his clothing—and instead savaged their caretaker?

Even now, the animals continued to tear at the corpse, their muzzles coated with gore.

That the houndsman was dead was not in question… and Caius supposed the apprentice's hysteria made sense now. The boy had sunk to the ground behind him, his back pressed to the wall near the door through which they'd entered. He didn't beg Caius to stop what was happening. Any fool could see there was no point in even trying at this late juncture. Instead, the lad merely looked on with unblinking horror as the animals fed on what had, mere minutes ago, been his master.

A living person.

Practicality reared its head. "Is there another whip?" Caius asked. "We should try to get them off the body while there's still something left to bury..."

"No. Let them eat." The raspy voice came from the hunched figure in the back. The prisoner hadn't moved until that moment, but with those words, he let his hands slide free of his hair and looked over his shoulder at Caius. "They're starving. And since I imagine that man was the one who starved them, there's a kind of justice to it, I suppose."

Caius buried the prickle of unease running up his spine. "You. Why aren't you dead?"

The prisoner rose, a bit unsteadily. He seemed either unaware or uncaring of his nakedness as he turned to face Caius and walked toward him.

"I always had a way with dogs," he said. His voice sounded detached. Far away. Around him, the animals parted like water, making way for his passage as he approached the barred door. His chest rose and fell on a deep, unsteady breath. "It's been a while, though. Wasn't sure if I still had the knack or not. Guess I do."

Caius' sense of unease didn't lift, though its flavor shifted incrementally as he became acutely aware of the other man's body. The prisoner stood barely more than arm's length away from him, separated by the heavy iron bars. Caius judged him to be in his mid-twenties, though he looked older than that. Not surprising, after what had probably been years spent languishing in prison for the crime of being born an emperor's illegitimate son.

It was apparent from his skin color and his unusual hair that his mother must have been from one of the southern lands—perhaps Kulawi. His eyes were a rich brown shade, heavy-lidded and accented by dark lashes. His body was hairless except for thatches of black at his armpits and groin. There wasn't an ounce of fat anywhere on his frame, but rather than appearing frail, his arms and legs were corded with lean muscle and sinew. It was the body of someone who'd been used on the prison work crews rather than kept chained in a cell day in and day out.

When he spoke, his accent was provincial, but not unpleasant to the ear.

"So, are you going to kill me now, soldier?" he asked, sounding more tired than fearful. His eyes landed rather pointedly on Caius' drawn sword. Around him, several of the hounds looked up from their grisly meal, and Caius heard the low rumble of warning growls as the beasts sensed the sudden change in atmosphere.

Caius' disquiet over the entire situation coalesced into a sharp, burning point beneath his ribcage. "Do you even know why you're here?" he asked, in lieu of answering the man directly.

The prisoner still looked unutterably weary. "Some nobleman or the other couldn't keep his prick where it belonged, and nine months later, there was me. No clue why someone suddenly decided to turn me into dog meat after ten years of wasting perfectly good food and clothing on me in prison, though."

Caius blinked.

Good god.

The poor bastard didn't even realize who his father was, did he?

An idea both terrible and wonderful in its simplicity percolated through Caius' mind, pushing his heartbeat into a gallop.

"You haven't answered my question," said the prisoner. "Will I die now at your hands, instead becoming food for the pack?"

For a long moment, Caius stood poised on the cusp of what would arguably be an act of treason, wavering. He had watched in silence for the past three years as the empire his family had served for generations slid ever downward, spiraling into corruption and depravity.

The emperor—once a military and organizational genius well on his way to conquering the known world—was losing his wits and his health in equal measure. Of the emperor's three legitimate sons, one was a drunkard, one was a sadist, and one was a manipulative bootlicker. Between them, they threatened to tear Alyrios apart with their power struggles.

And Caius, once a respected general in the Alyrion army, had somehow become the man whose job it was to make sure that the bones of a dead imperial bastard were cleaned up after being devoured by His Highness's hunting dogs.

Almighty Deimok, how had his life come to this?

Twenty-nine years of loyalty and military discipline creaked under the accumulated strain, like rotting timbers on a bridge giving way beneath the force of a flood-swollen river. Caius met the eyes of the man standing on the other side of the bars. The prisoner's gaze was dull with resignation.

"No," he croaked, barely recognizing his own voice. "I'm not going to kill you. Though we may both end up dead if we're not careful."

TWO

The prisoner stared at Caius for a beat before replying, "Sorry, but I can't tell if that's supposed to be reassuring or not. Because if it is, I hate to say it, but you're very bad at reassurance."

"It's not meant as reassurance," Caius said curtly. "It's just the truth. Has anyone inside the palace grounds seen your face?"

The man looked at him like he was trying to peel back Caius' skin so he could examine what lay beneath. "No. The guards who delivered me from the prison kept a bag tied over my head except when they fed me. And I haven't been fed since before I got here. Why?"

Caius ignored the question, his thoughts running fast and hot. "What's your name? Do the guards know it? Does anyone here know it?"

Dark brows drew together in confusion. "It's Decian. And no, they don't. Except for the handful of cellmates who bothered to ask over the years, no one's called me anything except 'prisoner' or 'bastard' since I was sixteen."

This could work, Caius thought, still with no idea why it suddenly seemed so important that it did. *It could work... or it could end up with my neck on a block beneath the executioner's axe.*

"Congratulations, Decian," he said gruffly. "You are now His Imperial Highness's master of hounds—temporarily, at least. You obviously have a knack for the work."

Decian stared at him for a long beat.

"What in the gods' names are you talking about?" he asked slowly.

And... *oh, good.* The emperor's part-Kulawi bastard son was apparently a heretic as well as a perceived threat to the succession. Because *of course* he was.

"There's only one God," Caius said, more sharply than he intended. "And you'll do well to remember it if you want to stay alive in this palace. Now, try to keep up. That sad pile of meat and bone is you—successfully executed, just as Princep Kaeto ordered. However, it appears the houndsman didn't have had the stomach for using his dogs to kill people. He walked off the job right after the deed was done, and promptly disappeared to who knows where. You're his temporary replacement."

"His temporary—?" Decian began, only to cut himself off. He stared at Caius with an incredulous expression. "Seriously... you just decided out of the blue to spare my life, and *this* is your plan?"

Caius' lips twitched into a scowl. "It is until I can get you away from the palace without arousing suspicion. Or... I suppose I could just run you through the heart right now, instead of risking my own position to save the neck of a condemned bastard."

"You think no one's going to notice what an odd coincidence this is?" Decian shot back. "The houndsman disappearing, and a random stranger taking his place?"

Caius' scowl grew. "I think you vastly overestimate the number of people that give a rat's arse about who performs their menial labor for them. No one cares who's tending the dogs, as long as the dogs get tended."

Decian's gaze moved from Caius to the huddled form of the apprentice, who was watching the exchange with wide, red-rimmed eyes. Tear streaks cut through the grime on the lad's cheeks.

Caius sighed.

All right. Perhaps there was at least *one* person who gave a rat's arse.

"You. Boy. Did the houndsman treat you well?" he demanded. "Was he a friend to you?"

The lad's face crumpled for a moment before he steeled himself to speak. "Not really," he said in a tiny voice. "He was a drunkard, and cruel when he'd been at the wine too much. But I didn't... I didn't want..." His gaze wandered toward the bloody mess in the cell, only to jerk away quickly.

"Of course you didn't," Caius said, forcing his voice into something less gruff.

"Did he have a wife?" Decian asked. "A mistress? Children?"

"No," said the apprentice. "I think he went to whores sometimes, though. And he played cards at the Wooly Ram most nights."

Caius cursed himself for not even considering those questions—for assuming that everyone in the world was as alone as he was. Still, the situation should be manageable enough. Prostitutes and gamblers were used to people disappearing as soon as their money dried up.

"Where are his rooms?" he asked, thinking that Decian and the unlucky houndsman were close enough in height and build that the dead man's clothing would probably suffice to replace Decian's shredded prisoner's rags.

"There's a lean-to at the far end of the building," said the boy, still looking on the verge of leaking more tears. "He sleeps there. *Slept* there. I sleep here in the kennel, to watch for thieves." He tipped his chin toward a corner furnished with a stool and a sad little bedroll on the dirt floor.

"All right," Caius said slowly. "Go to the man's room and fetch some of his clothing." He reached awkwardly for the purse hanging at his belt, his bad shoulder giving a warning twinge at the movement. "Here's a silver piece. There will be more if you keep quiet about what you've seen. But if I hear that you've flapped your tongue to anyone, you won't like what happens next."

The child's pale face grew paler, and he gulped audibly. Nonetheless, the coin disappeared quickly into a pouch at the boy's waist, and he hared away without another word. Caius figured he'd either return shortly with clothes, or he'd run for the hills and never be heard from again. The first option was more immediately useful, but he wasn't strictly opposed to the second.

"Do you often threaten children?" Decian asked, once the lad had gone.

"Only the ones who could get me executed with a careless word." Caius threw the other man a hard glance, aware that he would probably be finding this conversation easier to navigate if Decian's cock wasn't hanging out.

The physique of a prisoner who'd spent years breaking rocks and hauling ore had no business looking so appealing—at least from this angle, when they were facing each other and the whip scars on Decian's back were hidden.

"Look—here's a counteroffer," Decian suggested. "Tell me where the nearest palace gate is, and you'll never see or hear from me again."

Caius scowled. "It's not that simple."

Decian scowled back. "Yes it is. All I've ever wanted was to be left the hell alone. Whichever highbred arsehole sired me, they've got nothing to worry about from me. The *last* thing I want is more attention."

Caius' jaw was growing sore from how hard he was clenching it. "Believe me, I'd like nothing better than to send you on your merry way. But if there's one shredded body, no houndsman, and no prisoner, suddenly this farce becomes a *mystery*. There would be an investigation."

"Let them investigate," Decian said tiredly.

"On top of that," Caius continued, "since the guards at the gates won't recognize you, they're as likely to arrest you as let you through. Access into and out of this place is tightly controlled—unless you know the guards personally, you'll be subject to scrutiny you don't want. A lot of the laborers in the palace compound are slaves— escape attempts aren't uncommon."

Decian's eyes narrowed. "And my skin color makes me look like a slave, does it?"

Caius shrugged. "Not really. It does make you stand out, though. Slaves are as likely to be Alyrion as foreign, and I've known plenty of freemen from Kulawi and the southern reaches. But none of that will help you if the guards at the gate start asking the wrong questions."

The younger man subsided, though he still looked unhappy. Small surprise there, Caius supposed. After all, he *was* locked in a cage with a pack of starving dogs busily consuming a human corpse, and Caius had just told him he'd have to stay in the palace compound with his would-be executioners for an unspecified amount of time.

"It should only be for a few days," he offered. "Spin some story about being an acquaintance of the houndsman. Tell anyone who asks that he suggested you take the job before he left. Once the guards learn your face and your story, head into the city for some evening entertainment and keep going. Get as far away from Amarius as you can and never look back."

Decian stared at him with a piercing gaze the color of rich, freshly turned earth. He lifted his chin, and the weak light filtering in from the doorway caught his eyes oddly for an instant, making them almost seem to glow.

"Why are you doing this?" he asked. "Why put yourself at risk for a condemned man?"

Honesty tugged at Caius, drawing out words better left unsaid. "Because I no longer recognize my own country. Alyrios should not be a place where men are thrown to ravenous dogs because of the circumstances of their birth. It's wrong. This is not the empire I pledged to serve."

There are a number of dead bastards who probably wish you'd reached that conclusion a bit sooner, observed a razor-sharp little voice in the back of Caius' mind.

Decian still watched him with that oddly penetrating gaze. "So this is your grand act of rebellion, is it?" Silence stretched for an uncomfortable beat before he shrugged, snapping the tension. "Fine, I'll take it. It's certainly better than the alternative."

Caius' attention slid toward a pair of hounds snarling over what was probably a thighbone. "I should think so, yes."

The boy chose that moment to return, creeping through the door with a bundle of clothing under his arm.

"Clothes! Well, thank the gods for that," Decian said, apparently oblivious to his recurring blasphemy.

Caius swallowed a growl of frustration, along with the growing concern that he'd just made the worst mistake of his life.

"Is the cage door locked?" he asked gruffly.

"I don't think so," Decian said. "Though I suppose if I'm to be the new master of hounds, I'll still need the keys."

He looked around the cage, his attention landing on the floor near a handful of dogs tearing at a nearly bare ribcage. He walked over without hesitation and shoved the animals off. All but one slunk away. The holdout gave a low growl of warning, teeth clamped around its prize.

"Oh, *hush*," Decian said, glaring down at it for the space of a couple of heartbeats. "Let me get the damned key ring and you can go back to your meal in a minute."

Caius held his breath, but the standoff broke abruptly and without drama a moment later. The massive hound whimpered and dropped the hunk of human torso, crawling away on its belly. Decian stepped forward and picked up a jangling metal ring of keys, giving it a brisk shake to dislodge bits of gore.

Only when he turned and headed away did the animals cautiously return to the bones, watching him warily as he moved off. There was a low trough of water along one side of the cage. Decian sloshed the key ring in it and returned to the cage door.

He paused with his hand on one of the iron bars. "No second thoughts about running me through with your sword and saving yourself the trouble?"

"Several, actually," Caius said truthfully. "So don't try my patience. Get out here and get some damned clothes on, assuming you can do so without any of the dogs getting loose."

Decian scoffed, pushing a couple of hounds out of the way with his leg. They made no attempt to bury sharp teeth into the offending appendage. Caius experienced another sharp flash of disquiet over his abrupt loss of sanity as Decian eased the door open and slipped out, leaving the dogs huddled meekly inside their cage.

Distantly, Caius remembered a young man in the village where he'd grown up who'd seemed to have an almost uncanny affinity for horses. Perhaps he was seeing a similar talent now, but with dogs. The dead houndsman had been a diffident, beaten-down figure. If nothing else,

Decian's frankly bizarre fearlessness in the face of the slavering beasts probably worked in his favor.

Decian took the bundle of clothes from the red-faced apprentice, who was still watching both of them with wide eyes. Caius felt the tension in his shoulders ease incrementally as he pulled on a pair of trousers and a shirt—as though Decian's nakedness were truly his most pressing problem right now.

"Right," Decian said, as he straightened from pulling on the dead man's spare boots. "What's your name, lad?"

"Everyone calls me Pip," the apprentice mumbled.

"Great," Decian said. "So, Pip—why don't you show me where the meat for the dogs is kept?" His eyes slid to Caius and held. "And once they've been fed properly, *you* can help me gather up the *unfortunate prisoner's* remains." A sharp-edged smile drew Decian's full lips back, baring white teeth.

It wasn't a pleasant expression, and it shouldn't have felt like a dagger sliding painlessly home below Caius' ribcage, spreading heat in its wake. He cleared his throat. Under the circumstances, Caius supposed he couldn't exactly order anyone else to clear away the bones. Not unless he wanted that person asking the wrong kind of questions—specifically, questions that had no good answers.

"Oh, good," he replied without enthusiasm. "What a coincidence. That's *exactly* how I'd hoped to spend my evening."

THREE

Hours later, Caius returned to the palace to offer a succinct report on the prisoner's supposed death. A brief visit to his quarters followed, and now he lay sprawled on a comfortable divan in Saleene's suite of rooms. He'd bathed and changed before coming to the brothel, wanting very badly to divest himself of all reminders of his recent, abrupt descent into insanity.

Well… that, along with the smell of blood and dog shit.

If nothing else, showing up at Saleene's door while reeking like an abattoir would have been unforgivably rude — and there were not so many prostitutes in the city of Amarius who catered to Caius' tastes that he could afford to piss her off for no reason.

Saleene blinked up at him with kohl-lined eyes from her position between his thighs, her lips sliding along his length in a slow, firm glide. Two blunt-tipped fingers had also been crooked inside him for some time now, rubbing firmly. Caius was aware of his pleasure rising — but distantly, as though it were happening to someone else.

His mind was stubbornly elsewhere, but after a slow, protracted buildup, the sensation eventually peaked. When it did, he spent over Saleene's tongue with a shudder, his eyes sliding shut as some of the tension flowed out of his body in tandem with his seed.

She pulled off his softening prick with an obscene pop, sliding her fingers free at the same time. Caius swallowed a grunt of discontent at the sudden feeling of emptiness, slinging his good arm across his face to block out the low light of the oil lamp. He was aware of Saleene rising from her place between his thighs to clean up, returning a few moments later to perch on the end of the divan.

"My, my," she began in her familiar low tenor. "You know, I'm not sure I've ever seen a man less interested in the fact that his cock was being sucked. Deep thoughts tonight, *Legatus*?"

The undertone of mockery behind the military title was nothing new, but it was nevertheless unwelcome right now. Caius lowered his arm to shoot her an unimpressed look. She didn't back down from it, tossing her thick mane of wavy black hair over her shoulder. Square-jawed and broad-shouldered, Saleene was a study in contrasts. Her sharp cheekbones were dusted with rouge, and her thin lips were painted red—smudged, now, after her slow and underappreciated seduction of Caius' prick. Her bearing was sultry and inescapably feminine. But her chest was flat muscle beneath the artfully draped folds of her dress, and Caius was more than passingly familiar with the thick length hanging between her legs. It was a cockstand that could, for the right amount of money, take someone apart from the inside out.

In a society where the exposure of homosexual liaisons could ruin a man, Saleene had carved out a niche providing a very particular service, shielded behind a veil of plausible deniability. Caius—whose interest in soft thighs and yielding bosoms had waned significantly after his wife's death in childbirth many years ago—found Saleene's services decidedly to his tastes these days.

Tonight, though, such a diversion still failed to distract him from his own idiocy.

"I'm a fool, Saleene," he said, because in the end, if a man couldn't unburden himself to his favorite prostitute, what had the world come to, really?

"Oh, yes?" she replied in a noncommittal tone. "Have you behaved foolishly, then?"

"Almost certainly," he told her with a sigh, letting his head fall back to stare at the beams in the ceiling. "I tried to right an injustice."

"And trying to right injustice makes one a fool?" Saleene asked. "I think I must've missed that part."

"Not universally, no. But in this case, the attempt amounted to treason," he explained, wondering for the dozenth time what in heaven's name had possessed him.

He felt Saleene shift on the other end of the divan, as though leaning forward in interest. "Treason? Really? And do you regret serving the cause of treasonous justice?"

He closed his eyes again, attempting to banish the vision of Decian's blank look of shock when he realized he'd just been offered a chance at survival. At *freedom*, if he could hold out for a few days without being discovered.

"That remains to be seen," he admitted.

"Hmm," Saleene said.

She rose again, a clink of goblets signifying the imminent offer of wine. It wasn't kindness; Caius would be paying for the drink and the sympathetic ear right along with the sex. Perhaps it was pathetic of him. However, the alternative was to be utterly alone in the pit of vipers that made up the Alyrion royal court. Most days, Caius felt as though he fit in amongst the schemers and the arselickers of Amarius about as well as an aging carthorse fit in during a chariot race.

He supposed it was surprising that he'd lasted as long as he had without buckling. Maybe the events of this afternoon — or something like them — had been inevitable.

Saleene nudged his hip with her knee to get his attention and pressed a goblet into his unresisting hand. He transferred it from left to right and sipped. Meanwhile, she eased herself to sit on the thick fur rug, resting her back against the front of the divan with her skirts spread out before her.

"The city is rife with talk of the upcoming Council, you know," she said conversationally, as though they were resuming a previous discussion. "It takes up more and more of the conversation every day."

He grunted, not sure what he was expected to say to such an opening gambit.

The Council of Amarius had been called in response to the growing tension between the followers of Deimok and the pagan holdouts who still insisted on following the old ways, even though the emperor himself had declared

Deimonism the true religion of the Alyrion Empire. It was no wonder the city was speaking of little else in the run-up.

"At least once the Council rules, things will finally be decided," Caius offered. For all that he had more reason than most to distrust pagans and their dark magic, he had limited interest in—or patience for—religion in general. He kept to the form of the thing... performed the religious duties expected of a respectable advisor to the emperor, and didn't give it much thought beyond that. He found ideologues on either side more than a little incomprehensible.

"*Decided*, yes," Saleene echoed in a tart tone. "And then we shall see whether the zealots who believe it's the Church's duty to execute pagan heretics will hold sway over the moderates who prefer to leave such punishment in Deimok's hands."

Caius raised an eyebrow at her and took another sip of his wine. "You have opinions on the matter, I take it?"

Saleene snorted. "Everyone in the damned city has opinions, my dear Legatus." She lifted her chin, regarding him with a level gaze. "I did have a point to the observation, however."

"Oh?" he asked blankly.

She sighed. "The point is, Caius, that change is coming, and when it arrives, it won't be gentle. You're an advisor to the emperor and his family. Like it or not, you'll eventually have to pick a side in the endless skirmishes between factions, rather than continuing to play both ends against the middle."

Caius stiffened, the barb hitting home with perhaps more force than Saleene had intended.

"I don't know what you mean," he said, swinging his legs over the opposite side of the divan and rising abruptly. He set his goblet on a side table before moving to retrieve his clothing. Saleene watched him with an impassive gaze as he pulled on his smallclothes, stockings, and breeches, not commenting on the awkward double shoulder-shrug required to get his linen shirt over the ugly twist of scar tissue that limited the range of motion of his left arm.

He was lying, of course—to Saleene, and probably to himself as well. He knew exactly what she meant, though it bothered him that he'd apparently become so transparent. Over the years, Caius had come to despise the royal family he was sworn to serve—but rather than do anything about it, he merely seethed silently over the slow collapse of the empire he loved while corruption unfolded around him, unchecked.

At least, he had done nothing about it until today.

Today, he'd taken action to try to save a single life… yet even in this, he'd only been moved to act after the fact. He'd stood at parade rest while an innocent bastard had been thrown, quite literally, to the dogs… and he'd stayed silent. Only when Kaeto had retired with his cadre of fawning sycophants, and the dogs had miraculously spared their intended victim, had Caius stepped up to the task of seeing justice done.

Taking only what action could be achieved with minimal risk.

Playing both ends against the middle.

"It's late. I must return to the palace," he said, the words clipped. He fumbled in his coin purse for payment, tossing the money onto the table next to the wine.

Another whore might have scrambled to smooth her client's ruffled feathers, but Saleene only watched him pull on his boots with a neutral expression. Caius held no illusions regarding their relationship—not in this regard, anyway. Saleene might appreciate him as a man who paid well and gave no trouble, but should he walk out of her brothel and never return, there would be a dozen other men lining up to take his place.

Besides, he would be back within a fortnight when the pall of loneliness once more grew too stifling. They both knew it. None of which changed the fact that he was in no mood to appreciate having his very palpable shortcomings thrown in his face tonight, either intentionally or unintentionally.

He left her suite without another word, heading down the stairs to retrieve his sword belt from a little room off the main receiving parlor, where the clients' weapons were held for safety. He'd made it roughly halfway down when the sound of raised voices reached him from below. A low growl of irritation from the room he'd just left alerted him to Saleene's rapid approach behind him. She brushed past him on the stairwell, all lean grace, her skirts held up with one hand.

When Caius arrived a few moments later, it was to find a four-way standoff in the brothel's parlor. Saleene and her partner Zuri—a dark-skinned Kulawi woman with a ready smile and a vicious temper—formed two corners of the square. The richly dressed woman forming the third corner was a stranger to him, but Caius vaguely recognized the young man who seemed to be the target of the others' ire.

He was attached to the brothel in some capacity… a lad of perhaps nineteen with a face too pretty for his own good. Caius didn't know his name, but he'd occasionally been the one to take Caius' weapons before he went upstairs to Saleene's rooms. He had the sense that the lad was well aware of his good looks and had a rather high opinion of himself.

Having no interest in whatever sordid incident had precipitated the argument, Caius averted his eyes from the group as the rich woman gestured at the young man angrily. By the time he'd retrieved his sword belt from the wide-eyed girl in charge of watching over the patrons' belongings tonight, the finely dressed female client had stormed out, leaving through the tavern that fronted the street.

As he moved to follow suit, however, he couldn't help overhearing Saleene's hissed, "I told you, Tullio, *one* more angry noblewoman and you're out on your ear—" followed by the lad's querulous words of self-defense. Caius let the door swing shut behind him, heading through the busy tavern. Rather than leaving through the main entrance, he made his way to a back door leading into an alleyway that would, in turn, take him to the main *vaia* running north toward the palace complex.

The scuff of a boot against cobblestone in the dimly lit alley made him pause and look back. A cloaked figure in the shadows froze in place. Caius stared at the man for the space of a handful of heartbeats before dismissing the oddness of the moment and continuing toward the busy road ahead.

Amarius was not enemy territory. There were no scouts hiding in the shadows, waiting to spring an ambush. No doubt the man had merely been a drunkard stepping out behind the tavern for a few moments, surprised to find he didn't have the privacy he'd expected for a quick piss.

Caius put the momentary flash of disquiet from his mind. Tomorrow, he would once more have to face his duties, while also checking that Decian hadn't done anything foolish and drawn attention to himself. Tonight, however, there was a bottle of strong brandy in his rooms that very much had his name on it.

FOUR

The following morning, Caius stood at attention in an echoing meeting chamber near the heart of the palace. Dressed impeccably as befitted his rank, he was surrounded by opulence and excess as he waited for the assembly to come to order. He couldn't think of anyplace he less wanted to be.

Proclus was late. *Again.* It was anyone's guess whether the emperor's eldest son would bother to make an appearance at all. He was probably passed out drunk in his bedroom, drooling all over a naked serving girl or three. Caius wondered if anyone had been sent to wake him. Perhaps Bruccias had gone to get him, since the youngest son, too, was conspicuous by his absence.

That left sharp-eyed Kaeto seated at his father's left hand. As was often the case these days, the Emperor Constanzus seemed distracted, his attention on something in the middle distance that only he could see. The courtiers and advisors in attendance at the day's meeting buzzed among themselves, speaking of the latest gossip. Here, too, all attention was focused on the upcoming ecumenical council.

For all that he hated politics and religious wrangling, Caius was no fool. There were undercurrents roiling in the city, beyond the very real questions surrounding the continued practice of paganism within the empire. Those undercurrents were doubtless at least part of the reason Caius had attended more than a dozen grisly executions of royal bastards in recent weeks. It was also the reason Princep Kaeto had been front and center at every meeting and advisory session since the conclave was first announced.

With no valid path to the throne unless his elder brother conveniently decided to choke to death on his own vomit during a drunken fit, Kaeto sought to gain influence and support among the clergy by exhibiting the kind of leadership that his father and brother weren't.

It was not, in the end, a terrible strategy.

Caius had no desire to serve a wine-swilling fool as the ruler of an empire spanning a quarter of the known world. He had even *less* desire to serve a poisonous sadist in that same role. As things stood now, they'd be lucky to avoid a civil war on the way to either one of those options.

The doors of the chamber swung open and the herald entered, staff in hand. "Your Imperial Majesty, I present to you Episkopos Philian of Narvonne!"

Caius swallowed a sigh. Philian was a high-ranking member of the Church—a thin-featured older man with a silver tongue that was probably forked like a serpent's. With his arrival, any hope of a quiet and productive meeting fled.

The episkopos stopped before the massive table dominating the room and bowed perfunctorily to the royals at its head. Several of the courtiers bowed to him in turn. Caius did not join them, trusting that his military garb would make him functionally invisible to the churchman—a nameless guard rather than the trusted advisor he allegedly was. It wasn't a stretch. He might have saved the emperor's life once upon a time, but these days there seemed to be little enough interest in his counsel.

"Emperor Constanzus," Philian began, "I have come today to enjoin you to better control the rabble in the capital. You may be unaware of this, but there are reports of pagan heretics marching openly in the streets after dark. With the date of the conclave approaching, I'm sure I don't have to tell you how inflammatory such unrest appears to an outside observer."

The emperor frowned in evident confusion, tapping his fingertips restlessly on the marble tabletop as silence stretched. As ever when confronted with the stark changes between the man he had once followed into battle and the fading shell before him, Caius felt his stomach twist.

Constanzus was roughly the same age as Caius, and yet his mind was visibly failing week by week.

Kaeto stepped in before the pause could grow any more uncomfortable than it already was. "His Imperial Majesty appreciates your report, Episkopos Philian. This is yet more proof that the heretics lack respect for their rulers, both secular and spiritual."

Philian looked mollified, though his eyes flicked to Constanzus briefly. "I trust the issue will be addressed in a satisfactory manner before the Council convenes." He hesitated, his eyes sweeping the figures at the head of the table. "Forgive me, but... is Princep Proclus well? I would have expected him to be present this morning."

"My brother is indisposed, I fear," Kaeto said evenly, allowing the barest hint of disapproval to color the words.

"Yes," Constanzus echoed in a tone of distraction. "Indisposed."

With a mere handful of words, the emperor's middle son had drawn attention to the fact that his father was slipping and his elder brother was unreliable. Caius might have been impressed, if Kaeto weren't such a damned viper.

"Indeed," Philian said, and his expression grew speculative. "Well, thank you for hearing my concerns, Your Majesties. My secretary will convey the latest details regarding the preparations this afternoon."

He bowed again, clearly preparing to leave, but the emperor straightened in his chair.

"Do you enjoy the hunt, Philian?" Constanzus asked, his gaze clearing.

Philian blinked. "I... beg your pardon, Your Imperial Majesty?"

"The hunt," Constanzus repeated. "Do you enjoy riding to the hounds?"

Caius twitched at the mention of *hounds*. He couldn't help it.

The episkopos merely looked confused. "I fear I have never hunted, Emperor Constanzus."

"What, never?" the emperor replied in disbelief. "Why, we must remedy this immediately! Caius"—he gestured Caius forward—"organize a royal hunt for two days hence! I tire of this endless nattering across tables."

A sinking feeling took up residence in Caius' stomach. He hesitated for the space of a heartbeat, in hopes that Kaeto would step in and redirect his father's attention to more pressing matters before the order stuck and became real.

It was a vain hope. Kaeto was all in favor of anything that highlighted the emperor's growing mental confusion. The princep merely looked on impassively.

Caius cleared his throat. "Of course, Your Imperial Majesty. I will see to it."

Dear god. A hunt. In two days. A hunt... *using the royal hounds.*

The houndsman was dead, and an imposter now ran the kennels. Decian wouldn't have the first idea how to manage the pack during such an outing.

It was all Caius could do to keep one ear on the meeting as Philian left and talk turned to preparations for the arrival of the remaining Church dignitaries. The advisors droned on, and he managed to answer a couple of basic questions about security around the site of the conclave.

The only saving grace was that the emperor's order gave him a perfect excuse to speak with Decian privately. He'd been struggling to think of a reason why a military advisor to the emperor's family would be rubbing shoulders with someone so far below him in station. Now he had one.

The interminable palaver finally wound down. Caius neatly avoided the two courtiers who tried to draw him into conversation about the emperor's obvious befuddlement, and another who accosted him with questions about Proclus' whereabouts. As much as he wanted to flee straight to the kennels and attempt to determine how badly fucked they were going to be, there were other duties that also required his attention.

He made himself take a deep, centering breath, and headed toward the training grounds at the north end of the palace compound. There, he found Aelio drilling the men who were not on guard duty that day—running them through intricate sword forms in the bright sunlight.

"Tribuni," Caius called, once he was in hailing distance.

The Amarian commander looked up, and immediately spoke to the subordinate standing next to him. The soldier smoothly took over the drills, while Aelio crossed to meet Caius halfway.

"Good morning, Legatus," the tribuni greeted. "Escaped from the palace already? Surely that bodes well for the day."

Aelio was a good-tempered fellow—blue-eyed and sandy-haired, with a glint of humor that tended to surface often and easily. Were Caius inclined to make friends of subordinates, he might have considered that Aelio would be an agreeable drinking companion. Since he was not thus inclined, he contented himself with the pleasure of not being constantly at odds with a disobliging palace commander.

"Every day has its own set of problems," he replied, by way of greeting. "I need to discuss the upcoming guard assignments for the arriving Council members. It may be necessary to requisition additional men from the Amarian Guard."

To his credit, Aelio immediately fell to business. "I see. Does this mean we're expecting a degree of trouble beyond the scope of your common- or garden-variety security detail?"

Caius' felt his expression settle into hard, unhappy lines. "These days, I expect little else besides trouble."

Aelio nodded. "Understandable, considering the growing unrest in the city. Very well, I will send a message to Laurentin and advise him that we'll be needing some of his troops. I'm sure *that* will go over well."

"I don't care if he likes it. I just need him to do it," Caius replied.

"Then you will probably be in luck, on both counts," Aelio said solemnly. "Now, while you're here, do you have a few minutes to go over the disposition of the palace troops during the talks? I have some questions about the best placement of the household guard, since I have a feeling Princep Kaeto will be spending more time at the Council than in the palace..."

Caius joined Aelio under the awning abutting the practice field to hammer out a usable plan for the coming weeks, knowing that the situation would be subject to change depending on the progression of the pagan unrest. It was a relief to deal with someone competent and plain speaking after time spent in the company of royals, churchmen, and courtiers. Nonetheless, once the main points had been addressed to both their satisfaction, Caius prepared himself to play the role he was ill equipped to play.

"I don't suppose you've met the new master of hounds?" he asked, striving for a casual tone, and feeling ridiculous.

Aelio appeared taken aback. Not surprising, since Caius wasn't prone to either gossip or personal conversations.

"Er... no. I wasn't aware there *was* a new master of hounds. What happened to the old master of hounds?"

"Walked off the job, I gather," Caius said. "Though he did have the good grace to bring on an acquaintance to take his place when he left. The emperor has ordered a hunt in two days. I'm on my way to speak with the new man next."

The seed was planted. Caius was loath to get further into it, for fear of the conversation coming across as completely out of character.

Aelio's face took on the same look of disbelieving bewilderment that Caius suspected he had worn upon receiving the orders. "A... hunt?" he echoed. "*Now?*" The tribuni ran a hand over his face. "By the One God... he's getting worse, isn't he?"

Such an utterance was dangerously close to treasonous—not that Caius held the moral high ground regarding such things these days.

"His Imperial Majesty's priorities are perhaps different from ours," he replied carefully. How he hated this cautious verbal dance. This sense that speaking plainly was akin to signing one's own death warrant.

"That's putting it mildly," Aelio muttered, apparently less concerned with the dance than Caius was.

"Be prudent with your words," he warned, less harshly than he probably should have. "The emperor commands. We obey. I must leave now for my meeting with the houndsman. I'll let you know by tonight what sort of security we'll be needing for the royal hunting party."

"Of course, Legatus," Aelio replied, once more the picture of professionalism. "Our lives are ever at the emperor's disposal."

Aren't they just, Caius thought, as he nodded and took his leave.

FIVE

Decian was easy enough to find, playing dice with a group of workmen in the same courtyard where he'd been dragged in as a condemned prisoner a mere day before. A number of hounds lolled around the little group—tongues hanging out, sunning themselves contentedly. Caius gave them a wary look as he approached.

He was halfway across the yard when one of the men noticed him and straightened abruptly from the game. "Legatus," he said, bowing stiffly as his companions looked up and quickly followed suit. All but Decian, seated facing away from him, who straightened but did not crane around to look.

He'd cut his hair. The wild mats and spirals were gone, leaving tight black curls hugging his head like a sleek helmet.

"I need to speak to the new houndsman," Caius told the others. "Return to your duties."

The men scattered, leaving him alone with Decian and the lazing dogs. The day was balmy, the air carrying the scent of animals. Decian finally turned and met Caius' eyes.

"I was winning before you interrupted that game, you know," he said mildly. "And wasn't it you who told me to make friends with the men in the palace?"

The strange sense of unease from yesterday had returned to Caius' chest within moments of arriving in Decian's presence. He forced it aside. "I'm not sure taking their coin is the best way to make friends with them. Where did you even get money to gamble?"

Decian raised an eyebrow. "I inherited a coin purse that had been stuffed inside my predecessor's palliasse. Pip and I split the contents, since it's not as though dear old

Jona is going to need money now that he's moved to greener pastures... so to speak."

"So, the lad stuck around, then?" Caius asked, surprised. Though maybe he shouldn't have been—between the bribe Caius had given him and his share of the spoils in the coin purse, Pip was on course to become the highest paid houndsman's apprentice in all of Alyrios.

"He did, yes," Decian confirmed, stretching a hand out to scratch the ears of the nearest dog. "So, it turns out you're not just any old soldier. You're a *Legatus*, of all things. Tell me—what can I do for you today?"

It occurred to Caius that he hadn't introduced himself at all during their previous interaction... not even to the extent of offering his rank. An instant later, he decided that was probably for the best, under the circumstances. The fewer personal details Decian knew about him, the better.

"The emperor has ordered a royal hunt the day after tomorrow," he said simply. "Given your... recent introduction to this role, is that going to be a problem?"

Decian blinked at him. "That's a good question," he said after a short pause. He lifted his voice. "*Oy, Pip!*"

The apprentice stuck his head out of the door to the kennels and jogged toward them a moment later. Caius saw the boy's face go pale as he recognized him.

"Yes, Decian?" he asked, flicking a worried look in Caius' direction.

"There's going to be a hunt in two days," Decian told him. "Do you know what that entails?"

Pip swallowed. "Y-yes, sir. I've been on four hunts, helping out with Jo—" He trailed off, his gaze slipping to his feet. "With... the old master of hounds."

Decian shrugged. "That's good enough for me. You can talk me through it between now and then."

One of the hounds rolled onto its back, and Pip reached down absently to rub its belly. None of the beasts looked remotely ready to take down a boar or a hart. Nor did they look remotely like the kind of animals that could tear a man limb from limb—which only proved that appearances could be deceiving.

"So… a hunt." Decian looked speculative. "Which, presumably, takes place outside the palace grounds. Somewhere remote, I'm guessing?"

Caius heard the question he wasn't asking. "Yes. This will be your chance to slip away and never look back—assuming your apprentice here can get the pack back to the kennel on his own, without anyone getting bitten." He raised a pointed eyebrow at the lad.

Pip looked offended, his earlier nervousness forgotten. "Of course I can!" he snapped, and quickly added, "*sir*."

Decian snorted in wry amusement at the near-slip.

Caius held Pip's gaze, frowning. "You're not afraid of the dogs after what you saw yesterday?"

A hint of mulish anger hardened the boy's face. "*I* know better than to starve them for a week, no matter what some *nobleman* says."

"Good lad," Caius and Decian said, practically in unison.

Decian gave another small huff of amusement. "It's settled, then. Two more days and I'll be on my way. Now, if that's all, *Legatus*—why don't you get out of here so I can focus on learning all about royal hunts?"

The casual dismissal shocked Caius for a moment. But why should it? His rank meant nothing to Decian. As far as Decian was concerned, Caius was the crazy soldier who had disobeyed orders to save him—nothing more. All Decian wanted was to be far away from here, alive and free from imprisonment. Now that a path to freedom was almost within his grasp, that would become his whole focus, just as it should be.

As it should be for *both* of them.

"Very well, then. A fair afternoon to you both," Caius said, and left him to it.

⸙

The following day passed in a flurry of meetings, along with frantic scurrying to reschedule the important things that had been preempted by the upcoming hunt. By nightfall, Caius was twice as exhausted by the endless palaver as he would have been after riding with the hounds for half a day. He fell into his bed with a vaguely directed prayer for uninterrupted sleep. Instead, he dreamed.

He was in the forest, searching. Warm brown eyes set in a dusky-skinned face beckoned him forward silently before slipping out of view behind the bole of a massive tree. Caius followed, steadying himself with a small hand against the rough bark, dampened by humidity.

A child's hand.

It was too quiet — no birds chirped, rustling leaves with their flight. No dapples of ever-shifting sunlight reached the layer of decaying leaves at his feet. Caius circled the tree trunk, but the lithe figure with the deep brown eyes was already gone, disappearing behind another tree perhaps ten paces away. Caius crashed through the leaf litter in pursuit, his sandaled footsteps shockingly loud in the muffling silence. Always, his quarry remained just at the edge of vision. A glimpse here, a flicker of movement there — nothing more.

Eventually, a clearing opened ahead of him, and Caius stumbled to a halt. Gray clouds choked the sky, except for a single patch of brilliant blue. A narrow beam of yellow sunlight illuminated the trampled grass at the edge of the clearing, broken stalks painted red. A great stag lay crumpled on the ground. Its antlers jutted up like the bare limbs of a dying tree, crimson at the tips. Stripes and splatters of red crisscrossed its tawny coat, three spears jutting obscenely from its body. Its tongue lolled from its open mouth, swollen and dark purple with trapped blood.

Caius didn't want to look at the shapes arrayed around it on the ground. If he looked, it would be real. No, no, no, he chanted, with a child's desperate hope that wishing for something with enough conviction could make it true. His dream legs moved without his command, one in front of the other, bringing him forward until the splayed shapes around the fallen stag became men.

No, he thought again, but it didn't make any difference. His feet continued to propel him closer, until he was standing over the nearest man. A familiar face stared up at the sky sightlessly. His father's expression had frozen into lines of horror. Sticky blood trailed from a rip in the side of his throat to a puddle drying on the ground. His blade was still clasped in one hand, his fingers gripping the hilt like claws.

In the next moment, Caius felt himself falling, tumbling down into a dark pit of boyhood terrors. He tore his eyes away from the body of the man who'd bounced him on his knee as a babe and played at wooden swords with him, looking instead at the stag. It stared back at him with dead eyes, pinning him in place. Caius caught his breath as a blood-red glimmer began to kindle in the depths of those dark orbs, growing until the scarlet glow spilled from them like torchlight.

Horror caught him in the chest like a kick from a mule. He cried out, staggering backward —

—and woke abruptly, jolting upright in bed. His bad shoulder flared with pain at the sudden movement. Sweat beaded his brow. His heart hammered, the breath in his lungs coming fast and shallow. Beyond the open window, the stars twinkled down at him mockingly.

It had been years since the childhood nightmare had plagued him in such a way. His father had been a guardsman in the administrative district encompassing the village where Caius had grown up. Even four decades ago, reports of pagan shapeshifters had grown rare within the empire's borders, as most of the warlocks who could transform into dangerous beasts had already been hunted down.

Rare… but not unheard of.

When the elders in his village accused a man of transforming into a stag and damaging the crops, Caius' father and two of his comrades had been sent to hunt him down and determine the truth of the allegation. Instead, they'd been gored to death by a murderous supernatural creature. Caius—eight years old at the time—had snuck after his father that morning, in hopes of witnessing what he'd childishly assumed would be a grand adventure. Instead, he'd become lost in the woods during the chase, unable to regain his bearings as the sound of screaming echoed through the distant trees. He'd eventually stumbled across the blood-soaked bodies at the edge of a clearing.

As a youngster, he'd revisited that horror in the form of frequent night terrors, though they'd gradually faded as he grew older.

He shook his head, trying to clear it. No doubt it was all the talk of pagans surrounding the upcoming Council that had dredged up memories better left buried. Caius cautiously eased himself down to lie flat on the mattress once more, grimacing at the sensation of damp sweat cooling on the sheets. Blinking up at the darkness, he silently chastised himself for letting the current situation get to him.

It was ridiculous to lose sleep over such things, when there were far more tangible and immediate threats to be dealt with. He closed his eyes and forced his breathing to slow, intent on getting enough sleep so that he wouldn't be totally useless the next day.

SIX

Morning came far too soon after a night spent tossing and turning restlessly. Nevertheless, Caius was ready and waiting on horseback in the main courtyard before the sun breached the eastern wall of the Amarian imperial quarter. A hunt, it turned out, was one of the few things that could rouse the royal household before dawn, drawing them from their comfortable beds with the promise of excitement and the glory of the kill.

Even Proclus had managed to overcome his hangover, appearing bleary-eyed and snappish, laced into his clothing and hoisted onto a mount by his small army of servants. Sharp-eyed Kaeto was there as well, of course, and the youngest—Bruccius—skulked in the background on a round-barreled chestnut mare.

Caius experienced a frisson of disquiet when Kaeto's incisive gaze flickered over the new master of hounds. Decian had just arrived with Pip. Both were mounted on common roan ponies, with the hunting pack milling excitedly around them. But there was surely nothing for Kaeto to latch onto. At worst, he might make note of the fact that the emperor's new houndsman shared the same rich skin tone that he could have glimpsed on the bound hands of one of the nameless bastard half-brothers he'd ordered to their deaths over the past few weeks. That was all... and it was nothing. There were countless men of foreign birth or bloodline living in Amarius.

As the sun crested the palace walls, illuminating the courtyard by the main gates, they awaited only the emperor himself. Caius' gray gelding pawed the cobbles restlessly, eager for the chase. The dogs clustered around their two handlers, many of the beasts gazing up at Decian adoringly. He hoped that expression of canine loyalty boded well for the next few hours. It would be maddening to come so close to success in his self-appointed task of getting Decian away safely, only to have everything collapse around them in the last few moments.

Finally, the approach of many hooves heralded the arrival of Constanzus and his retinue of guards. Aelio rode at the emperor's right hand, sitting astride his bay courser. Another five soldiers flanked Constanzus' white stallion, silent sentry against any who might wish him harm.

The emperor had grown gaunt in recent months, as whatever illness or curse had befallen him took its toll on his body as well as his mind. Nonetheless, he sat straight in the saddle, the prospect of the hunt bringing a light to his eye that little else could manage these days.

"Everything is prepared?" he called to the assembled group, his voice a pale echo of the battlefield roar that had once commanded legions. "Then let us depart!"

On his command, horses and hounds headed for the gates and the open land beyond the edges of the city. The company was a large one, consisting of not only the hunters and dogs, but also an entourage of servants and wagons carrying the pavilions that would be set up for refreshments. Additionally, there were the palace guards commanded by Aelio, numbering perhaps two dozen, who would follow them on the hunt with eyes for the royal family's security, rather than the quarry.

Amarian citizens in the streets stopped what they were doing and moved aside for the small army of horses, hounds, and wagons. Most of them bowed deeply, avoiding eye contact. However, Caius' neck prickled as he noted the way that a few looked up from their obeisance with hard, angry expressions. He caught Aelio's gaze for a moment, seeing the same awareness reflected back at him in the palace commander's eyes.

Unrest was growing within the city, coiling in the shadows like an angry serpent hiding under a log. Still, no one was foolish enough to attempt any overt action against the large, well-armed royal party. When the tension inevitably erupted into the open, Caius suspected the city would tear at its own flanks long before aiming its venomous strike directly for the head.

They rode through the outskirts of the capital. Buildings gave way to fields, and eventually to pristine forest unspoiled by human habitation. The air grew sweeter as they left the stench of the city behind. The Silver Wood was royal land, set aside for the emperor's pleasure. Poaching within its boundaries was grounds for having an eye put out or a hand removed. Repeat offenders were executed.

As a result, the place was teeming with wildlife of every description. Deer and hare were thick in its dappled depths. Many a farmer cursed the woods as a breeding ground for wolves, boar, and foxes that roamed abroad, damaging cropland and killing livestock in their smallholdings.

The hounds wrestled each other and yipped excitedly as they entered the forest, eager to explore the myriad of scents drifting on the breeze. The pack moved like a stream of choppy water around Decian and Pip's stocky mounts, little waves of excitement cresting here and there. Caius could not help noticing how utterly ill at ease Decian appeared on horseback, bouncing stiffly in the saddle with the reins held awkwardly high.

He winced at the younger man's lack of skill, and chastised himself for it a moment later. What did he expect, for god's sake? It was almost as if Decian had been raised as a commoner and then stuck in prison for the last who-knew-how-many years, rather than learning to ride and hunt like the son of nobility he was.

With luck, his lack of experience on horseback wouldn't matter. The master of hounds controlled the hunting pack with the curled horn hanging from his saddle. No doubt Pip had spent the last two days tutoring Decian in the various signals and commands. He wouldn't need to keep pace with the dogs at all times.

It would be fine, surely. At this point, all Caius could do was hope.

They ventured deeper into the woods, the dense stand of trees cut through with meticulously maintained trails and paths. The dogs sniffed eagerly along the edges of the smooth track along which they were riding, but did not scatter into the forest. Before long, the group passed into a large clearing where the pavilions would be erected. The wagons came to a halt, servants immediately swarming over them to unload and ready things for the royal party's comfort. Aelio spoke to his men, going over final plans for the coming hunt, while Caius forced himself to stay out of the tribuni's way.

He was no longer a soldier in the same sense as Aelio and his underlings. His fighting career had ended four years ago on the western border, with the wet thud of a barbarian battleaxe embedding itself in his flesh. He stood back and let the palace commander do his job, instead watching surreptitiously as Decian and Pip disappeared into the maze of trails with the dogs, seeking a covert where game worth hunting might be flushed out.

Caius turned at the approach of another horse, surprised to find Bruccias sidling his mare within conversational range. Constanzus' youngest son was a dark-haired, well-favored youth of nineteen who'd inherited something of his father's square shoulders and stubborn jaw line. He was also as oily as a mink, adept at greasing the wheels of power whenever he thought that doing so might somehow benefit him.

"A pleasant day for a hunt," said the young princep, as though he and Caius were old drinking friends engaging in casual conversation.

Caius wondered what Bruccius sought to gain from him today. It didn't even occur to him that the friendly gambit might be genuine.

"His Imperial Majesty has always had an excellent eye for the chase," he replied, noncommittal. "It's good that your elder brother was able to join us this morning."

Bruccias laughed lightly, as though at an inside joke. "Oh, indeed." He cleared his throat, and Caius thought, *now we come to it*. "Jesting aside, I must admit, I've been wondering what you make of my brother's recent... *crusade*, Legatus."

There was absolutely no reason for the question to make Caius' heart beat faster, or make prickles of sweat break out across the nape of his neck.

"Proclus has undertaken a crusade?" he asked, being deliberately obtuse. "I can't say I'd noticed, Princep."

Bruccias stared at him unblinkingly. Had Caius been either younger or less jaded than he was, he might have found that flat gaze disconcerting.

"Playing the fool doesn't suit you, Caius," Bruccias said shrewdly. "It's clear you disapprove of Kaeto's private war against our father's bastards. Proclus disapproves as well. So do I. We thought you should know that."

Privately, Caius doubted whether Proclus had even *noticed* the steady stream of young men entering the palace gates over the past weeks, never to leave again. He also wasn't certain what, exactly, Bruccias was getting at.

He summoned a suitably noncommittal reply. "Prisoners in the empire serve their sentence at His Imperial Majesty's pleasure. My opinion on the disposition of that sentence carries no weight."

Still, Bruccias continued to watch him with unnerving intensity. "His Imperial Majesty's pleasure had nothing to do with it, Legatus — as I suspect you well know. Kaeto has been taking liberties."

Caius wished mightily for a convenient exit from the conversation. "I wouldn't presume to comment on matters of which I know nothing, Princep," was all he said.

Finally, Bruccias blinked. "Of course not. I only wish to know whether Proclus can count on your support, should our dear brother attempt to reach even higher for things beyond his grasp."

So that was it. Bruccias was feeling out the sentiment of the inner court… not anything more sinister that that. Nothing relating to Caius' recent actions in saving Decian, as his paranoia had tried to suggest.

"I serve the rightful succession," Caius replied gruffly, wondering if that was truly the case anymore. Soldiers who served the empire loyally tended not to disobey the direct orders of the second in line to the throne.

"As you have done for far longer than I've been alive," Bruccias said with oily graciousness. "Forgive me, Legatus, for implying it could be otherwise."

Caius was reminded, not for the first time, of the many reasons he so disliked the emperor's youngest son. It was a great pity that he also disliked the emperor's *other* sons — though for different reasons. Thankfully, he was saved from having to come up with a diplomatic reply by the sound of a hunting horn echoing through the trees.

"Ah!" Bruccias cried, a smile lighting up his handsome face. "It seems the chase is on! Come, Caius — let us see what the dogs have scared up for us."

The young princep wheeled his mare and galloped off, while Caius followed at a more sedate pace, reining in his eager mount. His gelding would happily have charged ahead at full speed, but Caius was well aware that he was included in hunts such as this only as a courtesy these days. He carried no weapon except the ceremonial sword and dagger at his belt — neither of which was a generally preferred method for dispatching game.

Since his injury, he could no longer fire a crossbow or hurl a spear reliably while also controlling a horse. And while some soldiers might revel in hurtling after a deer over ditches and logs, risking a fall or a mount's broken leg for the sake of meat that could be more easily acquired elsewhere — Caius was not one of them. He headed toward the sound of the horn at a sedate canter, the gray horse champing impatiently at the bit.

Members of the hunt tended to sort themselves into two groups fairly quickly — those for whom the chance to make the kill represented glory and increased status, and those who either felt that they had to make an appearance, or who genuinely enjoyed a morning's canter through a forest with the occasional stream to splash through or fallen tree to leap.

On his best days, Caius might count himself among the latter group. The Silver Wood was undeniably a beautiful place, and having the wind in one's face and a good horse between one's legs for an hour or three was not an unpleasant proposition. Unfortunately, today was not destined to be numbered amongst Caius' best days.

Or... perhaps it should be, given that he had finally made some small stand against the many injustices surrounding him. Whatever the case, Caius' main concern on this particular hunt was ensuring that Decian got away cleanly. He was confident that once away from Amarius, the young man would be good to his word, disappearing never to be heard from again.

Lucky man, he caught himself thinking.

Riding near the front of the less ambitious group of hunters, Caius registered a downed tree ahead, its trunk lodged across the trail at an angle. He steadied his gelding and approached the lower side, shifting his weight forward and giving the animal its head as powerful muscles bunched beneath him, launching them over the obstacle.

He absorbed the impact of the landing with his knees — something else that had been considerably easier a few years ago. Several other riders followed his lead, but then he heard a commotion behind him indicating that someone's horse had balked, or otherwise caused a problem.

Caius didn't look back, since it wasn't his job to babysit soft courtiers who couldn't properly sit a horse over a low jump. Unbidden, his thoughts flashed to Decian, bouncing in the saddle with the reins held stiffly in front of him. Thankfully, Decian struck him as a man with enough sense to ride around any obstacles he wasn't confident of mastering on horseback.

Ahead, more hunting horns sounded, indicating the quarry was in sight.

"What do you think they've got?" puffed a pale courtier riding at Caius' right flank.

"Does it really matter?" Caius replied.

Suddenly unwilling to pretend enthusiasm for this hunt that should never have happened in the first place, he allowed his eager horse to stretch into a gallop that left his companions behind. The animal leapt across the next ditch almost gleefully, its breath coming in rhythmic snorts.

Ahead, he could hear the excited cries of the hunters, and he gathered that the lead riders had caught up to whatever prey the dogs had flushed from cover. In the confusion of trees and crisscrossing animal trails, it took some time to find the main party. By the time he finally did, the day's excitement appeared to be over. Caius could make out no details across the length of the clearing where the final confrontation had taken place—only the dogs milling around whatever creature had been brought down, while Pip and Decian on their fat ponies waded into the midst of the pack to call them off the carcass.

The emperor's white horse trotted toward him, and Caius straightened to unthinking attention in the saddle.

"Your Imperial Majesty," he greeted.

"Ah, Caius!" The emperor's eyes shone with an almost fanatical light from within his gaunt face. "A good hunt! Kaeto and Bruccias brought down the beast together— though I think it was Kaeto's spear that pierced its heart."

"I'm pleased to hear it," Caius managed.

Constanzus waved an airy hand. "Yes, yes. Well, do carry on, Legatus."

Already, the emperor's customary distracted expression was reasserting itself. Caius felt the increasingly familiar sense of a heavy weight clenching cold and clammy inside his gut. The leader of an empire that spanned continents was failing before his eyes, and no one worthy of the title stood waiting in the wings to replace him.

He swallowed hard. "Yes, Your Majesty." But Constanzus had already wandered off.

Across the glen, the dogs had clustered around Pip, who led them away from the kill with a shrill whistle and a snap of his whip. Decian trotted toward Caius, and a new, much more pleasant kind of tension coiled in his chest. The younger man smiled at him with a sort of wary hopefulness as he approached. Something about that smile made Caius' throat ache.

"Greetings, Legatus," Decian said with a sense of formality that didn't quite ring true. "It looks as though I'm missing two dogs. I figured I'd send the rest of the pack back with Pip while I nip off and look for them. I assume you'll let the others know, in case anyone wonders where I've disappeared to?"

The wink that accompanied the words was so quick Caius almost missed it.

"As long as you think you can manage it without falling off that pony," he returned.

That startled a huffed breath of laughter from Decian. "I won't lie—my arse may never recover from the last couple of hours," he said. Then his tone softened into something more genuine. "Thank you for everything you've done."

Caius made a concerted attempt to ground himself in this moment—appreciating the fact that he'd helped an innocent man to freedom, while ignoring the impulse to stare too long at the aforementioned man's square, hard-muscled shoulders and slender waist.

"Call me Caius," he replied. "I'll pass on the message to anyone who asks. Good hunting, Decian."

"Good hunting… *Caius*." Decian smiled his crooked little half-smile again, before reining the pony around with exaggerated, unpracticed movements. Caius watched him go, finding himself oddly surprised by the anticlimactic nature of it all.

SEVEN

After ensuring that Decian was safely away, Caius rejoined the main party and dismounted, handing his horse off to a servant so he could stretch his legs for a bit and try to unknot the cramped and twisted muscles in his bad shoulder. Unfortunately, this tactical decision had the unintended consequence of exposing his metaphorical flank to a bevy of over-excited young whelps who thought a beast hounded to its death in the forest was somehow worthy of awe.

"It's magnificent, is it not?" crowed one. "Quite the largest I've ever seen."

"You *must* come and see before the butchers start hacking at it!" exclaimed another.

And so it was that Caius found himself being chivvied along to look at a dead animal lying in the grass at the edge of a glen. He let the inane chattering of the courtiers wash over him — wishing only for the peace and privacy of his quarters, now that Decian was gone and the thing was finally done.

The little knot of men approached the site of the kill, and the courtier on Caius' right said, "Look at those antlers! They must be six feet across, at least!"

Caius' feet brought him to an abrupt halt at the edge of the circle of trampled grass. Blood coated the broken stalks, and his vision swam for a moment as the image before him blurred double with the image from his dream.

From his *memory*.

A great stag lay in the bloodied grass, its hide smeared with crimson. Spears jutted from its ribs and flank. Its dark eyes stared through Caius, and its tongue jutted obscenely from its mouth, swollen and purple. For a moment, the play of shadows from the overhanging branches darkened its antler-tips, making them appear shiny with gore to his addled gaze.

He took a single, involuntary step back before catching himself and blinking rapidly.

No.

This was not the otherworldly abomination that had killed his father when he was a boy of eight. There were only two spears, not three—hurled by the hands of Kaeto and Bruccias. The stag's antlers were not blood-soaked; it was merely a trick of shadow and light. Its eyes did not glow as they had in his dream.

He glanced around furtively, his breath coming fast and shallow. No one had noticed his lapse. They were all too busy fawning over the supposed greatness of the two princes who had ridden down an exhausted hart and killed it, as though the feat had been some enviable battlefield victory.

"Is it not a majestic creature?" sighed the man who had waxed poetical earlier about the stag's antlers. He glanced at Caius, clearly expecting a response.

It probably was, but it's not anymore, Caius thought.

"I need a piss," he said aloud, aware that his voice emerged hoarse. Before anyone could express outrage at his lack of appreciation for the carcass bleeding onto the dirt, he turned and escaped into the trees—ostensibly to find some privacy so he could relieve himself.

His heart still thundered painfully against his chest. He kept walking until the sounds of the hunting party faded to a distant buzz behind him, and fetched up against the sturdy bole of an ancient oak tree.

It was ridiculous. He'd seen dead stags before, many times. Hell, he'd taken a few himself in his younger days. If it hadn't been for that *fucking* dream last night…

Caius growled in frustration at his unruly mind, fumbling with the laces of his breeches and smallclothes— as though following through with his feeble excuse for fleeing the glade would somehow erase the lapse that had preceded it. He stepped back and aimed a weak stream of piss at the base of the tree, silently cursing himself, his nightmare, the failing emperor who thought this hunt had been a good idea, and stags who were too stupid to escape a pack of baying hounds.

A twig snapped somewhere off to his left, and he turned his head sharply toward the noise.

It might have been another member of the hunting party come to relieve his bladder. It might have been an animal. But the fine hair at the back of Caius' neck prickled unpleasantly, and he tucked himself away as quickly as he could without making it look like he'd noticed something amiss. He turned casually in the direction of the sound, his right hand resting on the hilt of his dagger.

A breath of air caressed his cheek as a crossbow bolt flew past and embedded itself in the tree with a sharp *thunk*, two inches from his temple.

In an instant, the heady awareness of imminent death sang through his veins, dispelling his earlier disquiet between one heartbeat and the next. Caius was already in motion, putting the tree trunk between himself and the archer's position. His thoughts flew — was this an attack on the royal family? Or had he merely stumbled upon a poacher desperate enough to add murder to his crimes if it meant silencing a witness who might drag him before the imperial magistrate?

A second arrow sliced through the loose sleeve of his linen shirt, drawing a burning line across his left bicep before burying itself in wood. He cursed and ripped it free, darting sideways into the trees. That one had come from a completely different direction.

This was no poacher.

He could cry out for help — attempt to shout a warning — but he'd purposely wandered far away from the main party. It would take them some time to find him, especially now that he was on the move. It was also unlikely that he'd be able to convey the nature of the threat effectively enough to keep any responders from stumbling into a hail of arrows.

How many assailants were there? *Damnation*. If there were any possibility of this being an organized, large-scale attack, there was nothing else for it.

"*Ambush!*" he roared in his best battlefield bellow — rusty now, after four years of palace life. "*Guards!* Protect the royals!"

Caius ducked and dodged through the trees, not following any established path or trail. If he could take down one of the two currently hunting him, he could make his way back to the clearing with less chance of being cut down for his troubles.

Another crossbow bolt whizzed past, going wide in the confusion of tree trunks and brush. He tracked its direction and altered course, heading for the source of the shot. Distantly, he could just make out the sound of shouting as the hunting party and its guards reacted to his cry of warning.

Closer, the sound of a would-be assassin on the move held his attention firmly on his goal. It was impossible to move silently in this tangle of branches and underbrush, with piles of fallen leaves crunching underfoot. With luck, their surroundings would also negate much of the advantage his opponents held with their ranged weapons. Unfortunately, the forest was also a poor venue for sword fighting. Though naturally left-handed, Caius had made a point over the past four years of becoming competent as a right-handed swordsman. Now, though, his dagger was the best option in his limited arsenal.

He just had to get close enough to use it without getting skewered by a crossbow bolt first.

The assailant he was tracking changed course, cutting toward him at an angle that made Caius think he was attempting to get in front of him for an ambush. He increased his pace through the vines and thickets, his lungs burning from the unaccustomed exertion. Indeed, moments later he stumbled without warning into a small clearing. The bare patch in the woods had been obscured from view until he was practically upon it.

The archer stood at the far end, dressed in dark clothing, with a mask obscuring the lower half of his face. Perhaps a dozen strides separated them. The man whirled to face him, lifting a loaded double-bolt crossbow into position in the same motion.

Instinct had Caius flipping the dagger in his right hand to grasp the blade between thumb and forefinger, before letting it fly in an overhand throw. The reality of being both out of practice and naturally left-handed meant that the blade embedded itself in the meat of the man's arm rather than anyplace more vital.

The assassin cried out, the crossbow releasing one of its twin bolts with a twang as it slipped from his injured grasp. The bolt missed Caius by a hand's breadth, flying over his head to crash into the brush. Caius unsheathed his sword with a snarl and charged. The assassin drew a blade with his good hand, steel meeting steel as they clashed. Caius hacked at his opponent with the vicious recklessness that had earned him his reputation on the battlefield over the course of a military career spanning decades.

It didn't matter that he was well into his forty-sixth year, or that he'd not seen a battle since the one that had ruined his shoulder. It didn't matter that his left arm was largely useless for swordplay after the injury. His opponent, injured and outclassed, stood no chance fighting him blade against blade. Caius hacked and slashed, knocking the other man's sword to the side and kneeing him in the stomach.

The man stumbled back, his shoulders impacting a tree at the edge of the clearing. A moment later, he looked down in confusion at the slice that opened his gut. Caius watched the man's sword hilt slide from nerveless fingers. His hands came up to cradle the ruin of his stomach, uselessly. A moment later, he slid down the rough bark of the tree trunk to sprawl on the ground, groaning as he bled out.

Caius sheathed his sword. He moved cautiously, leaning down to retrieve the discarded crossbow, still with its single remaining bolt loaded and cocked. A rustle came from the underbrush to his right. When he straightened and whipped around, it was to find the second assassin aiming his own crossbow at Caius' heart.

EIGHT

Caius wouldn't have voluntarily chosen to engage in a duel of crossbows where he was forced to fire right-handed. His finger tightened on the trigger at the same instant as the assassin's. The twangs of two bolts releasing reached his ears simultaneously.

He grunted as nauseating pain flared in his left thigh, the impact spinning him to the side. His attacker slumped forward, free hand curling around the bolt bristling from his ribcage as he fell to the ground and started jerking. Caius tried to catch himself against the nearest tree trunk with his left hand, but missed, his scarred shoulder hitting it instead. The twisted muscles screamed, a throbbing counterpoint to the fiery burn of the arrow embedded in his leg.

His jaw ached with the force of his gritted teeth as he steadied himself, knowing he needed to stay alert and on his feet in the event of more archers hiding in the woods. A quick glance at the body near his feet confirmed that the first assassin had a quiver of crossbow bolts slung over his shoulder, but Caius feared that leaning down and trying to grab one so he could reload his stolen weapon might make him pass out. Before he could convince himself to attempt it anyway, the shouts of approaching guards and hunters responding to his raised alarm reached his ears.

"Here!" he cried hoarsely. "Look sharp—there might be archers in the trees!"

Aelio appeared first, sword drawn and blue eyes snapping fire. Then, to Caius' distant surprise, Decian charged into the clearing from the opposite direction, skidding to a halt as he took in the carnage and the arrow sticking out of Caius' leg. With the immediate crisis apparently over, Caius let the growing heaviness in his body drag him down in a semi-controlled collapse against the base of the tree, hissing a bit as the wound in his leg protested.

"The emperor?" he asked, directing the question to Aelio.

"Safe and well guarded," said the tribuni. "What happened here, Legatus?"

Caius raised a shaking hand to scrub at his face. "I went for a piss, and nearly took an arrow through the skull for my trouble. There were two of them… as you can see."

Decian seemed to wrench himself free of his paralysis. "You're hurt," he said, giving the downed assassin next to Caius a wide berth as he approached.

"It's not serious," Caius said, giving his leg a long look and sighing.

"There's an arrow sticking out of you," Decian replied rather pointedly.

Aelio snorted. "Definitely not for the first time, houndsman. Though, one might hope it will be the last. No offense, Caius, but you're supposed to be retired from active duty."

"Tell that to the random assassins roaming the woods," he grumbled.

Aelio shook his head and gestured at the arrow. "You want to take that out now? Or wait until you're back at the palace?"

Caius made a disgruntled noise and grasped the shaft right handed, yanking it free in a single, sharp movement. Decian flinched. Blood welled from the wound, but didn't spurt—as he'd known it wouldn't. He tossed the bolt aside and untied the decorative blue sash from his waist.

"It went in at an angle," he told Decian, who was looking decidedly pale beneath his tawny skin—especially for someone who'd barely batted an eye while a man was being torn apart by dogs a handful of days ago. "Don't worry, it mostly lodged under the skin rather than in the muscle. Someone help me bind it and give me a shoulder to lean on. Where's my horse?"

"Back at the clearing with the kill, I should imagine," Aelio said, as Decian hesitantly leant a hand to wrap the blue cloth around the wound and tie it tight. More people were arriving, and Caius cursed silently as he truly registered for the first time that Decian hadn't made it away as planned.

Aelio prodded the second assailant's body with the toe of his boot, looking down with a frown. "Next question—who were they, and what were they after?" He leaned down and tugged off the man's mask, revealing nondescript Alyrion features.

Leg bandaged—after a fashion, at least—Caius accepted Decian's hand up, steadying himself between the younger man and the tree at his back until his lightheadedness subsided.

"Not poachers, that's for sure," he gritted, carefully testing a bit of weight on the leg. It held, notwithstanding the stab of pain radiating outward from the wound. "Assassins after the emperor and his sons, probably. I must have surprised them as they were trying to sneak up on the main party."

Aelio's expression hardened. "In which case, we have an even bigger problem with security than we originally thought. It's not as though this hunting expedition was advertised to the public."

"As you say," Caius agreed. His wound flared as he took another step, still leaning on Decian. "*Fuck*, I should've killed the bastards slower. And a *lot* more painfully."

Aelio raised a wry eyebrow. "If it meant we could have questioned them before they died, I can't disagree."

"I can't believe you two are joking about this," Decian muttered.

Caius shot him a sideways glance, suddenly struck by the warm line of Decian's body pressed against his. He cleared his throat and looked away.

"Didn't you have some missing dogs to look for?" he prodded.

"They can wait for a bit," Decian replied grimly.

"Come, Legatus. Let's get you back to the others," Aelio said, before turning to the additional men who'd arrived. "Search the area. Make sure no one else is skulking around. Watch your backs." With that, the tribuni sheathed his sword. He and Decian maneuvered Caius between them, working around his bad shoulder as best they could.

"Your arm's bleeding, too," Decian pointed out, frowning at the line of red soaking Caius' left shirtsleeve.

"It's just a graze," he said, having forgotten all about it in the face of subsequent events.

"If you say so." Decian's tone was skeptical.

They hobbled through the underbrush, cursing as it dragged at them, until they reached a trail. Caius was pretty thoroughly turned around by that point, but Aelio seemed to know where he was going. Eventually, they did, in fact, reach the clearing with its bloody, trampled circle of grass at one edge. The butchers had continued their work despite the excitement, and the creature from Caius' bad dreams was now little more than a stack of meat and a pair of trophy antlers.

He still had to look away from it.

In the shade of the trees beyond, the members of the royal family were gathered together on horseback, surrounded on all sides by a tight pack of guards bristling with weapons. Caius ran his eyes over the four figures at the center of the circle out of habit, ensuring that they were all unhurt and accounted for.

"There were two assassins armed with blades and crossbows in the woods, Your Majesties," Aelio reported once they were close enough to be heard. "The legatus killed them, but was injured during the fight. I have other men searching the forest to make certain no others are hiding there, but we should return to the palace immediately for Your Majesties' safety."

Proclus ran bloodshot eyes over their sad little procession. "Old Caius killed them, eh?" He laughed, short and harsh. "Still a bit of life in the one-armed soldier after all, then. Who'd've thought?"

Irritation at the casual slight would have been unseemly. It also required more energy than Caius really possessed at the moment. Any ruffled feathers he might have suffered were quickly soothed by the way Constanzus looked at him, dark brows furrowing—clearly seeing him properly.

"Well done, Legatus," he said, sounding more like the man Caius had known, and less like the pale shadow he'd become. "Once again, you bleed to protect us."

"It is my duty, Your Imperial Majesty," he managed, taken aback by the degree to which such praise could still affect him. "Nothing more."

He wasn't oblivious to the fact of Decian supporting his right side, face to face with the father he didn't know and the half-brother who would prefer to see him dead. Kaeto sniffed, oblivious to the identity of his escaped victim standing mere yards away.

"Perhaps the legatus should retire for medical attention and rest after such unexpected exertion," the princep suggested, as though he had an ounce of care for anyone but himself.

"You're quite correct, Your Majesty," Aelio agreed quickly. His gaze flicked between Caius and the royal family uncertainly. "I could—"

"You are needed here," Proclus interrupted. "If there is danger to us, your place is guarding us during our return to the palace."

"I'll take care of him," Decian said immediately.

Caius grimaced. "The missing dogs…"

"*Will be fine*," Decian finished for him. "Pip can deal with them."

Kaeto looked down his nose from his elevated position on horseback. "And who is this?"

A chill ran down Caius' spine that had nothing to do with exertion or blood loss.

"He's the new—" Aelio began.

"No one of import, Your Majesty," Caius interrupted, speaking over him. "I will allow him to help me back to my quarters, and no doubt be recovered enough to return to duty in a few days."

"Yes, yes," said the emperor, waving an airy hand. "Do go on. You're suddenly looking rather pale, Legatus."

Caius bowed as best he could, elbowing Decian when he didn't immediately follow suit. As quickly as was feasible, he dragged Decian away as though he were the one with two good legs and Decian, the injured one.

Subtle, it probably wasn't, based on the look Aelio gave him as they left.

"So, was that...?" Decian started to ask.

"The Emperor of Alyrios and his three sons, yes," Caius muttered.

"Huh," Decian said. "Which one was the asshole who ordered me executed? I recognized his voice."

Caius pressed his lips together, and not only because his damned leg hurt. "That would be Princep Kaeto. The middle son."

Decian didn't reply.

It took a few minutes to track down someone who could retrieve Caius' horse. The gray gelding snorted mistrustfully at Decian, who eyed him with equal distaste.

"Your horse is very... big," he observed.

"Yes. Still, you'll forgive me if I prefer not to ride your pony back to the city," Caius sniped, aware that his tone sounded more than a little peevish.

Decian shrugged. "As you like. You're the one who has to figure out how to get into the saddle."

Caius looked at the tall gelding, and sighed.

NINE

The less said about the logistics of Caius getting mounted, the better. In the end, it required three men, a tree stump, and quite a bit of creative cursing. Meanwhile, a guard had retrieved the roan pony from the forest where Decian had abandoned it during the excitement. When they were ready to depart, however, Decian decreed firmly that he would walk back rather than riding.

Aelio's men had found no trace of anyone else hiding in the woods. Caius and Decian left ahead of the main party, since it would take time to pack up the wagons and organize the men for the return to the palace. Once Caius was confident they were well out of hearing range of the others, he turned a frown toward the younger man walking even with his horse's shoulder.

"You could still leave, you know," he said in a low tone.

Decian glanced up at him, eyes dark and guarded. "I heard you shouting about an ambush, back in the forest. Figured I owed you one after the kennels." He shrugged. "There'll be other hunts. And anyway, the guards are already getting to know me. It's not like this was my only chance to get away."

Caius swallowed another protest—knowing the other man was right, but still taken aback by the jolt of worry he'd felt when Kaeto had expressed casual interest in Decian's identity.

Decian raised an eyebrow. "So, are we going to look for a surgeon when we get back? Is there one in the palace? There must be, right?"

Caius felt his features twist with distaste. "Might as well have asked the butchers in the hunting party to have a go at me once they were done with the stag. The wound just needs cleaning and bandaging, that's all."

Decian glanced up at him with a raised eyebrow. "If you say so. Does this kind of thing happen to you often, then?"

Caius snorted. "I was a soldier for nearly three decades. The job comes with its share of wounds."

"Like your shoulder?" prompted Decian, who could hardly have failed to notice the defect during the awkward three-man shuffle back to the clearing earlier.

"Yes. I took a blow from a battle axe four years ago," he said. "Can't say I really recommend it."

Decian nodded. "I don't blame you. I managed to get through ten years of prison with only a single flogging and the occasional beating by the guards. Can't say I recommend any of it, to be honest."

Caius remembered the mess of scar tissue he'd seen on Decian's bare back in the kennels.

"What was the flogging for?" he asked.

"I helped another prisoner escape," Decian said.

Caius blinked at him. Alyrion prisons weren't exactly known for their leniency. "Surprised it wasn't more than a flogging, for something like that."

Bitterness crept into Decian's tone. "Being a nobleman's bastard comes with a few benefits, apparently. Right up until the day when it doesn't anymore."

Caius digested that for a few moments.

"What about the man you helped?" he asked eventually. "Did he make it out?"

"I'm not sure," Decian replied. "They didn't tell me. I never saw a body, so he might've done. Of course, I was also delirious with fever and blood loss for more than a week after the whipping, so I could have missed it. I hope he did get away. He was nice, and he had other people who cared about him enough to try to sneak in and smuggle him out."

Caius wasn't prepared for the sharp ache those words engendered. How long had it been since he'd had people in his life who'd cared for him that much?

Unbidden, Serah's face appeared in his memory—his sweet wife, rosy-cheeked, with long, brown hair and twinkling gray eyes. They'd both been so young when she'd died... matched in an arranged marriage that had hardly lasted long enough to blossom into more. Yet her loss had hollowed him out as nothing else ever had. Diminished him in ways he couldn't fully express, not even all these years later.

In the army, he'd had comrades, of course—men as close as brothers. He'd known the intimacy of trusting that the man next to you would lay down his life for yours, as you would do for him in turn. Sometimes, there had been intimacy of other kinds among the men, as well—in a setting where such liaisons were quietly overlooked since they helped with morale.

Too many of Caius' fellow soldiers had fallen at his side during battle. Too many had fallen while under his command. Eventually, he'd fallen in battle as well, in the course of protecting his emperor... and now he was alone in a world that didn't suit his talents, surrounded by people to whom he was either a useless relic or an embarrassing hindrance.

"Whether he made it out alive or not, your friend was still a lucky man to have such friends," he managed.

They continued in silence. Caius directed his horse down smaller side streets as they reentered the city, rather than staying on the main vaia with its milling crowds shooting them furtive, angry glances. Eventually, they arrived at the outer wall of the imperial quarter, where Caius made a point of introducing Decian to the pair of guards manning the east gate.

One of the men took a single glance at Caius' leg and asked if he wanted to send for the physician, but Caius waved him off with a growled negative. "Send a stableboy to meet us at my quarters and take my horse, though," he added grudgingly.

Passing through the gate, they continued into the maze of walls and buildings. The dwelling belonging to Caius was part of a larger block of tightly packed *insulae* located on the western side of the palace compound, housing courtiers and other advisors to the royal family. After half a lifetime spent bunking in various forts and encampments, Caius had always considered the house to be ridiculously grand with its atrium and colonnaded garden… but at least it was private. After his years of eschewing social contact, few people bothered him here. Even the middle-aged slave woman who cooked and cleaned for him knew enough to perform most of her work while he was out.

A fresh-faced stable lad jogged up while he was maneuvering himself out of the saddle—a process thankfully simpler than getting into it had been. Caius tossed the boy a copper coin as he led the gelding away, and accepted Decian's support to hobble inside.

Unnecessarily grand or not, Caius still felt a bit of tension unwind from his shoulders as he entered the familiar haven. It felt decidedly odd to welcome another person inside the house. Decian looked around with something uncomfortably close to awe. Caius directed him through the atrium with its burbling marble fountain, past the hallway with the kitchen on one side and his office on the other, and into the open garden surrounded by white columns.

His bedroom—along with three identical guest rooms that he never used—opened onto the airy space. Inside, wood and kindling lay ready in the grate, placed there by Tertia, the housekeeper, in anticipation of his return.

"How many people live in this place?" Decian asked, still taking everything in as though his neck was on a swivel-joint. "It's like a palace within a palace."

"Just me," Caius said gruffly, peeling himself away from Decian's support and limping across the room to his bed. He unbuckled his swordbelt and laid it on the table before sinking onto the edge of the mattress, his bad leg stretched out in front of him, heel resting on the floor. Once there, he realized that his ambition to care for his injuries had evaporated at some point during the journey. Left to his own devices, at this moment he would have done nothing more useful than collapse onto the feather mattress and sleep.

"Just you? *Seriously?*" Decian echoed. "Being a legatus clearly comes with a few more perks than being a nobleman's bastard, even on a good day."

"It's not so much being a legatus," Caius said, "as being someone who stood between the emperor and a barbarian's axe on the battlefield. That part does come with a few benefits, it's true."

Decian ran a weather eye up and down Caius' body. "You're about to keel over, aren't you," he observed, not really phrasing it as a question. "Get your shirt off so I can see that graze on your arm. Then we'll tackle the rest."

Unused to being fussed over, Caius felt his mind settle into relieved compliance despite his best intentions. He opened the row of hook-and-eye closures securing his leather jerkin and slid it off—right arm first, then the left. Next, he pulled the hem of his linen shirt free from his trousers and shrugged out of it, dipping his head to ease himself free of the wide collar without the requirement of raising his bad arm very far. The blood-stiffened linen had become glued to his skin as it dried. He winced as he pulled it away from the shallow wound where the second arrow had carved a furrow in his bicep.

Decian leaned close, grasping him above the elbow and gently turning his upper arm toward the light from the window. The fine hairs all over Caius' body stood up in response to the touch, and he cleared his throat to distract himself.

"There's a bottle half full of brandy on the shelf," he said in a tone that was purposely gruff. "Get it for me, please."

Decian gave him a wry look, his face somehow both too close and not close enough to Caius'. "Are you planning on drinking it or using it to clean the wounds?" he asked.

"Both," Caius replied without hesitation.

The huff of amusement he got in response did nothing to quiet his rattling thoughts, but at least Decian did as he'd asked. Left to his own devices for a few moments, he craned around to look, confirming that the slice in his skin wasn't ragged enough to require debridement. It was oozing again after he'd pulled the sleeve free of the clotting blood, but it would probably do better without a bandage, even so.

Decian returned and handed him the uncorked brandy bottle before gesturing at the wound. "You should leave that open to the air, assuming you can keep it clean. It'll scab in a few hours," he said, echoing Caius' thoughts.

"Agreed." Caius tipped the bottle to his lips right-handed, swallowing without decorum. The brandy burned going down, but it would take a lot more than what he had available to truly dull the pain of the next few minutes.

"Do you have anything here to bandage your leg?" Decian asked. "Anything *clean*, that is to say."

"There should be towels in the kitchen somewhere," he said. "You can use a couple of those."

Once Decian left to look for the linen, Caius gritted his teeth and sloshed a bit of the brandy over the graze on his arm. Pain flared, which was at least a momentary distraction from the insistent throbbing in his damned leg. He breathed through it, using his discarded shirt to mop at the rivulets of reddish brown spidering down his arm before they could drip onto the bedding.

By the time Decian returned with a bowl of clean water and the linen, Caius was fumbling at the tight knot of makeshift bandaging over the hole in his thigh with fingers that didn't want to cooperate. Decian batted his hands away. "Let me. Get your breeches unlaced."

Between them, they got him stripped down to his smallclothes, which had mostly escaped harm except for a bit of blood staining the bottom edge.

"Lie down," Decian ordered, pushing Caius onto his back and helping him lift his injured leg onto the bed. He perched on the edge of the mattress to examine the ragged hole. Caius draped his right arm across his eyes, wishing once more that he could just sleep for the rest of the day and deal with the wound later.

All thoughts of sleep fled in an instant when a callused hand closed on his thigh, resting a few inches below the wound. The touch was utterly innocent—a way to steady the leg as Decian prepared to clean up the injury so he could see it properly. Innocent intentions or not, the blood rushed urgently to Caius' prick, which twitched hard against his smalls, tenting the loose material.

Cursing his body's longstanding tendency to blur the lines between fighting and fucking—not to mention the effects of the brandy on his self-control—Caius let his arm slide away from his eyes so he could judge Decian's expression. Caius was both too old and too experienced to succumb to irrational panic over another man's reaction to his sexual proclivities… which wasn't to say that such reactions couldn't turn ugly, given Alyrion social mores. He didn't fear Decian. The man was unarmed, and in no position to make trouble for himself. Even so, Caius wasn't ignorant of his own vulnerability given the current situation.

Decian looked from Caius' cock to his face, his pleasant features tinged with wry surprise. "Well, well. So, there's a human being lurking beneath that gruff exterior after all, huh?" He quirked a crooked smile. "Though your timing could maybe use some work."

Caius relaxed and covered his eyes again. "'S just the brandy, that's all. Ignore me."

Decian snorted. "Ignore you getting hard for me? Bit of a tall order there, since it's been, like, a year since I last got laid. Too bad this next part is going to kill the mood stone dead. Here—bite down on this."

Caius lifted his arm enough to find Decian offering his thick leather belt, and grunted with discontent before taking it and biting down on it as ordered. The agony of strong spirits flushing out the rip in his flesh left by the crossbow bolt did, as promised, wipe every last thought of ardor from his mind. He arched and cried out around the makeshift gag, writhing until the pain subsided to more manageable levels.

He was barely aware of Decian wrapping the leg in clean linen and sliding the belt from between his gritted teeth. Cool hands lifted his head, supporting the back of his neck and holding the brandy bottle to his lips until it was empty. A wet cloth mopped at the sweat beading his forehead and chest, but somehow he was asleep before the soothing sensation truly registered.

TEN

Of course, on the one night when he truly needed some damned rest, Caius dreamed again. This was not the childhood nightmare of death in the forest. Instead, it was a soldier's dream of battle lost, and honor ground underfoot. Caius had barely turned eighteen when, fresh out of military training, he'd been sent as an oarsman to be part of the naval assault on the Eburosi port of Llanmeer.

At the time, the emperor had been set on adding the barbarian island of Eburos to his crown—a shining jewel of natural resources and productive mines that had somehow managed to cling to its independence up to that point. After the natives launched a series of ambush attacks on Alyrion troops pushing north into the wilder areas of the island, Constanzus had decided to move in with a larger force, attacking by sea.

As a freshly commissioned grunt with no battle experience, Caius had only learned the details of the assault later. At the time, he'd merely been told to row the damned boat and kill as many barbarians as he could skewer on the end of his sword once they reached the beach.

As tactics went, it had seemed straightforward enough.

Caius remembered the swell of pride he'd felt as part of the massive waves of sleek, six-man landing craft sculling through the water in well-disciplined lines. He also remembered the bewildering barrage of cloth pouches packed with rocks and choking powder raining down on their boats from lines of trebuchets arrayed along the cliff tops as they neared the shore.

Many of the pouches had burst open on impact, coating the boats and the unlucky men aboard them with fine gray dust. They hadn't understood what was happening until a salvo of flaming arrows followed the hail of powder filled pouches, and the dust-covered vessels had promptly exploded into fireballs, sinking with all aboard.

Caius had watched in disbelief as the boats surrounding him were decimated, only sheer luck keeping his afloat as other men screamed around him—burning and drowning, weighed down by their metal armor. The commanders had bellowed at the surviving men, driving them forward through the carnage of the sinking fleet and onto the shore.

The first wave to make it through had engaged the enemy barbarians on the beach, fighting their way up a rocky path carved into the cliff side to get to the city above. They were already halfway up, barbarians falling like cattle to the slaughter, when Caius' boat reached the shore and scraped to a halt against the sandy bottom. He'd barely had a chance to scramble out of the craft and draw his sword when the army of unnatural wolves had arrived.

On the voyage across the channel, the men had amused each other with tales of pagan Eburosi shapeshifters who could control the spirits of animals with magic. He'd laughed off the stories with the rest of the soldiers, pretending with a young man's bravado that they didn't chill him to his marrow… that they didn't fling his mind back to his childhood and a dead stag surrounded by the corpses of fallen guardsmen.

In the Alyrion homeland, one did not acknowledge belief in the power of pagan warlocks aloud. Not in the army. Not if one wanted to advance. Not even when one's own father had been killed by a shapeshifter.

On a beach in Eburos, however, the wolves came like a tide, ripping and tearing at Alyrion soldiers while leaving the enemy barbarians untouched… and Caius turned tail in fear, fleeing back to his boat. It would have been the most humiliating moment of his life, were it not for the fact that every other soldier still standing was doing exactly the same thing. Such cowardice during battle should have been cause for court-martial and expulsion, were it not for the fact that turning out so many soldiers at once would only have served to bring more attention to what was already a disgraceful defeat.

Caius jerked awake from a vision of two wolves closing on him as he stumbled toward his boat, his heavy armor slowing his footsteps until it felt as though he were slogging through treacle. He lay in bed, staring at the plastered cornices of his bedroom ceiling, his heart and his head pounding in time with each other.

Only when he tried to swing into a sitting position did the recent past swim into focus. His thigh screamed a protest at the movement. He swallowed a curse as he fell back — remembering the hunt, and the would-be assassins in the forest.

Remembering *Decian*.

The light filtering in through the window held the gray, uncertain quality of early morning. Caius took a deep breath and sat up more carefully this time, clutching his bandaged leg to steady it. His head protested the change in elevation… or, more accurately, it protested the amount of brandy he'd swigged the previous evening. He ignored the pounding ache, taking stock of the rest of his body as best he could.

The arm wasn't too bad. It had scabbed well while he slept, and since he already favored that arm as a matter of course, he was used to the restriction in movement that would be necessary to protect the wound for a few days. The leg would be more of a hindrance — but only a small amount of blood had seeped through the bandages overnight, and he was able to cautiously bend and straighten his knee without anything catastrophic happening.

The rest of his body felt like he'd run headlong through a forest full of underbrush and fought two men half his age. Which… was reasonable under the circumstances, he supposed. At least he'd fought two men half his age and *won*.

He let his gaze wander around the room, unsurprised to find it empty of anyone except him. Cautiously, he stretched the parts of himself that hadn't been recently injured, and levered himself onto his good leg. A bit of experimentation proved that as long as he was careful, the bad one would take his weight without buckling. With slow, hitching steps, he hobbled to the chamberpot and relieved himself.

As he was lacing up his smallclothes, he heard a shuffle of movement coming from the front of the house and stilled. Had someone informed Tertia that he'd been injured? The slave woman wouldn't normally be here to perform her duties until midday, and frankly, Caius couldn't picture her rushing to his bedside just because he'd taken a crossbow bolt to the leg.

Out of an abundance of caution, he limped to the side table and reached for his swordbelt. He'd just pulled the blade from its sheath when Decian wandered in with a hunk of bread piled with cheese held halfway to his mouth. He froze in the doorway when he saw the sword.

"Er... good morning?" he hazarded. "I assume this either means you're feeling better, or you're really, *really* unhappy with my bandaging job for some reason."

Caius let out a sharp breath and sheathed the sword. "I thought you'd gone."

"Oh, I did," Decian told him, taking a bite of the bread and cheese and pausing to chew before speaking around it. "I've been in and out a few times, making sure Pip was doing all right on his own with the dogs, and letting him know what was going on." He swallowed. "I met your house servant yesterday afternoon. Tertia, I think she said her name was? She's very... what's the word? Oh, yes. *Terrifying.*"

Caius snorted and sank back on the bed. Someone— either Decian or Tertia, presumably—had left a goblet of water on the table for him, sitting next to the swordbelt. He reached for it and drained it dry, knowing it would help with his head.

"Oh, she's fine, really," he said. "The trick is to avoid her completely. Though I have no doubt she'd say the same thing about me."

Decian smiled his crooked smile. "Well, she left you enough food for a small army, and said to tell you she'd be back around midday today. You should probably eat—I can bring you something, if you'd like?"

The way Caius' stomach protested the idea told him he probably *should* eat, if only to soak up the remnants of the brandy. He scrubbed a hand over his face, rubbing at his eyes. "Bread and cheese would be good, yes. And some more water, as well. Thank you."

Decian nodded and disappeared, leaving Caius to contemplate what it was about this situation that had him feeling so off-balance. Then he remembered the part where he'd nearly poked Decian's eye out with his erection while the poor man had been preparing to clean his wound.

Oh.

Yes… that would certainly account for it. Even more so, since Decian hadn't seemed put off by the idea at all.

His traitorous cock stirred with interest at the memory, just as Decian returned with a fresh slab of bread and a goblet. Caius ignored his body's distraction and accepted the simple meal with gruff thanks. Once he started eating, his vague sense of queasiness transformed into ravenous hunger—unsurprising, since he hadn't eaten anything in slightly over a day.

When he was done, he set the second empty goblet alongside the first and contemplated what to do next.

"You should rest more, if you can," Decian said, as though in answer to his thoughts. "Oh, and I should probably change that bandage before I head out again. You bled through it."

"I can take care of it." He didn't mean for the words to sound so brusque.

Decian lifted his eyes skyward. "Or I could take care of it, since I have equal use of both my arms and I'm here anyway."

For the second time in twenty-four hours, Caius found himself being pushed bodily onto his back on the bed, his bad leg lifted up to rest on the feather-stuffed mattress. And this time, he wasn't fighting post-battle shock and exhaustion.

Though his leg still hurt like damnation, blast it all.

The pain wasn't enough to keep his arousal at bay when deft hands unwrapped the linen cloth from around his thigh. Decian shot him a wry smile.

"And you can't even blame the brandy this time," he quipped.

"Maybe I can't," Caius shot back, taking in Decian's dilated pupils... the way his tongue darted out to wet his lower lip. "But what's your excuse?"

Dark eyes met his, unafraid and unapologetic. "Told you already. It's been a while for me—no mystery there." He blinked, and turned his gaze determinedly to the wound as he lifted the last layer of linen away. "Hmm... that seems to be doing decently well, all things considered. It's pretty swollen—"

"That's normal," Caius said.

"—but it doesn't smell like it's festering, and it seems to have clotted nicely," Decian finished. "Shall I flush it again?"

Caius waved him off. "No. Just bandage it, please. As long as the wound stays sound, there's no point in doing anything more to it. You'll only start it bleeding again."

"Hmm. You're the expert, I suppose." Decian retrieved fresh linen and rewrapped the wound, tucking the ends in and checking to make sure it wasn't too tight or too loose. Satisfied, he let his fingertips trail along the smallclothes covering Caius' inner thigh and brush over the length resting hard and heavy at the apex. "And now, I should probably leave before I'm tempted to take advantage of an injured man."

A jolt of raw lust sparked up Caius' spine in response the soft stroke of fingers. Before Decian could do more than yelp in surprise, Caius grabbed him by the shirtfront with his good arm and jerked him onto the bed, rolling them until Decian was on his back with Caius next to him, looking down at his startled expression. His leg and arm barked an indignant protest at the sudden movement. He ignored the flare of pain in favor of fusing his lips to Decian's, swallowing his gasp of surprise.

ELEVEN

Caius fumbled with the younger man's trouser laces right-handed, tugging and burrowing until his fingers closed around hard flesh, freeing Decian's cock from layers of clothing. Decian thrust up helplessly into the circle of Caius' fist, making a muffled, desperate noise into the kiss. Caius jerked him fast and hard and without finesse, not letting up with either lips or hand until Decian arched and came silently, spilling over Caius' fingers and his own clothing.

He gentled his movements as Decian shuddered beneath his touch, taking a moment to appreciate the length and weight of the other man's cock as it twitched a few more times and began to soften. With a final nip to Decian's lower lip, Caius pulled away from the kiss, but kept a proprietary grip wrapped lightly around his spent prick.

"Word to the wise," he said. "Never tease a soldier—even a wounded one."

Decian blinked up at the ceiling with dazed, unfocused eyes. Caius could see his pulse jumping beneath his jaw. His own cock throbbed with insistent need despite the pain from his leg. He ignored both sensations in favor of enjoying the view in front of him.

After a long moment, Decian swallowed, his throat bobbing. "Oh... I dunno," he said slowly, rolling his head to the side until he could meet Caius' gaze. "I feel as though it's working out rather well for me, so far."

Caius huffed out a startled breath of laughter, the impulse taking him by surprise.

Decian eyed him speculatively, a smile tugging at one corner of his full lips. "The problem is, I've no idea what I can do to reciprocate that won't end up jarring your leg in the process."

Caius raised an eyebrow at him. "Simple. You can lie back and look appealingly debauched for a few more minutes."

He let go of Decian's prick with a last slow stroke, enjoying the full-body shiver it elicited. With great deliberation, he untied the closure of his undergarment and took himself in hand, his fingers still slick with Decian's release. Decian caught his breath.

With a grunt, Caius levered himself into a more upright position to reduce the strain on his bad arm. He still ached all over after the previous day's abuse... but he was damned if that was going to stop him spilling his seed all over the sated man currently sprawled in his bed.

"*God*, you're beautiful when you've just come," he said, working himself steadily — feeling the exquisite tension gathering at the base of his spine, despite the discomfort clamoring elsewhere in his body.

"You're not so bad when you're getting ready to come, either," Decian said. "Keep going." He looked up with luminous eyes, his gaze traveling with leisurely slowness between Caius' face and his hand working his own flesh.

It had been an embarrassingly long time since Caius had been with anyone who didn't expect payment afterward. In the back of his mind, he was acutely aware that the emperor's bastard son was just about the most foolish choice of bed partner he could possibly have made. Yet, somehow his impetuous decision to save Decian in the first place appeared to have opened the floodgates when it came to making foolish choices that were also the *right* choices.

Decian's lazy half-smile turned wicked. The same clever fingers that had teased him earlier and precipitated all of this snuck between them and closed over Caius' grip on his own prick, guiding his movements. Decian's thumb swiped over the engorged head on the upstroke, sliding through the moisture beading there.

Pleasure punched hard into Caius' gut, cresting and spilling. He gritted his teeth, his cock pulsing in hot spurts that did, indeed, make his leg hurt like hell as his body jerked through the release. Thin ropes of pearly white splattered across Decian's softening prick and open trousers. Finally spent, Caius managed a marginally controlled collapse onto his back, lying shoulder to shoulder with the other man.

"Bloody hellfire," he muttered, as post-coital lassitude leached all the pain from his body, leaving him feeling limp as a used washrag.

Decian lay just as spent, his arm flopping down to lie at his side. "No respect for clothing," he said, sounding half-amused and half-exasperated. "That's your problem. Look at this mess. These trousers aren't even mine, you know."

Caius choked on another breath of laughter, even though the reminder of the dead houndsman should have been anything but humorous. "There's all the clean water you could want in the fountain. Sponge them off before the spunk dries, and no one will know the difference." He waved an uncoordinated hand in the air. "I'd offer to do it for you, but..." He indicated his compromised state.

"You're an injured man," Decian finished for him. "Yes, I can see that. Practically at death's door. It's tragic, really."

Caius nodded in sage agreement and let his eyes slip closed. "S'right," he agreed, and grunted when a lithe body crawled over him to get to the side of the bed, being careful not to jar his leg in the process.

He was on the cusp of dozing when Decian returned a few minutes later and crawled over him again, settling with his back against the headboard this time. Vague surprise motivated Caius to peel open one eye and peer at him curiously.

"What?" Decian asked. He indicated his damp trousers. "I'm sorry, but I'm not in much of a hurry to go outside looking like I've just pissed myself. Besides, your bed is *really comfortable*."

"It's too soft," he protested.

Decian made a disbelieving noise. "I recognize those words you're using, but they don't make any sense when you put them together in that order. How can a mattress be 'too soft'?"

"I spent too much time sleeping on hard pallets and tattered bedrolls in the army," he muttered. "It's what I'm used to."

Decian huffed. "And I spent ten years sleeping on dirty straw in a prison cell. What's your point?"

"I don't belong on a feather bed," Caius mumbled, slipping toward the siren call of slumber despite his best efforts. "Don't belong... in this place." Something important occurred to him in the instant before he would have drifted off with a man lying next to him in his bed. "Tertia—"

"Your house slave won't be here for hours yet," Decian reminded him. "Don't worry, O mighty soldier. Your virtue is safe with me. Safer than mine is with you, it appears."

"Oh. That's all right, then," Caius decided, and promptly fell asleep. This time, he didn't dream.

⚜

He wasn't sure if it was the sound of voices that woke him next, or the glare of sunlight in his eyes. He grunted and turned his head away, trying to escape the stabbing beam. It was early afternoon... apparently. Caius wasn't in the habit of being in bed at this time of day, and whoever had designed the windows in the house clearly agreed that use of the bedroom for sleeping after midday was something to be discouraged in the strongest possible terms.

It was, he reflected, a bit worrying that he'd slept through whatever conversation was taking place outside the room. He recognized both voices, and while neither of them belonged to anyone he considered a threat, the idea of both of them together did engender a faint sense of dread in the pit of his stomach.

Thankfully, he retained the presence of mind to check whether his smallclothes were laced up before he levered himself out of bed and went hobbling outside to confront the owners of the voices... because they weren't. His underclothes were, in fact, hanging obscenely open. He fumbled them into order with clumsy fingers, cursing the stiffness of his left arm.

Maybe he should have worried more about the propriety of wandering out to confront his middle-aged house slave while bare-chested and trouserless, but in truth, Caius doubted there was much he could do at this point that would lower Tertia's opinion of him any further than it already was.

He limped out to the enclosed garden, drawing the attention of both Tertia and Decian, who were conversing at the mouth of the hallway leading through to the atrium.

"You can go home, Tertia," he said, in lieu of a greeting. "You don't need to be here."

Tertia eyed him up and down, lifting her chin as she pinned him with an unimpressed gaze. Her iron gray hair was escaping its bun as it often did. Her unadorned stola had been stained dark at the bottom, as though the edge had fallen into a mop-bucket at some point in the recent past. Her mouth turned down at the corners, accentuating the wrinkles in her careworn face.

"Pompous fool," she said. "Go back to bed. Do you not have the sense Deimok gave a snail?" Then she turned back to Decian, dismissing Caius' presence as effectively as if she'd closed an invisible door in his face.

Caius felt his jaw tighten.

"I'm not an invalid, Tertia," he told her.

This time, her gray eyes flashed with irritation when she looked at him. "You're standing in the garden in your underclothes and keeping yourself upright by holding onto the wall, *Legatus*. Now, go back to bed before I pour a tincture down your throat that will put you out like a snuffed candle, and keep you out for the rest of the day."

Decian choked on a laugh and tried, unconvincingly, to turn it into a cough. Caius glared at him, the traitor.

"I'm going back to my room now," he said, with all the dignity he could muster. "But only because it's a more appealing prospect than continuing this conversation."

"I couldn't agree more," Tertia said. "I'll have Decian bring you bone broth and bread dipped in oil in a bit. Try to avoid getting in the way of any more arrows until then, eh?"

Caius gritted his teeth. "Tell you what. I'll do that, if you try to avoid acting like an objectionable old crone."

Tertia grinned at him, revealing crooked teeth. "I *am* an objectionable old crone," she retorted. "Which is still better than being a pompous fool. Oh, and by the way — the workmen will be here the day after tomorrow to repair the broken roof tiles from the storm last week. I told them what they were originally trying to charge was highway robbery, so they're doing it for half that."

"It's a source of amazement to me that any artisans are willing to work on this place at all, after dealing with you," Caius said.

"You're welcome," she told him, and pointedly turned back to Decian again.

Caius sighed and hobbled back to his room, defeated.

When Decian showed up some time later with two bowls of broth and a plate of sliced bread balanced on a tray, Caius was seated on the bed, sharpening his dagger with a whetstone. His sword hung in its scabbard, freshly cleaned and oiled after being bloodied by an assassin's entrails. Decian put the tray down carefully on the small table next to the bed and gave the dagger a pointed look.

"Tertia said she was leaving for the day and would be back in the morning. Out of curiosity, if you two really hate each other that much, why not get a different house slave?" he asked.

"Too much effort," Caius replied succinctly, not pausing in his brisk movements as the stone scraped rhythmically along the blade. "Besides, she keeps the floors clean."

"And saves money on roof repairs, I gather," Decian offered. "And makes sure you don't starve."

"That, too."

Decian took a slice of bread and one of the bowls before settling on the floor, his back resting against the side of the bed next to Caius' good leg. He dipped the bread in the broth and bit into it. Caius tried not to let the younger man's proximity distract him from his foul mood. He flipped the knife over and started work on the other edge.

"You know," Decian said around a mouthful, "There was a prisoner in the cell across from mine who managed to snap a piece off one of the door hinges where it had rusted partway through. He spent almost six months trying to sharpen that hunk of iron into a blade. *Scrape, scrape, scrape*, every night until I thought I'd go mad. He'd almost managed to get an edge on the damned thing when the guards found it and took it away. I always found that ironic. That's the right word, isn't it? Ironic?"

"Sounds right," Caius agreed, drawing the blade across the stone at an angle. "What happened to him afterward?"

"They beat him to a bloody pulp as an example to the rest of us. The broken fingers on his right hand never healed properly, and he could barely see out of his left eye when they were done with him. But at least the infernal scraping stopped."

"Do you think one of the other prisoners ratted him out?" Caius asked absently. He set the blade and whetstone on the table, in favor of taking up the second bowl and a hunk of the coarse bread.

"No idea," Decian replied. He jerked his chin toward the dagger resting next to the tray. "Are you expecting to fight off any more assassins in the near future?"

Caius scowled, focusing intently on his broth. "Not likely. That was the first real action I've seen in four years." And somehow, in the aftermath of that ugly two-on-one struggle, he'd never felt less at home inside the safety of the palace compound. "Like I said before, I don't belong in this place. I was never cut out to be a palace lapdog."

"Believe it or not, I can relate to that," Decian said, and took another bite of broth-soaked bread. He gestured around the room with the bitten piece. "Still. Nice digs."

Caius let out a breath of startled amusement. "I suppose so." He tipped the bowl to his lips, swallowing the contents and mopping up the dregs with the crust of bread before setting it back on the tray.

In truth, no amount of cleaning and polishing his weapons would erase the reality of the last four years. His soldiering days were over, and the odds of a repeat of the scene in the forest were about as likely as the odds of Proclus giving up drinking wine in favor of water. Frankly, it was a miracle he'd fared as well as he had against two younger opponents armed with crossbows.

"So… I was thinking this morning," Decian began.

"Always dangerous," Caius observed, battling his own memories of the morning. Specifically, the way the morning light had outlined his sated companion's body as he lay sprawled across this very bed.

"I was thinking that I could get used to having enough to eat and a place to stay that doesn't have a door made of iron bars," Decian continued, oblivious. "I could get used to having money and a job to do. You know?"

Unease coiled in Caius' gut, twining together with something lighter. Something hopeful.

"Staying in the palace grounds would be dangerous for you," he said carefully.

Decian craned around to meet his gaze. "Oh, yes? What happened to 'no one cares who feeds the dogs as long as the dogs get fed'?"

"That was before Kaeto showed an interest in you," Caius told him.

Decian's dark brows drew together. "He asked who I was. And then immediately got distracted. Which, I might add, is exactly how someone behaves when they don't actually care about the answer to the question they just asked."

"Even so—" Caius began.

"Am I right in thinking that after yesterday's debacle, there aren't likely to be any royal hunts requiring use of the hounds for a while?" Decian pressed.

Not unless the emperor descends even further into madness than he already has, Caius thought. Aloud, he only said, "Probably not."

"There you go, then."

Caius scowled. "And if Kaeto shows up at the kennels with another prisoner slated for execution-by-hound?"

Decian's expression hardened. "Then I'll hold the dogs off him and sneak him out the back when no one's looking." He raised an eyebrow. "It's a trick I just learned recently, you know?"

The sinking feeling in Caius' stomach grew. So did his selfish desire not to see the last of the emperor's half-Kulawi bastard son, who could control ravenous hounds with a look and who smiled so sweetly after spilling his seed over Caius' hand.

"It's a horrible idea," Caius said. "Really, truly horrible."

Decian raised an eyebrow. "Well, you could always turn me in as an escaped prisoner if it bothers you so much."

Caius snorted. "Right. And then I could explain how I mistook the houndsman's dismembered corpse for yours, and you for him."

"Good point," Decian acknowledged. "Best not, I suppose." A slow smile tugged at one corner of his lips. "Besides, if you did turn me in, you'd never find out what it's like to fuck me when you don't have a bleeding hole in your leg."

And just like that, the blood was rushing to Caius' cock again, as though he were a callow youth rather than a used-up soldier well into his fifth decade. He forced his body under control, and his expression to blandness.

"This is just an observation, mind," he said. "But when trying to convince an imperial advisor that the risk related to your staying in the palace grounds is negligible, offering to become his secret male lover in nearly the same breath doesn't really do much to bolster your argument."

Decian tilted his head, regarding Caius curiously. "This place has some seriously twisted views on sex. Just saying." He set his empty bowl on the floor and rested an elbow on the bed. "Doesn't that ever bother you?"

Caius shrugged. "It is what it is."

"Things are very different where my mother came from."

"Kulawi?" Caius hazarded.

Decian nodded. "There, they don't judge people for who they sleep with. As long as everyone involved is an adult and agrees of their own free will, who cares? What does it matter to anyone else?"

Caius wondered how Decian, of all people, could ask that. "It matters plenty to any man who needs an heir," he said, thinking of the steady stream of imperial bastards who *hadn't* escaped execution at Kaeto's hands.

But Decian only scoffed. "This may come as a shock to you, but I'm extremely unlikely to get you pregnant, *Legatus.* Or vice versa."

"That's not what I meant and you know it. If a woman can lie with anyone, then how can a man's title and property pass to his sons?"

"That's simple enough," Decian retorted wryly. "In Kulawi, wealth passes through the mother. That part is surprisingly easy to keep track of, no matter who's sleeping with who."

Caius blinked at him, trying to wrap his mind around the concept and failing.

"My point is," Decian went on, "I don't give two shits about what people in Alyrios think about sex." He gave Caius a long, assessing look. "And if *you* do—frankly, you've got a really strange way of showing it."

TWELVE

There wasn't much to say to that, since Caius had shamelessly fucked his fair share of fellow soldiers in the army, not to mention seeking out a prostitute in Amarius willing to cater to… multiple tastes, so to speak.

"I care enough not to advertise the fact in the middle of the Alyrion capital," he managed.

Decian exhaled sharply. "Well, it *would* be a pity to get yourself excommunicated and lose this lovely house, I'm sure."

"It would also be a pity to end up getting stoned in the streets by a jeering mob," Caius retorted.

"Agreed," Decian said. "I'm not a big proponent of gruesome execution, as you may have guessed. All of which makes me wonder why you'd choose to risk it in the first place? Why not find yourself a nice young widow to marry, and avoid tumbling random men into bed in the future? Problem solved, surely."

"I had a wife once."

The words hung in the air, surprising Caius since he certainly hadn't meant to say them aloud. Decian twisted his upper body to regard him more directly, resting his chin on his forearm at the edge of the too-soft feather mattress.

"Oh? What happened to her?" His tone made it clear that he'd picked up the subtext beneath Caius' use of the past tense.

"She… died in childbirth." Again, the words seemed to be pulled from him, rather than exiting his lips voluntarily. "She was twenty-one. I was twenty-three. We'd been trying for more than three years. It was her first pregnancy."

His voice sounded… not like him.

Decian must have noticed as well. "You loved her?"

He swallowed. Nodded. "I did. It was an arranged marriage, but we were well matched." With a jolt, he realized that at age forty-six, he'd lived exactly half his life since Serah and their infant daughter had died. "I'd like to think she loved me as well," he finished.

Silence settled for a long moment before Decian spoke again. "And in the time since, you never considered marrying again?"

An unwelcome vision of Serah's pale, sweat-soaked face as she labored to bring a dead child into the world before it killed her flickered through his memory, and Caius shook his head slowly.

"No."

He had no desire to risk such a thing a second time. It was much easier to tumble the occasional soldier or prostitute when the need for companionship became too distracting.

Decian stared up at him with a somber expression. "I shouldn't have jested about pregnancy earlier. Forgive me."

But Caius waved him off with an irritated flick of the hand. "Don't be ridiculous. It was decades ago."

The room descended into thoughtful silence once more. Caius found himself studying Decian's dark eyes... his sleek black helmet of closely shorn hair... the noble line of his Alyrion cheekbones and jaw paired with a nose that was wider and flatter than was usual in this land. He had to consciously stop himself brushing his own lips with his fingers as the echo of the kisses he'd stolen from Decian tingled along the skin.

Decian's gaze dipped to his mouth as though he were somehow privy to those private thoughts. The tip of his tongue darted out to wet his full lips, and his gaze lifted to meet Caius' again.

"I need to get back to the kennels," he said. "Is the bandage all right? I can check it again before I leave."

Caius took a slow breath and let it out silently, dragging his wandering thoughts under control. "No, leave it. It's fine — better to disturb the wound as little as possible unless it starts to fester."

Decian nodded and made to rise. "Fair enough. You've already proven you can get around if you need to, but I'll bring a jug of watered wine and a plate of food in here for you to eat later so you don't have to get up. You'll be all right on your own for the rest of the day?"

A small smile tugged at one corner of Caius' mouth, though he covered it out of old habit. "I've managed this long. I expect I'll survive until tomorrow."

He looked up as Decian moved to stand in front of him, unused to being seated while someone else loomed over him. Decian reached out a hard-callused hand and tipped Caius' jaw up with a gentle touch, thumb playing over his cheekbone and leaving a trail of heat in its wake.

"See that you do," Decian told him.

⚜

It was several days before Caius' leg recovered enough for him to walk unaided, without the need for something or someone to lean on. By that time, he was slowly going mad with boredom despite regular visits from Decian and Tertia. Every blade in the house was sharp enough to split a hair, whether its intended use was the battlefield or the kitchen.

On the fourth day, an administrator from the palace had showed up at his door to inquire about his health. The man took one look at Caius balancing his weight against the doorframe and told him he would inform His Imperial Majesty that the legatus needed more time to recover before returning to his duties at court.

Caius had bristled, ready to snap that he was as capable of standing in the corner and being ignored with an injured leg as with a sound one. He stopped himself, realizing with a jolt that he had absolutely no interest in returning to his duties before he was forced to do so. As much as it went against his nature to malinger, the truth was that he had taken a moderately serious injury in defense of the imperial family. If recovering meant he would be spared a front row seat to the slow dissolution of the empire for a few more days...

It wasn't an unappealing prospect, even with the associated boredom.

On the eighth morning, Decian showed up at the house with an air of purpose. He let himself in without knocking, as he'd grown accustomed to doing over the past few visits.

"Get dressed for riding," he called. "We're taking the dogs out for a run. I had a stableboy bring your horse along." He poked his head into the bedroom as he spoke the last few words, a broad smile gracing his attractive features.

Caius felt his mood lighten at the prospect. This, despite his nagging, ever-present pall of worry related to Decian's decision to stay on as royal houndsman rather than fleeing to obscurity in the hills.

"Oh? Are we indeed?" he asked, lifting a skeptical eyebrow — mostly for the form of the thing.

"Yes we are," Decian said with finality. "I didn't manage to acquire a winch to help get you into the saddle, but I expect we can muddle through somehow."

"Arse," Caius said without heat. Already, he was relishing the thought of leaving the confines of his house. For one thing, the walls had been closing in on him at odd moments lately whenever his thoughts began spinning in tight circles.

"Come on, now… you don't want to miss the spectacle of me bouncing around on that damned pony's back like a fool, do you?" Decian teased.

Caius let out a breath of laughter. "Well, when you put it like that…"

"So get dressed," Decian insisted. "Do you need help?"

The flare of stubbornness that prickled along Caius' spine was probably misplaced, but he'd spent enough time feeling like an invalid in the past few days.

"No, I am actually capable of dressing myself, thank you," he said tartly. "I'll join you in a few minutes."

Decian shrugged agreement and went out to wait for him.

Fortunately for Caius' pride, he was able to successfully pull on his riding breeches and boots without making too much of a hash of things. Which wasn't to say the process was painless—it very much wasn't. At this point, however, he was happy to bear a bit of pain as long as it meant getting back to something closer to normalcy.

When did riding out with the palace houndsman to exercise the dogs ever constitute normalcy?

Caius scowled at the unwelcome prodding of his niggling internal voice. Riding was normal, he told himself firmly. Getting out of the blasted house was normal. The details of where, why, and with whom were irrelevant.

He limped outside to find Decian and the stableboy waiting for him. His gray gelding tossed its head and nickered, lifting one front foot to paw at the cobbles. Beside it, the apathetic roan pony dozed in the sun, muzzle drooping and one hind leg cocked at the hip. Both animals' saddles were hung with waterskins, and the pony carried a pair of bulging saddlebags as well.

Decian looked Caius up and down critically. "Hmm. Looks like you were telling the truth. Boots on the correct feet... breeches laced up... shirt on the right way around. I concede that you are, in fact, able to dress yourself. Ready to go?"

Caius caught the stableboy's look of bug-eyed horror at seeing someone speak to a palace advisor—an imperial legatus—in such a way. He scowled at Decian because it was expected of him.

"I may owe you for helping when I was injured, houndsman," he said with mock severity. "But someday soon, someone's going to shove something in that smart mouth of yours to shut you up."

He saw the double entendre hit home—saw Decian cover a smirk, and caught the faint darkening of his brown eyes.

"Many have threatened," he replied in a tone of amusement. "Yet here we stand, bantering. Let's get you mounted. How would be best?"

Caius greeted the gelding, rubbing his mount's muzzle affectionately before gathering up the reins and facing the saddle. "A leg-up should suffice... if you've got the shoulders for it."

"Didn't I tell you we'd muddle through?" Decian teased. "So, how do I—oh, I see."

Caius bent his bad leg at the knee and Decian cupped it in both hands, heaving upward at the same time Caius pushed off with his good right leg and pulled himself up with his right arm. The maneuver was every bit as painful as dressing himself had been, but Decian was strong and Caius had been scrambling onto horses' backs since he was knee-high to one. With a grunt of effort and a bit of shuffling, he was in the saddle. He settled himself into place, fished around for the stirrups, and arranged the reins in his right hand.

"I have him now, lad," he told the boy, who'd been steadying the gray's head during the inelegant mounting process.

Decian clambered onto the pony with approximately the same lack of grace Caius had just demonstrated. The aging beast snorted awake and rolled a baleful eye at his rider before yawning widely.

"Maybe I'll train a couple of the dogs to pull me around in a cart and save both of us the trouble, you horrible little beast," Decian muttered, fumbling with the reins one handed and reaching down with the other to twist the offside stirrup leather so he could get his foot into it.

"That I'd like to see," Caius said. He flipped a coin into the stableboy's waiting hands and urged his gelding into motion. Decian kicked his heels into the pony's ribs a couple of times and followed him.

The scab across Caius' upper arm was barely a hindrance at this point, though his bad shoulder was not expressing much appreciation for the recent stretch of inactivity. Meanwhile, his injured leg ached and throbbed in time with the easy movement of the horse beneath him. It was, he knew from long experience, the kind of pain that would diminish as his flesh continued to knit itself back together. Not the kind that warned of further damage being done to a fresh wound.

Decian jounced along next to him, glancing over to meet his eyes. "So, are you truly feeling better, or just putting a brave face on it?"

"It's an annoyance at this point; nothing more," Caius assured him. He tried not to think about how much faster he'd healed from similar injuries a decade ago... much less *two* decades ago.

"Well, whatever you do, don't fall off. If you do, I'll make you ride the pony so I don't have to heft you onto that monster's back again."

Caius' lips twitched. "That assumes you'd have any more luck climbing onto this *monster's* back than I would, after that performance to mount the pony. Now... look here. You're holding the reins like you're driving a plow horse. Hold them like this instead, but with one rein in each hand."

He lifted his right hand, demonstrating the rein position. Decian studied it and changed his own grip to match.

"Better," Caius said. "Now lower your hands. Keep them close to the pommel—that's the front of the saddle. Only move one of them at a time when you need to steer. Set your hips and squeeze your fists closed to slow or stop. Though honestly, I expect you could just stop kicking him in the sides. That would work, too, since I'm fairly certain that pony's default speed is 'asleep.'"

"I'm fairly certain you're right," Decian grumbled.

They made their way through the palace grounds to the royal kennels, with Caius offering occasional tips and corrections to address the more egregious points of Decian's riding form.

"I'm going to be sore for a week," the younger man complained. "Which isn't something you'll have much sympathy for, I suppose."

"It comes with the territory," Caius told him. "Competence on horseback requires hundreds of hours spent in the saddle."

"Hmm. Sounds awful," Decian said, just as the pony gave an irritated little cow-kick.

Pip was waiting to meet them in the kennel courtyard, surrounded by two-dozen excited hounds whose shoulders came up past the level of his waist. "They're ready for a good run," he said by way of greeting, offering Caius a wary dip of his head in acknowledgement. "Do you know the fields east of the river gate, sir? That's where Jona always used to take them for exercise."

"I do," Caius assured him. The area was used for grazing by many of the freemen with smallholdings outside the city, but only during winter. It was a good place for a gallop — or for running a pack.

"Lead on, in that case," Decian said. "Pip, after the kennels are clean, feel free to take a few hours for yourself. We'll be back by mid-afternoon."

Pip brightened. "All right. I will, thanks."

Decian smiled at him, open and easy. "Enjoy… but don't get into trouble. See you later."

He gave a low whistle, and the dogs trotted toward him, surrounding the bored-looking pony. Caius steadied his own mount, who wasn't quite so accustomed to being hemmed in by predators at close range.

"This way," he said, and headed toward the river gate.

THIRTEEN

The eastern fields stretched across hundreds of *arpennes* of gently rolling hills bounded by forest. The place was peaceful and empty, which suited Caius well. It wasn't so much the bustle of the city that he'd missed while cooped up in his rooms, as it was the open sky and a sense of freedom. Decian was as agreeable a companion as one could ask for, and the dogs were eerily well behaved as they trotted along, tongues lolling, sniffing the air occasionally.

"I trust they can get their exercise without us needing to keep pace with them the whole time," Caius said wryly.

Decian might be acquiring a basic grasp of steering and changing the pony's speed, but he still had no kind of seat. And Caius had no desire to test his leg's mettle at a faster gait unless he was forced to do so.

"I think they're going to have to," Decian replied in the same dry tone. He pulled a curled hunting horn from his saddle as they approached the top of a hill—one that gave a good view of the grasslands stretching all around. Lifting the horn to his lips, he blew two short blasts, and the dogs exploded forward in a riot of excited baying.

"And away they go," Caius mused, enjoying the play of the sleek hounds' muscles as they raced down the hill, leaping and jostling with each other.

"They needed this today," Decian said, watching them indulgently.

So did I, Caius thought.

They watched together until the dogs wore themselves out. Decian redirected them with the sound of the hunting horn whenever they threatened to wander too far away. Eventually, they began to return to their master, panting and bright-eyed. Once the whole pack had rejoined them, Caius led the way toward a stream that ran along one of the wooded boundaries. The dogs and horses sated their thirst, several of the hounds splashing noisily into the water to cool off.

"Is that food in your saddlebags, I hope?" Caius asked.

Decian nodded. "It is. Hungry?"

"I could eat." Caius cautiously tested his thigh muscles to see how they were faring, and looked around to catalogue their immediate surroundings. Satisfied, he swung his good leg over the front of the saddle and slid down slowly, landing with his weight on his right foot.

"*Hey*. Didn't I warned you about getting down?" Decian protested.

"You warned me about *falling off*, which I don't intend to dignify with a response." Caius gestured to a fallen tree trunk nearby. "There's a downed log I can use to mount again when it's time to leave. Don't fuss."

Decian looked skeptical, but he did step down from his pony, wincing as his feet hit the ground. "*Oww*."

"Don't whine, either," Caius told him.

"The bottom of my spine is in imminent danger of poking through the fabric of my trouser seat after the pounding it's just taken. I'll whine if I want to, thanks."

Caius hid a smile. "You'll live."

"You think so? Well, I suppose that's more than could be said about me a couple of weeks ago." Decian stretched gingerly from side to side, his vertebrae popping audibly.

It was a sobering reminder of Decian's situation, but Caius tried not to let it spoil his pleasant mood. He led his gelding over to a tree with a sturdy branch just above head height and tied him there, showing Decian how to use a slipknot that wouldn't tighten if the animal startled and pulled back. When both mounts were settled and the dogs had flopped down around the clearing to rest in the dappled sunlight, Caius joined Decian by the downed tree. He carefully eased himself to sit on the ground, resting his back against the sturdy log and stretching his bad leg out in front of him to ease it. Decian sank down next to him with food and drink, sitting shoulder to shoulder.

They shared cold salted meat and brown bread, soft cheese and an early apple that Caius sliced into pieces with his dagger. The fact that it was the most pleasant morning he'd passed since coming to Amarius almost four years ago was something he didn't care to dwell on.

"This is nice," Decian said, echoing his thoughts. "Really, *really* nice. Do you know how long it's been since I had a day like this?" He let his head fall back against the log, looking up at the sky through the thin covering of overhanging branches. His expression grew far away.

"More than ten years?" Caius offered.

"Yes. More than ten years," Decian confirmed, rolling his head to the side to meet Caius' eyes. "Thank you for this."

"Don't thank me," Caius told him. "If it was up to me, you would have left Amarius already. You could leave right now, in fact. We're outside the city. No one's around to see you go."

Decian let out a little huff of laughter. "I'm not leaving yet. For one thing, if I tried to make a run for it now, I'd have a pack of royal hunting hounds stuck to my tail." His expression grew serious. "And for another, I'm not ready to give *this* up."

He leaned forward, and Caius felt a small jolt go through him as their lips brushed together. His eyes slipped closed, his entire focus narrowing to that slow slide of skin against sensitive skin.

It was gentle. Easy. The kind of kiss traded by young sweethearts in the first flush of attraction. It made Caius' chest hurt, but not with the sort of pain that would convince him to stop. Pursuing this dalliance was the worst kind of foolishness. He knew it in his bones… yet he made no move to pull away. Decian's lips were a drug—a sweet herbalist's concoction that made warmth and lassitude crawl through Caius' veins, unknotting his muscles and soothing his nerves. He never wanted to move from this spot… never wanted this day to end.

They were in the open, some distant part of him tried to warn. *Anyone could ride by and see them kissing, see their hands wandering in slow caresses.*

But the dogs would warn them if anyone approached. There was no track or road leading past the area. The likelihood of anyone else coming this way was small. And it had been far too long since Caius had kissed anyone like this.

He ran his fingers through the closely trimmed spirals and waves of Decian's unusual hair. It was softer than he'd expected, springing back from his touch as he stroked it. Decian made a low noise of enjoyment into the kiss. His full lips wandered to Caius' jaw, then lower — following the tendon that ran down the side of his neck.

It was such a simple touch, but Caius *felt* it... felt more than he had in years... felt so much that it hurt with a pain to rival an arrow through the leg. *God,* how had he lived for so long without *feeling*? He clutched at Decian's shoulder, at the back of his head, as though Decian were somehow in danger of leaving and taking this raw sensation of awareness with him. A choked noise wrenched free from his throat as Decian laved his collarbone, nosing aside the loose collar of his shirt.

He trailed lower still, kissing through fabric, pulling Caius' good leg to the side to make room for himself without jostling his injury overmuch. As he settled in, Caius became instantly, desperately aware of his cock pressed hard against the lacing of his breeches, throbbing with need. His fingertips kneaded the nape of Decian's neck as the younger man freed Caius' hard length from his clothing. Mission accomplished, he settled his body in the soft grass between Caius' legs.

The first touch of Decian's lips and tongue to his cockhead was so intense, so *immediate* that it drove every other thought from his head. It was cool water after a trek through the desert; a warm bath after hours spent in the cold. It was the sight of camp after a battle hard-won. It was home after a long journey.

He stroked that soft, springy helmet of hair, letting his head fall back as Decian's lips slid down his shaft with confidence, tongue swirling in complicated patterns against his skin. Leaves rustled above him in the light breeze, the sound of birds competing with the rhythmic *shush-shush* of his own heartbeat in his ears. Decian made a soft noise of enjoyment, the pleased hum resonating along

Caius' nerves and sending a wave of gooseflesh across his skin.

Decian stoked the fire of his pleasure with slow deliberation, neither teasing nor hurrying. Time lost meaning, until Caius felt his approaching climax begin to coil, hot and insistent at the base of his spine. He steeled himself, sliding his fingers to cup Decian's jaw and guide him up and away. The younger man looked at him with a question in his eyes — lips wet and swollen, cheeks flushed beneath his dusky complexion... a slight furrow forming between his brows.

"Let me finish you," he said.

Caius urged him upright. "Come up here and let me finish both of us," he retorted.

He guided Decian to straddle his thighs, sitting high enough that their hips pressed together and the younger man's weight rested well above the bandages covering his crossbow injury.

"Your wound—" Decian began.

"Is fine," Caius insisted. A lie, though not a very large one — the pressure of Decian straddling his leg did cause him a bit of pain, but it also worked to pull him back from the edge of release long enough for him to accomplish his goal.

Between them, they got Decian's breeches and smallclothes open. His cock sprang free, hard and leaking at the tip. Caius made a low noise of appreciation and hitched Decian forward another fraction so their lengths slid against each other — swordplay of an altogether enjoyable kind. Caius spit into his right hand and gathered their shafts together in his grip, jerking them slowly at first, then faster.

Decian groaned, bracing one hand on Caius' good shoulder and the other against the fallen tree trunk. His hips flexed in time with Caius' stroking, and he curled forward a bit awkwardly until he could catch Caius' lips in a kiss every bit as sweet as the one that had started all this.

It wasn't long until Decian shuddered and spilled, coating Caius' hand and smoothing his grip to something warm and liquid. The pleasure that had been lurking beneath Caius' skin gathered into a tight knot and held... held... growing and heating until it finally broke free in a warm rush. The kiss had grown sloppy as Decian lost control, but Caius curled into it regardless as his seed pulsed and spurted between them.

They breathed against each other's lips, panting as their muscles uncoiled into sated languor. Decian slid halfway off his body, leaning against Caius' uninjured side with their legs still tangled together.

"You're very good at that, you know," he said.

"So are you," Caius managed.

Decian waved one hand in a vague, uncoordinated gesture. "There wasn't much to do in prison. One of my cellmates loved sucking cock. He was a bit of an arse most of the time, really. But it was... educational, I guess?"

Caius wasn't sure what to say to that, so he made a noncommittal noise and settled Decian closer against him. They lay together for some considerable time, boneless in the midday warmth. Somehow, this part was both new and painfully old in its familiarity.

In the military, occasional relations among the men were tacitly accepted, but they were generally pragmatic affairs not laden with emotion. Two men agreed to get each other off, after which they parted and went about their business. But this... casual warmth, this shared moment of post-coital vulnerability—it reminded him of lying curled together in bed with Serah after their lovemaking. And that realization frightened Caius more than battles, or treason, or assassins with crossbows in the woods.

"I should wet a cloth in the stream so we can clean up," Decian mumbled, making no move to actually get up and do so.

"For what it's worth, I think my clothing took the brunt this time," Caius said, with an equal lack of ambition to move. Perhaps it was a function of age and experience— or mere jadedness—but Caius couldn't raise much worry over the prospect of a random person in the street examining his crotch for evidence of dried spunk during the ride home. In the end, most people didn't pay that much attention to their surroundings.

Decian craned down to look at his breeches. "Huh. So it did."

They lay together for a bit longer, until one of the hounds wandered up and sniffed at Caius' face. He waved it off, trying not to think about the fact that the same dog had probably been picking bits of Jona out of its teeth not so long ago.

"I suppose we should get back," Decian said with clear reluctance.

Caius made a vaguely affirmative noise, surprised by the sense of loss he felt when Decian untangled their legs and levered himself upright. He put his clothing to rights, then went to rummage in his saddlebags, retrieving a rag and dipping it in the stream. He offered the damp cloth to Caius, who took it and made a half-hearted effort to clean himself up. When he'd tucked himself away and done up his undergarments and breeches, he accepted a hand up from Decian. They brushed grass and bits of bark off each other, and Decian brought Caius' horse to stand next to the downed log for mounting.

With Decian holding the gelding's head to steady him, Caius was able to clamber aboard without too much trouble. Decian gathered up the remains of their meal and got on the pony, whistling to the dogs to call them to heel.

The ride back to the palace was uneventful, but Caius couldn't escape a sense of melancholy. This was stolen time, he knew. Things wouldn't always be this easy, and he was asking for future strife by not resisting his attraction to Decian more strongly. This was not a world in which an imperial legatus and a palace houndsman could dally their days away curled together in the woods, with no one being the wiser.

He needed to stop this foolishness and convince Decian to leave before disaster struck. But when they arrived at his house after returning the dogs to the kennel, instead of saying '*You shouldn't spend time with me anymore,*' he found himself saying, "Come with me to the gymnaestra tomorrow."

Decian gave him a curious look. "You're going to a gymnaestra with your leg only half healed? Is that a good idea?"

"It's for my shoulder, not my leg," he explained. "It gets worse when I don't work it regularly."

The pleased, slightly crooked smile that Caius was beginning to crave like a drug lit Decian's face. "Then I'd enjoy that a great deal. I can have your horse here about the same time as today."

Caius nodded. "Until then."

He watched as Decian took up the gray gelding's reins and rode off on his pony, heading for the royal stables. He told himself that the gymnaestra would be a good place to speak to Decian at length about the wisdom of leaving Amarius… and knew it was a lie.

FOURTEEN

That evening, Caius sent a message to the palace to inform them that he would be returning to duty in two days. Briefly, he entertained the fantasy of leaving Amarius with Decian and moving to some idyllic and doubtless fictional rural paradise. Perhaps they could return to the village of his youth. Upon his mother's death a few years ago, he had technically inherited the land that his parents had lived on—though in his absence it had probably been taken over by squatters.

One way or another, they could find a place somewhere—raise horses and hounds while pretending to be nothing more than business partners running a venture together.

He scoffed. *Yes.* And then the locals could run them out of town with pitchforks and torches after catching them in some indiscretion—either before or after the empire tore itself apart from the inside out during a fight over the royal succession.

He was a fool. Worse, he was quickly becoming an *old* fool, bewitched by a beautiful younger man who only looked twice at him out of gratitude for Caius having spared his life.

Morning rolled around, and Decian arrived as promised to accept Caius' ill-conceived invitation to the gymnaestra. He decided to allow himself this last day of self-indulgence. At the end of it, he would lay out his concerns and try one more time to convince Decian to leave the city. After that, the decision would be up to him. Caius would put distance between them, and if Decian still insisted on staying in Amarius, no doubt some younger, more charming companion would eventually catch his eye.

Caius hadn't thought to ask if Decian was inclined toward women as well as men. In the end, he supposed it wasn't really his business. Best-case scenario, Decian would end up somewhere far away with a sweet wife who loved him, living in safety and obscurity. Caius would do everything he could to make that happen.

"Have you ever visited a gymnaestra before?" he asked, not wishing to make assumptions.

"Never," Decian said. "The town where I grew up with my mother wasn't far from Amarius, but it was small. We didn't come into the city."

Caius wondered what had become of the emperor's Kulawi mistress after her son was thrown into prison at the age of sixteen, but it seemed insensitive to ask. He doubted the story had a happy ending.

He focused on the practical instead. "This one has a combination of areas set aside for athletic training, along with public baths," he explained. "Only men are allowed. Most will be naked. It's a more relaxed atmosphere than most in the capital, but discretion is still necessary."

Decian shot him an amused glance. "Are you worried I'll proposition someone?"

Caius flushed, realizing how his words had probably sounded.

His companion gave him an assessing look. "The prospect of being outed as an invert really worries you, doesn't it?"

Caius hesitated, framing his answer carefully. "I'm an advisor to the imperial family—in name, at least," he said. "If such a scandal were to come out, it wouldn't go well for me... but it would go far worse for you."

The corner of Decian's mouth quirked up, but it wasn't an expression of humor. "Yes," he said lightly. "I mean— heavens above—they might even decide to execute me or something."

Caius winced.

"On a related note," Decian went on, "if I'm going to be parading around in this gymnaestra with my bits on display, is anyone going to make a fuss about the state of my back? I've never seen it directly, but I imagine it's not a suitable view for polite company."

Caius shook his head. "No, you don't need to worry about that. It's not that sort of gymnaestra."

Indeed, the gymnaestra at the corner of Vaia Condora and the Pradi Imeno wasn't frequented by nobles and courtiers. It was a haven for old soldiers, former gladiators, and other rough characters who lived and died by the strength of their muscles. That was why Caius came here. People rarely asked questions beyond superficial small talk, and seldom offered opinions on anything of substance. They came, they took exercise, they made use of the bathing facilities and rubdowns. Then they left, and didn't spare much thought for any of their fellow members.

Caius led the way to a line of hitching posts. They tied the horses securely next to a trough filled with fresh water and went inside. The building, while large, wasn't grand. The man watching the door nodded at Caius in recognition and waved them through, not commenting on Caius' obvious limp. Inside, the sound of weights clanging and the occasional grunt of effort echoed off the tiled walls.

"Changing room's over here," Caius said, gesturing Decian inside. At this time of day, the place wasn't well attended. Nevertheless, a gray haired man looked up from one of the bench seats where he was lacing up his boots.

"Caius!" he exclaimed. "Don't normally see you here so early. Bringing a new friend, I see?"

"Hello, Olivio," Caius said. "An acquaintance, yes. This is Decian. I thought he might appreciate this place."

Olivio gave Decian a thorough onceover. "Fellow soldier, are you?"

Decian offered him a pleasant smile and shook his head. "No, nothing like that—I'm far too headstrong. Even if they'd let me join in the first place, I'd have been drummed out in fairly short order, I expect."

Olivio laughed. "At least you're honest about it. Well, I'm off home to the missus. Make sure old Caius here doesn't overdo it after whatever the hell he did to his leg."

"I'll try," Decian agreed.

After he left, Caius showed Decian where he could stow his clothing and belongings. Some gymnaestra had fancy padlocked compartments in the changing rooms to discourage theft. The Condora gymnaestra engendered a strong sense of brotherhood among its members. That, combined with an owner who made it known that anyone caught stealing in his establishment would be hunted down and murdered in his bed — *slowly* — meant that problems with theft were rare.

After they'd both disrobed, Caius led the way to the main exercise chamber and its attached courtyard. Decian looked around the place with fascination, taking in the grizzled men sparring with heavy leather punching bags, lifting and lowering spherical metal weights with handles, and engaging in bodyweight exercises.

They were a motley bunch. One might almost say disreputable. The fact that Caius was more comfortable here than in the echoing marble halls of the palace neatly described the state of his life these days.

He saw Decian's eyes light up, his attention falling on the circle laid out for wrestling. In it, two men close to his age were grappling, hands clutching and slipping against oiled skin.

"Seen something that interests you, I take it? Go on, then," Caius said. "I'll be over by the weights. Don't do anything I wouldn't do."

Decian shot him a knowing smirk, and Caius cursed himself silently. *Damn it*, he was supposed to be talking Decian into leaving Amarius... not lobbing double entendres at him.

"We both know that's not much of an admonition," Decian pointed out, and left to investigate the wrestlers.

Once he was out of hearing range, Caius sighed gustily and went to claim a bench and a weighted ball. Because he apparently enjoyed torturing himself almost as much as he enjoyed sabotaging himself, he sat down so he had a clear view of the wrestling circle. His left shoulder was a mess after so many days of complete inactivity. He began the familiar, painful process of forcing the damaged muscles into use — first by stretching, and then by lifting the weight, circling his arm through its limited range of motion.

Decian quickly fell into conversation with the two men who'd been grappling. Inevitably, before long he was oiling himself up, laughing at something one of the others had said. The clear noise carried over the sounds of men at exercise, trapping Caius' attention almost as much as the sight of his long, lean muscles glistening tawny in the light.

He was good, too. Caius might have expected him to be competent at brawling after years spent in prison, but this clearly wasn't the first time he'd wrestled in the classical style. Caius watched, rapt, as Decian held his own against his more experienced opponent by means of sheer strength and flexibility.

"He's a tough one. Where'd you find him, anyway?"

Caius blinked, startled, as the man who'd addressed him sat down on the end of his bench. He was a familiar face in the gymnaestra, but Caius didn't have a name to put to the face. More importantly, he didn't have a prepared answer to the question.

Good god above… what had happened to him over the past few years? He'd commanded troops during wartime, for fuck's sake—devised military strategy, won major battles against seasoned opponents. Now he floundered for words after being caught staring at a younger man engaged in a wresting clinch.

"On the wrong end of trouble," he managed after a brief hesitation.

The man laughed. "That I can believe. You're the legatus, aren't you? The one from the palace?" He gestured at Caius' bandaged leg. "Looks like you and trouble have been spending too much time together lately."

Something about the fellow's interest prickled at his instincts, but Caius only shrugged. "I don't go looking for it," he said. "But there's not much I can do when it comes knocking on my door."

Liar, said the little voice that lived in the back of his head.

With his shoulder aching and his thoughts oddly disturbed after the brief exchange, he excused himself and returned the weight to its shelf. Decian was still with the pair of wrestlers, and appeared to be getting instruction on a specific move. Suddenly unwilling to watch Decian's long limbs twining with his opponent's any longer, Caius excused himself and headed for the steam room. It was empty, and he took advantage of the opportunity to stew both physically and mentally. After a few minutes, the door opened and Decian joined him.

"There you are," he said. "How's the shoulder?"

"Hurts like hell, which means it will be easier to use tomorrow," Caius said gruffly. He steeled himself. "We need to talk about you leaving."

Decian settled back and looked at him, brow furrowing. "Do we? I thought we already talked about me leaving. I distinctly remember pointing out that I now have food, a place to sleep, and a job I rather enjoy doing for the first time in a decade." He paused. "Not to mention... the other benefits."

The other benefits need to stop, Caius wanted to say. He opened his mouth, even drew breath to utter the words — only to have them wither and die on his tongue.

"It's not safe," he said instead.

Decian's expression turned intent. "Life's not safe. I'm not sure that's a good enough reason to stop living it."

Caius stared at him... at the sweat and oil making his skin shine dark bronze. His eyes were guileless — without artifice, but full of conviction. Caius felt himself giving in to their magnetic pull, cursing his weakness all the way down. If he was enough of a fool, would he eventually be able to convince himself that succumbing to this temptation was some grand act of rebellion against society's injustice, rather than the base cowardice and selfishness he knew it to be?

"It will end badly," he said, not sure which of them he was warning.

"Then it ends badly," Decian replied simply. "In my experience, most things eventually do."

Caius held his gaze, unblinking. "That's a grimmer outlook than I've come to expect from you."

Decian didn't look away. "I said *most* things end badly. Not *all* things."

The little quiver of yearning that bloomed in Caius' chest as the words hit home hurt more than hopelessness ever had.

FIFTEEN

They lingered in the steam room for a little longer, then moved to the bathing room. An attendant poured water from an amphora over each of them to wash away the oil and sweat. Caius declined the cold pool—not wanting to submerge his leg wound until it was healed more fully—but Decian waded in and dunked beneath the surface to cool off.

Both of them skipped the warm pool. Returning to the changing room, they dressed and headed out to the street. A young man entered as they were leaving. He paused, his gaze landing on Caius and sticking there for longer than seemed appropriate. When the lad's attention moved to Decian, Caius felt his expression darkening into a scowl.

The lad noticed and flushed, jerking his eyes downward and squeezing past them to enter without a word. It was only as he disappeared inside that Caius recognized him as the young man from Saleene and Zuri's brothel—the one who'd offended the noblewoman somehow.

"Someone you know?" Decian asked curiously. He lifted an amused eyebrow. "Should I be jealous?"

Caius shook himself free of his moment of preoccupation. "He works at a brothel in this part of the city. I didn't expect to see him here, that's all."

"Ooh, now I'm *definitely* jealous," Decian teased, and Caius turned the scowl on him.

"Not like that," he said severely. "I think they must throw him at the occasional frustrated wife who comes in for relief."

Decian let out a bark of surprised laughter. "Oh, dear. Never mind, then." He glanced up to gauge the position of the midday sun. "So, what's next? How's your leg holding up?"

In a refreshing change of pace, his leg actually hurt less than his shoulder at that moment.

"It's all right," he said. "Do you need to get back to the kennels?"

Decian smiled and shook his head. "Not until mid-afternoon. As long as the dogs are all healthy and not needed for a hunt, it's mostly a matter of feeding and exercising them in the courtyard twice a day. Well—that and keeping everything clean. But Pip's the apprentice, so he gets stuck with most of the dirty jobs."

Caius snorted. "If he's still taking half your pay, I would certainly hope so."

"He's a good lad," Decian said. "Without him, I doubt I'd have been able to pull this off to the extent that I have. He's young, but if I do end up having to leave on short notice at some point, he should have the job… not someone else. The dogs trust him, and he's got a steady hand with them."

If Decian ended up having to leave against his will, Caius suspected that the dogs would be the least of their worries. Aloud, he only said, "I'll keep it in mind if it ever comes to that. Come on—if you don't have anywhere else to be just yet, let's go get a drink and a meal."

⤙ ♕ ⤚

Choosing the Cock's Crow tavern for their meal was, perhaps, a mistake. At the very least, Caius supposed it meant that he'd capitulated to the inevitability of Decian staying in Amarius for now. The modest drinking den fronted Saleene's brothel—someplace Caius hadn't been since the evening after Decian had crashed into his life almost two weeks previously.

"I have to say," Decian observed as they entered through the main doors, "your tastes aren't what I would have expected."

Caius shot him a sidelong glance. "What would you have expected?"

"After seeing your house?" Decian gestured vaguely with one hand, as though trying to outline something grand. "I dunno. Rich places. White marble and mosaics everywhere. Pies made of hundreds of swallows' tongues and wine with flakes of gold floating in the goblets."

"Good god," Caius muttered. "It's bad enough that I have to make an appearance at those kind of functions a few times a year at the palace. Why on earth would you think I'd seek out that sort of ridiculous frippery during my time off?"

Decian let out a breathless laugh. "Well, consider me thoroughly disillusioned. Not to mention a bit relieved. For one thing, I have no idea if you're actually supposed to drink the gold flakes in the wine, or what."

A smile pulled at one side of Caius' mouth. "If you have to ask, you're generally not invited to those sorts of parties in the first place. In this tavern, however, if there are flakes of anything floating in your goblet, I would definitely advise against drinking them."

It was something of an exaggeration, honestly. While far from grand, the Cock's Crow served decent food and drink at a reasonable price. If the place had been horrible, Saleene wouldn't have set up shop above it... and Caius wouldn't frequent it.

Decian scoffed. "Oh, *please*. Hello — ten years in prison? I've swilled more weak wine with mysterious chunks floating in it than you've had hot dinners. And probably swilled more weak *vinegar* with chunks in it, as well."

It still struck Caius as surprising how little bitterness Decian seemed to harbor when it came to his years of unjust imprisonment. It would have been easy to let the quip ruin his mood, reminding him of the dark circumstances surrounding them. Instead, he forced himself to reply in kind, keeping things light. "If that's so, then you should already know the answer to your original question. Of course you drink the gold."

"And shit it out the next day?" Decian asked in disbelief. "Seems wasteful."

"I think that's probably the point," Caius mused.

He glanced around the establishment, looking for an empty table. Instead, his eyes landed on a familiar, distinctive pair of faces seated in the corner. Saleene caught his eye, raised her eyebrows in mild surprise, and jerked her chin in a brusque motion, beckoning him over. Beside her, Zuri—her dark-skinned partner—looked up curiously, following the direction of her gaze.

Caius weighed the possible pitfalls involved in introducing his new male lover to his favorite prostitute for only an instant before making a strategic decision. He glanced at Decian and indicated the table. "Over here. There's someone I'd like you to meet, if you're amenable."

Decian shrugged agreeably, giving the pair at the table a curious look.

There were hazards here, to be sure. For one thing, Caius had no idea how Decian was likely to react to Saleene… but Saleene could take care of herself in that regard. The cold, tactical part of him—the same part that had deserted him earlier—was working overtime now. If the meeting went smoothly, Saleene and Zuri could potentially act as a safe haven for Decian in the event that he had to run, at least for a night or two. Whether they'd be willing to do so was another question, of course—especially since Caius wasn't about to offer details of Decian's true identity as a condemned bastard son of Emperor Constanzus.

"Hullo, Saleene," he greeted, as he limped up to the table. "Hullo, Zuri. We just stopped by for a drink and a meal."

Zuri gestured at the empty chairs. "Join us, Legatus. Who's this?"

Decian beat him to the punch, dipping his head in a shallow bow of greeting. "I'm Decian. You're friends of Caius', I gather? It's a pleasure to meet you."

Saleene's smile was cool. "Business associates, more accurately. Pleased to meet you, Decian. Have a seat, both of you."

Caius pulled out a chair and lowered himself into it carefully, grimacing as his wound twinged. "Saleene and Zuri run the brothel upstairs. I met Decian recently, when he became the new master of hounds at the palace."

A wry smile wrinkled the corners of Decian's eyes. "Oh, yes. The legatus and I hit it off immediately. He's been showing me around the city."

Saleene smiled back, her incisive gray eyes taking them both in with a look of speculation. "Has he, indeed? Well, our dearest Caius *is* widely known for his geniality and convivial nature."

"Uh… he is?" Decian asked, giving her an odd look. He turned to Caius. "You've certainly been keeping *that* part quiet. You should have mentioned."

Zuri let out a short bark of laughter.

Caius took it in good humor, not offended by the teasing. "You always seem to have enough bonhomie for both of us, so I never felt it was worth the effort."

Saleene raised an eyebrow at the banter. "Goodness. If nothing else, you've certainly managed to lighten his mood since the last time I spoke to him, Decian. I'm impressed."

Zuri gestured toward Caius. "What happened to your leg, anyway?" she asked, fearlessly direct as always.

"I got between an assassin and his intended target," Caius replied.

"You got between *two* assassins and their intended target, you mean." Decian frowned. "Whoever that was supposed to be. Do you even know?"

"No idea," Caius said. "By the time I was in a position to ask, they were already dead. The imperial family, presumably."

Zuri raised a hand and beckoned a serving girl over. "Bring us some more wine, Fassa. And two more bowls of stew, please."

The girl nodded and hurried off to fetch their meal.

Saleene leaned back in her chair. "Hmm. Still leaping between Constanzus and danger, Caius? I'd have thought you'd had enough of that job after the first time."

Caius regarded her curiously, his brows drawing together. "I wasn't aware you even knew about that. It was a long time ago."

"People talk," Saleene told him. She flicked her fingers in a dismissive gesture. "But enough about our illustrious emperor. How did you come to work at the palace, Decian? I take it you're not originally from Amarius?"

"No, I grew up in a village some distance outside the city," Decian said. "Mostly, I was in the right place at the right time when the old master of hounds left the position."

"He has a way with the dogs. Far more so than the previous houndsman," Caius added, with a flash of inappropriately dark humor.

"What about you, Zuri?" Decian asked, neatly redirecting the conversation. "You're Kulawi, aren't you? That's where my mother came from, you know."

"That's right," Zuri said, easily enough. "I arrived here with my father on an extended trade mission when I was young. Grew up here, really—so when he left to return to our village, I decided to stay behind."

Her dark eyes flicked to Saleene, glowing with a look of affection that hinted at the real reason she'd stayed. Caius had noted the obvious devotion between the pair on many occasions over the years. He didn't claim to understand how their relationship worked when both of them slept with random men for money, but there was little question that somehow, it did.

Decian nodded, shifting his attention to Saleene. "And what about you? You're... cross-spirit, is that right? That's what my mother used to call it, I think. A woman born into a man's body?"

It was direct to the brink of rudeness, but Decian's tone made it clear he wasn't judging, just curious.

Saleene—who'd doubtless heard far more insulting descriptions on too many occasions to count—replied with good grace. "Yes, that's what Zuri calls it, too. When I was younger and living as a man, I was a soldier in a rebel army across the border in Utrea. I was captured during a skirmish with Alyrion forces and brought to Amarius as a slave."

"The businessman who bought her owned a string of brothels in the city," Zuri went on. "She was good with numbers and accounting, so after a few months, he put her in charge of several of them."

Saleene shrugged. "Like you, Decian, I had a natural affinity for the work. I eventually earned my freedom and bought my own brothel. Now I can live as I choose."

"That's important," Decian said. "Sometimes I think it might be the most important thing of all."

The wine and food came as he was speaking, and once it was settled in front of them, Zuri lifted her goblet. "I'll drink to that," she said.

SIXTEEN

They all raised their drinks, tapping the rims together in solidarity. Caius looked around the table, wondering how he could feel envious of a pair of prostitutes and an escaped prisoner when he lived in an extravagant house and rubbed shoulders with the nobility.

Now I can live as I choose, Saleene had said. And that was the thing, wasn't it?

Could Caius choose something different? Again, the ridiculous vision of a quiet smallholding in the country slid across his thoughts—some magical, fantastical place where politics didn't exist and no one cared who he bedded. Again, the vision of Alyrios crumbling to dust beneath his feet followed close on its heels.

He blinked the moment of self-indulgence away and began to eat. The conversation slowed as they shifted their focus to the food.

"Oh—by the way," Caius said into the lull, "we ran into your troublesome pretty boy at the Condora gymnaestra this morning. It surprised me—he doesn't really seem the type."

"Pretty boys need to keep their pretty physiques," Zuri said around a mouthful of stew.

Caius considered pointing out that his particular gymnaestra didn't tend to cater to boys, much less pretty ones... but the subject was unimportant. It had been a minor coincidence, nothing more.

Outside, the sound of an angry, chanting crowd cut through the buzz of conversation in the tavern, growing loud enough that Decian craned around to look toward the door with a frown.

"What's that about?" he asked.

"Protesters," Saleene replied in a level tone. "There are more on the streets every day."

"A mob nearly burned down the temple on Vaia Sacrii last night," Zuri added. "Did you hear about it?"

"*What?*" Caius said, and unpleasant jolt of surprise hitting him in the chest. The Temple of Deimok on Vaia Sacrii was one of the largest churches in the capital. The idea that a pagan mob would dare attack it spoke of a level of unrest far beyond anything Caius would have predicted.

"I did tell you that change was coming—and that it wouldn't be gentle," Saleene reminded him dryly.

Decian looked between them. "Why do I feel like I'm missing something here? What exactly are the protesters protesting?"

Both Zuri and Saleene shot him odd looks.

"You don't know? How long did you say you'd been in Amarius?" Zuri asked.

"Not long enough to get embroiled in this morass," Caius answered for him.

"The Church is convening an ecumenical council to discuss the fate of pagan practitioners who refuse to convert to Deimonism," Saleene said. "The pagans take exception to the fact that they're not even to be allowed a voice during the discussion."

Decian's expression settled into lines of distaste. "Oh. *Religion.* I'm sorry I asked."

Zuri stared at him. "People will die if the radical wing of the Church gets its way."

"People *always* die when they start arguing about whose god is better," Decian retorted.

Caius was still struck with unease over the idea that things in the capital had deteriorated to such a degree while he'd been sitting at home, nursing a wounded leg. "Burning down temples won't help their cause."

Saleene turned a hard expression his way. "I find it fascinating when people are more appalled by the idea of a building being burned by a mob than the idea of a person being burned at the stake by a judge."

"Is that what's going to happen?" Decian asked. "People being burned at the stake?"

"Not if the moderate voices inside the Council prevail," Caius said firmly. "Which would be a more likely outcome if the pagans would stop provoking them."

Outside, the volume of chanting reached a crescendo, then began to fade as the protesters passed them by and continued down the street.

"Pagan lives hang in the balance, their fate to be decided by a body that refuses to so much as hear their testimony or allow them to be present for the debate," Saleene pointed out. "How do you expect them to react?"

"I expect them to be angry and afraid," Caius shot back. "Which doesn't change the fact that by marching through the streets and openly attacking Deimonist temples, they increase the chances that the zealots within the Council will ultimately hold sway."

"And if that happens, hundreds will die at the hands of the Church, if not thousands," Saleene finished.

"Even if the worst happens, they could always just agree to convert," Caius said. "It's better than dying."

Saleene and Zuri's faces were unreadable, but Decian's quiet voice broke the silence. "My mother worships the old gods from her homeland. She has since she was a little girl. Her beliefs have always been important to her."

Caius turned to him, the twisting discomfort in his stomach that accompanied any discussion of the upcoming Amarian Council intensifying as the words hit home. Decian's mother was Kulawi. *Of course* she worshipped the Kulawi gods. Did Zuri worship them as well? Was that why Saleene appeared to hold such strong opinions on the matter?

"I'm sure many in the capital feel the same way," he said carefully, aware that he'd never personally understood the level of passion and stubbornness that religion seemed to bring out in others. "But if it came down to it, would you not prefer to see her convert rather than have her fall afoul of the Church and risk death?"

Decian frowned. "I'd rather see a world where people didn't talk about burning other people alive because they disagree on a point of theology."

"Yes. Wouldn't *that* be a lovely world?" The tone of Saleene's reply was deeply sardonic. "In fact… while we're at it, I can think of a few other things I'd like to change as well."

So can I, Caius thought, though he didn't voice the sentiment aloud.

"Is your mother still living in your old village?" he asked Decian, realizing even as the words left his mouth that Decian might not know the answer to the question. He'd been locked up. It was quite possible he hadn't seen or heard from his mother in more than a decade.

His mouth quirked down. "I expect she's returned to Kulawi by now," he said.

"Then she's safe," Caius told him firmly, "no matter what the Council decides."

Decian shrugged, still looking unhappy. "I suppose so."

Was Zuri safe, though? And what would happen if Decian casually invoked the pagan gods in front of the wrong person at the palace, as he was occasionally wont to do?

Unsurprisingly, the conversation fizzled after that, each of them retreating into their own thoughts. They finished their meal with only a desultory back-and-forth about trivial matters, though Saleene continued to cast assessing glances at Caius when she thought he wasn't paying attention. When his bowl was empty and his wine mostly drunk, she tilted her head, regarding him openly.

"Since you're here, might I have a quick word in private, Legatus?" she asked, pausing to give Decian a brief smile. "You don't mind, do you?"

Decian blinked at her, then seemed to shake himself free of his reverie. "No, of course not. Zuri, maybe you could tell me more about where you came from in Kulawi? My mother was from one of the river tribes…"

Zuri shrugged and nodded, launching into a tale of her home village in the land across the Southern Desert. Saleene rose and gestured toward one of the private rooms in the back, indicating Caius should follow her. They entered the dim area with its single large table dominating the central space, and she closed the door behind them.

He limped over and turned to face her, crossing his arms and hitching a hip against the heavy wooden table to take the weight off his leg. "What's this about, Saleene?" he asked, genuinely curious.

Their relationship had been a fairly lengthy one for a prostitute and client, spanning all but the first few months of the four years he'd spent in Amarius. However, that wasn't to say they were friends, exactly. Saleene was nothing if not businesslike, and Caius was generally ill suited to conviviality — as she herself had pointed out not long ago.

Saleene leaned back against the wall next to the door and crossed her arms as well, mirroring him. "Am I right in thinking that Decian is your foolish cause, Caius? Your act of treasonous justice from a couple of weeks ago?"

Damn, but the woman should never be underestimated.

"What would make you think such a thing?" he asked blandly.

"The fact that I'm not a fool, mostly." She lifted her chin, looking down her patrician nose at him. "You've bedded him as well, haven't you."

Caius let a hint of a smile curl one corner of his lips. He knew it didn't reach his eyes. "I'm not certain our business relationship entitles you to ask me questions like that."

She matched the smile. "It wasn't a question. And if you're bringing him around to the Cock to try to ingratiate him with me, I'd say that entitles me to some answers." She paused, her expression growing serious. "He seems lovely. He's been good for you, too. So… where does the 'treason' part come in?"

Caius sighed, capitulating. "I can't tell you that, Saleene. I don't even think *he* knows the details."

"You're trying to make contacts for him, aren't you? To give him options, if whatever game you're playing unexpectedly goes tits-up. Come on — give me something to work with here."

Caius hesitated. "He was a prisoner unfairly slated for execution. He escaped death—mostly by pure chance—and I helped him hide in plain sight rather than killing him myself... or turning him in."

"Execution? What was his crime?" Saleene asked, her tone neutral.

"Being born," Caius told her.

Silence settled over the room. Eventually, Saleene broke it.

"As I said, people talk," she said. "There have been mutterings about prisoners being brought to the palace for execution in recent weeks. Some say they're imperial bastards who've recently become... *inconvenient*."

Caius shook his head. "I'm sorry, but I truly can't say any more about it." He hesitated. "Well... maybe this much. He was thrown in with the palace hounds after the beasts had been starved for a week. That was supposed to be his method of execution—getting torn apart by ravenous dogs."

Her eyebrows shot up. "God's *balls*, Caius. And you somehow installed him as *master of hounds*? That's... a bit on the nose, don't you think?"

"It's a long story," he said, feeling suddenly, unutterably tired. "I'll concede that when I saw you and Zuri dining today, it occurred to me that the two of you might be useful acquaintances for Decian to make. But you'll have to take my word that it was an impetuous decision, not part of some grand, overarching strategy. I appear to have lost my facility for grand strategy quite thoroughly in the years since I left the battlefield."

She studied him, doubtless taking in the tired slump of his shoulders and the way he leaned against the table to coddle his injured leg. After the past two weeks, he felt every inch the used-up old warhorse that he was—lame, and overdue to be put out to pasture.

"Are you in love with him?" she asked.

He exhaled forcefully, taken by surprise. "In *love* with him? What the hell kind of question is that, Saleene?"

She didn't back down or break eye contact. "Oh, don't mind me—I'm just trying to figure out if I've lost a client permanently or not. That's not a complaint, by the way. Like I said before, it seems he's been good for you."

Caius gave a single, frustrated shake of the head. He turned away from her, in favor of examining the rough-plastered wall as though it were the most fascinating thing he'd ever seen. "Let's put it this way. When this situation inevitably comes crashing down around my ears, I'll pay you whatever you ask to bugger me so hard that I forget my own name for a week. Assuming my head is still attached to my shoulders and not severed by an executioner's axe, of course."

"You're still trying to play both ends against the middle, Caius," Saleene said. "Though I at least get the impression that you finally know which side you *should* be playing, now."

"I don't have a side, Saleene," he replied. "I'm fairly certain the side I want to play doesn't exist anymore."

"Caius, you absolute fool. You *do* have a side," she retorted. "He's sitting out there with Zuri as we speak."

To that, he had no reply.

✸

Caius returned to the front room of the tavern to find Decian and Zuri chatting amiably. It was anyone's guess whether their tentative affinity would survive the full report Saleene was certain to give her partner as soon as they had privacy to speak.

Decian looked up at his approach with a smile. "Everything all right?"

"As much as it ever is," he replied.

"Right. Not a terribly reassuring reply, but whatever you say," Decian told him. "Are you ready to go? I should probably be getting back to the kennels soon, but I can drop you at your house and return your horse to the stables on my way."

"Yes, let's be going," Caius said. "Saleene... Zuri. Always a pleasure. Perhaps we can share a table again soon."

"Oooh, careful with the charm, Caius," Saleene warned. "Someone will mistake you for a gentleman."

Decian swallowed a laugh, and even Zuri cracked a smile.

"Fortunately, everyone at this table already knows me too well to make that particular mistake," Caius told them dryly. "Good afternoon, both of you."

They paid for their meal and left the tavern. Outside, Decian shot him a sidelong glance laced with humor. "I notice you didn't tell *them* not to do anything you wouldn't do."

"I wouldn't dare," Caius said.

The younger man seemed to have already forgotten their earlier, uncomfortable exchange about religion. Caius hadn't, though.

"I apologize if I was out of line earlier. I'm afraid I've always taken a practical approach to religion rather than a theological one."

"So I gathered," Decian said, though Caius could detect no anger in his tone. "Personally, I have very little use for any of it, even though I suppose some of what I grew up with must have stuck with me."

Caius only hoped the parts that had stuck with him didn't end up getting him in trouble.

"Still, it was thoughtless of me," he insisted. "I'm frustrated... with the Council, with the protesters... with all of it, I suppose. I watch events unfolding like two runaway wagons heading for a collision. And if any of the involved parties would simply step back for a moment and behave rationally, the disaster could be averted. But they won't. None of them will, and in the end, people will die. It only remains to be seen on how large a scale."

Decian nodded, thoughtful. "I've always been more concerned about the events immediately around me than with politics or religion... or any of the rest of it. I've had to stay focused on the here-and-now to survive. This is the first time I've really had a taste of the larger picture, and I can't say I envy you. Not one bit."

They reached the horses. Caius accepted a leg up, suppressing a pained grunt as he swung into the saddle and gathered up his gelding's reins.

"I suppose it's one thing when you have the kind of power that allows you to shape the larger picture to your liking," he said, as Decian untied the pony and scrambled onto its back. "But standing just outside the sphere of influence while watching everything go horribly wrong? Well, let's just say it grows old quickly."

They headed for the palace compound, winding through the back streets of Amarius. Caius couldn't help feeling on edge—watching their surroundings for any hint of trouble. Citizens went about their business. Wagons, riders, and people on foot crowded the roadways. The sound of clattering wheels and hooves against cobbles filled the air, along with the smell of people and animals, food and smoke and rotting garbage.

There was nothing out of the ordinary, although they did catch up to the crowd chanting anti-Church slogans at one point, riding parallel and a couple of blocks north of the marching protesters. Eventually, the mob turned onto a crossroad leading into a different part of the city, the sound of their voices gradually subsumed by the sounds of daily life.

When they'd successfully reentered the palace grounds and reached his house, Caius dismounted, looking at the familiar edifice with a combination of relief and dread. He had almost certainly pushed himself too hard today, before his wound was sufficiently healed. He knew on an intellectual level that he needed to rest, but he was also sick to death of staring at his own walls.

Decian leaned down and took the gelding's reins, ready to lead him back to the stables. He met Caius gaze and held it. "I could come back here tonight?" he offered. A sly smile slid across his face. "In case there's anything else you need help with, I mean."

The words *that's not a good idea* formed on the back of his tongue... but what came out was, "I'd like that." He frowned at himself, and quickly amended, "I'll be resuming my duties at the palace in the morning, though. After that, my time won't be my own. Not like it has been these past several days."

Decian only shrugged a shoulder. "I understand. Just try not to overdo it, all right? No more battling armed assassins until you've recovered from the last skirmish."

"I'll inform the assassins that they'll need to reschedule their dastardly plans to accommodate me," he said.

"You do that," Decian told him with a firm nod. "See you tonight, Legatus. Thanks for showing me around the city today." With a quick wink, he urged the pony around, leading the gelding alongside.

"Until then," Caius said to his retreating back, hating himself just a little bit more for his continuing weakness of will.

SEVENTEEN

When Caius entered his house, he was greeted by the sound of clattering pots and pans in the kitchen. Tertia poked her head out as he approached, giving him a brief head-to-toe inspection.

"You're looking better," she said. "Have you been out all day on that leg?"

"Since mid-morning," he told her. "I've already eaten, by the way."

"What, so you'll never need to eat again?" she asked. "Well, that *does* save me some trouble."

He huffed out an irritated breath and started past the kitchen, with the intention of returning to his room. After a few hitching steps, he paused and turned back. "Tell me something, Tertia. Would you say sympathies among the common people in Amarius lie more with the Church, or more with the pagans?"

She lifted her eyebrows in surprise, probably because he'd never asked her a question like that before. "About half and half, I'd say. Why?"

He shook his head, dismissing his own line of questioning. "Just a conversation I had with someone today in a tavern. Don't mind me—forget I asked."

"Minding you is my *actual job*, you dolt," Tertia said without heat. She took a breath as though to speak, but held it for a moment as she chose her words. "Outside of the imperial quarter, things are... complicated right now. Up until recently, I don't think most people gave a rat's testicles about what the pagans got up to—not until this Council nonsense came up, anyway. Now, everyone's got an opinion. The ones who were inclined to be worried are more worried, because there are pagans marching in the streets demanding rights. And the ones who were inclined to be sympathetic are more sympathetic, because they've got a better idea what's at stake now."

Caius took a moment to digest that, even though it basically confirmed his suspicions. "And what about you? What do you think?"

She straightened her spine, and Caius watched her walls going up before his eyes. "I'm just a lowly slave, *Legatus*. I don't discuss religion with my betters. I'm sure the emperor and his Council will decide what's best for all of us."

It was as clear a rebuke as if she'd told him to go straight to hell, and it brought the power imbalance between them into sharp relief. Caius was a respected general, seeking information about a matter important to the empire. Tertia was a slave who could be punished or even killed if she said the wrong thing to the wrong person.

"I understand," he said. "Thank you, Tertia. I'll retire to the garden for a bit while you finish what you were doing."

She scowled at him, as though fighting an internal debate. As he turned to leave, she said, "Most people in the palace don't look at things the same way as you, Legatus. You'd do well not to forget that."

He paused, not looking back at her. "Believe me," he told her, "there are days when I wish I *could* forget it."

⚜

Caius spent the rest of the afternoon and the first part of the evening turning the problem around and around in his head. The ideal outcome, as he saw it, would be for the moderate wing of the Church to prevail. Under their leadership, the pagans would be left more or less alone, in the belief that Deimok could sort them out as He saw fit after they died. As far as the moderate voices were concerned, the unbelievers would still end up suffering eternal torment for their wicked heresy — it would just happen a few years later than it otherwise might have.

Caius had no opinion on the disposition of souls after death, but he had some fairly strong opinions about rounding people up and setting fire to them because their neighbors claimed they were divining the future using chicken entrails or dancing under a full moon, or what have you.

There were genuinely dangerous pagan practitioners in the world, obviously. Caius had lost his father to one, and could easily have lost his life to another on the beaches of Eburos, during the botched invasion at Llanmeer. After what he'd seen during his forty-six years, if a shapeshifting pagan warlock ever found himself at the end of Caius' sword, Caius would run the fucker through without a second thought.

But that kind of real magic was vanishingly rare in Alyrios. The imperial family would have people believe that it had been wiped out generations ago—though Caius knew that to be a whole different kind of propaganda. It sure as hell hadn't been wiped out on Eburos. In addition, dragons had returned to the neighboring land of Utrea in recent years—and while the animals themselves might not be magical in the purest sense, the bonds their riders used to control them smacked heavily of witchcraft.

Caius hadn't heard of any shapeshifters infesting Alyrion lands in recent years. Not, in fact, since the one his father and the other guardsmen had killed at the cost of their own lives when he was a boy. That didn't mean none existed, but it certainly argued they weren't common. In the context of the current struggle, the term 'pagans' simply referred to people who still followed the old gods.

As long as they weren't hurting anybody, in Caius' view they didn't deserve a sentence of execution—no more than Decian deserved a sentence of execution for being born a bastard. But the pagans were angry. They were afraid for their lives, with good reason. And so they were making trouble, which only succeeded in fanning the flames of sentiment against them within the Council. That, in turn, fanned the flames of protest against the Council… and so the wheel turned.

Caius could see no practical way to break the cycle. Certainly, nothing that could be implemented by a single aging Legatus standing at the fringes of a ruling dynasty riddled with infighting.

The sound of someone entering through the front door broke him free from his thoughts. It had grown dark outside as he pondered the empire's troubles, the garden now illuminated only by the torches Tertia had lit before she left. They flickered in their sconces, casting a warm glow over Decian as he entered the open space. Humidity choked the air.

"You're going to get wet if you keep sitting there," said the younger man, by way of greeting. "There's a storm rolling in."

As if in response to his words, a gust of wind blew through the open area, whistling past the columns and rustling the leaves on the plants. Several of the torches blew out, and a fat raindrop splattered on the bench next to Caius' leg.

"Good thing you arrived in time to warn me," he said. "I might have drowned otherwise." He hauled himself to his feet as more raindrops followed. "I expect there's food in the kitchen. Hungry?"

"Always," Decian said, retreating under the cover of the hallway.

Caius followed him, joining him just as the skies opened. They were overdue for rain, and he enjoyed the sound of it overhead as he ushered Decian into the kitchen to investigate whatever food Tertia had left for him.

"Did your roof get repaired, I hope?" Decian asked wryly.

"As far as I know. At least, there was a fair amount of crashing and banging going on up there a few days ago."

"This ought to test the quality of their work, if nothing else," Decian said over the din of rain against baked ceramic tiles.

They put together plates of salted pork, pickled greens, and soft cheese, along with hunks of Tertia's ever-present bread — standing at the worktable to eat. The initial deluge eased into the pattering drumbeat of a steady shower, and by the time they were finished, it had slowed to a drizzle.

After hours spent brooding over a problem that couldn't be fixed, Caius resolved to set aside his worries until tomorrow, when he would once again be back in the vipers' den at the palace and unable to ignore the situation. Tonight, he was alone with a pleasant companion and nothing else to occupy him until morning.

"So," Decian began, affecting a long-suffering tone. "Have you thought of *anything at all* I could help you with, since I walked all the way out here and nearly got caught in a rainstorm?" His eyes dipped suggestively to a point below Caius' waist, before lifting again to meet his with a mischievous twinkle.

Caius let his lips twitch into a smile. "Well, for a start you can bar the front door so we can be certain we won't be interrupted."

"Why, Legatus—are you about to suggest something *scandalous?*" Decian asked. "I am *shocked.*"

"I haven't even told you what I have in mind yet," Caius pointed out.

"True," Decian allowed. "But I'm certainly waiting with bated breath to find out."

He disappeared into the atrium and returned a few moments later, errand complete. Caius took a quick mental inventory—the back door would already be barred, and Tertia would have closed and secured all the shutters before she left. They were alone, their privacy bolstered further by the unpleasant weather outside. Nothing short of the death of the emperor himself would be likely to bring anyone to his residence in the dark and the rain.

He limped over to the shelves arrayed along one wall of the kitchen and ran his fingers over the array of bottles and jars stored there.

"Still hungry?" Decian teased.

Caius chose a glass vial of pure, uninfused oil and plucked it from the shelf. "Not exactly," he said. "Though I'm not averse to swallowing something else before the night is through. Tell me—have you ever fucked another man... or been fucked?"

Decian went still. "You mean penetrated?" He paused. "No, I..."

Caius turned to look at him, struck by the sudden hesitation.

Decian shook his head briskly, recalling himself from whatever thoughts had distracted him. "It happened sometimes in the prison. Not to me personally, although I did have to fight off other prisoners on a handful of occasions. It... uh... wasn't exactly the kind of thing you did for fun."

Realization struck, and Caius covered a wince. "*Ah.* Yes, I see what you mean." He paused, debating for a moment before continuing. "You're aware that some men take enjoyment from the act, when it's approached with proper care?"

Decian tilted his head. "You're one of those men, I take it?" His tone was more curious than wary.

Caius consciously relaxed his stance. "I am, yes. Which isn't to say I indulge all that often—and we needn't tonight, obviously. Not unless you're interested. If you are, I'm more than happy to receive, rather than giving. I enjoy both variations with the right partner."

Decian tilted his head, considering. After a moment, he shrugged. "Bring the oil, at least. I'll admit to being intrigued."

"Very well. Just don't expect me to oil myself up and wrestle you," Caius told him, remembering the way the younger man's skin had gleamed as he grappled with the pair in the gymnaestra. "You'd probably win, and my pride doesn't need the blow."

Decian snorted. "Another time, then. Maybe once your leg is healed."

Even with his bad shoulder to consider, it wasn't an altogether unappealing offer. "We'll see. Come on—even *I* draw the line at fucking in Tertia's kitchen."

EIGHTEEN

Caius turned and headed for his bedroom. Decian's surprised laughter followed him, making something in his chest grow lighter. Rain pelted them as they exited the interior hallway, slanting down beneath the overhang that ran around the edge of the garden. Caius led the way into his room and set the oil on the bedside table. He took a few moments to light several of the lamps hanging evenly spaced on the walls, wanting enough illumination for both of them to be able to see what they were doing.

Decian, by contrast, made straight for the feather mattress, flopping down on it with a groan of pleasure. "See, now… that's what I'm talking about. It's criminal that you don't properly appreciate this bed."

"Oh, I don't know about that. Its appeal is growing as we speak," Caius assured him, looking over his shoulder to enjoy the show as Decian wriggled around in search of the perfect position. He finished with the final lamp and turned. "Clothes off," he ordered, tugging at the lacing of his own shirt and shrugging it awkwardly over his bad shoulder.

While there was something to be said for slowly unwrapping a lover's layers, the truth was that their two previous encounters had both occurred with Decian more or less fully clothed. Caius had seen him bared, but only in the gymnaestra. Tonight, Caius wanted him naked while they were in a place where he could touch as well as look.

"Hmm," Decian mused, even as he toed off his boots. "Do I call you *sir* when you order me around like that?"

Caius barked out a laugh and started work on his trouser lacings. "*God*, no. You were right before — you'd make a horrible soldier. Which is not, I hasten to add, a criticism." He was able to get out of his own boots — albeit painfully — with the aid of the carved wooden boot-pull sitting on the floor in the corner. At that point, however, he was stymied… his leg having grown too stiff over the course of the day for easy removal of the rest of his clothing.

He sighed. "Well, this is embarrassing."

Decian had already shimmied out of his layers and tossed them onto the floor next to the bed. He looked up, intuiting the problem with a single glance. "Not to worry. I *did* ask earlier if there was anything I could help you with, after all."

He rolled off of the too-soft mattress and prowled toward Caius, stopping so close in front of him that a deep breath would have brushed their chests together. His hands skimmed down Caius' sides—catching his waistband, sliding the breeches over his hips and down. He crouched, unselfconscious in his nudity, and Caius' cock twitched with interest at the memory of those full lips wrapped around his length.

Decian helped him step out of his trousers, smallclothes, and stockings, throwing them carelessly aside once he was done. He stood in a single, smooth movement, his skin sliding against Caius' on the way up. A self-satisfied little grin crinkled the corners of his eyes, and Caius couldn't help but pull him in for a kiss.

Decian made a low noise of appreciation. Caius swallowed it greedily, winding his good arm behind Decian's back to pull their bodies flush from chest to knee. He felt the ropy scar tissue from the flogging where it crisscrossed the younger man's skin, but the unusual sensation was swallowed beneath the jolt of their cocks brushing together. Decian's hips flexed, rutting against Caius shamelessly. He was already hard, and Caius wasn't far behind.

Caius let him continue for a bit, not immune to the appeal of simple frotting. Eventually, though, he eased Decian back until he could meet his eyes in the lamplight.

"Come on. Let's adjourn to that bed you're so fond of," he said. "You can put that oil to good use, if you're still interested."

Decian regarded him intently for a long moment before replying. "Actually, I think you should put it to good use on me, instead. You've got me curious now." He gave a small half-shrug. "If you like it enough to ask for it, then there must be something to it, right? I trust you."

Perhaps those three simple words shouldn't have affected him so, but Caius couldn't deny the sudden catch in his throat. He thrust the sentimental reaction aside, determined to ensure that Decian reaped generous rewards for his trust.

"As you like," he said. "There's often a small amount of discomfort involved at first... but if you decide at any point that it's not to your taste—"

"I'll let you know," Decian said with an easy smile.

Caius nodded. "It also requires the answer to an awkward question or two. Have you relieved yourself recently?"

Decian snorted. "Shortly before I came here. You're right, that is awkward."

"Not nearly as much as the alternative would be," Caius replied wryly, and Decian laughed outright. Caius decided there and then that he would never grow tired of hearing the sound of his laughter.

"Ever the practical military man," Decian teased, amusement still lurking in his tone. "Go on, then. How do you want me?"

Any way I can have you, Caius thought. He gestured to the bed. "Lie on your back. Get comfortable—we're going to be here awhile."

While Decian did so, he found a shallow bowl and poured a generous measure of oil into it. He arranged himself at Decian's hip and set the bowl within easy reach before leaning down to resume their earlier kiss.

If there was one advantage age had granted him, it was patience. He lavished attention on Decian's lips until the other man was panting against him, before moving to tease his nipples into taut brown points. Those, he plucked and tortured until Decian was writhing on the bed. Eventually, Decian reached for his own cock—pushed past his limits of self-control, though Caius had barely started on him.

"No," Caius said, grasping the wandering hand and placing it back on the bed.

Decian let out a frustrated groan. "This isn't at all what I'd pictured, just so we're clear," he said unsteadily.

"I know it's not," Caius told him, unrepentant, and went back to pinching and tugging the closest nipple. "Trust me."

Only when Decian stopped writhing, lying still except for the occasional full-body tremor, did Caius move lower. Decian's cock was a thing of beauty, hard and twitching—already leaking little dribbles of seed onto his flat stomach. Caius ran his finger lightly up its length from base to tip, gratified when the feathery touch drew a strangled noise and another pulse of pearly white.

He dipped his fingers into the oil—pleased that this, at least, was something he could still do left-handed—and cupped Decian's balls, kneading and tugging them lightly.

"F-*fuck!*" Decian stammered, thrusting up helplessly against nothing.

Caius let his fingers explore further, teasing sensitive skin until Decian's legs fell open of their own accord. More oil, and he slid down the final inch, brushing over the pucker he found there. Decian stilled as though suddenly unsure.

Caius met his eyes, sliding a single finger in slow circles around his tight rim. "All right?"

His companion's attention turned inward. He was silent for several moments before he nodded. "Yes. Don't stop."

Rather than reply with words, Caius leaned down awkwardly until he could kiss the tip of Decian's cock, which had softened a bit from its earlier ardor. Decian let out a sharp breath, his hips twitching. Caius indulged him with a long, slow suck of the head, licking the clinging drops of bitter saltiness clean. The pucker beneath his finger fluttered, and his fingertip sunk in a fraction, coming up against a second barrier of resistance.

Decian gasped.

Caius continued describing small, circular motions until Decian's last line of defense fell, allowing him inside. For several moments, he rested there without moving, sucking and laving Decian's cock until his body relaxed.

"That's... a decidedly odd sensation," Decian said, when Caius released his cock and started carefully stroking his way deeper.

"It is," Caius agreed. "Though it does get better."

Unhurried, he continued to tease Decian open until he was buried to the third knuckle. He was out of practice at the next part—it took a couple of attempts at curling his finger in a beckoning motion before Decian stiffened and arched, his hard prick jumping.

"*What* was that?" Decian demanded in an unsteady tone.

Caius smiled a predator's smile. "Oh, you mean this?" He curled his finger again, drawing an undignified noise from his partner. "Didn't I tell you it got better?" With that, he turned his attention to the highly enjoyable task of taking Decian to pieces without a single touch to his cock.

In the end, it took perhaps half an hour, three fingers, and roughly a third of the oil from the bowl to wring the first climax from him. He arched like a bow, his stomach muscles jerking as he stifled a cry. Caius' cock throbbed and twitched in sympathy as seed dribbled from the slit of Decian's prick, but did not spurt.

When he'd wrung as much as he could from his companion, he slid his fingers carefully free. Decian shuddered and went limp.

"Holy gods," he breathed. "That was... that was..."

Caius smirked down at him and rubbed an oily hand over his hard length, slicking himself thoroughly. "Oh, dear," he teased. "Did I somehow give the impression that we were done?"

Rain drummed against the roof over their heads. Decian blinked up at him, dazed and open and stunningly lovely in the warm, flickering light. "You're going to kill me, aren't you? I'm going to expire right here on this bed and sing your praises with my dying breath."

"Don't be ridiculous," Caius told him, rising from the bed on aching legs. Ignoring his nagging injuries, he manhandled Decian's unresisting body around until his hips rested at the edge of the mattress. "I've gone to far too much trouble to keep you alive."

Decian's head flopped back as Caius positioned himself between his legs, hooking his right elbow under Decian's left knee to tilt his hips up a bit. He lined himself up, nudging against Decian's entrance with steady pressure.

"Bear down for me, Decian," he ordered gently. "I promise to make it worth your while."

Decian groaned and did as he was told. Caius held his breath as his tip slid inside impossibly tight, silky heat. He froze, resisting the urge to thrust deep—instead waiting for Decian's body to adjust to him. Decian, too, was holding his breath. After a few seconds, his lungs emptied on a gusty sigh, and he wriggled his hips in Caius' grip. Caius slid a little deeper, and both of them gasped.

Caius worked into him by fractions, taking his time until he was fully seated. Beads of sweat had broken out on Decian's chest. "Move," Decian demanded. "Before I go mad."

He moved—cautiously at first. Decian flexed his hips, trying to meet him. Caius changed the angle, seeking, until he was rewarded with Decian's full-body shudder.

"There we go," he said. The heat and pressure was indescribable, demanding he seek more of it—deeper, faster. He refused to give into the urge; not until he'd wrung a second release from his lover.

There was a reason he'd avoided Decian's cock earlier, but now it was time. He freed the hand that wasn't supporting Decian's knee. Decian's other leg wrapped around his waist, pulling him in... keeping him close. Caius' fingers closed around Decian's cock, still hard despite his earlier climax. Decian keened, his hands scrabbling against the bedclothes for purchase as Caius worked him steadily, in time with the shallow thrusts that were driving both of them toward climax.

Decian broke first, his muscles clenching hard as his spine arched. His seed spurted from his pulsing cock in thick ropes, painting his chest and belly. His passage clamped around Caius like a warm vise, pulling his release from him in waves of rippling pleasure. Caius breathed through it, savoring every second. Eventually, with Decian growing lax beneath him, he slid out. Both of them flinched at the loss, and Decian made a small, discontented noise that went straight to Caius' heart.

"Shh," Caius soothed, ignoring his unsteady legs long enough to help Decian sprawl full length onto the bed. "I'll get a cloth to clean us up and be right back."

He did so, aware that he'd pushed his body too hard today and not regretting it one bit. When he'd completed at least a cursory attempt to prevent them from becoming glued together by drying spunk as the night progressed, he set the cloth aside and climbed stiffly into bed, arranging the covers over them both.

Decian made a noise of happiness, sprawling along Caius' right side with his head resting on Caius' shoulder and a leg hooked possessively over his. Tawny, work-roughened fingers drew abstract patterns across Caius' chest, raising a pleasant shiver of gooseflesh in their wake. It had been… too long since Caius had something like this. So very, *very* long. Every circling thought in his mind was quieted; every physical ache and twinge buried beneath the warm, woolen blanket of affection and sexual lassitude.

He curled his good right arm around until he could stroke Decian's temple, fingertips caressing soft skin still dampened by cooling sweat. Decian's muscles—already lax with afterglow—melted completely against him. His wandering fingers stilled against Caius' chest, his palm coming to rest warm and heavy over Caius' heart.

"Mmm," Decian breathed, as Caius continued to stroke his temple and cheek. Above them, a new burst of rain pelted the tile roof. Wind whistled past the closed shutters, and a huff of soft laughter fluttered Decian's ribcage. He craned his neck to look up at Caius in the low lamplight. "You know—somewhere out there, an incompetent cutpurse is getting soaked to the skin right now. Serves him right, too."

Caius gazed down at him in mild confusion, trying to pull his wits together enough to decipher the statement. "A cutpurse? What do you mean?"

Decian lifted his hand, waving it vaguely in a 'doesn't matter' gesture before letting it fall back to rest on Caius' sternum. "It's not important. A man tried to follow me when I was on my way here earlier. A thief, I reckon. As soon as I noticed him, I doubled around to the stables and lost him." He yawned. "Anyway, he would have been disappointed. I've got nothing to steal. Not that I was carrying with me, at least."

A chill swept down Caius' spine, washing away his lethargy as effectively as if he'd stepped into the garden to stand under the downpour. He sat up, ignoring Decian's sleepy noise of protest.

"You were *followed*?" he demanded. "From the kennels? Describe this man to me. Decian—tell me *every single thing* you can remember."

NINETEEN

Decian rolled onto an elbow, a frown furrowing his brow. "Describe him? There's nothing much to describe. He was average looking. Dark clothing — nothing fancy. Why does it matter? There must be hundreds of petty thieves in a city this size."

"Did he follow you all the way from the kennels?" Caius asked urgently. "Was he armed?"

Decian blinked at him in the lamplight, clearly having no idea what had upset him so badly. "I mean... I wouldn't have thought so. I didn't notice him until I was about halfway here, anyway. And I didn't exactly stick around to see if he was armed."

Caius felt his pulse throbbing in his temple. Dread pooled in his stomach. "This is bad. Don't you *see*? Someone suspects you. You need to leave."

"What?" Decian shook his head sharply, as though to clear it. "Wait. Back up for a minute. Why would you assume this was anything more sinister than someone after a few coins?"

"*Think*, Decian!" Caius said. "We are *inside the palace compound*. There are no cutpurses roaming the emperor's grounds."

"This place is like a city inside a city," Decian protested.

"A *city* with high walls surrounding it and guards on every gate, day and night," Caius said grimly. "Guards who don't let anyone in or out unless they either know them personally, or they're carrying signed papers granting passage."

"That's..." Decian began, only to cut himself off. "So, you're saying someone was... what? Sent to follow me specifically?"

"Yes," Caius said, the chill of dread spreading from his stomach to his heart. "Someone is suspicious enough to want to know more about your comings and goings."

"And I led him here," Decian said slowly. "Well... I mean, I don't think I actually *did* lead him here. I stopped in and talked to the stable lads for a bit, and then snuck out the back to come the rest of the way to your house. I didn't see any sign of someone following me after that."

It was something, Caius supposed. But in the end, it wasn't where Decian had led his pursuer that was the issue. It was the fact that he was being shadowed in the first place.

"It doesn't matter," Caius said. "It's no secret that you've been spending half your time here since I was injured. The fact that you came here again tonight wouldn't gain them any new information. Though, normally I'd tell you to leave before it got any later, because seeing you slink out in the morning like a thief *would* give them information they could use against both of us."

The rain increased in intensity, battering against the roof.

"But tonight," Decian said slowly, "It would look stranger if you threw me out in the rainstorm, instead of letting me stay in one of your fancy guest rooms until the weather cleared."

"Just so," Caius agreed. He scrubbed his right hand through his close-shorn hair, thinking hard. "This isn't a game anymore—we have to get you out of the city. It was one thing when no one suspected you. But if someone is willing to make the effort to have your movements tracked inside the palace grounds—"

"They must know I'm not who I'm pretending to be." Decian looked as though his entire life had just been pulled from beneath him.

Which, of course, it had been.

It was a life crafted in the space of a mere couple of weeks... but for someone who'd been hauled off to prison at the age of sixteen, it was almost certainly the best life he'd known since childhood. Caius ached for him... or perhaps he ached for himself, selfishly, at the prospect of Decian being gone from his life. More likely, it was both, he decided.

He closed his eyes and took in a steadying breath. "Leave early in the morning and go back to the kennels. Act as though nothing is wrong. Don't breathe a word of this, not even to Pip. I'll beg off early tomorrow at Court—claim my wound is still paining me, or some such. Come here in the evening, just as you did tonight, but bring horses with you. If anyone asks, tell them you're taking me into the city to drink. If anyone follows you here, don't try to throw them off your trail. Don't let on that you've noticed them at all."

Decian frowned, still looking as though he'd been gut-punched. "What? Why not?"

"I don't want them on their guard. If we're followed beyond the palace gates, we'll lose them in the backstreets of the city. I'll take you to the port; buy you passage down the coast on the kind of ship where they ask no questions. I'll give you what money I can—enough to establish yourself somewhere far away from here." His chest tightened around the words, but he held his voice steady by force of will.

The expression on Decian's face gutted him.

"I don't want to leave," Decian whispered.

Caius lifted a hand, cupping the side of his face. "I don't want you to die," he said.

Decian's eyes slid closed. After an endless moment, he nodded.

"So. This is our last night, then." His voice sounded distant.

Caius swallowed. "It has to be. I'm sorry."

Decian leaned forward, his hand coming around the nape of Caius' neck. He pressed their lips together, and Caius squeezed his eyes shut at the desperate intensity of the kiss. He returned it as best he could, still cradling Decian's cheek in his palm, trying to convey not only his regrets, but also his gratitude for the gift of companionship Decian had given him.

After what might have been minutes or hours, Decian lowered his head to rest in the crook of Caius' shoulder. Throat aching, Caius wrapped his good arm around Decian's scarred back and held him tightly.

The door was barred. The shutters were closed. Even if Decian's shadow had decided to stand around in the rain for hours in hopes of catching a glimpse of his target, there was nothing for him to see from a vantage point outside the house. Caius would not force Decian into a guest room for appearances' sake. Not on their first and only night together. He eased the younger man down to lie with him on the bed as they had been before, and resumed his slow stroking of Decian's temple once they were settled.

Whereas the younger man had been sprawled across him in total relaxation before, now, he was clinging. Caius rested his chin on top of Decian's head, trying to ignore the heavy weight of grief settling across his shoulders with the familiarity of an old, tattered cloak. He couldn't give in to melancholia. Not yet, when he still had to get Decian away to safety. Right now, helping Decian escape Amarius was his only goal... the only important thing in his world.

The night grew deeper, the rain continuing off and on. Eventually, half a lifetime of soldiering came to the fore, and Caius slept despite the dull, gray pain of heartache.

He was in the forest, searching. Warm brown eyes set in a dusky-skinned face beckoned him forward silently before slipping out of view behind the bole of a massive tree. Caius followed, steadying himself with a child's hand against the rough bark.

It was too quiet... always too quiet in the deep woods. No birds chirped. No leaves rustled. No dapples of ever-shifting sunlight reached the layer of decaying leaves at Caius' feet. He circled the trunk, but the lithe figure with the deep brown eyes was already gone, disappearing behind another tree perhaps ten paces away. Caius crashed through the leaf litter in pursuit, his sandaled footsteps shockingly loud in the muffling silence. Always, his quarry remained just at the edge of vision. A glimpse here, a flicker of movement there – nothing more.

Eventually, a clearing opened ahead of him, and he stumbled to a halt. Clouds choked the sky, turning it flat gray except for a single patch of brilliant blue. A narrow beam of golden sunlight illuminated the trampled grass at the edge of the clearing, where the broken stalks were painted red. A great stag lay crumpled on the ground. Its antlers jutted up like the bare limbs of a dying tree, crimson at the tips. Stripes and splatters of red crisscrossed its tawny coat, three spears jutting obscenely from its body. Its tongue lolled from its open mouth, swollen and dark purple with trapped blood.

Caius didn't want to look at the shapes arrayed around it on the ground. If he looked, it would be real. No, no, no, he chanted, with a child's desperate hope that wishing for something with enough conviction could make it true. He walked forward despite his fervent desire to turn and run away, until the splayed shapes around the fallen stag became men.

Please, no, he thought again, but it didn't make any difference. His feet continued to propel him closer, until he was standing over the nearest man. A familiar face stared up at the sky sightlessly. Decian's expression had frozen into lines of horror. Sticky blood trailed from a rip in the side of his throat to a puddle drying on the ground. He held no weapon in his hand, but his fingers curled in the air like claws.

The corpse stared up at him with dead, unblinking eyes, pinning him in place. Caius caught his breath as a blood-red glimmer began to kindle in those brown depths, growing in intensity until the scarlet glow spilled from them like torchlight —

He jolted awake from the dream with a gasp, flailing blindly in the darkness. His elbow thudded against something warm and solid as he scrambled into a sitting position, eliciting a startled grunt from the figure beside him.

"Caius?" A hand closed around his upper arm, half steadying and half restraining. "What is it, what's wrong?"

The dream images dissipated like mist, leaving him clammy with sweat, his heart thudding painfully against his ribs. The rushing noise in his ears resolved itself into the sound of his own gasping breaths.

"*Hey,*" the voice said, and the hand on his arm gave him a little shake. "You were having a nightmare. Come on—wake up."

"I'm all right," Caius croaked, his voice emerging nearly unrecognizable to his own ears.

"Yeah, I can see that," Decian said, not scrimping on the irony. "It must have been quite a dream. Does this happen often?"

Caius swallowed. Once… twice. He licked his lips and shook his head, only to realize that the last of the lamps had gone out at some point, and it was dark as pitch in the room. "No," he managed. "Not… recently, anyway."

If it hadn't been for that thrice-damned hunt—the stag in the forest, staring at him with Kaeto and Bruccias' spears buried in its side…

"It's fine," he said. "I'm fine. I'm sorry I woke you."

The hand that had been gripping his bicep loosened in favor of rubbing up and down his arm before falling away. "Don't worry about it. When I'm sleeping somewhere far away and missing your presence beside me, I'll remind myself of the way you tried to break my ribs with your elbow the first night we spent together."

The choked laugh that broke free of his control sounded wrong, but it was better than any of the other options that might have come out of his mouth.

"Sorry," he said again.

"You should go back to sleep." Decian hesitated. "It's early, but the rain's stopped. I might head back to the kennels now, actually."

Caius' heart still pounded against the inside of his chest, convinced that danger lurked all around. It took him a moment to put Decian's words into context. When he did, his pulse stuttered in response to the sinking feeling in his stomach. He was leaving. It had been their first night… and also their last night. Now it was about to be over.

They would see each other one more time, publicly and with no chance to say or do any of the things they might wish to before their final parting.

"All right," he said faintly.

The silence stretched long enough to grow heavy. His eyes adjusted to the point that he could make out Decian's lean form as a darker shadow amongst the gray of the room.

"All right," Decian echoed eventually.

Warm fingers caught Caius around the nape of the neck and reeled him in. The kiss was clumsy in the dark until Caius' hand blindly found Decian's cheek to steady him. He adjusted the angle, fitting their lips together and taking possession of Decian's mouth. It was a bad idea, since once he'd started he didn't want to stop.

Ever.

After long seconds, they were forced to break for air. Decian ducked his head, resting their foreheads together, his fingers still curled around the back of Caius' neck.

"I'll see you this evening," Decian murmured against his lips.

His hand slid away, and Caius let him go. Decian slid out of the bed, the faint rustling as he found his clothing and pulled it on sounding loud in the dark. He was surefooted in the low light, navigating around the furniture easily. Caius heard him pause at the door.

"Goodbye," Decian said.

Caius found he couldn't answer, and after a moment, Decian left. He lay back in the bed, listening to the sound of the front door being unbarred. It opened and closed, leaving Caius alone in the echoing dark.

TWENTY

Returning to Court would have been a form of torture, even without the knowledge of what was going to happen later in the day. Caius dressed himself with care and dragged his aching body to the main palace, where he was greeted largely with indifference from the various courtiers and adjuncts.

Apparently, the march of days that had passed since the royal hunt had been a sufficient stretch of time for most people to lose interest in the presence of assassins bent on murdering members of the imperial family. Caius wasn't surprised, though he did take more grim satisfaction than was probably seemly in coming up with increasingly ridiculous answers to people asking him where he'd been or what had happened to his leg.

"My horse kicked me. He's always foul-tempered after a hunt," he told the emperor's valet.

"My tailor was adjusting a new pair of trousers to fit, when the needle slipped," he told the wide-eyed head of the armory. "Terrible things, needle sticks—it festered immediately, and the surgeon thought for several days that I might lose the leg."

"An asp bit me. It must have crawled beneath my blankets at night to get warm," he told the adjunct to the treasury. "God knows how it got in the house."

Unfortunately, there were other things to worry about besides scandalizing the palace staff. The date of the Council was almost upon them, with most of the Church dignitaries having already arrived in Amarius. Their presence required significant added security, day and night.

Aelio was at his wits' end, and Caius imagined Laurentin was, as well. The two tribuni were in charge of the palace guard and the city guard, respectively. While their roles didn't often overlap, there was still a degree of rivalry between them at the best of times. Now, they were essentially forced to work together, as the emperor's important guests arrived to find a city in upheaval over their presence.

"If we get through this without a major diplomatic incident, it's going to be a miracle from Deimok himself," Aelio told him privately, as they went over the final plans for security around the formal Council meetings.

They were interrupted by a harried looking pageboy, who bowed low when they turned to him. "Legatus? I come bearing an invitation from the empress. She wishes to speak with you in her private gardens."

Caius and Aelio shared a look. Such a summons was highly unusual, and not something anyone in their right mind would ignore—not unless they harbored a death wish.

"Does she require my presence immediately?" Caius asked.

The page bobbed again. "Yes, Legatus. If you would accompany me?"

Caius turned back to Aelio with a small shrug. "It appears I must take my leave. You might consider redirecting some of the city guard to watch over the larger temples at night. Perhaps we could speak more on the matter tomorrow."

Aelio nodded. "Indeed. I look forward to it."

Caius followed the page through the sprawling interior of the palace, leaving the public areas behind and entering the residential wing. On any other day, he would doubtless be devoting more energy toward wondering about the purpose of the summons. Empress Stasia was not usually a public figure. Caius had met her before, but only in the context of important functions that required her to appear briefly on her husband's arm.

The page led him to a pair of double doors inlaid with colored glass, which opened onto a meticulously appointed garden. The air was perfumed with sweet, floral scents. Flowering plants and elegant statues flanked a path leading to a central area set with stone benches and firepots. There, the empress herself sat primly on one of the seats, looking out across the vista of exotic blooms.

"Your Imperial Majesty," the page said, bowing until his hair nearly brushed the ground. "The legatus is here as you requested."

Stasia turned, taking Caius in with a quick sweep of her pale gray eyes. "Thank you, Jules. You may go."

Her voice was delicate, as was her appearance. She wore an ivory-colored stola—simple in design, but made of rich cloth embroidered with fine designs. Her dark brown hair had been pinned artfully atop her head; soft curls framing her thin face. This was the woman who had wed an emperor… borne him three healthy sons, and managed to avoid falling out of his favor over the course of more than a quarter century.

Idly, Caius wondered what her feelings were regarding the parade of Constanzus' bastards that had entered the palace in recent weeks, never to leave again. Did she even know about them—either of their existence or their fate? Only a fool with very little attachment to his own head would dare to ask such a question.

"Empress," he said, bowing with as much courtly grace as he could manage, given the stiffness of his injury.

"Caius Oppita," she greeted, surprising him with the use of his name rather than his title. "Please… sit."

She indicated another of the benches, and Caius limped over, lowering himself onto it.

"You have saved my husband's life," she said, without further preamble.

"It was my duty," Caius replied by rote, unsure if she were referring the recent hunt, or the battle four years ago. He hesitated before adding, "And it has always been my honor to serve under my emperor's command."

He refused to examine the statement's truthfulness too closely. For years, it *had* been an honor. Constanzus would doubtless go down as one of the great military minds in history. Caius only hoped history would not end up recording a final footnote about the great conqueror's ignominious decline and fall.

"He is not who he once was," Empress Stasia said, eerily echoing his thoughts.

Caius looked up sharply and did not reply, since any reply would either be an admission of disloyalty or a blatant lie.

Stasia waved her hand, dismissing the awkward position in which she'd placed him. "Forgive me, Legatus. You need not answer that, obviously."

"May I ask why you've summoned me here today?" he asked.

She raised an eyebrow. "Is expressing gratitude for your continued service to my husband not reason enough?" The question was coy, and did nothing to settle his misgivings.

"No gratitude is necessary," he told her. "As I said, it is my duty."

Stasia nodded, watching him closely. "Of course. And your duty to the empire is important to you, is it not?"

Oh, what a loaded question that was.

"Yes, Your Imperial Majesty," he said, his voice even.

"What if I were to tell you that the empire now faces a danger greater than it has ever known before?" she asked.

These were turning into deeper waters than Caius was prepared to navigate, on today of all days. He fervently wished he'd slipped away from the palace before the page had managed to find him.

"Then I would express confidence that Alyrios will ultimately prevail, thanks to the strength of its institutions and the loyalty of its citizens." The lie burned against his lips, even as he spoke it.

Stasia tilted her head thoughtfully. "I wish I shared your confidence, Legatus."

Exhaustion washed over him without warning. He was so tired of all this—tired enough that it made him bold. "Please speak plainly, Empress. I fear I am not well-suited to subtle insinuation."

If his recklessness in addressing her in such a way surprised her, she didn't show it. "Tell me your opinion of my sons. One of them will be the next emperor of Alyrios. What do you think of them?"

Fucking hell. Did this endless family scheming extend to the empress as well? He tried not to let the depths of his disquiet show.

"They are ambitious and canny young men," he said neutrally, since saying *'One is a drunkard, one is a terrifying sadist, and one is a slimy arselicker'* probably wouldn't go over too well.

"I have reason to believe that at least one of them is plotting against me," Stasia said, her eyes still burning holes in him.

And... *of course* this meeting would end up being all about her. Not about her husband's reign. Not about the empire. No—one of her sons was plotting against *her*.

"Which one?" he asked.

"I have suspicions, but I do not know for certain." Her brow furrowed. "You are a trusted advisor. I wish to know if any of them have said things to you that you found... unusual or suspect."

Abruptly, he found that he couldn't be done with this conversation fast enough.

"No, Your Imperial Majesty," he lied. "Nothing like that." *Not unless you count their obvious maneuvering to take control of the throne upon their father's death.*

Stasia looked disappointed, as though she'd genuinely expected him to spill some sort of incriminating evidence at her feet. "I see. Very well, Legatus. If you should overhear any useful information related to this matter, I will make it worth your while to pass it on to me. In private, of course."

Yes, of course—I'll get right on that, he thought. Aloud, he only said, "As you wish, Empress. If that is all, I should return to my duties at Court. I've been absent too long as it is."

Stasia looked troubled, but she nodded her assent. "Certainly, Legatus. I don't wish to keep you from the important things you must have to do."

He took his leave from her with another low bow, wondering—not for the first time—what would happen if he purchased passage for two people rather than one at the docks tonight. As always, duty prevented him from giving the idea more than passing consideration.

He'd served Alyrios since he was a lad of seventeen — almost thirty years, now. Somehow, that duty had never felt like such a prison sentence before.

As he'd promised Decian, Caius made his excuses in the middle of the afternoon and left for the day. To maintain appearances, he accepted the offer of a carriage to see him home, even though he could have managed it on foot. As it always had after an injury, getting back to some sense of normalcy acted as better medicine than any tincture or concoction a physician might offer.

Normalcy. He scoffed at himself. There was nothing normal about any of this. He dreaded the coming hours.

As he clambered down from the carriage and approached his front door, a figure on the far side of the street melted into the shadows of an alley between two rows of insulae. Caius took note of the man's presence, but made a point of not staring after him. Clearly, whoever had been following Decian had decided to station a watcher here in anticipation of his return. He wasn't surprised; as he'd said last night, only a fool wouldn't have noticed how much time Decian had been spending here since Caius had been injured.

Let them spy. None of it would matter in a few hours.

Caius had already concocted his cover story, ready for use whenever it might become necessary. Decian was a lively and pleasant drinking companion. He'd lured Caius out for a few hours of merriment in the city despite his sore leg. When Caius was ready to call it a night, Decian expressed the desire to stay out longer, and that was the last Caius had seen or heard from him.

He would suggest moving Pip into the position of houndsman, and bringing in a new lad to work under him. Beyond that, Caius intended to put the whole thing behind him as thoroughly as he could manage. Maybe he'd make good on his threat to spend a night letting Saleene pound the sentimentality out of him, assuming he could afford her rates after giving most of his spare coin to Decian.

He entered the front door, only to find Tertia waiting inside.

"Someone's been watching the house all afternoon," she said by way of greeting. "Should I be worried?"

He sighed. "No. I'll deal with it tonight. It won't be an issue after that, and I guarantee their interest doesn't extend to you, even now."

She held his gaze intently. "You seem very sure of that."

"I am."

Her mouth turned down. "You should take more care, Legatus. Sometimes I worry that you're not as good at these palace games as you think you are."

His face settled into a matching frown. "I don't need to be good at playing them, Tertia. I just need to know how to finish them." He scrubbed a hand through his short hair, tired beyond measure of the whole sorry mess. "Finish up whatever you were doing and go. Everything will be back to normal tomorrow."

He left without waiting for her reply, heading to his room and pointedly closing the door behind him. His sturdy wooden moneybox rested in a concealed compartment in one of the interior walls. The key to the iron padlock securing it was hidden in a specially sewn pouch in one corner of his stupidly soft feather mattress. He hauled out the box and unlocked it, lifting the lid on creaking hinges and assessing its contents.

Money to purchase Decian's passage to safety went into the coin purse hanging at his belt. Most of what was left he poured into a second silk-lined bag, tying it shut and adding that to his belt as well. He locked the box and returned both it and the key to their hiding places. Then he went to test the edges on his sword and his collection of daggers.

Considering the amount of time he'd whiled away sharpening them during the past week, it wasn't surprising that they were all keenly honed. He stowed an extra dagger in his weapons belt and one in each boot. When

Decian finally arrived some time later, Caius was in the garden, running through basic sword exercises by torchlight to test the state of his leg—just in case.

"Hullo?" Decian called from outside.

He sheathed his sword and set the sword belt aside for the moment. After limping to the front door to meet him, Caius braced himself against the sight of the younger man's downtrodden expression.

"Hello," Caius said, trying not to remember the lurid details of the previous evening—especially the way Decian had lain relaxed and sated in his bed, curled intimately against his side. "Have you come to drag me out for a drink?"

This, for the benefit of the stableboy who had once again accompanied Decian to help with the horses. Tomorrow, the lad could act as a supporting witness to bolster Caius' story, should such a thing become necessary.

Decian tried on a smile, unconvincing though it was. "You already know me too well," he said. "How's the leg doing?"

"Sore," Caius said, which wasn't a lie. "I had to leave the palace early today to rest it."

"Hmm," Decian mused. "You know what's good for a sore leg? Ale. *Lots of it.* So come with me anyway."

"You certainly do make a persuasive argument," Caius told him, aware of the stable lad watching the exchange with limited interest. "Eh, why not? Give me a minute, and I'll come along despite my better judgment."

He went to retrieve his sword belt from the garden, where he'd left it rather than wearing it to answer the door. After all, he was supposed to be resting—not ready and waiting to leave his house on a moment's notice. With a deep, centering breath, he returned to the entryway— prepared to see this through if it meant Decian would finally be safe from his vengeful half-brother, Kaeto.

"Leg up?" Decian offered, gesturing to Caius' gray gelding.

"Thank you," Caius replied politely. He tried not to notice how his skin tingled where Decian's hands touched him, even through his clothing.

Making it into the saddle was a bit easier today than it had been yesterday. The stableboy held Decian's pony while he, too, clambered up—exhibiting a little more grace than the last time Caius had seen him mount. Caius tossed the stable lad his customary copper coin and sent him on his way. The boy dipped his head in a sloppy bow and jogged off, leaving him alone with Decian... and whoever was watching from the shadows.

"Come on, then," Caius said, wheeling his horse in the direction of the nearest gate leading out of the palace compound. "Let's go see if we can lose ourselves in a tankard."

"And lose anyone following us along the way," Decian muttered, too low to be heard by whoever might be listening.

TWENTY-ONE

The lamplighters had already been out with their long poles, ensuring that the roads running through the sprawling palace compound were lit with flickering orange light. Caius pretended not to be aware of the figure following them on foot. He maintained the easy pace of someone wandering out for a night on the town with a friend, rather than goading his horse into a faster gait in an attempt to outdistance the man behind them.

Decian was a tense presence at his side. Caius could tell that he, too, was making an effort not to look over his shoulder—but he was evidently finding it a struggle. They weren't alone on the streets at this hour, but it wasn't crowded by any means. The mood in the imperial quarter was subdued these days, with the growing unrest and the upcoming Council to worry about.

By rights, Caius should probably be making small talk for the sake of appearances. However, since small talk wasn't a particular skill of his at the best of times, he and Decian rode side by side in grim silence. The only saving grace of the situation was that the awareness of danger helped him push aside the reality of Decian's imminent departure from his life.

The southern gate leading into the city loomed ahead, guarded as always. The portcullis was down, as was generally the case after dark. It would only be lifted for those who had legitimate business inside, and who could prove it—or for those that the guards recognized and trusted. Idly, Caius wondered where the man following them fell along that spectrum.

"Ho, there," called one of the guards, raising a hand as they entered the half-circle of brighter torchlight surrounding the gate. "Who goes there, and what is your business?"

Caius led the way closer and halted his horse. "Legatus Caius Oppita, heading into the city for a few hours with the master of hounds."

"Our business is ale," Decian added, and the guards chuckled.

"Serious business, indeed," said the one on the left. He touched his helm in acknowledgement of Caius' rank. "A good evening to you, Legatus. Houndsman."

Without fuss, he gestured to the men stationed at the gate mechanism. They turned the massive crank, machinery creaking as the heavy portcullis rose. Decian watched it nervously despite his earlier witty quip, as though worried that someone would drop it on their heads as they tried to pass through.

Caius nodded to the guards. "Thank you, guardsmen. We'll be back at some point, I expect." *Or one of us will be, at any rate.*

"I'll let the next shift know," said the man, giving another small salute as he and Decian rode past.

Behind them, Caius heard the gate clank as it was closed. It was possible that would be that, as far as their pursuer went... but Caius had been a soldier for a very long time before becoming a palace lapdog, and he wasn't about to assume things would be so easy.

"Come on," he said, urging his gelding into a jog. "We wouldn't want the Wooly Ram to run out of ale before we get there."

He glanced around to see Decian gritting his teeth as he jounced up and down in time with the pony's jarring trot. Caius' bad leg was none too pleased about the faster pace, either, but the sooner they left the open area surrounding the walls of the imperial quarter and lost themselves in the dim streets and alleys of Amarius, the happier he'd be.

The open space was specifically designed to leave anyone approaching the imperial quarter without cover. It had never been put to a military test in the city's long and storied history, but Caius could now confirm that it succeeded in its stated purpose of making him feel uncomfortably exposed.

On the positive side, the lack of cover made it easy enough to be sure that they were not, in fact, being followed by anyone from within the palace compound. Their shadow from earlier hadn't exited through the gate after them.

"We'll head in the general direction of the Wooly Ram," Caius said, confident no one was within hearing range. "Once we get into a busier area, we can make for the backstreets and take an indirect route to the docks."

Decian gave a tight nod.

The first buildings appeared on either side of the vaia along which they were riding. This area was an administrative district—a quiet place after dark, with all the bureaucrats either resting at home or frequenting the bars and taverns in the southern quarter. The cobbled road was wide and well kept, lit sparingly with street lamps that left large swathes of shadow between the pools of flickering illumination.

From the distance, the sounds of a restless city reached their ears as an undifferentiated din. Caius' horse tossed his head and shied a step sideways as they passed the first of the towering marble edifices. The fine hair on the back of his neck prickled. He cast a glance at the dark space between one building and the next, but could make out nothing.

He looked up to assess the sky. Lingering clouds leftover from the previous night's rain obscured the moon, which would otherwise be waxing gibbous tonight. On a clear evening, it might have offered enough light to be useful, though the buildings would still cast dark shadows. As it was, the darkness beyond the reach of the street lamps was impenetrable.

"Look sharp," he murmured, maintaining a brisk pace toward the more frequented areas of the city that lay ahead. As the buildings became shabbier and the streets around them more active, Caius cast his senses outward with the wariness of the battlefield.

"There are hoofbeats coming from behind us," Decian said, still maintaining the kind of stiff posture that said he was working very hard not to crane around and look over his shoulder.

"I'm well aware," Caius replied grimly. "Don't worry... we're getting into an area where it will be easier to disappear into the alleyways and circle around."

The port was on the northern edge of the city. Caius had purposely left by the south gate, heading toward the southern quarter to further confuse anyone who might be following. That did, however, mean that they would have to travel the entire breadth of the city to get where they were going. Fortunately, the docks never slept. Sailors and longshoremen would still be about their business after even the most tenacious drunkards had abandoned the taverns for the night.

From the sound of it, there were at least two riders on their tail, which was worrying. Something about the entire situation niggled at his instincts. If Kaeto or anyone else suspected Decian of being an escaped prisoner, why not simply arrest him at the kennels and drag him before a tribunal?

Aspects of the situation made no sense, and Caius *hated* things that made no sense.

Now, though, they were entering a narrower street lined with shops and inns. The Wooly Ram was located off an intersection perhaps three blocks away, and they were no longer the only people of horseback. Some distance ahead, Caius could make out the familiar sounds of chanting.

"Sounds like our pagan friends are back," Decian said. "Can you tell if those riders are still behind us?"

Caius frowned. "They'd have to be complete incompetents to have lost us already."

If the protest ahead was large enough, it would add to the confusion and might aid them in slipping away. If it was *too* large, there was a risk of getting bogged down—hemmed in by an angry crowd. He headed for the noise anyway, trusting to their ability to skirt around it on horseback rather than getting caught up.

"If there's a crowd around the protest, we'll mix with the edges and use the confusion as cover to disappear into an alley," he said. "If we can make it a couple of roads over without being seen, we should be able to slip away and head north for the docks."

Decian nodded his understanding, clenching his pony's reins with determination.

Two blocks ahead, they did indeed run into the back of a crowd of gawkers gathering to watch the protest. Most were on foot, which was less than ideal for use as cover, but there were a few carts and wagons mixed in, along with a handful of other riders. Were he not still recovering from his leg wound, he would have been sorely tempted to ditch the horses at that point... but he was, and they would have a lot of ground to cover to reach the docks.

He contented himself with trying to use the shadows to their advantage as they wove between wagons and drays, getting as far into the confusion of excited people as they dared without attracting too much attention. Before long, Caius slipped into an alley running between two large buildings, with Decian right on his heels.

The alley led to a smaller road one block over. Caius turned onto it only long enough to find another alley leading to an even more disreputable looking street. "Now we're getting somewhere," he muttered.

Decian looked around. "This is definitely... somewhere."

The houses surrounding them were dingy and ill kept, some of them leaning drunkenly at odd angles. Caius led the way to an intersection and turned left, their horses' hooves plop-plopping through puddles of filth in the road. At the next intersection he turned right, aware that they were entering an older area of the city where the roads did not meet at neat right angles, but wound around curves and bends with little logic.

They rounded one such bend, only to be confronted by two riders standing at the next crossroads, facing them with swords in hand. Caius felt a moment of disbelief, quickly lost in an instinctive rush of battle-readiness leftover from years of campaigning. Their pursuers should not have been able to get in front of them. Not unless they had the demons' own luck. It seemed... physically impossible.

"Back the way we came," he snapped, aware that this was a far worse area for a confrontation than someplace with crowds and witnesses.

He wheeled his horse; Decian yanked the pony around beside him. Two more riders appeared in the intersection they'd just passed through, and Caius felt his stomach drop.

"Alley," he ordered, riding for the nearest gap between rows of slatternly houses.

Decian cursed under his breath and followed. The previous night's rain had turned the garbage-strewn ground in the alley to muck, the horses feet slipping in it as they turned into the claustrophobic space.

The clouds chose that moment to part, moonlight spilling in from above. It illuminated two more riders as they entered the far end of the alley, blocking it. Caius' heart sank, even as he reached right-handed for his sword hilt and drew steel. He looked over his shoulder just as the four riders from the road entered behind them, pinning them.

Caius met Decian's wide eyes. "We're charging the two at the other end," he said in the calmest tone he could muster, painfully aware of how poor their odds were against even two armed opponents... much less six. "Stay behind me as best you can. If you see a chance to get past them, take it. Don't let them unhorse you unless it's unavoidable."

"This is a horrible plan!" Decian said, wrestling with the nervous pony's reins. "*Why are all of your plans horrible?*"

Unfortunately, Caius didn't have an answer to that. Time was not their friend, so he pointed his gelding at the far end of the alley and dug his heels in. The horse half-reared, startled, and bolted forward. The gray wasn't battle-trained—Caius could only hope the same was true of their enemies' mounts. Already, the gelding was hesitating, wary of rushing directly at a pair of unfamiliar animals in the dark.

Caius slapped it sharply on the haunches with the flat of his sword, sending it scrambling forward again in the slippery muck. He dared a quick glance behind him in the moonlight. Decian was kicking the pony in the ribs, urging the reluctant beast after Caius' mount. The other four riders had already entered the alley, two abreast, preparing to pincer them.

All Caius could do was commit to the strategy he'd initiated. With a roar, he lifted his sword and propelled his mount into the other two. In the brief moment before the clash, familiar battle-lust sang in his veins, banishing the aches of age and injury.

Horseflesh thudded against horseflesh. The rider on the right took most of the brunt of the impact as the other horse skittered sideways. Caius' sword was already in motion, but the terrible footing betrayed him. Both animals' legs went out from under them, sending horses and riders alike to the ground in a tangle.

Caius kicked free and rolled, aware of the shriek of agony from his injured leg. The pain was distant. Unimportant, because to acknowledge his body's condition would result in the battle being lost before it had properly started. These men weren't playing. It was pretty clear that if Caius didn't prevail in this fight, he wouldn't be in a position to feel pain—or anything else—ever again.

He stumbled to his feet, covered in filth but with his sword hilt still gripped firmly in his right hand. The gray gelding staggered upright and bolted from the alley, disappearing from sight. The other horse was still down, legs flailing without coordination, its rider trapped beneath it.

One down.

Caius parried a clumsy strike from the second rider. "Go! *Go!*" he shouted at Decian, forcing his opponent into a defensive block with a wild slash.

To his immense relief, Decian kicked and prodded his terrified mount through the gap Caius had made, barely avoiding the downed horse's thrashing legs. There might be more men waiting beyond the alley mouth, but that was not something he could control. For now, Decian was free.

Caius just had to keep the five remaining combatants from getting past him to pursue the aging pony with their faster mounts.

He ducked to avoid a slash that would have taken his head off, cursing both the horrible footing and his leg's weakness. Grabbing the dagger from his belt with his bad arm, he distracted his opponent with a right-handed sword lunge. The man parried, and Caius took the opening to drive the dagger point into his calf muscle. The move pushed the boundaries of his strength and range of motion on that side, but it was enough to make the rider cry out and curl instinctively toward the injury—at which point Caius' sword edge took him across the throat.

Unfortunately, the other four attackers were already upon him, even before the dead man's body slid from the saddle. There was only room for two of them to engage him at once in the narrow space, but even so, his options were limited. He grabbed the reins of the horse whose rider he'd just dispatched, dragging the animal in front of him to use as a physical barrier. His bad shoulder screamed in protest at the strain as he yanked the beast into position, but the front two riders pulled up, unable to get within sword-range.

The panicked horse he was holding bucked and plunged in the confined space, trying to get free. Caius held onto it grimly. Metal flashed in moonlight and it staggered, blood spraying from its throat. With a gurgling scream, the animal stumbled to its knees and collapsed, its body floundering as it rapidly bled out.

The two riders in front dismounted and climbed over the twitching horse on foot, weapons raised. Caius backed away, his own sword held ready even as he reached for one of his boot daggers with his left hand. He was limited in how much ground he could afford to surrender before he hit the end of the alley. Honestly, his chances of survival might be better in the open, but as soon as the battle spilled into the street, there was nothing to stop the two remaining riders from going after Decian.

"Who are you? Who sent you?" he growled. He didn't hold out much hope of getting them talking as a distraction. He didn't hold out much hope, *period*. Still, every second's delay was one more second's head start for Decian.

Unsurprisingly, the men did not reply.

"Stop dallying, you pair of cretins," said one of the riders. "*Take him.*"

The two on foot attacked in unison. Caius blocked and dodged, dreading the moment when his leg would fail him or his feet would slip in the muck at the wrong instant. *Parry, lunge, whirl, retreat… keep them both in front… don't let them get past and out of the alley.*

It started to go wrong almost immediately. His heel hit one of the downed horses' legs as he gave ground—not hard enough to make him stumble, but enough to rob his parry of power as his center of balance shifted unexpectedly. The rhythm of the two-on-one fight faltered. He jerked one opponent's sword to the side, but the movement left an opening for the other that was outside the range of motion of the parrying dagger held with his bad arm.

He braced for the strike, teeth gritted, only for the man to go down with a cry under the force of a dark, heavy shape. Whatever it was, it had barreled past Caius without slowing, running low to the ground. The remaining horses in the alley screamed in terror, rearing and bolting toward the opposite end. One of the riders fell to the ground with a grunt, unseated. The other rider struggled to regain control and galloped away, fleeing the scene.

Eerie red eyes and sharp teeth gleamed in the moonlight as the attacking creature savaged Caius' downed opponent. The sight almost made him drop his guard against the second swordsman. Fortunately, the other man was just as shocked as he was—unable to take advantage of the opening.

Caius pushed past his clamoring instincts as they shouted *bad, wrong, get away,* and managed a clumsy swing that caught his opponent in the side. Blood spurted, and Caius jammed his dagger through the man's ribcage before kicking him to the ground. He whirled toward the thing with the red eyes, his weapons raised defensively.

The... *creature*... seemed almost to glow in the darkness—a wavering aura like phosphorus light surrounding its pitch-black hide. Its eyes were burning coals, lit from within. It was doglike in outline, but larger and more heavily muscled than any dog Caius had ever seen in his life.

It held its victim's throat clamped in its jaws, shaking the downed man like a terrier with a rat. As Caius watched in horror, the beast's outline seemed to shift and separate into two. A ghostly, translucent version plunged muzzle-deep into its victim's chest. Its jaws snapped closed, and it dragged out a shimmering smear of a shape. There was no substance to the wavering, smoke-like figure, but dark holes forming the shape of eyes and a mouth opened in a silent, existential scream. The spirit-hound snarled and flung the diaphanous form into the void. As it disappeared, the man's physical body abruptly went limp within the creature's grip.

TWENTY-TWO

The thing lifted its bloody jaws, the ghostly form and the physical form merging into one. Its glowing eyes pinned the unlucky man who'd fallen when his mount bolted moments before. Caius stumbled backward to put distance between them, tripping over the tangled limbs of one of the dead horses. Agony flared in his leg as his arse landed in the muck. He clutched his weapons in a tight grip, unable to properly feel his fingers. His mouth hung open in shock, every single thought frozen in solid ice as he watched the hellhound lunge for the injured rider.

The man made a clumsy swing for the creature with his sword, only to scream as massive jaws closed around his forearm and bore him down. The screams grew louder, and again the strange double-vision image of the physical hound and the ghostly hound separated. As before, the ghost hound ripped something intangible and essential from its victim's body, flinging it into the darkness.

The man slumped, obviously dead. Silence fell over the alley, broken only by Caius' harsh gasps and the pained groaning of the attacker still trapped under his horse.

The hellhound looked up from its dispatched prey, its red eyes falling on Caius. Every hair on his body stood up, gooseflesh shivering across his skin as that unearthly gaze met his. A sense of something weighty and unavoidable thickened the night air. Caius' numb fingers tightened on the sword.

The two stared at each other, moonlight limning the scene with silver. As Caius watched, the beast's outline twisted, reality shifting around it until a human figure crouched opposite him in the alley's filth. Red light spilled from the man's eyes, and Caius' heart stuttered, skipping a beat before pounding painfully into triple time. In that instant, he was transported back to the forest of his youth—staring at a dead shapeshifter as his father's corpse cooled in the grass nearby. Caius forced himself to his feet, ignoring the treacherous weakness in his knees as terror and hot rage flooded him in equal measure.

The crimson glow faded from the shapeshifter's eyes, and Decian looked up at him. He was naked, surrounded by bodies, with human blood running down his chin. Nausea slammed into Caius' gut as images of kissing those gore-stained lips played across his mind's eye. When his awareness flickered back to the present, he was standing with his sword under Decian's chin, and he couldn't quite remember putting it there.

"You," Caius rasped. "You're... you're a..."

He couldn't get the words out.

Decian lifted his chin, the bite of the blade having forced him up to his knees. "Caius," he began.

"*Shapeshifter*," Caius hissed, the sound like a curse.

The moon was too bright. He didn't want to see the details of this; didn't want to see the way Decian's brown eyes shone with a look of betrayal as he knelt, disheveled and bloody, with Caius' weapon at his throat.

"Caius," Decian said again. "Please... I don't understand what's happening to me. Before, with the dogs—"

In a flash as bright and abrupt as a lightning strike, Caius remembered Decian crouched naked among the royal hounds, safe and untouched as they savaged their caretaker. He remembered the unnatural way the beasts had submitted to him, practically abasing themselves to avoid antagonizing him.

"*What are you?*" he demanded, distantly aware that his grip on the sword hilt was trembling.

"I don't know!" Decian said. "That's what I'm trying to tell you! That day in the kennels... that was the first time it's ever happened. And this was the second! Caius—*I don't know what this is!*"

"You're an abomination," Caius whispered hoarsely. "A killer."

The look of betrayal grew deeper for a moment, before Decian's expression settled into blank lines. His lip curled into a bitter half-smile, made grotesque by the blood on his face.

"An abomination." The words were a low monotone. "And after all of this, will I die now at your hands, soldier?" he asked, echoing the question he'd posed when Caius had found him alive among the dogs, having miraculously survived his own execution.

After his father's death... after the slaughter on an Eburosi beach... Caius had vowed that if any shapeshifter ever ended up beneath the point of his sword, he would run the bastard through without a second thought. He stared down at his lover. His secret. His *act of treasonous justice*.

... and he could not move the blade a finger's width. His stomach cramped, churning with a poisonous slurry of grief, self-loathing, and bitter anger.

"Go," he said. The word tasted like bile. "Leave Amarius. Leave the empire, and don't look back. Because if I ever see you again, I'll kill you."

"*Caius.*" Decian's voice was pleading.

"*Don't.*" Caius jerked the sword up a fraction, forcing Decian's head back. "Don't use my name. Don't look at me like I should somehow have mercy on *what you are.*" His voice rose to a shout. "Go! *Get out of my sight, damn you!*"

Decian scrambled upright, away from the sword at his throat, and fled the alley.

Caius stood frozen, breath coming in great, shuddering gasps. He wanted to collapse in a heap on the filthy ground, but he was afraid if he did, he might not get up again. Almost against his will, practicalities began to flutter and peck at the edge of his awareness. One of the attackers had fled the scene. It was conceivable he might eventually return with reinforcements.

He turned slowly, following the sound of weak groaning. The trapped rider was still alive, his leg pinned beneath the crushing weight of his dead horse. The animal's neck was broken, snapped during the fall. Caius channeled all of his bitter rage and betrayal into his trembling muscles, forcing them into action. He limped toward the man, sheathing his sword along the way. After kicking the fallen rider's sword out of reach, he fell to his knees, grabbed the brigand by the hair, and jerked his head around.

"Who sent you?" he demanded, barely recognizing his own voice.

The man clenched his jaw, panting shallowly past the pain of his crushed leg.

Caius let his head go in favor of pinning his left wrist with a knee. Ignoring the muck coating the ground, he grabbed the man's thumb and sawed through it with his dagger, feeling the joint crack as the tendons gave way. Screams echoed against the walls of the tenement buildings.

"Who sent you?" he asked again.

The man flopped like a fish. Caius grabbed his index finger and twisted it until it broke.

"Who sent you?"

"I don't know!" the man shrieked, snot and spittle flying in the moonlight.

Caius twisted his middle finger until it snapped, then waited until the fresh round of high-pitched screaming subsided into whimpers.

"Try harder," he suggested.

"I d-don't know, I swear!" The man choked and gagged for a moment before regaining control of his voice. "The orders c-came anonymously. That's how they always come!"

Caius changed tack. "Did your paymaster know Decian was a shapeshifter? Is that why they came after him?"

The man stared up at him, sniveling and bewildered. "Who?"

"The houndsman!" Caius snapped, and broke the man's ring finger, setting off another round of hoarse screams. "Did they know he was a shapeshifter when they sent you after him, *yes or no?*"

The man's eyes were growing hazy with pain, but the confusion in his face was unsettlingly real. "We weren't after him!" he gasped. "We were after you!"

Caius blinked, going utterly still as the events of the last couple of weeks reshuffled themselves in his mind, like a child's painted puzzle pieces coming together to form a completely new picture.

The assassins in the woods.

The shadowy figure outside the Cock's Crow.

The men stationed outside his house to monitor any comings and goings.

Oh.

Oh.

Dear god. *He was such a fool.*

Wrenching free of his sudden paralysis, he looked down at the shuddering man trapped beneath him. "Right," he said. "That makes sense. Well, I can only hope you got paid up front."

Grabbing the man's hair again, Caius forced his head back and slit his throat with a single, efficient slice. He let the body fall, convulsing in the mud, and forced himself to unsteady feet. Every single square inch of his body ached—a welcome distraction from the sharp pain in his heart that throbbed and pulsed fresh blood with every beat.

Calling on three decades of battle experience, he packed that pain into a tight, dark ball and put bars around it, resolving not to spare another thought for the dangerous shapeshifting warlock he'd unknowingly let into his bed. Into his *life*. Decian would either run, and Caius would never hear from him again... or he'd succumb to his dark nature and kill more people, in which case the Amarian guard would hunt him down.

Either way, he wasn't Caius' problem any longer. Now, he had a *new* problem. Someone inside the palace apparently wanted him dead, and was prepared to go to extraordinary lengths to make that happen. Battle fatigue dragged at him as he trudged to the end of the alley, heavily favoring his left leg.

He looked around warily, but there was no sign of Decian. In a much-needed burst of good fortune, he found his gelding wandering aimlessly in the roadway perhaps two hundred paces away. To his relief, the horse did not attempt to flee when Caius approached and caught him. The animal was caked in mud, bleeding sluggishly from scrapes and cuts along his right side, but he appeared sound otherwise.

The shutters of all the houses along the street were tightly and pointedly closed. In this area, the clash of a sword battle and the screams of someone being tortured were clearly a reason to huddle inside with the doors locked, rather than venturing out to investigate. All of which meant that Caius was on his own when it came to mounting his damned horse so he could ride away.

He looked at the saddle, which might as well have retreated to a distant mountaintop when it came to how accessible it appeared from the ground. There was nothing nearby to use as a mounting block. For lack of any other options, Caius dragged himself onto the animal's back mostly by virtue of willpower, his vision wavering in and out for a disconcerting few moments as his leg protested the exertion.

He was aware that more assassins could appear at any time. If they did, he was as good as dead. With this thought firmly in mind, he rode toward the distant sound of shops and taverns and *people*, making for the most crowded area he could find. Once he had his bearings and was safely surrounded by witnesses who might object to someone being assaulted in the street for no reason, he doggedly headed for the imperial quarter, riding for the same gate he and Decian had left by.

There was a degree of fierce stubbornness involved in his decision to return to his own quarters rather than attempting to flee — but it was not the irrational decision it might have appeared on the surface. Had the emperor himself wanted Caius dead, he would have ordered him arrested at his home, or inside the palace when he was attending the Imperial Court. Whoever was after him, Caius was confident they didn't have official sanction.

Moreover, they obviously wanted the deed to occur somewhere far away from the palace, where it might be easier to convince people that his death was an unfortunate random act.

The guards at the gate were the same ones from earlier in the evening, and they reacted with alarm at the sight of him and his horse, muddy and blood-covered.

"Send a boy to my house to take my horse back to the stables and care for him," he ordered.

"Sir," said the guard who'd spoken to them when they'd left. "You weren't alone earlier. What of the houndsman?"

"I wasn't alone then, it's true," he agreed in a flat tone. "But I am now."

The man didn't push for an explanation, either out of respect for Caius' rank, or because he looked like he was in danger of falling out of the saddle at any moment. Caius passed beneath the portcullis and headed for his residence, only vaguely curious as to whether someone would be lurking outside to take note of his arrival.

His *survival*.

Indeed, as he approached his front door, movement in the shadows across the street registered in his peripheral vision. He ignored it, trusting to his earlier assessment that if his unknown nemesis thought they could get away with having him killed here, they'd have done so long ago. Dismounting was not quite as fraught as mounting had been, but he had to clutch the saddle for a moment until his knees agreed to take his weight. Once he was steady, he tied the horse outside for the stableboy to collect and let himself in the front door.

His house was eerily unchanged from a couple of hours ago when he'd left. It felt as though everything should be upended, torn apart and thrown to the four winds. He shrugged off the irrational feeling and limped toward his bedroom, unbuckling his weapons belt as he went. It was heavy with the coins he hadn't thought to give Decian before he'd driven the younger man away. With the door closed behind him, Caius shed what muddy, filth-encrusted clothing he could. He managed to get his boots off with the help of the boot-pull, but the trousers defeated him.

The bottles of wine in the kitchen called to him, but he resisted their siren lure. Enough wine might help with the clamoring pain of muscles and joints pushed past their endurance, but he'd need his head clear in a few hours. Instead, he slumped onto the ridiculous feather mattress, letting his aching body sink into it. Drawing from the same deep well of stubbornness that had allowed him to haul himself onto his horse's back after the battle, he closed his eyes and banished the events of the evening to a dark corner of his mind.

Thankfully, he still possessed the soldier's skill of sleeping whenever the opportunity arose, no matter what else might be occurring at the time. Unfortunately, that talent did nothing to prevent the nightmares from coming, even if his body's exhaustion ensured that he did not wake from them. He lay in bed, alone, twitching as dream images tortured him behind his eyelids. Outside, the moon that had illuminated horrors both earthly and unearthly in an unremarkable Amarian alley slid slowly across the western sky.

When morning came, there would be a reckoning... whether Caius was ready for it or not.

TWENTY-THREE

Decian fled the blood-soaked alley, scrubbing madly at his face and jaw with muddy hands. Inside his chest, something horrible swelled. If it broke free, he wasn't sure what would happen—whether he would wail, or weep, or stand in the middle of the street and scream at the sky until his throat bled.

He was naked. The beast had taken over his mind and body again, pressing his humanity aside—filling the space with something... *other*. And then Caius—

Decian's breathing stuttered, growing fast and shallow.

No. He quashed the memory, instead casting his gaze around the street until he found the pile of torn fabric that had, up until recently, been his clothing. The shirt had been reduced to rags. The trousers were ripped—almost shredded in places—but he pulled them on anyway. His boots were intact. He tugged them onto his bare, muddy feet, since he couldn't find his stockings.

The sobering realization that he had no idea where he was—and no idea where he could go—washed over him like cold water. In the next instant, a scream of agony echoed from the alley mouth. Decian whirled toward the sound, heart pounding. Seconds later it came again, desperate and high-pitched.

He cursed himself for thinking that it might be Caius screaming. Caius had been fine a few moments ago—on his feet, angry and armed. One of the men who'd attacked them had still been pinned under his horse, injured and unable to get free.

More shrieks echoed, interspersed with the sound of choking and retching.

Caius had called *Decian* a killer, and now he was dragging those sounds from the throat of an injured man.

Decian's stomach turned over. With no other options that didn't involve the threat of immediate death beneath his lover's sword, he turned his back on the shrieks and started walking. Ahead, Caius' gray gelding paced restlessly near the next intersection. Decian slowed. He briefly considered stealing the horse before deciding that even if he could successfully catch the animal and scramble onto its tall back, he probably wouldn't be able to control it.

He reluctantly passed the gelding by and turned right at the intersection, heading toward the distant sounds of human activity. He'd barely gone twenty paces when his eyes lit on a fat pair of haunches and a scruffy tail poking out from between two buildings. The pony radiated tense sullenness, resembling nothing so much as one of the giant flightless birds from Kulawi that his mother used to tell him stories about, which dealt with danger by sticking their heads in the sand so they couldn't see the threat coming.

"Hey, you," Decian said hoarsely, approaching the pony's pudgy rear end with caution. True to form, it didn't move or acknowledge him in any way, so he squeezed past it to reach its head. The pony's reins had snapped at some point, possibly because it had stepped on them in its haste to get away. The two ends were still attached to the bit, however, so he tied them together and urged the animal backwards, out of its ridiculous hiding place.

The pony complied with mulishly pinned ears. Its lips curled in disdain as Decian checked the girth and gathered up the reins, but it didn't try to evade him as he stuck a foot in the stirrup and levered himself onto its back. He directed it toward the sounds of life coming from the distant business district, keeping a nervous eye out for additional attackers lurking in the shadows.

There was, he decided in short order, really only one place he could go. He had no money, no food, no water, and his clothing—what there was of it—was in tatters. Saleene's brothel would only be a haven for him as long as Caius didn't show up to tell them what had happened... and that assumed they'd even let him through the door in the first place. But it was still something, and without it, he had nothing.

If his nebulous idea to seek shelter and assistance there didn't work out, he would have to try to sell the pony—and hope no one realized it had been stolen from the imperial stables. He wasn't even sure what kind of money the little beast would bring—being locked in prison for a decade wasn't exactly conducive to staying on top of the latest livestock prices.

He rode through the city for some time, looking for any familiar landmarks that he could use to orient himself. Finally, he stumbled across the road leading to the Wooly Ram, and from there he was able to find the Vaia Condora and the gymnaestra he'd visited with Caius. After that, it wasn't too difficult to retrace the route they'd taken to the Cock's Crow. Good gods, had it only been *yesterday*? Surely that was impossible…

He tied the pony outside the building, trying to ignore the strange looks he was getting from passersby. Bare-chested and with gaping holes ripped in his trousers, he'd be lucky if he wasn't arrested by the nearest city guard for being a vagrant, or a public nuisance or something. Rather than attempting to enter through the front, he skirted around the side of the building, trying to ignore the frisson of disquiet he felt at once again being in a darkened alley.

The side door was unlocked, so he ducked inside the tavern and made for the unobtrusive interior door at the back. Caius had said that Saleene and Zuri's brothel was located above the Cock's Crow, and since there had been no staircase visible in the front of the house, it stood to reason this must be the way in.

Or… it might be the kitchen. That was also a possibility.

He poked his head in, ready to duck out of the way to avoid being mowed down by a serving wench carrying a loaded tray. Inside lay a quiet parlor rather than a busy kitchen, populated by a bored looking young man who looked vaguely familiar, along with a pair of pretty girls wearing sheer, thigh-length stolas and nothing else.

The oddly familiar young man looked up and frowned. "Come in if you're coming."

Decian stepped through the door sheepishly, and the man's frown deepened. The girls tittered nervously at his half-clothed, mud-spattered appearance. He took a moment to be thankful that any blood on him would have dried to a rusty, unremarkable brown by now—or else the girls would doubtless have been doing more than giggling at him.

Even so, the man rose, stepping forward aggressively, and it was only then that Decian finally placed him. He was the one from the gymnaestra, that Caius had called Saleene's *pretty boy*.

"Nuh-uh," he was saying. "No way. You can't come in here looking like that. You've got no money, you get no girls. *Out.*"

"Wait," Decian said breathlessly. "I'm not here for that. I need to speak to either Zuri or Saleene—it's important!"

"Yeah, *sure* it is," said the pretty boy, slapping a hand flat against Decian's chest and shoving him back a step. "I said, *out.*"

Decian gritted his teeth, scrambling for any kind of a story that might get him past the gatekeeper.

"Stop!" he insisted. "Look—you saw me at the gymnaestra yesterday with the legatus, right? Caius? He's the one who sent me here! He's in trouble, and I urgently need to get a message to your employers on his behalf!"

The pretty boy hesitated, wavering.

"*Please,*" Decian pressed. "I'm begging you—it's life or death!"

The girls had been watching the exchange curiously. After that dramatic declaration, one of them spoke up.

"I could take him to one of the empty rooms and let Saleene know he's here once she's done with her client," she said. "Caius has been coming here for years, and this sounds serious, Tullio."

Pretty boy—*Tullio*—chewed his lip for a moment before giving her a reluctant nod. "Yeah, I guess."

Decian let out the breath he'd been holding. "Thank you," he whispered.

The woman rose gracefully from her seat and gave him a wary look as she slipped past him, heading for the staircase at the back of the room.

"Not so fast," Tullio said as he made to follow her. "You got any weapons on you?"

Decian gestured at himself. "Are you joking? I don't even have a damned *shirt.*"

Tullio only grunted skeptically, and Decian submitted without comment to having his boots and waistband checked for hidden blades.

"Come on," said the girl, once Tullio waved him on.

He followed her upstairs to an empty room furnished with a bed, a chair, and a divan. She left him there and closed the door behind her. Decian heard a lock click. He lowered himself gingerly onto the chair, painfully aware of how filthy he was, and settled in to wait—one leg jiggling impatiently.

Time dragged. He wasn't sure how long it had been when the lock finally turned and the door opened, admitting Zuri. She took one look at him and scowled.

"Great ancestor spirits, whatever has befallen you?" she asked, closing the door again to give them privacy.

Decian opened his mouth, only to realize that he had no earthly idea what should come out of it. A choked noise emerged instead of words, and he wrapped his arms around himself as he realized that tears had started running down his cheeks. Mortified, he turned his face away from her, trying to get hold of his emotions. Fingers grasped his jaw, forcing him to lift his gaze and meet her dark brown eyes.

"I'm sorry," he whispered. "I didn't know where else to go. It's all gone wrong…"

"I can see that," Zuri said wryly, taking in his battered appearance. "Are you injured?"

He shook his head back and forth within the confines of her grip, and she let him go. The magnitude of everything he'd just lost hit him anew. His eyes burned almost painfully as the intensity of his grief threatened to escape its cage, and Zuri breathed in sharply, straightening away from him in surprise.

She opened her mouth to speak, but the sound of someone else entering the room interrupted her. Saleene swept in, her expression hard-edged. She was fully dressed, but the smell of sex clung to her as she strode up to Decian and loomed over him.

"What's happened?" she demanded. "I just got a garbled message about Caius, and a matter of life and death. Start talking. Where is he?"

"I don't know," Decian said wretchedly. "I'm sorry. Six men attacked us in an alley, but as far as I know he's all right. They… they were after me, not him."

Saleene's expression turned even grimmer. "Ah. So the chickens have come home to roost, then. If he survived, why didn't he come here with you?"

A tight band settled around Decian's chest, constricting his breathing. "We… fought, afterward," he managed, aware of how inadequate the word was when it came to describing what had happened. "He sent me away, and I didn't know where else to go. I can't go back to the palace — I'd be killed on sight."

Saleene's gray eyes narrowed. "You fought off six men and then had a *lovers' quarrel*?"

Decian swallowed, painfully aware that there was nothing he could tell her that wouldn't dig himself deeper into a hole. "… yes?"

She crossed her arms, staring down at him from her considerable advantage of height. "You're lying about something — or omitting something, at the very least. And I have limited patience for liars."

Zuri had been watching the exchange closely, but now she spoke up. "Haartlam," she said, addressing Saleene, "we need to take him in."

Saleene looked at her sharply. "What? Zuri, I'm not in the business of cosseting jilted lovers. If you want to give him a few coins to buy some clothes and a meal, that's one thing —"

"No," Zuri said evenly. "You're not listening, my love. We *need* to take him in."

Saleene stared at her, and Zuri held her gaze with a meaningful look. An entire wordless conversation seemed to pass between the pair—one that Decian wasn't privy to. Eventually, Saleene blinked.

"You can have a room and two meals a day in exchange for cleaning and odd jobs," she told Decian, though her eyes never left Zuri. "*For now.*"

Decian's chest hitched on a shudder of relief. Even so, he couldn't help picking at the scab. "And if Caius comes here?" he asked.

"I have no earthly idea," Saleene said with brutal honesty. "One thing at a time. Go clean yourself up. I wasn't born yesterday, and not all of that mess on you is mud. Zuri can show you the bathing area and find you some clothes. After which, she and I need to have a talk."

For her part, Zuri seemed unfazed by Saleene's rather dire tone. "That we do, beloved. Come on, Decian. Let's get you cleaned up and find you a place to sleep. You look like you need it."

He nodded, exhaustion washing over him as though her words had conjured it from thin air. "Thank you. Thank you both. I came here on a pony—it's tied up outside. Is there anyplace it can be cared for and fed for the night?"

"I'll have Tullio see to it," Zuri said. "Don't worry. Now… follow me."

Decian rose beneath Saleene's watchful eye and did as he was told, feeling some tiny fraction of the tension in his shoulders begin to unravel. It was a precarious perch—but at least he'd found someplace safe to land, rather than crashing headfirst into his own grave.

TWENTY-FOUR

Outside Caius' bedroom window, dawn painted the street golden. He lay on his back, covered in bruises and scrapes, every joint and muscle feeling like a wagon wheel that had been neglected too long and rusted into immobility.

Decian was a murderous, shapeshifting hellhound who could rip men's souls from their bodies and fling them into the void.

Someone inside the palace wanted Caius dead.

His thoughts circled back and forth between the two catastrophic revelations, making no headway toward dealing with either one. What had he ever done to deserve either of these things? He'd never asked for a lover. Never wanted one, since Serah had died and left him alone. It was outrageous to think that he'd somehow fallen for the same kind of unnatural creature that had butchered his father when he was a mere boy.

And the imperial family. He'd served them faithfully for well over half his life. He'd sacrificed his blood to keep them safe, and he carried the scars to prove it. Until mere weeks ago when he'd spared Decian's life, he had never once questioned them; never defied them or worked against their aims.

It had to be Kaeto. There was no other explanation. Kaeto, the second son with ambitions above his station, and a cruel streak that found joy in the suffering of others. If Caius were truly seen as loyal, Kaeto might reasonably assume that he would support the lawful succession. That would place him firmly in Kaeto's way. And if Kaeto saw him as an obstacle, might he secretly plot Caius' assassination?

It made more sense than any other option that Caius could see.

Caius blinked up at his ceiling, dreading the prospect of rising from his bed. He needed to take action… but what kind of action?

He could pack a bag, get on a horse, and disappear from Amarius. Maybe try to find that elusive rural idyll of which he'd been dreaming, only without the complicating factor of a male lover to court scandal among the townsfolk. It would require slipping past whatever surveillance was currently in place and evading or overpowering anyone who attempted to trap him as they'd done last night.

With planning, he was confident he could manage it. Before, he hadn't understood the nature of the threat facing him. Now, he did, and could react accordingly.

It was tempting. *Deeply* tempting.

But he knew he could never do it.

Icy rage had been gathering in his stomach since the moment the assassin had confessed to Caius being the target. Part of that rage might have been directed toward the attack on the empire's integrity. Mostly, though, it was personal. He knew if he fled with his tail between his legs in an attempt to save his own skin, that decision would curdle and fester until it ate him alive from the inside out.

After his humiliating cowardice on an Eburosi beach, Caius had vowed never to flee in the face of fear again. His life since then had been defined by his willingness to stand and fight, even against overwhelming odds. In the four years since his arrival in the capital, faced with battles that took place with words and scheming rather than swords, he'd begun to lose that part of himself.

It was time to reclaim it.

With a growl, he forced his body into motion… into compliance with his will, as he'd done so many times before. His aches and pains didn't matter. His bruises and scars didn't matter. His limp didn't matter. All that mattered was what needed to be done next.

He rolled out of bed and stripped himself of his filthy clothing from the previous night, ignoring every warning twinge of muscle and sinew as his body protested. He bathed. He dressed as befitted a respected imperial advisor. He ate the food that Tertia had left for him, strapped on his sword belt, and walked to the palace, because he was damned if he'd arrive in the back of a cart like an invalid.

On his way, he detoured to the kennels. As he approached, mournful howling could be heard emanating from the low building that housed the hounds. Pip emerged from the door just as Caius walked up.

"Decian's not here—" the lad began, sounding more than a little harried. His gaze caught on Caius, and he cut himself off, staring for a long moment. "What in the One God's name happened to your face?" he blurted.

"Decian had to leave unexpectedly," Caius told him, ignoring the question. "Unless someone with more authority tells you otherwise, you're the new master of hounds. If you know another boy who can take on the apprentice position, hire him."

Pip gaped at him. Eventually, he seemed to come back to himself. "Is he all right, though? Decian, I mean?"

Images of bloody jaws and red, glowing eyes rose in Caius' memory. "He was, the last time I saw him." He felt physically ill as he said the words, but Pip didn't need to know about any of that. "You'll hear talk saying otherwise, I expect. Just nod and play along, and do your best to forget about him. He won't be coming back."

Pip's eyes were very wide, but after a moment's hesitation, he nodded. "If you say so."

"I do." More eerie howling echoed around the courtyard. Caius frowned. "What's the matter with the dogs?"

"Dunno," Pip said. "They've been like this since late last night." He shrugged. "Maybe they can tell he's gone an' left us."

The nauseated feeling grew worse. "You should know that it wasn't his choice to leave."

"Didn't think it was," Pip retorted.

"Congratulations on your promotion," Caius told him, and walked away.

When Caius arrived at the palace, he couldn't help but hear the pages and household servants whispering behind his back. As he approached the throne room, the imperial herald's eyes bugged—presumably because he looked like he'd come out on the wrong end of a bar brawl.

"Sir!" the flustered man protested, but Caius pushed him aside and strode into the great chamber, ignoring his impotent fluttering.

Inside, Emperor Constanzus sat upon his throne, flanked by Kaeto and Bruccias, and surrounded by buzzing courtiers. As the commotion of Caius' arrival registered, all eyes turned to him.

"What is the meaning of this?" wheezed one elderly hanger-on, who apparently had an inflated view of his own importance.

Caius strode up to the group, his uneven footsteps echoing in the vast hall.

"The master of hounds and I were attacked by half a dozen brigands last night while riding into the city for an evening of drinking," he declared, his gaze landing firmly on Kaeto to judge his reaction. "As you can see, I survived. He did not, since competence with a sword is not a prerequisite to throwing meat to a pack of dogs twice a day."

Kaeto's face might have been carved from marble. However, since it was likely that the escaped assassin had already reported back to him about the previous night's events, his lack of reaction meant little.

"I've seen to the houndsman's replacement," Caius continued. "But given the imminent commencement of the Council and the number of important persons currently lodging in Amarius, one does have to wonder about security. I would like carte blanche to deal with the situation before a diplomatic incident arises."

Kaeto raised a slow eyebrow.

Another of the officious arselickers hovering around the throne like buzzing bees raised his voice querulously. "Brigands attacking palace officials in the streets? Yes, something must be done, and quickly!"

Several other voices joined in agreement, and Constanzus waved a careless hand in Kaeto's direction. The emperor's expression was distant; Caius would have bet money that he had no real idea what subject was being discussed. Kaeto, however, knew very well what was being discussed. He offered Caius a thin smile that came nowhere near his cold eyes.

"Why, of course, Legatus," he said. "We can only thank our good fortune that you managed to escape. Speak to the palace tribuni about whatever you may need for your... *investigation*."

Caius dipped his chin in a nod. "Of course. Your Imperial Majesties..." He forced his battered body into a courtly bow, and turned on his heel with military precision, striding from the hall.

Outside, he asked around until he was successfully able to track down Jules, the pageboy who had conveyed him to his secret meeting with the empress the previous day. It seemed like a century ago.

Jules looked up from the tray of drinks he was arranging, and his eyebrows shot up in surprise. He bowed quickly, recovering his poise. "Legatus? How may I serve you today?"

Caius felt his jaw tighten, remembering his conversation with Stasia in stark detail. Her fears for the empire... her unshakeable certainty that one of her sons was plotting against her. He met Jules' eyes, knowing that his own were as hard as flint.

"I need you to arrange another meeting with your mistress for me," he said. "Tell her it's urgent."

End of Book 1

MASTER OF HOUNDS: BOOK 2

ONE

The Empress' gardens were as fragrant and lovely as they had been the previous afternoon, when Caius Oppita—respected former legatus in the Alyrion army—had been summoned there to discuss Her Imperial Majesty's suspicions that one of her sons was plotting her downfall.

Less than twenty-four hours later, Caius was the one doing the summoning. The fact that he had been granted an audience so quickly spoke to the depths of Empress Stasia's misgivings about the situation. Though, to be fair, she'd been the one to ask him to report back to her if he acquired any new information, and had offered to compensate him handsomely in exchange for spying for her.

Taking her up on the offer had been the last thing on Caius' mind, once he'd managed to politely extricate himself from their previous meeting. Now, everything had changed during the course of a single evening. The foundations of his life had shifted, and he'd barely survived the resulting collapse.

An attack that he'd assumed to be directed at his lover had in fact uncovered betrayal on two fronts. Decian, the condemned imperial bastard Caius had saved from execution in a moment of insanity, was actually a murderous pagan shape-shifter—some kind of slavering hell-beast that could tear men's souls out by the roots, killing them instantly. As if that wasn't enough, the assassins Caius had assumed were sent after Decian had, in fact, been sent to kill *him*.

Despite a lifetime spent in service to the royal family, someone in the palace wanted Caius dead. He had some very particular ideas about who that person might be, and after their conversation the previous day, Caius intended to discover if the Empress Stasia's suspicions mirrored his own.

As before, the empress awaited his arrival in the center of her private gardens, seated on a bench and surrounded by exotic blooms.

Jules, her trusted pageboy, cleared his throat as they approached. "Legatus Caius Oppita, Your Majesty." He bowed low, gesturing for Caius to approach.

Stasia didn't rise, but her eyes widened as she took in his battered appearance—his bruises and scrapes courtesy of a vicious fight against six armed men in a dark alley.

"Legatus," she said, unable to keep surprise from coloring her tone.

"Empress," he replied, managing a stiff bow that sent his various injuries clamoring. "We need to speak. *Privately.*"

It was not the way a palace advisor spoke to the wife of the emperor. Indeed, the correct response to such presumption would have been for her to rebuke him and have him removed from her presence. Perhaps she saw something in his expression, though, because her delicate brow furrowed. She turned to the young servant with a wave of dismissal. "Leave us, Jules."

Jules bowed again, even lower than before. "Yes, Your Majesty," he replied, and slipped silently away.

Caius waited until he heard the door to the palace open and close. When he was certain they were alone, he returned his attention to the woman who had wed an emperor and borne him three duplicitous sons.

Stasia examined his battered face with the distaste of one who rarely had direct exposure to violence or its aftermath. "Legatus, are you quite well?" she asked.

"Someone inside the palace means to assassinate me," he told her without preamble. "Last night, they nearly succeeded. I suspect Princep Kaeto."

She drew in a sharp breath, the small noise escaping her control. "What evidence do you have to support this claim?" she asked.

"None, as yet. It is supposition only," he replied in a crisp tone. "Kaeto seeks openly to suborn his older brother's support among the clergy and the nobles. He might reasonably assume me to back the rightful succession to the throne, which would make me an obstacle in his eyes."

"That is pure conjecture," Stasia said, but something haunted lurked behind her gaze.

He pressed on—reckless in the grip of the cold rage that had overtaken him after the events of the previous night. "Kaeto has also been systematically executing all of your husband's illegitimate sons over the course of the last several weeks. According to Bruccias, he has done so without consulting his father or elder brother. It's clear he is intent upon removing as many potential barriers standing between himself and the throne as possible."

The blood drained from Stasia's face as he spoke.

He regarded her intently. "I would appreciate any information you might have to either support or refute this."

For a long moment, he thought she would not answer.

When she did, her normally melodic voice was hoarse. "I suspect Kaeto of plotting to remove me from my husband's good graces."

Caius stared at her, taken aback. The empress had been married to Constanzus for twenty-five years, with never so much as a hint of scandal against her name. Did Kaeto truly think he could poison the emperor against her with whispers and rumor?

Stasia looked positively ill. "Constanzus is not the same man I married. The curse that has stolen his health and his wits has also made him endlessly suspicious of those closest to him. I believe, as you do, that Kaeto is working to remove obstacles standing in his path to the throne. He may perceive that my absence from the field of play would weaken Proclus' position, as I—like you— would support my eldest son in the succession."

Caius did not, in point of fact, support the idea of Proclus' drunken arse getting anywhere *near* the throne, but it seemed impolitic to say so, under the circumstances. "Then it appears we are in accord. Do you have any solid proof of Kaeto's betrayal?"

"No," Stasia said distantly. "He is canny, and he knows I am watching him closely. It will be up to you to acquire evidence against him to present to the emperor, Legatus."

Caius nodded, secretly doubting that the emperor would be of much use to either of them in his current state. "I have already requested and received cart blanche to investigate the failed attack on my person last night. I will assist you in this matter, Your Imperial Majesty, but information must flow in both directions. I require any evidence you are able to uncover, as well."

Stasia still looked like someone who wasn't ready to have her worst fears confirmed, but she nodded in turn. "As you wish, Legatus. Please keep me informed of your progress. You may do so through Jules—he is trustworthy."

No one in this damned pit of vipers is trustworthy, he thought. But aloud, he only said, "Very good, Your Majesty. In that case, I will take my leave. You may expect a report from me as soon as I have new information."

⁓⁓ ♛ ⁓⁓

Caius spent the rest of the day watching everyone in the palace like a hawk, for all the good it did him. Proclus, the eldest son, made an appearance after midday had come and gone—bleary-eyed, and looking as though the light streaming into the meeting chamber pained him terribly.

With the Council of Amarius convening two days hence to determine the Church's stance on the disposition of pagan heretics, things were in a state of controlled chaos. All but a handful of the religious dignitaries on both sides had already arrived in the capital. Because the Church had refused to hold the ecumenical council within the palace grounds—on the basis that doing so would damage the appearance of independence from the crown—it had become necessary to assign additional security forces in the city to protect them.

Aelio, the tribuni of the palace guard, was at his wit's end. Laurentin, the tribuni of the city guard, had shown up at one point in the proceedings to shout at everyone, because his forces were overextended between trying to protect the dignitaries and trying to protect the city itself. With pagan protesters marching in the streets, Amarius was quickly approaching a crisis point.

Caius could barely bring himself to care about any of it. At least, not until Proclus and Kaeto butted heads in an uncharacteristically public matter. At that moment, Caius became all ears.

"Just kill the bloody protesters and be done with it," Proclus said, as though he found the entire situation tiresome beyond all bearing. "That will be the ultimate outcome once the Council has talked itself out, will it not? I fail to see the point of letting this pagan rabble burn the city down while we wait."

Kaeto turned to his older brother sharply. "As you have missed all but a handful of the daily briefings on the situation, *Brother*, you may not be fully apprised of the nuance. If the protests erupt into violence, half of the city will rise up against the other half."

Proclus gave Kaeto a look of utter boredom and covered a yawn. "You overstate the matter. Besides, that's what the bloody guard is *for*—putting down dissent. You are too timid, Kaeto. You always have been."

Watching the exchange, Caius had to suppress a familiar lurch of nausea at the thought of what the future of the Alyrion Empire would look like once Constanzus was gone. That evening, he took himself back to the peace and quiet of his house with a sense of real relief. Not that his home didn't hold its own ghosts these days, but his body ached with injury and strain, and his mind ached with the weight of everything he'd learned.

Tertia, his house slave, was waiting for him when he arrived. The smell of cooking food wafted from the kitchen. Her eyes widened when she took in his battered appearance, but—rather unusually, for her—she said nothing about it.

"You're back late," she offered in a neutral tone.

"And you're here late," he retorted. A frown furrowed his forehead as he noticed the gray cast of her complexion in the firelight. "Are you well, Tertia? You look ill."

"It's nothing," she said. "I made you roast fowl and preserved vegetables for dinner. Shall I serve you before I leave?"

Cauis' appetite had been thoroughly spoiled by the events of the past couple of days. However, he'd also been a soldier for nearly half his life. He had learned early and well the importance of fueling the body, even during hard times.

"Yes, thank you," he said. After a pause, he added, "And regarding that unpleasantness yesterday, I might have spoken too soon when I promised it would be dealt with. It's still nothing that should concern you directly... but you might want to take extra care, just in case. In fact, should you wish to take a few days off and lie low, I would encourage you to do so. Especially since you do, in fact, look rather unwell."

At his words, she looked even more unwell, but she lifted her chin in response. "Worry about yourself, Legatus. I've work to do, and I'll do it as I always have."

He watched her for a long moment. She didn't back down, though she did seem reluctant to hold his gaze. Not for the first time, he found himself acutely aware of the difference in their stations, and he wondered what unseen pitfall of protocol he'd stumbled across this time.

"As you like," he said eventually. "Dinner sounds good. I'll go clean up and be ready to eat shortly."

"You do that," she murmured, and turned back to the kitchen.

After retiring to his room to splash water on his face—in the vain hope of washing away the stench of palace politics and intrigue—he returned to find the table set and Tertia gone. Perhaps she'd taken his words to heart after all, and would rest at home for a few days. Alternately, perhaps she was merely finished with her work and had no desire to spend more time in his presence than necessary.

He ate, barely tasting the fowl or the vegetables, and washed it down with a goblet of full-bodied red. It was the same vintage he'd shared with Decian on their last night together. Now, it tasted bitter.

Irritated with himself, he thrust the unwanted memory away and tried to focus on the task currently before him.

The brief skirmish between Kaeto and Proclus today had been... interesting. It was no secret that the pair hated each other. However, for that hatred to bleed through in such a public setting was unusual. Even more unexpected had been the thrust of the exchange itself. Kaeto had shown little else but contempt for the pagans in the capital. Yet his words today had demonstrated a more nuanced understanding of the consequences to political security in Amarius, should the radical wing of the Church hold sway during the upcoming ecumenical council.

Perhaps that should not have surprised him, though. Kaeto had never been lacking in intelligence — only in moral character. Meanwhile, his older brother demonstrated all the political nuance of a drunkard set loose in a brothel. While both Kaeto and the Empress might believe Caius' support lay with Proclus, they were mistaken. At this point, if someone had held a knife to his throat and demanded he choose a side, he'd probably throw his support behind Bruccius, the youngest. While there was a difference between diplomacy and self-serving oiliness, it wasn't quite as wide a gap as either cruelty or idiocy.

He knocked back the rest of the wine, grimacing. How was it possible that the same man who had sired Decian had also sired the three abhorrent princeps?

With a growl of irritation, Caius pushed away from the table and stood. Thoughts of Decian were the last damned thing he needed right now. The young man's facade of good-natured innocence covered the soul of a monster. And Caius had allowed that... that *creature* into his bed. He'd kissed lips that had later been stained with human blood.

He paced restlessly through his house, trying to dislodge the memory of the previous night.

What are you? Caius had demanded, standing in that fateful mud and blood-soaked alley, amid the carnage of dead and dying assassins.

I don't know! The ghost of Decian's voice rang in his memory. *That's what I'm trying to tell you! That day in the kennels... that was the first time it's ever happened. And this was the second! Caius — I don't know what this is!*

An unpleasant knot tightened in Caius' gut. As he had done at the time, he pushed the anguished words away, refusing to consider them. How could a shapeshifter reach the age of twenty-six without knowing *exactly* what sort of abomination lived inside him? Shifters were cold-blooded killers—every goddamned, miserable one of them. His father had learned that lesson the hard way, and so had Caius, long ago on an Eburosi beach.

The only good shapeshifter was a dead shapeshifter.

So why didn't you kill him?

The nagging internal voice prodded at him; its presence as irksome as a blistered heel during a long march. Caius had no answer beyond the obvious—that he was a sentimental fool. Heading for his bedroom, he attempted to refocus his thoughts on more immediate matters. He needed a plan to outwit Kaeto and expose his machinations to the court.

Hours later, stomach still churning, he drifted into a restless sleep despite having made very little progress on the matter.

TWO

Before the age of sixteen, Decian had never been to a brothel. After the age of sixteen, he'd *also* never been to a brothel because he'd been stuck in a prison cell for the crime of being a nobleman's bastard. Now, apparently, he *worked* in a brothel… albeit, not in the fun way.

In prison, he'd had a few serious run-ins with guards or fellow prisoners over the years—enough to recognize this current dull-witted, disconnected feeling as a form of shock. Miraculously, he'd emerged from a battle against half a dozen armed men on horseback last night with nothing more serious than a couple of scrapes.

But that was only on the outside. He wasn't quite ready to examine the bleeding wounds hidden on the inside.

It was fortunate that Saleene and Zuri had only set him to cleaning and tidying in exchange for temporary room and board in the brothel. It was mindless drudgery, if a bit sticky and unpleasant, at times. After letting him sleep uninterrupted for several hours, Zuri had returned and given him a bowl of porridge for breakfast. When he was finished eating, she showed him what needed doing— mostly cleaning and changing the linens in the bedrooms used for assignations.

While he was admittedly rusty after so long spent sleeping on dirty straw in a prison cell, it didn't take long for the chores from his childhood to come back to him. He swept and dusted and tucked fresh sheets around the corners of straw-stuffed mattresses. All the while, his mind floated somewhere just out of reach of his feelings, the distance preventing him from poking at the fresh, bleeding wound in his heart.

When the last bedroom was once more in a nominally respectable state, Zuri reappeared. Decian realized he had no earthly idea what time of day it was. He'd started work late in the morning. Since then, he'd been putting one foot in front of the other as he made his way through the list of simple tasks.

"You're finished?" Zuri asked. "Good. Come with me. There's a bowl of stew from the tavern waiting for you. After that, we need to talk."

Decian nodded agreement, even as the dark mass of *very bad things* hovering around him circled restlessly. He followed her, not to the communal area where the working girls and Tullio took their meals, but instead to a private room at the back of the building. From the piled ledgers and sheaves of vellum scattered across the heavy desk and tables, he gathered the place was Saleene's private office. The woman in question sat behind the desk, her painted face looking a bit careworn in the late afternoon light slanting in through the single window.

She glanced up as they entered.

"Ah. Decian. There's dinner for you on the side table. Eat, but don't dawdle." She gestured toward a covered bowl waiting on a table by the wall that was less cluttered than most of the rest of the room. A spoon, a cup, and a carafe of water sat next to it.

"Thanks," Decian managed. Somehow, the atmosphere of the room reminded him of the handful of times in his childhood when he'd been called before the tutor his mother had hired for him, to account for some misdeed or shortcoming.

He crossed the room and sat wordlessly in the wooden chair that had been set out for him, uncovering the bowl and pouring water into the cup. Saleene and Zuri talked business as he ate, discussing the previous night's takings and whether they should bring in another girl to keep up with demand.

By rights, Decian should have been hungry after several hours of steady physical work, but the stew sat in his stomach like a lump of lead. He finished it anyway. When he was done, he rose, figuring whatever was about to happen, he should probably be on his feet.

Both women's attention immediately fell on him, and he was once more transported back to the times when he'd stood before his strict tutor.

"You've both been very kind," he began, attempting to get out in front of whatever was coming next. "But I don't intend to abuse your hospitality for any longer than necessary—"

Saleene cut him off with a wave of her manicured hand. "I didn't bring you here to make pretty speeches, Decian," she said.

He closed his mouth, taking that on board for a second or two before responding. "Then... why *did* you bring me here?"

She sat back in her chair, regarding him.

It was Zuri who replied, however. "You're a shapeshifter. I saw your eyes glow."

Saleene shifted in her seat, still watching him intently. "*That's* why I brought you here. It's also why Zuri insisted you be allowed to stay in the first place. Which, I should add, is more than a little bit awkward—since I don't personally believe in shapeshifters." She titled her head, assessing him. "So. Anything to say?"

Decian's knees chose that moment to stop supporting his weight, and he sat down abruptly in the chair he'd vacated earlier.

"No," he whispered.

Zuri looked ceilingward, as though for strength.

Saleene continued to drill holes through Decian with her gray gaze. "I'm going to need a bit more than that. Try again."

He shook his head mutely, aware on some level that this was the prelude to him getting tossed out on his ear if he was lucky or turned in to the magistrate if he wasn't.

In Alyrios, anyone credibly accused of having or using magic was executed. For most of Decian's life, that had been an abstract concept that didn't affect him personally. But now...

Zuri blew out a breath. "For the gods' sake, Saleene— the boy is terrified. Stop glaring at him." She turned her attention to Decian. "We're not going to drag you before the authorities."

"Oh," he said blankly, still feeling as though his mind was running at a slight lag from the rest of reality. "Well, that's... good?"

"'*Good*,' he says," Saleene muttered.

Zuri glared at her, but her words were for Decian. "Like I told you, I already know. I saw it last night. The question is, why in the ancestors' names would you stay in Amarius when you could have run, instead? And not just in Amarius, either. But the *imperial palace*? That's madness, and I don't believe you to be mad."

Decian wavered, before desperation to spill his story to someone who might listen and understand won out over caution. He curled forward in his chair, elbows on knees, face in hands, addressing his words to the floor.

"Whatever it is, it's only happened twice. I have no idea what's happening or how to control it." He glanced up nervously, to find Zuri crossing her arms as though to say, *now we're getting somewhere.*

"Last night, when you and Caius were attacked?" she asked. "It happened then?"

He nodded miserably.

"And the legatus saw?" Zuri pressed. "That was what you meant when you told us you had a fight and he sent you away?"

He swallowed hard, remembering the feel of Caius' sword blade pressed beneath his chin. "Well... it was less of a fight and more of a..." He trailed off, unable to think of a suitable word.

"You mean he didn't take it well," Zuri suggested, when it became apparent he had no idea how to finish the sentence.

The problem with spilling his guts, Decian realized too late, was that it threatened to tear away the gray cloud of dissociation that had been muffling his emotional reactions until now.

"You could say that," he whispered.

"Stop," Saleene said. "Both of you. I've known Caius the better part of four years. He doesn't go in for this kind of woo-woo religious nonsense any more than I do. Zuri, I know this is what you were raised to believe—and fate knows I agree that in general, pagan beliefs are less noxious and stultifying than Deimonist beliefs. But we live in the real world, and people do not spontaneously turn into animals. They just... *don't*."

The look Zuri turned on her was one of patience. "Most people don't, it's true. But some do. And in the empire, if they're caught, it does not go well for them."

The pair squared off. "You mean if they're *accused*, it doesn't go well for them," Saleene said. "I know how it goes. Someone has a grudge against someone else. Or maybe a person is mentally ill, behaving irrationally. And, *whoops*, somehow a whisper reaches the magistrate's ear—and suddenly, that person becomes a dangerous pagan magician." She held up a hand to stave off whatever Zuri was about to say in response to that. "No, let me finish. I'm not claiming there aren't things in the world we still don't understand, my love. But at its heart, the world is a rational place. Shapeshifters are just a story people tell to make pagans seem more dangerous, and foreigners seem more threatening."

"You know I adore you, haartlam," Zuri said without heat, "but you're wrong about this."

Saleene let her hand fall to the desk with a soft slap. "Have you ever seen a shapeshifter?"

Zuri raised an eyebrow. "Aside from the one sitting in this room, you mean?"

Saleene only stared at her.

Zuri huffed. "*Fine*. No, I have not. But the healer in my grandmother's village was a shapeshifter. She told me how he could turn into an eagle—which is also how I learned that shapeshifters' eyes glow when they're roused. Just as Decian's eyes glowed last night when he became upset."

"Right," Saleene said. "Of course. That's a much more sensible explanation than the idea that the lamplight hit them oddly for a moment."

The dark-skinned woman's lips twisted. "There's a simple enough way to confirm it."

"Is there?" Saleene asked.

"We take him with us tonight and introduce him to Licinius."

Saleene's mouth turned down as well. "I'm not completely convinced that Licinius isn't one of those pagans who falls under the 'mentally ill' category."

"He's a powerful practitioner," Zuri countered. "Even if he is a bit… eccentric. He will be able to tell if Decian is a shapeshifter."

"Erm…" Decian said, his eyes following their verbal volleys back and forth like watching a sporting event.

They both looked at him. "Yes?" Saleene snapped.

He licked his lips, trying to organize his muddled thoughts. "Three things. First, where are you planning on taking me? Second, who the hell is Licinius?" He paused. "And third… do I get a say in any of this?"

Saleene still looked irked as she began counting the answers off on her fingers with exaggerated patience. "*One*. Someplace your friend Caius certainly wouldn't approve of. *Two*. An eccentric pagan who's approximately the same age as the catacombs he lives in, and three— you're free to walk out that door at any time," she said. "In fact, please do. It would save me an untold amount of trouble."

"He's not leaving," Zuri said with finality. "Decian, you said you don't understand what's happening to you. If you want to find out, you'll come with us tonight and talk to Licinius. Now, what do you say?"

Decian drew breath to tell them thanks but no thanks, and to apologize for imposing on Saleene's hospitality. Before he could form the words, however, the memory of another consciousness wresting control of his body from him rose up. It smothered the words, making him choke on air. If Zuri truly knew someone who could help him untangle the madness of the past few weeks, he'd be an idiot to turn down the chance.

He let his breath flow out in a sigh of resignation.

"Fine," he said. "I'll come."

THREE

The catacombs and ossuaries beneath Amarius were practically a city unto themselves. Decian had heard about them, of course. Everyone had. They were a staple of frightening childhood stories, spread from one youngster to another with the intent to send a chill through the blood. He'd never expected to see them firsthand.

As the population of the capital city grew over the centuries, the bodies of the poor and unwanted had been buried in tunnels that were expanded as the ranks of the dead swelled. At some point, an enterprising engineer raided the bones of the long-deceased to shore up the structure. Over time, the practice came to be part of the ritual of death in Amarius, as older bones were moved to make room for fresh bodies and used as supports for the ever-growing labyrinth of underground passageways.

Decian looked around him in wonder. Something about the place called to him in a way he couldn't explain. He was standing in a corbelled vault with walls made of skulls and long bones, lit by flickering torches. The space echoed, flattening nearby sounds while enhancing distant ones. The sickly-sweet smell of death tickled the back of his throat, but it had largely been overpowered by the musty smell of great age.

He'd come here with Zuri and Saleene. They were dressed in hooded cloaks that threw their features into shadow, as were most of the other people present. The entrance they'd brought him through had been in the basement of a building that backed up to the Cock's Crow tavern—not a proper door with a stairway, but rather an irregular hole chipped out of the brickwork, with the rubble piled in such a way to allow someone to make their way down to the catacombs lying beneath.

Zuri had led the way down with a lantern to light their surroundings, but once they'd entered the warren of the ancient under-city, torches had guided them toward this manmade cavern of bone. Decian counted a crowd of perhaps three score and ten milling around the area, speaking in muted tones as smaller groups formed and broke apart.

"I trust it goes without saying that you'll become very unpopular, very quickly, should you decide to start flapping your mouth about what you see here tonight," Saleene said in a dry tone.

Decian gave her a look. "What am I going to do—run back to the palace and tell the guards?"

"Good point," she replied.

Zuri met his eyes. "You said your mother worships the old gods, Decian… and you have magic. These are your people. They're here because they're trying to survive."

He raised an eyebrow. "Would I be likely to find the organizers of the protest marches here?" he asked. "Is it the same group?"

In the run-up to the Amarian Council, set to decide the fate of pagan practitioners in the empire, protests had been growing throughout the city. Some were peaceful, others less so.

"I expect there's overlap, certainly," Zuri said. "This is where the unofficial spiritual leaders in the city gather to discuss strategy. That includes public protests, but also other things."

Decian sighed. "Have I mentioned how little use I have for religion?"

Saleene's face settled into a frown. "I feel your pain, believe me. However, I also have very little use for people being burned at the stake, if the Church decides to take matters into its own hands."

I have enough problems of my own without taking on other people's, Decian wanted to say… but he swallowed the words. Zuri hadn't dragged him here because she was trying to recruit him. She'd dragged him here because the mysterious Licinius supposedly knew something about shapeshifters.

Zuri led them from group to group, asking for the man. Eventually, someone pointed to a figure holding court in one corner of the echoing space. Unlike most of the others, his hood was down, revealing a balding pate ringed by white hair. Zuri took Decian by the arm and more or less dragged him toward the elderly man. Saleene tagged along behind, with a look of resignation coloring her sharply drawn features.

Licinius smiled as they approached, gesturing to the group around him. They gave Decian and his companions a curious look, but dispersed without comment.

"Greetings, sisters," Licinius told them. "I received your message, Zuri. Is this the young man in question, then?"

Decian stood warily between his two escorts, studying the elderly figure. He seemed harmless enough, with kind brown eyes and smile lines etched into his wrinkled features. Still, Decian had seen too many kindly grandfathers thrown into prison for gruesome offenses over the years to let his guard down completely.

"Greetings, Elder," Zuri said, dipping her chin in respect. "Yes, this is Decian. Marella told me you would be the best one in the city to ask about the old magic."

Saleene almost managed to cover her scoff, but Decian still caught it. Licinius didn't acknowledge the brothel-owner's obvious skepticism, instead turning his intent gaze on Decian.

"Well, now. Why don't you start by telling me exactly what you've experienced? Then we'll go from there."

Decian fought the sudden desire to tell the old man 'Never mind,' and run for the hills. Surely if he made a point of avoiding near-certain death in the future, he could forget about all of this and pretend it never happened? He closed his eyes and took a centering breath, because in reality, nothing in his life had ever been that easy.

When he opened them again, the old man was still watching him closely, waiting for him to speak.

"I... was... about to be executed," he began in a halting tone. "They threw me in with a pack of ravenous hunting hounds and left the houndsman behind to make sure the dogs finished the job. But... the dogs didn't attack me. I remember the houndsman opening the door to the cage and coming inside. He cracked his whip to get the dogs even more worked up, and... something inside me changed."

Licinius nodded. "Go on."

Decian's eyes lost focus as he tried to remember that horrific day. "My memories don't make a lot of sense after that. There was screaming. The hounds were howling and baying. I remember thinking that while the houndsman wasn't a *good* man, he wasn't wholly evil, either. The next thing I knew, I was crouched in the back of the cage, naked, and the dogs were tearing apart the houndsman's corpse."

Decian risked a glance at the others. Zuri's expression was unreadable, but Saleene appeared taken aback—as well she might, he supposed.

"And the second time?" Zuri pressed.

He really, really didn't want to think about the second time.

Licinius gave him a look of sympathy. "It will help to speak of it, brother. The memory obviously pains you."

Swallowing against the sudden tightness in his throat, he managed a jerky nod. "I was with a... friend... who was trying to get me out of the city. We were heading for the docks in hopes of finding a ship so I could leave, when we were accosted by six armed men on horseback. They trapped us in an alley. Caius charged the men at one end so I could get past, and he stayed behind to delay them while I got away."

Saying the name aloud was surprisingly painful.

"At least, that was the plan," he continued. "I remember thinking he was going to die. He was already injured, and badly outnumbered. He just wanted me to get to safety, but I couldn't make myself ride away."

"What did you do?" The old man's tone was soothing.

"I... I don't know," Decian managed. "It was like the first time—one moment I was me, and the next moment I was... something else. I remember slamming into one of the attackers. He smelled... *rotten*. I wanted him gone, so

I... made him go away, where he belonged. Then I did the same thing to another one. When I came back to myself, there was"—he choked on the words—"there was... blood... running down my chin... pooling in my mouth. And Caius was... looking at me. His eyes—"

Decian's voice broke. At the same moment, his knees threatened to stop doing their job of holding him upright, and he wavered on his feet. Saleene let out a low, filthy curse, as she and Zuri each grabbed one of his arms. They lowered him to sit on the rough stone floor, trading a look over his head.

"I see," Licinius said, seemingly unperturbed by the grisly tale.

"What do you think, Elder?" Zuri asked. "I saw his eyes change myself, when he was upset."

"I think you've had a difficult time of things, brother," Licinius replied, crouching in front of Decian on creaking knees. "Perhaps it would be best for you to rest while the meeting finishes. I brought along two tinctures. One of them will calm your mind. Would you like it now?"

Foolish, Decian's inner voice warned. *Foolish to take an herbalist's mixture from someone you don't know.* He nodded anyway, reaching for the vial the old man produced from a fold of his robe.

It was bitter against his tongue. He drained it and handed the empty vial back to its owner.

"That will begin to work in a few minutes," Licinius told him. "Rest here. No one will bother you. Do you have other business here tonight, sisters?"

Saleene met Zuri's eyes. "You go. I'll keep an eye on him. You can fill me in on the rest of the meeting later."

Zuri nodded. "I'll return soon, haartlam. Don't snap at the boy while I'm gone." With that exhortation, she left, heading for one of the larger groups. Licinius went with her.

Left alone with him, Saleene let out a sigh and lowered herself to sit on the floor next to him.

"I'm twenty-six, you know," Decian said absently, staring at the geometric pattern of bones in the wall. "I'm not a *boy*."

"Don't take it personally. She's like that with everyone," Saleene replied. She hesitated, then continued, "You know, when I was a mercenary, there was a man in our company who went berserk whenever we were forced to fight hand to hand."

Decian glanced sideways at her, not sure where she was going with the story.

She shrugged. "The rest of us were just trying to stay alive, while hopefully also sticking to the battle strategy, if there was one. But Cotyar… he was different. Something snapped in his mind, and he became a bloodthirsty animal. Nothing could stop him. By the end of the battle, he'd be covered in blood from head to toe—including his teeth. I watched him bite someone's ear off once."

"He sounds like a real charmer," Decian said, not thrilled with the direction of the tale.

"We knew enough to give him a wide berth after the fighting was done. I always got the feeling he wasn't totally clear on who was an enemy and who was an ally when he got like that—though to be fair, I'm not aware that he ever went for anyone in the regiment. But at some point, if you were watching, you could see his eyes snap back to the present, like he was once more aware of his surroundings beyond looking for the next person to kill. At which point, he'd go dunk himself in the nearest river or lake to wash the blood off, and then fall asleep for ten hours straight."

He stared at her. "I'm not a berserker."

She didn't back down or break eye contact. "Sure about that, are you?"

After a long moment, Decian looked away. "I don't want to talk about this."

Saleene's tone turned tart. "Then you might have been better off walking out the door when I gave you the chance."

Decian grunted and didn't reply. An odd sense of lethargy was beginning to creep up on him. It brought welcome apathy in its wake, as the herbalist's draught kicked in. He closed his eyes and let it wash over him, relieved.

Happily, Saleene appeared content to stay silent. Time moved oddly as the drug did its work. The hum of muted conversation around the vault grew distant and unimportant. When it disappeared altogether, Decian pried heavy eyelids open to find everyone gone except Saleene, Zuri, and Licinius. They were surrounding him in a half-circle, looking at him.

"What?" he slurred.

Licinius pulled a second vial from his robes. "I would like you to drink this now, Decian."

Decian frowned at the little bottle before taking it. The first tincture had been… really good. Maybe if he drank this one, it would make all of this go away completely.

"What is it?" Zuri asked, but Decian was already tipping the vial to his lips and swallowing.

"It will force the shift," Licinius replied.

"Is that a good idea?" Zuri asked sharply.

Decian turned to look at her, drawn by the sudden worry in her tone. But something inside him was twisting, making the outline of the vault waver in his vision.

"Without the sedative first, perhaps not," Licinius replied. "But this will be the easiest way to see what we are dealing with, since he has no control of the transformation at present."

A moan forced its way up Decian's throat, and Saleene grasped his shoulder.

"What was in that drink?" she snapped.

FOUR

The thing inside Decian writhed, forcing its way free. His joints cracked, limbs contorting into a new shape—strong and compact, covered with a velvety pelt of dark fur. A shocked gasp pierced the air next to him, the grip on his shoulder falling away. His vision was changing, but he saw the cross-spirit human scrambling backward across the floor, putting distance between them until her shoulders thumped against the wall of empty-eyed skulls behind her.

The umber-skinned human and the old, brittle-boned one watched him warily, but did not flee. The sedative still held its grip on his body, even though his essence had changed. But he would not have attacked, with or without the drug. The three souls surrounding him smelled pure and clean. None of them were completely untouched by darkness, but they were not indelibly marked by it, either.

The cloth wrapped loosely around his body was irksome, but this time he couldn't summon the energy to rip it away with his teeth. Instead, he wriggled free of most of it, and ignored the rest. Lowering his muzzle onto his front legs, he let out a mighty yawn and closed his eyes. It was safe here. Sleep beckoned, and he followed it down into peaceful blackness.

When Decian woke, it was to find himself lying half-naked in a pile of his own rumpled clothes, on the stone floor of an ossuary vault, with three people staring at him. His head was fuzzy, and his mouth felt like someone had stuffed cotton in it.

It took a few moments for the day's events to sort themselves out in his memory. Something about Saleene's bloodless complexion and the new lines etched into her face brought back the most pertinent bits.

"Oh," he said. "Right. Maybe don't let me drink that stuff again without warning me first?"

"You're a shapeshifter," Saleene stated, in the tone of one who was hoping that saying the words aloud might force the situation to somehow make sense.

"That does seem to be the consensus," he agreed. "Could someone please tell me what *kind* of shapeshifter?"

"A dog," Saleene said, still sounding faint and shocked. "At least, if dogs weighed as much as a solidly built man and had glowing, red eyes. *God's fucking balls*, Decian." Her voice was shaking.

"I did try to warn you, haartlam," Zuri said, before turning her attention to Decian. "Tell me something. When you described the change to us before, you mentioned that the men who attacked you smelled rotten, and that you made them go away. You described another man as neither fully good nor fully evil. Do you remember thinking anything like that tonight?"

Decian cast his fuzzy mind back. It was surprisingly difficult. "Er... not exactly? All three of you smelled fine, so I figured I was safe. Though that might have been the drug talking." He shot what he hoped was a pointed glare at Licinius, though he probably just looked bleary-eyed and half-asleep.

"Interesting," said the old man. "I have never encountered a creature like you before, Decian. But I take it you have, Zuri?"

Zuri shook her head, looking thoughtful. "Encountered? No. But I grew up with the stories, as do all children in Kulawi. Decian, I believe you are a rhitsaaru—a spirit hound that shepherds souls to the afterlife."

Decian blinked at her.

She gave a small shrug. "A huge hound, as black as night, but with glowing red eyes? One who can sense the balance of good and evil in living souls?"

He continued to stare at her as the silence stretched. "I don't know what I'm supposed to say to that," he replied eventually.

"Perhaps nothing," Licinius offered. "You came here seeking answers, and you have received at least one—even if other questions remain."

Decian considered that for a long moment. "So... I'm just supposed to shrug off the fact that I randomly turn into a huge black hellhound?"

"*Rhitsaaru*," Zuri corrected.

He opened his mouth to speak, only to hesitate and close it again. He had vague memories of his mother telling him those kinds of stories when he was very small—tales about fantastical beasts that served the old gods as helpers and guardians.

"One thing is clear—it is not safe for you in Amarius, young man," Licinius said gently. "If you cannot return to Kulawi, then perhaps you could book passage to the island of Eburos instead. Shapeshifters enjoy a degree of acceptance in the barbarian lands, or so I hear."

"I'm not from Kulawi," he said. "I'm from... well... *here*. A village near here, anyway. And I don't want to live among barbarians on Eburos."

"He's right, though, Decian," Zuri said, her dark brow furrowed in worry. "The Church is whipping itself into a frenzy ahead of the Council. No one with magic is safe in the capital these days."

Decian lifted his hands, indicating himself. "Zuri, look at me. I have no money. No possessions, beyond a few borrowed clothes and an ancient, ill-tempered pony. A *stolen* pony." He paused, before adding, "Plus, there's the small matter of whether I might accidentally shift into a murderous beast while I'm stuck on a ship full of strangers."

Licinius contemplated him with a birdlike tilt of the head. "You know, you *are* quite unusual, in the sense of being an adult at the time of your first shift. The magic normally comes upon a person in childhood or adolescence."

"I really think I would have noticed if it had," Decian pointed out.

But Licinius shook his head. "Do not misunderstand. It's not that I doubt your account of things. My point is that most shifters learn to control the transformation at a relatively young age. Which is not to say that you cannot learn now, of course; merely that you will need practice and guidance."

Decian frowned. "So, you've known other shapeshifters?" he asked. "Personally, I mean?"

"Oh, indeed," Licinius replied. "They are not quite so rare as the Church and the government would have people believe. Though, you must understand that I cannot share personal details about the others, any more than I would speak to other people about you."

"Can you help him learn, though?" Zuri pressed. "Teach him how to control it, so he can stay safe?"

Licinius nodded. "I'm certainly willing to lend what knowledge I have. It is in no one's interest for him to continue as he is, with little mastery over the change."

He and Zuri turned to each other, falling into a discussion of logistics. Decian realized that Saleene had been uncharacteristically silent for some time now and examined her closely for a moment.

"Saleene, are you… all right?" he asked, tentative.

Zuri's partner was sitting on the floor of the vault a short distance away, hugging her knees beneath the flowing skirt and cloak she wore. Her face was still drawn into pale, haggard lines.

"No," she said flatly. "No, I'm not all right. I just watched a person turn into some kind of… nightmare creature, and magic is *fucking real.* Which means the rational world is a lie, but *damn it,* I'm quite fond of the rational world… and what the ever-loving *hell* am I supposed to do with *any of this*?"

Zuri peeled away from Licinius and crouched next to her, a look of concern on her face. "Haartlam, take a moment and breathe, yes? You've grown very pale."

"Look, I'm really sorry," Decian told Saleene, not sure what else to say.

She let out a harsh bark of laughter, waving both of them off. "*You're* sorry? What do you have to be sorry for? You're the one stuck changing into a giant dog." She scrubbed a hand over her face. "Tell me—what did Caius do, exactly? When he found out, I mean?"

A sick, empty feeling settled in Decian's gut. Despite feeling more or less all right mere moments ago, now his eyes burned with the same grief and frustration he'd felt in that fateful alley, when everything in his life had unexpectedly fallen apart in the space of a single night.

"He held a sword to my throat and threatened to kill me if he ever saw me again." His voice sounded dull and flat to his own ears.

Zuri's expression tightened in sympathy. "He was upset. He probably didn't mean it," she said.

Decian swallowed a choked laugh that lacked even a single shred of humor. "No. Actually, I'm pretty sure he did."

Saleene took a deep breath, visibly getting control of herself. "Licinius," she began, looking up at the elderly pagan, "you have my deepest apologies for thinking you mad. Which is to say... if you're off your head, I'm clearly right there with you."

He chuckled. "Think nothing of it, my dear. It's true that most manifestations of the old gods' magic aren't quite so... *striking* as this."

"I sincerely hope not," Saleene agreed. "Tell you what—if you'll come to the Cock's Crow at midday tomorrow, I'll buy you a meal to make up for it. While you're there, you and Decian can arrange when and where to meet for dog training lessons, assuming he's amenable."

"If you can help me learn to control this, I'm amenable," Decian said.

"Very well," Licinius told them. "I will be there. Now, though, perhaps we should follow the others' example and depart before the last of the lamps and torches go out."

"Agreed," Zuri said, reaching a hand down to Saleene and hefting her to her feet when she took it. "I have no desire to travel these catacombs in the dark."

Saleene gave a delicate shudder. "I'll pass on that prospect as well, thanks very much. Decian, get your clothes on properly and let's go."

Whether his weariness was due to the remnants of the sedative draught, or just... *everything*, Decian had to drag himself to his feet. A fleeting sense of something *other* in the back of his mind promised him that darkness held no terror, and he would be able to navigate this labyrinth with or without the torches, should the need arise.

The same thing couldn't be said of the others, though. Pushing through his lethargy, he pulled his disarranged clothing into a semblance of respectability and followed his companions through the catacombs. Licinius split off at the second junction, presumably heading for a different entry point to the tunnels than the one they had used.

Once his footsteps faded and they were alone, Zuri drew a pensive breath.

"What is it?" Saleene asked.

"Forgive my indelicacy, but is no one else going to bring up the small matter of the *emperor's illegitimate son* being a shapeshifter?" Zuri asked.

Decian nearly stumbled over his own feet as he came to an abrupt halt in the tunnel. Saleene also stopped walking.

"Oh," she said blankly. "Oh... *fuck.*"

"Wait," Decian demanded. "Stop. Back up for a minute. *What* did you just say?"

FIVE

The two women exchanged a glance. "He doesn't know?" Zuri asked.

He stared at them. "Look. I am *literal moments* from losing my composure in an unpleasantly explosive way. And lately, that hasn't been going terribly well for me — or for the people around me. So would someone please *start talking?*"

Saleene blew out a breath. "You arrived at the palace as part of Princep Kaeto's efforts to round up all of his father's bastards and have them executed. We assumed you already knew."

"How the hell would I know that? I was a prisoner — they didn't offer me a running commentary of palace gossip!" he shot back. Then something terrible occurred to him. "Hang on. Did Caius know about this? Did he know the whole time, and couldn't even be bothered to tell me?"

Saleene's expression was grim in the flickering light of the torches. "He didn't tell me so explicitly. But I'm confident he did know about it, yes."

Decian knew a moment of utter, impotent rage at the man who'd apparently thought he was good enough to fuck, but not good enough to know the truth of his own origins. Saleene took a hasty couple of steps backward, and Zuri looked suddenly wary. The odd reaction was enough to knock him out of his own thoughts, and he scowled at them.

"What?" he demanded.

"Your eyes," Zuri said.

"They're glowing red," Saleene clarified. "So... if you could refrain from turning into a giant rabid dog and eating us, that would be helpful right now."

He blinked, taken aback.

Saleene relaxed. "That's better. Come on—walk and talk. I truly don't have any desire to navigate this warren without light."

Many of the torches had, in fact, burned themselves out already. Decian tamped down his growing frustration and headed to the entrance with the others, though Saleene continued to shoot him occasional nervous looks as they walked.

Only when they were back in the safety of Saleene's private office in the brothel did Decian pick up the topic again.

"All right," he began. "So, let's say I believe you, and it was the emperor himself who stuck his dick in my mother to get her pregnant, rather than some random provincial nobleman. So what? I'm still no one—a bastard is a bastard is a bastard. What does any of it matter, in the end?"

Saleene's smile was a pinched, twisted thing. "Oh. It matters, believe me. Why do you think one of the emperor's legitimate brats was so keen to make sure all of you were dead?"

"I have absolutely no idea," Decian said, with some asperity.

"To ensure that none of you could make a grab for the throne when Constanzus shuffles off this mortal coil, of course," she said patiently.

He shook his head, bewildered. "On my list of things to do, angling for the imperial throne of Alyrios is actually quite far down," he told her. "To be clear, I'd place it somewhere below singlehandedly invading Utrea, and draining the Northern Sea like a bathtub."

"If anyone in this city found out who and what you are, it could spark a civil war right here in the capital." Saleene looked positively queasy at the prospect.

He looked at her, uncomprehending. "That's crazy. I'm still nobody."

Zuri spoke up. "*Think*, Decian. Half the city secretly supports the pagans against the Church."

"Or not so secretly," Saleene muttered.

"But if they had proof that magic resides in the bloodline of the emperor himself?" Zuri went on. "What do you *think* would happen? You'd become the figurehead for every pagan and pagan sympathizer in the entire empire."

Dazed, Decian shook his head slowly back and forth. "But that's not... I don't..." He trailed off, unable to string words together properly. With a deep breath, he tried again. "I'm not anyone's figurehead. I just want to find somewhere I can make a decent living with honest work. Somewhere I can be left alone, in peace."

What a fool he'd been to believe he'd found such a place in the capital. Of course, he'd been an even worse fool to believe for a fleeting moment that he could have something better than '*alone*.'

"Then I would strongly suggest letting Licinius help you get your furry little problem under control, so you can disappear somewhere and never look back," Saleene said with brutal honesty.

Unfortunately, none of this addressed his lack of money or useful contacts. Running was easy when you had money to live; less so when you had nothing.

"I'll have to sell the pony," he said. "Would that be enough to buy passage somewhere on a ship, do you think?"

"Probably not," Saleene said. "But let me worry about that part."

Zuri sighed. "There's to be another protest march tomorrow evening. Let's hope it doesn't stop the punters from coming into the brothel for a tumble. It sounds like we'll need the money."

Saleene groaned. "Another march? What in sanity's name do they hope to accomplish beyond stirring things up more than they already are?"

"It's the only way their voices can be heard," Zuri said with a shrug.

"Well, it's horrible for business," Saleene snapped. "And things are tense enough as it is."

Decian scrubbed at his face, his earlier exhaustion returning. "Look. It must be almost dawn by now. If I'm supposed to meet Licinius tomorrow at noon and also get the rooms cleaned, I need to get some sleep while I can. I hope it goes without saying that assuming I even believe this nonsense about the emperor and my mother—which I'm not sure I do—I don't want it spread around."

"No," Saleene agreed. "That's the last thing we need right now."

He nodded, appeased. "Good. Like I said, all I want is to find someplace where I can live my life and be left alone. Maybe down the coast somewhere, near the Utrean border. Although at this point, I'm not sure I even care where it is."

"Get some rest, Decian," Zuri said. "We'll figure something out."

He left them to it and headed for his cot. He could hear their low voices through the closed door as he went—no doubt they were still discussing him. The brothel was quiet and dark at this hour, offering nothing to distract him from his churning thoughts. Knowing sleep would be a hopeless prospect until he got his emotions under control, he fell back on the tricks he'd used in prison to clear his mind—picturing a future where things were better than they were now.

Tomorrow, he would meet with Licinius and learn how to control the creature that lived inside him. The rhitsaaru wasn't evil—he was confident of that much, at least. It had protected him when his life was in immediate peril... and, gods help him, it had also protected Caius. Once Decian could be confident that he wouldn't shift unexpectedly the next time he was in danger, it would be fine.

Entering the little storage room with the cot Zuri had brought in for him to sleep on, he pulled off his outer clothing and slid beneath the rough blanket in his smallclothes. Somewhere out in the world, there would surely be a place for him. He imagined a pleasant little town not unlike the one where he'd grown up. Perhaps he could find a job tending dogs, or even some other kind of animals. He'd enjoyed that, during his brief stint at the palace.

With that picture firmly fixed in his mind, he fell into a restless sleep despite the evening's disturbing revelations.

A few hours later, he dragged himself out of bed, ate his bowl of porridge, and finished as many of his assigned duties as he could squeeze in before Licinius arrived at the Cock's Crow for his lunch with Saleene and Zuri.

Decian did not join them, since showing his face in public more than absolutely necessary would be asking for trouble. He was still a marked man after escaping death at the hands of his half-brother's armed assassins the other night.

His alleged half-brother.

He thought of the haughty princep he'd briefly met in the forest after the disruption during the royal hunt. It was inconceivable to picture the man as *family*. This whole crazy situation was inconceivable… and yet, here he was.

Licinius suggested retiring to the catacombs for their practice sessions, since they had easy access to the warren of tunnels from the building behind the one that housed the tavern and the brothel. Decian accepted readily, having felt oddly at home among the walls of old bones.

"It is your other nature at work," Licinius observed. "Most people find the underground ossuaries disconcerting, to put it mildly."

Decian found them peaceful, but he merely shrugged in easy agreement. He spent the next few hours learning the feel of the shift, with the help of Licinius' mysterious herbal concoction—but without the sedative this time. Shortly before they called a halt due to low oil levels in the lamps Licinius had brought along for light, Decian was able to shift form purposely, without the aid of the tincture.

Shifting back was harder. It seemed that after twenty-six years locked inside its invisible cage, the rhitsaaru wasn't eager to give up its hold on him once it was allowed out.

"When your other nature comes to trust that you will give it the freedom it needs, this will become easier," Licinius assured him, after Decian finally regained control of his body.

Or, more accurately, *their* body. It was a surprisingly difficult idea to incorporate into his worldview, even though the rhitsaaru appeared to mean him no harm.

"I wish I could see it," Decian mused. He'd heard the others' descriptions, but it was nevertheless very difficult to picture himself as a massive, heavily muscled black dog.

"When your control has improved, perhaps Saleene can provide you with a looking glass," Licinius suggested.

"That could work," Decian agreed. "Or even a still pond, or a lake."

The old man gave him a grim smile. "I fear you'll do better to avoid shifting in the open, young man. While your other form's general appearance may resemble a large mastiff, the glowing eyes do rather give you away as more than that."

Decian tried to set aside his disappointment. Then, his brow furrowed in thought. "You know, I'm sure I'm beginning to feel the difference when my eyes change. I think with practice I might be able to control the red glow in both forms."

Licinius hummed, noncommittal. "It's worth a try, to be sure. That would be a useful skill to master, should you ever be caught in your shifted form by other people."

With a sigh, Decian stood and went to retrieve the sputtering oil lanterns. "I do wish you could tell me more about the other shapeshifters you've known," he said. "Even though I understand why you can't."

They made their way from the open gallery where Decian had been practicing, toward the entrance leading to the basement of the building behind the Cock's Crow.

"There are places where knowledge about shapeshifters is far more public," Licinius offered. "But here, it is not safe."

"Places like Eburos, you mean?" Decian asked, remembering their earlier conversation.

"Just so," Licinius agreed. "The Wolf Priest of Draebard is practically a legend, after the emperor's failed invasion of the island. You would have been a mere babe—if you were even born yet—but it was the talk of the capital for a time. And more recently, when the slaves in southern

Eburos rose up and toppled the king of Rhyth, they say there was a lion shifter at the head of the rebellion."

"Both normal animals, though," Decian couldn't help pointing out. "Not unnatural ones."

Licinius tilted his head in acknowledgement. "Yes and no," he said. "It is true I've never come across a creature like yours… but what is the true line between natural and unnatural? Dragons have returned to the land of Utrea in recent years. Had they not survived the king's attempted purge, the species might have fallen into myth within a generation or two. Giant, flying creatures that can breathe fire and form unbreakable mental bonds with their riders? Is that really less believable than an unearthly hound that can reap men's souls?"

"Maybe not," Decian mused.

After the two of them parted ways, Decian hurried through the rest of his cleaning and tidying, ensuring the rooms in the brothel were ready for the evening trade. He was just finishing up when the sounds of a chanting crowd floated through the second-story windows at the front of the building.

"Here we go again," he muttered, and went to see how close they were getting.

He found Saleene standing at the window that gave the best view of the street and joined her there. Outside, a throng of protesters snaked along the block, taking up the entire width of the road and a good part of the walkways on either side. It extended as far back as Decian could see.

"There goes the evening's takings," Saleene observed, her tone sour. "No one's going to fight their way through that chaos just for a meal or a fuck."

Indeed, the crowd's progress was slowing to a crawl, and then to a complete stop. It appeared the protesters were going to set up camp directly on the Cock's doorstep.

"There certainly are a lot of them," Decian said, as the volume of chanting grew louder. "And they seem very… *irate* tonight."

Saleene's square jaw worked. "As long as they don't start throwing rocks and setting fire to things."

Zuri joined them. "Goodness," she said. "That's a lot of people."

Abruptly, Saleene's shoulder's tensed, her spine snapping straight. "Oh, no."

"What?" Zuri asked sharply, as both she and Decian craned to follow Saleene's gaze toward the other end of the block.

Armed men on horseback, wearing the uniform of the Amarian Guard, were turning onto the street. Decian watched with a sinking feeling as more and more appeared until he'd counted at least two dozen—and they were still coming. They rode abreast, bearing down on the stalled crowd of protesters, unhurried but inexorable.

Zuri cursed sharply in Kulawi.

Saleene's fingers gripped the window frame so hard the knuckles turned white.

"Zuri, get downstairs and have the owners bar the tavern doors," she snapped, sounding more like the soldier she'd been in another life than the languid brothel-keeper Decian had come to know. "Decian, round up Tullio and the girls. Move them to the parlor at the end of the hall and have them lock themselves in. If anyone from the Cock wants to shelter in the downstairs receiving room, we can bar that door as well."

"The alley door," Zuri said.

Saleene nodded, already going. "I'll barricade that one. Now both of you, move!"

Decian's heart kicked into double-time as he shot a final look at the approaching guardsmen and hurried off to round up the brothel's employees. Inside him, the rhitsaaru stirred, restless. He consciously attempted to calm himself, knowing that the last thing he needed right now was to turn into a dangerous beast.

Not now, he chanted silently. *Not now, not now...*

He jogged down the stairs behind Zuri, bursting into the large room where a few of the girls and Tullio were lounging around, waiting for customers.

"Everyone get upstairs," he said breathlessly. "Saleene's orders."

Tullio scowled at him. "What are you talking about? We can't leave the receiving room unattended."

"There's a mob of protesters outside—" Decian began.

"So?" Tullio asked. "It's not the first time. They're only chanting slogans. Who cares?"

"I do," said one of the girls. "We're not gonna make any coin with them blocking the door."

Decian clenched his jaw. "There are city guards bearing down on them, blocking the end of the street. Dozens of them."

The girls rose in alarm, and Tullio's expression fell.

"Get upstairs," Decian said again. "Zuri and Saleene are barring all the doors. Saleene said to go to the upstairs parlor at the back and lock yourselves in, once everyone's there."

Tullio's jaw firmed. "Right. You take the rooms on the west side. I'll take the ones on the east. At least there's no punters here yet."

Decian nodded, following the girls up the stairs and going room to room to make sure no one was missed. He met Tullio at the entrance to the parlor just as Saleene hurried up, looking grim-faced.

"Is that everyone?" Decian asked, trying to do a head count in the crowded room.

"Everyone except Zuri," Tullio said.

"I'm here," Zuri said, jogging down the hallway to join them. "All of the ground floor doors and windows are as secure as they can be. Women and children from the tavern are inside the receiving room with the door barred. What's happening outside?"

The sound of chanting had broken down into confusion and angry shouts. Tullio moved to the room's single window.

"The guards are still coming," he said. "They're not even slowing down—just heading right for the marchers in front."

Some of the girls were huddling around Tullio, trying to see outside as well.

"Come away," Saleene said. "Tullio, close the shutters."

The words were quiet, but they carried the unmistakable tenor of a command. Saleene's employees huddled around her as Tullio pulled the wooden shutters shut, throwing the room into dimness.

Moments later, the screaming started.

SIX

Caius awoke with a splitting headache and a churning gut, silently cursing Tertia for having brought her accursed mystery illness to his doorstep. Unfortunately, despite his ever-growing collection of physical complaints, malingering wasn't an option.

After a morning spent in yet more endless meetings, the afternoon marked the first time the Council of Amarius convened. It was more of an orientation session than anything—the council members would not take up any real business until the following morning. Nonetheless, Caius traveled to the site of the gathering with Aelio as part of the emperor's contingent of observers.

After much negotiation, the Council had decided to convene in the building belonging to the Guild of Spice Merchants—presumably because they had been able to offer the largest bribe. While the surroundings were spectacular, it was safe to say that Aelio and his counterpart in the Amarian Guard, Laurentin, would have been happier holding the affair in some remote, defensible mountain fort. As it was, security had been—and would continue to be—a logistical nightmare.

"They couldn't just swallow their bloody pride and hold it inside the imperial quarter," Aelio grumbled as he and Caius made their way past the lines of armed guards and into the gaudy three-story building.

Caius only grunted, as a fresh wave of nausea assailed him. Aelio shot him a sidelong look.

"Forgive me, Legatus, but you really don't look at all well today," he said.

Irritated, Caius waved him off. "My house slave is down with some kind of ague, which she thoughtfully shared with me. It's nothing."

Briefly, Caius entertained the fantasy of passing the illness to every dignitary and official in the building, then watching as they all spent the next several days groaning and puking their guts out. Of course, if such a thing happened, no doubt the radicals among the group would insist it was Deimok's wrath for not punishing the pagans with sufficient severity.

"Bad timing," Aelio commiserated. "Though with luck, maybe you can nap through most of the proceedings today."

Caius snorted. "Tempting."

They found seats in the massive meeting hall with its white marble columns and gold-leaf cornices. After what felt like endless delays, the great and the good of the Church settled in to hammer out procedures and schedules for the rest of the conclave. It was, as expected, painfully boring, leaving very little to distract Caius from his general misery.

The afternoon dragged. Aelio sat next to him, the picture of respectful propriety, his sharp eyes doubtless cataloguing the same security vulnerabilities in the building and the chamber that were making Caius' neck itch. Outside, the sun slanted low through the spectacular leaded glass windows as afternoon deepened into evening.

When a guardsman entered unobtrusively and made his way to Aelio's side, bending to speak with him, the interruption came as something of a relief—right up until Caius heard the man's muttered words.

"Sir, there has been a clash between protesters and the city guard in the Southern District, on the Vaia Meretricia. There are reports of civilian deaths numbering in the dozens."

Aelio stiffened, his expression falling. "*What?*" he hissed.

He and Caius exchanged a wide-eyed glance, even as Caius' stomach plunged in a way that had nothing to do with the ague. The Cock's Crow—and Saleene's brothel above it—were located on the Vaia Meretricia.

Aelio jerked his chin, indicating they should leave the meeting hall. Caius was already on his feet, ignoring the disgruntled look from the people around them at the disruption. As soon as they were away from the echoing chamber, Aelio rounded on the messenger.

"How did this happen?" he snapped. "Laurentin had *specific orders* to use a light hand with the protesters. Where is he?"

"I'm sorry, sir—these are all the details I have," the man said stiffly. "I believe another messenger was dispatched to find Tribuni Laurentin and inform him of the incident."

"*Incident?*" Caius echoed, already picturing all the ways the situation could spiral out of control.

"I need to get there and take control of the scene," Aelio said. "Have someone fetch my horse immediately. Dispatch as many of the palace guard as can be spared to the site, with orders to secure the area, while avoiding conflict with the citizens who might still be present."

"I'm coming with you," Caius said. "Have my horse sent here as well."

The man dipped his chin in acknowledgement and hurried away.

Aelio ran his hand through his short-cropped, sandy hair, a noise of frustration escaping his throat. "What a fucking disaster. Someone had better have a damned good explanation for this—and by *someone*, I mean Laurentin."

"It's possible the crowd grew violent," Caius offered, remembering the arson attempt at the temple on the Vaia Sacrii not long ago.

"Possible, yes," Aelio agreed. "And there's still a rather large gap between controlling an unruly crowd of people and massacring them by the dozens."

"That there is," Caius said grimly, trying not to think about Saleene, and Zuri, and the elderly couple who ran the Cock's Crow.

They waited in heavy silence until a stableboy arrived with their mounts saddled and ready. Caius waved off Aelio's offer of assistance and dragged himself into the saddle, feeling like an old man with one foot already in the grave. His gray gelding stood motionless for the painfully clumsy performance, which somehow only succeeded in irritating him more.

With a sense of deep foreboding, he reined the animal around and headed for the Southern Quarter, Aelio a grim and stiff-backed figure at his side. The city beyond the perimeter erected around the site of the conclave was quiet—unusually so. It felt as though Amarius was holding its collective breath, waiting to see which way the dice would fall.

As they entered the business district, the usual bustling crowd of shoppers and tavern-goers had dwindled to a trickle of furtive-looking people walking with hunched shoulders, shooting worried glances at their surroundings as they headed quickly toward their destinations.

The lamplighters had already made their rounds, and pools of unsteady illumination lit the roads as the sun disappeared beneath the horizon. Ahead, the intersection with the Vaia Meretricia loomed, blocked by several armed guardsmen. Aelio rode up to them without hesitation.

"What happened here?" he demanded with the snap of command.

By the uniforms, the men were city guard rather than palace guard. "Dunno, sir," said the one on the left. "When we got here, the decurian in charge told us to keep the civvies from wandering in and gawping at the mess. Looks like there was a battle."

A muscle in Aelio's jaw ticked. "It's not a battle when only one side is armed!" he snapped, his voice cracking like a whip. "Where is Tribuni Laurentin?"

The guardsman covered a flinch. "Just arrived a few minutes ago, sir. I believe he's getting a report from the unit commander."

Aelio's gaze slid past the men, as though his mind had already moved on to the ways in which he intended to verbally eviscerate his Amarian Guard counterpart.

"Let us pass," Caius commanded, pitching his voice into something authoritative, rather than the sick rasp it wanted to be.

The guards made way for them, and Caius let Aelio take the lead as they turned onto the road.

It was a site of carnage. The moans of the injured joined the wails of those grieving the dead. Their messenger had not exaggerated the scope of the slaughter. It would not have surprised him if the number of unmoving bodies numbered a hundred or more. The worst of the devastation lay at the far end of the block, where Caius could see people in civilian clothing moving among the corpses — presumably searching out those still living and readying the dead for removal.

Aelio rode directly for the knot of uniformed figures gathered across the road from the intersection where they'd just entered.

"Tribuni!" he called, as soon as they were within hailing range.

Caius reined to a stop and dismounted, as Aelio did the same. A guard hurried up to them and took their horses. Laurentin looked up at their arrival. The Amarian commander had been speaking to a red-faced decurian, and it clearly hadn't been a pleasant conversation. The unit commander's forehead was beaded with sweat, and he wore the expression of someone whose career was balanced on a knife's edge.

"Legatus. Tribuni." Laurentin's tone was tightly controlled.

"What happened here?" Caius demanded, figuring it would be quicker for him to start asking the questions, since Aelio and Laurentin technically shared the same rank and did not answer to each other.

Laurentin's jaw clenched in frustration. "That is what I'm attempting to determine, Legatus. *Decurian* — tell them what you just told me."

The decurian snapped to attention. "Sir!" A rivulet of nervous perspiration trickled down the side of his face, and he swallowed hard. "We were patrolling the Southern District when a messenger found us and relayed your orders to disperse a crowd of demonstrators marching toward the Vaia Sacrii. The messenger said they were going to make another attempt to burn the temple."

"I issued no such orders," Laurentin growled. "And there has been no such intelligence regarding an arson attempt."

The decurian paled, but his posture remained straight, his hands clasped behind his back as he stood at parade rest. "Tribuni, I examined the orders myself. They were marked with your personal seal."

"Where are these orders?" Caius asked.

The man looked straight ahead. "In my saddlebags, sir."

Laurentin gestured sharply to another guard standing nearby. "You. Get the scroll and bring it here."

The decurian took a deep breath and continued talking. "The mob was marching east along the vaia when we confronted them and told them to disperse. Those at the front started throwing rocks at us. Some of the men… might have been a bit overzealous in their response."

Caius could practically hear Aelio's teeth grinding together.

"It was a huge crowd," the decurian said. "Much bigger than any of the previous demonstrations. The ones at the front panicked, and before we could do anything about it, there was a stampede. Most of the ones who died were trampled by their fellows, we think."

"You *think*," Aelio echoed flatly.

The man Laurentin had dispatched to retrieve the purported orders returned and handed a loosely curled sheet of vellum to him, before bowing and hastily removing himself from any potential crossfire. Laurentin unrolled the scroll and examined it, his brow creasing in a frown.

"This is not my handwriting."

Aelio snatched it from him and scanned the contents. "It's damned close, though." He flipped it over to check the wax seal. "The seal's too damaged to make a determination one way or the other. It could be a forgery, I suppose."

"Of course it's a bloody forgery!" Laurentin snapped.

"I'm not doubting your account," Aelio snapped back. "I'm saying it's impossible to tell whether the seal was a deliberate copy or merely a similar design."

Laurentin subsided, at least partially mollified.

Caius sighed. "Which leads us to the question—who benefits from the city guard massacring dozens of pagan sympathizers in the street?"

The others fell silent for a moment.

"Who wants civil war?" Aelio asked after a pause.

Kaeto.

Caius kept the thought to himself... but the princep was the obvious choice when it came to people who might benefit from existing power structures being thrown into chaos.

"It doesn't matter right now," he said. "What matters is getting enough loyal troops into the city to control any uprising before it spreads. How quickly could we recall the nearest auxilia stationed in other cities?"

Aelio's expression firmed. "That depends on how quickly I can talk the emperor into putting his seal on the orders, and how fast the messengers can ride. Let's find out."

Laurentin blew out a slow breath. "You do that. I'll try to keep a lid on things here. How many more palace guards can you send me to add to the patrols?"

Aelio gestured for his horse to be brought. "None, unless you want me to leave the conclave unguarded. Just... do your best." He mounted and looked down at Caius. "Are you coming, Legatus?"

Caius glanced down the street, at the building that housed the Cock's Crow. Streaks of soot blackened a section of the facade. "I'll follow you shortly."

Aelio nodded and spurred his horse into motion, heading toward the palace. Laurentin was already deep in conversation with several of his guardsmen, so Caius left him to it—making his way further down the street.

Several of the people milling around gave him wary looks as he skirted the worst of the killing ground. There was very little in the way of blood, bolstering the decurian's account of trampling deaths. The Cock wasn't the only place to show evidence of attempted arson, but with the exception of one building that was still smoldering, none of the fires had taken hold.

A line of men passing buckets along had that one almost under control. Meanwhile, other men and women moved among the bodies, covering them up and readying them for removal. Already, a wagon drawn by two strong horses had pulled up to a line of sheet-wrapped corpses, and men were hefting them into the back, one at a time.

Caius looked away. His eyes fell once more on the bucket line, just as a cloaked figure near the end turned to take a newly filled pail from a lad running back and forth to the pump. His hood slipped back, revealing a painfully familiar profile, and a jolt went through Caius' chest.

As though he'd sensed eyes on him, the man reached up to pull his hood forward, turning as he did so. As though drawn by a magnet, his brown gaze met Caius' across the fifty paces or so separating them, and they both froze.

SEVEN

"Legatus?" A hand fell on Caius' arm, jerking his attention away from Decian, and toward the guardsman who'd approached without him noticing. "Tribuni Laurentin requests your counsel on a matter of security."

Caius whirled back to the line of men fighting the smoldering fire, but Decian had disappeared without a trace.

"I'll join the tribuni shortly," he snapped, and hurried toward the place where Decian had been standing.

"Legatus—" the guard called after him.

He ignored the man, scanning the area for the shapeless brown cloak. There was nothing. With a hand on his sword hilt, he approached the narrow alley where Decian might have fled for cover. Light from the many torches and lamps that had been brought into the street penetrated partway into the claustrophobic space. Caius paused, trying to listen for movement or breathing over the thudding of his own heart.

There was nothing. Feeling sick and dizzy from the combination of shock and whatever benighted illness Tertia had given him, he entered the alley cautiously.

It was empty, ending in a blank wall at the back. There was a door on his left. He tried it, but it was barred from the inside.

Defeated, he returned to the chaos of the street, where he promptly began second-guessing himself. Had it really been Decian? They'd been separated by quite a distance, and it had only been the barest glimpse. Would the idiot truly have ignored Caius' ultimatum to leave the city and never return?

Caius turned slowly in place, his gaze falling on the Cock's Crow. Realization hit him like a bolt of lightning.

He'd sent Decian away with no money… without even proper clothes on his back. And afterward, he hadn't so much as asked himself where Decian might go. All of this, after Caius had made a point of introducing him to Saleene *so that he'd have somewhere to run if he ever needed to.*

Dear god. He was such a fool.

Dread pooled in his aching stomach. But before he'd taken three steps toward the building housing the brothel, the guardsmen from before caught up to him.

"Sir, forgive me — but the tribuni's request is urgent…"

Caius clenched his teeth and looked at the disaster area around him, duty warring with fear over what he might have sent scuttling to Saleene and Zuri's doorstep. He made himself take a deep breath. If Decian had fled straight to them the night of the attack, that meant he'd been there for a couple of days already without any… *incidents.* It was in his best interest to control his murderous nature around his new benefactors. After all, the shapeshifter had nowhere else to go.

The city was poised on the cusp of chaos, and Caius' presence was required. Warning Saleene would have to wait until he'd seen what Laurentin needed of him.

"Yes, guardsman," he forced out. "I'm coming."

⤳ 🐚 ⤳

Hours later, after Caius and Laurentin had hammered out the disposition of the available security forces in the city and all of the bodies had been cleared away, Caius dragged himself to the side door of the Cock and let himself in.

The outside of the building was a bit battered, with smoke damage on the front wall and some of the wooden window shutters hanging cockeyed on their frames. Given this fact, he was relieved to find that the interior appeared undamaged. Apparently, none of the panicked mob had succeeded in getting inside, which hopefully meant that no one inside had been hurt.

The interior door leading to the brothel's downstairs receiving room was closed, but not barred. He pushed it open, only to be confronted by the sight of Saleene's pretty boy—the one she kept around for the occasional female client—holding a rusty shortsword.

Caius raised an eyebrow at him.

"Oh," said the lad, relaxing. "It's just you."

"Word to the wise," Caius said. "If any of the guardsmen come here to check on things and find you brandishing a sword at them, things could go badly for you."

A flush stained the young man's high cheekbones. "Zuri said to make sure no one tried to come in and cause trouble."

Caius' visit might well end up causing more trouble than any of them wanted to deal with, but he only said, "Do you even know how to use that thing?"

The lad's chin lifted defiantly. "Put the pointy end between me and anyone trying to get in, right? How hard can it be?"

Rather than reply to that somewhat bewildering statement, Caius sighed and asked, "Would you get either Saleene or Zuri down here, please? I urgently need to speak with them."

A mulish look crossed the boy's pleasant features. "Can't. I'm supposed to—"

"Guard the door," Caius finished for him. "Right. In that case, may I go upstairs? Preferably without risking a case of lockjaw from the rust on that blade."

The lad appeared to mull that over for a few moments. "Yeah, all right. Just don't scare any of the girls. They're fretting enough as it is."

"Given what happened tonight, I don't really blame them," Caius said, and limped past him toward the stairs.

He was lightheaded by the time he reached the top, but he stopped the first girl he found and asked once more for Saleene or Zuri.

"We're not taking customers tonight," she said—looking pale-faced and grim, but hardly a picture of maidenly distress.

With his head still pounding, it took him a moment to understand what she meant. He shook his head. "This is business, not pleasure."

Even as the words left his mouth, he realized that for her, pleasure *was* business. She must have understood what he meant by it, though, because she jerked her chin toward the far end of the hall. "I think Saleene's in the parlor. Not sure about Zuri."

"Thank you," he told her, and went to beard the lioness in her den.

He found the proprietress standing in front of the room's window, looking down at the torch-lit confusion below.

"Saleene," he said.

She looked up sharply, her gray eyes falling on him with heavy weight. "Legatus," she greeted in a flat tone. "I certainly didn't expect your custom tonight."

He met her gaze and held it. "That's not why I'm here, and you know it. We need to talk about Decian.

One sharp eyebrow climbed toward her hairline. "Your cause of treasonous justice? Forgive me if that's not foremost in my thoughts right now. I'm more interested about what is to be done regarding the city guard engaging in wholesale slaughter of citizens in the street."

The words could have peeled varnish from wood.

"An investigation into the incident is already underway," he told her. "And, in the course of that investigation, I happened to see Decian among the crowd. If he's staying here, you need to make him leave."

Her face might as well have been carved from marble. "I am not in the habit of inserting myself into the center of lovers' quarrels, Caius. Assuming that's what's going on here."

"He's a shapeshifter, Saleene. He's killed people. He's not safe to be around." The words hurt, scratching like emery powder along his throat.

She scoffed. "A *shapeshifter*? Really, Caius. To think I had you pegged as a rationalist."

He didn't break eye contact. "I am a realist. Specifically, a realist whose father was slaughtered by a shapeshifter when I was a boy. I saw this with my own eyes. Decian is dangerous. If you don't want to worry about yourself, then think of your employees."

Her expression didn't shift an inch. "I don't take in strays, Legatus. He came here; I sent him away. End of story."

"Apparently not, since I saw him outside."

Saleene waved a dismissive hand. "You claim he is a shapeshifter? Then why would it be a surprise to find him among a crowd of pagans? I've told you he's not here. I'm not certain what else you expect me to say."

Something about the exchange sat uneasily in Caius's stomach… or perhaps that was merely his illness. But to push the issue further would be to call Saleene a liar, and he couldn't see the conversation magically becoming more productive should he do so.

"If he comes here again, please inform me," he said stiffly.

"Fine," she told him. "And if the Amarian Guard intend to cut down any more pagans on my front doorstep, you can inform me of that, as well."

The reality of the current situation settled heavily across his shoulders. "Given the circumstances, I can't entirely rule it out," he said. "Please stay safe."

Her hard gaze softened incrementally, but only for a moment. "Go home, Legatus. In case no one else has mentioned this, you look like hell puked up a two-week-old corpse."

Caius nodded his farewell and went home.

⚜

Unsurprisingly given the late hour, Tertia had already gone back to her quarters by the time he arrived. He picked at the plate of cold meat and cheese she'd left him, eating it slowly while nursing a single cup of wine. His stomach complained vociferously about both, but he at least managed to keep everything down.

Sleep was slow to come. When he woke the following morning, he felt even worse than the day before. Nevertheless, he dragged himself out of bed and headed for the first full day of the Council. The question of pagan suppression was, if possible, even more critical than it had been before the previous night's massacre.

Even as muddle-headed and feverish as he was, he could sense the brittle tension in the city. That tension would snap, and soon — it was only a matter of what form the backlash would take.

When he arrived at his destination, the area around the building was bustling with activity. After checking in with Aelio and learning that no new violence had erupted overnight, he confirmed that everything was in order as far as the security around the meeting chamber. It was as good as it could be under the circumstances, even though the remaining vulnerabilities made Caius' skin prickle with disquiet.

His stomach cramped as he made his way toward the seat that had been arranged for him along the wall of the chamber. It was bad enough that he had to fight to keep from doubling over, his footsteps stuttering beneath the onslaught of pain. Gritting his teeth, he pushed through it and sank down onto the cushioned chair.

Around him, the other observers found their places, settling in for the beginning of the day's business. Both Proclus and Kaeto were seated at the long table along with the church dignitaries, and Caius caught sight of Bruccias settling into the first row of seats in the central audience area.

The emperor was notably absent. So was Stasia, though that was less surprising. Empress she might be, but that lofty title did not give her leave to flout the Church's rules barring women from participation in matters of religious policy and governance.

After the last few weeks, Caius was so weary of religion — in all its various forms — that he could weep.

Episkopos Phillian of Narvonne rose from his seat at the table and tapped his staff of office on the marble floor three times. The sound echoed around the room, the murmur of voices falling silent as it did.

"Let the Council of Amarius come to order," he said. "We have gathered to decide once and for all the question of the disposition of heretics. The Church has long tolerated unbelievers in its midst, in the knowledge that their souls would eventually be judged by the Almighty

Deimok Himself. Recently, however, those same unbelievers have grown brazen in their disrespect for the True Faith. A coalition of patriarchs from the southern reaches now wishes to alter the Church's official position, allowing for the trial and disposition of accused heretics by a dedicated group of inquisitors. Arguments will be heard for and against, followed by a period of debate and a vote."

The murmuring of low conversation rose again as Phillian sat down. Caius blinked against the growing blurriness of his vision as his headache pounded in time with his pulse.

Proclus rose. "I speak as emissary of the Emperor of Alyrios. The empire has tolerated religious dissent from heathens for too long. One need only look to the recent violence and unrest in the capital to see it. Put the blighters down like the vermin they are and be done with the matter. Alyrios will be the better for it."

Several voices were raised in agreement.

When they died down, Kaeto cleared his throat. "One wonders what the benefit of setting half the population against the other half might be, when Alyrios already faces numerous threats outside its own borders."

Again, Caius was taken aback by the show of restraint. He knew Kaeto must have some kind of angle when it came to his apparent softening of stance toward the pagans, but he was damned if he could figure out what it was.

"And how are we to face those threats while the empire is corrupted from within?" Proclus drawled. "One might almost think you sympathized with the heretics, *Brother*."

An elderly dignitary Caius didn't recognize rose at the far end of the table. "The matter is not one of secular politics, but of spiritual purity!" he insisted. "The coddling of heretics is an affront to Deimok himself—"

Shouts and screams from outside cut off the old churchman's tirade, and Caius surged to his feet. Across the chamber, Aelio did the same, shouting orders to the line of guardsmen standing along the back wall, behind the table of dignitaries. The men immediately charged forward, placing themselves between the council members and the entrance to the chamber. Some of the audience members were also on their feet now, adding to the confusion.

Caius craned to see the huge double doors, his battle instincts kicking in even as his head and stomach protested the sudden movement. The doors creaked open on their massive hinges, and Caius caught the glint of light off the sleek outline of a crossbow.

"Get down!" he bellowed, directing the command toward the council full of aging churchmen and imperial heirs.

Several people dropped behind the sturdy cover of the wooden table, reacting to the barked order without thought—Proclus and Kaeto among them. Bruccias abandoned the pew where he'd been seated, darting behind the nearest marble column.

Crossbow bolts hissed through the air. In his peripheral vision, Caius saw several guards and one episkopos who'd been too slow to take cover go down beneath the assault. He was already searching for something that could be used as a weapon—cursing the decision to forbid all blades within the chamber except those carried by the guards.

It had been an attempt to reduce the risk of an attack by anyone in the audience, but now it meant the intruders were largely unopposed as they drew swords and began hacking at members of the panicking crowd.

Caius couldn't get a good count on how many there were, but he thought it was a relatively small number. A sharp whistle caught his attention, and he barely managed to catch the sword that Aelio tossed him hilt-first.

There was blood on the grip. It must have belonged to one of the downed guardsmen. Knowing Aelio would group his surviving men around the princeps and council members, Caius gritted his teeth and threw himself into the carnage in the crowd. If he could take out a couple of the assassins before they had time to reload their crossbows...

He waded in, heading for the nearest screams, and started slashing. Before long, fresh city guards poured into the chamber, and with the additional help, the half-dozen or so intruders were overrun. Most of the audience who'd been there to watch the council proceedings had managed to flee by that point. For the second time in the past twenty-four hours, the moans and sobbing of injured civilians echoed in Caius' ears.

As the battle lust faded from his muscles, he turned toward the front of the chamber, intending to check on the status of the emperor's sons and the visiting dignitaries. Before he managed two steps in that direction however, his legs gave out. The pain of his various half-healed injuries was a dull and faraway thing as his knees hit the unforgiving marble floor. A flat buzzing like the sound of angry insects drowned out the confusion of noise around him.

His stomach cramped again, and he pitched forward, barely managing to catch himself on his hands as his guts heaved. The vomit that splattered onto the pristine tiles was red and black with clotted blood.

That's not good, he though distantly, in the instant before the world went dark.

EIGHT

Caius awoke to the sound of a woman's stifled weeping. His eyes didn't want to focus properly, but the room around him was dimly lit by oil lamps, and the mattress beneath his back was far too soft.

If they've already hired the paid mourners, it must be even worse than I thought, he reflected, blinking rapidly in hopes of clearing the fog obscuring his vision. His unseen female companion inhaled sharply, a congested noise that was decidedly unladylike. A callused hand closed on his forearm.

"You're awake." The voice was unsteady and tearful. It unquestionably belonged to Tertia, of all people.

"You don't have to sound so surprised about it," he rasped.

Focusing inward, he tried to take stock. Everything that had hurt before still hurt. His stomach, in particular, now felt like he'd swilled an entire glass of green vitriol without stopping for breath.

The fingers clasping his arm squeezed convulsively.

"I've done something terrible," Tertia whispered.

A sinking feeling made Caius' lungs hitch, as he waited for her to tell him that the damnable illness she'd given him was some kind of incurable plague.

"It's poison," she breathed, barely audible. "I put it in the wine."

He shook off her grip and struggled upright in the bed, ignoring the way it made his head swim. "You *what?*"

She hunched forward, burying her face in one hand as her shoulders shook. After a moment, she straightened and visibly pulled herself together, meeting his gaze with the air of one steeling herself for her fate.

"Three nights ago, men came to the slave quarters and kidnapped us from our beds," she began.

"Stop," Caius said immediately. "Back up for a moment. Who's '*us*'?"

Her chin trembled, and she clenched her teeth to control it.

"My two daughters and I. They tied cloth hoods over our heads and threw us in the back of a goods wagon. I could smell the bags of rye flour we were lying on. They took us outside of the imperial quarter, to an abandoned building." Her voice broke, and she let out a choked noise.

"Keep talking," Caius ordered, wishing like hell that he had something to wash the taste of stale vomit away.

Tertia swallowed hard and continued, unable to keep the quaver out of her voice. "After they took us inside, they forced me to watch while Ennia and Helvii were chained to the wall and beaten. One of the men gave me a vial of poison and told me how to use it. He said if I didn't use it on you, they'd kill my girls." Her breathing stuttered, and she curled forward again, hugging herself. "Oh, god. They're going to kill my girls, Legatus."

Caius silently cursed the fog of pain and exhaustion slowing his thoughts to the consistency of molasses. Hand shaking with weakness, he reached out and clasped his house slave's thin shoulder.

"Tertia, look at me," he said, waiting until she met his eyes. "They're not going to kill your daughters. As far as they know, you've done exactly as they said, and I'm at death's door after collapsing in the council chamber today." He paused, realizing he had no idea how much time had passed since then. "That was... today, wasn't it?"

She gave a jerky nod and swallowed again. "You're not going to turn me in to the magistrate?" she asked.

"Good god, no," he told her, trying not to be offended by the sheer disbelief coloring her tone. "What in hell's name would that accomplish?"

Her mouth opened, only to close again a moment later. He tried to remember if he'd ever managed to render her speechless before. He was reasonably certain the answer was no.

"These men," he went on. "Did you recognize them? Were they wearing uniforms? Livery? Did they say who they were working for?"

"N-no," she managed. "I'd never seen them before. They were dressed in dark clothing. Very plain. They didn't mention any names."

Something flashed in the back of his mind at the mention of dark clothing, but it was gone before he could grab hold of it—lost to the mist of weakness.

"Very well," he said. "Here's what's going to happen next. You're going to go home, because I'm a heartless bastard and you honestly don't care if I live or die. If these men ask you about my condition, you can tell them I was fading fast when you left me alone to choke on my own vomit. Speak to no one else of this."

She stared at him for a long moment, unblinking.

"Why are you doing this?" she rasped, sounding unutterably old and tired.

He raised an eyebrow at her, shocked to find that even such a tiny movement hurt. "As it happens, Tertia, you're not the first person to try and kill me in the past month. In fact, I believe you're the... eighth? No, I'm wrong. Actually, you're the ninth. You are, however, the first one that had to be blackmailed into doing it. You're also the first one to feel bad about it afterward."

Her eyes were bloodshot from crying as she continued to hold his gaze. "I didn't know what else to do," she told him. "I can't lose my daughters, Legatus. They're all I have in this world."

The thought of adding yet another impossible task to his list of things to do made the invisible weight pressing down on his shoulders grow heavier.

"Leave it to me," he said. "Now go home and let anyone who asks know how close to death's door I was when you left. I'm going to disappear for a bit while I figure out what the hell to do about this mess. As far as you know, I've crawled off somewhere to expire in peace. Keep coming here every day at your normal time. I'll contact you as soon as I can do so safely."

She nodded reluctantly. A moment later, her gnarled hand settled on his forearm again. "I'm sorry," she said.

He hesitated for a moment before covering her hand with his. "No. *I'm* sorry. I only realized what was truly going on a few days ago. And even then, I was *so certain* none of this would touch the people around me. I'm a fool."

She broke eye contact and slid her hand away, fiddling with her apron instead. "You are, yes. But I still don't want to be a murderer."

"Not dead yet," he pointed out, trying to ignore the way his body was screaming at him. "Now get out of here. I'll get news to you soon."

She chewed her lower lip for a moment, as though debating saying something else. Apparently deciding against it, she rose and departed, leaving him alone with his failing body and clamoring thoughts.

"God help me," he muttered to the ceiling—with no expectation whatsoever that any god in residence was likely to lift a finger on his behalf at this point.

Getting to his feet was harder than he'd hoped, but once he was there, his legs held him. When he was certain Tertia had gone, he checked the contents of his coin purse, donned a shapeless, hooded cloak, and left by the back door. There were probably men watching the house, but there was fuck-all Caius could do about it at this point.

He did his best to disappear into the shadows and byways of the Imperial quarter at night, knowing it might not be good enough to lose anyone following him. The stomach cramps were nearly constant now, and he had to stop twice to retch, bringing up nothing but thin bile both times. It was too dark to tell if there was blood in it, which was probably just as well.

When he finally reached Aelio's dwelling, he found the servant's entrance and pounded on it. In truth, he didn't even know what time it was. It could have been late evening or the small hours after midnight. Fortunately, a wary looking manservant opened the door before he ended up rousing the entire neighborhood.

"I need to speak with your master," he said. "Tell him it's Caius, here about something urgent."

The servant brought him inside to wait, and Aelio strode in moments later. His blue eyes fell on Caius and widened in alarm, making him wonder how closely he resembled a walking corpse.

"Legatus!" the tribuni exclaimed, hurrying forward to take him by the arm. "Good god, man—come sit down. What are you even doing out of your bed?"

Caius swallowed whatever paltry pride he might have left and let himself be steered to a wooden chair in the kitchen.

"I appear to have a small problem," he said weakly, pushing back the hood of the cloak.

Aelio gave him a critical onceover. "My dear Caius— don't take this the wrong way, but any problems you may have don't appear to be of the *small* variety."

Caius sighed. "As you say. Very well, then—I appear to have a *large* problem. Someone in the palace is trying to kill me. In fact, they've become rather single-minded in pursuit of that goal in recent days."

Aelio was silent for a long moment. Then, he pulled up a second chair and sank down in it, his full focus on his unexpected houseguest. "Tell me," he said.

With a deep breath, Caius pulled his thoughts into order as best he could and relayed all of it, starting with the mercenaries in the forest during the royal hunt, and proceeding to the attack in the alley before finishing with the report from his house slave. He glossed over Decian's involvement—not entirely sure why—and gave no indication that the former master of hounds was anything other than dead.

"You need to take this to the Magistrate," Aelio said when he was finished.

The tribuni's expression was deadly serious. Caius was mildly surprised that he'd accepted the entire unlikely story without question.

Still, he choked on an ugly snort of laughter. "Right. There's only one small problem with that."

A furrow formed in Aelio's brow. "What sort of problem?"

Caius scrubbed a hand down the length of his face, irritated to find that his fingers were shaking with weakness. "It's very likely that the assassination orders originated one step below the throne."

Aelio sat abruptly straight in his chair. "One step below—" He cut himself off. "You mean... one of the princeps?"

"Kaeto, most likely," Caius confirmed. "He may be plotting against the empress as well."

The tribuni appeared lost for words, his mouth hanging open. After a few moments, he recovered. "Go to the emperor, then."

For the first time in years, Caius met the gaze of a fellow palace official and spoke plainly. "We both know Constanzus is too far gone to deal with something like this."

Aelio's pleasant features went pale. "So," he said. "I take it we're finally speaking the words aloud, then."

NINE

"Looks like we are," Caius agreed tiredly. "Aelio, I'm telling you this because one of these days, Kaeto is going to succeed in putting my bones in the ground. When that happens, someone else needs to know what's happening. Someone besides the empress—because he's coming for her, as well."

Aelio watched him closely for a long moment, and Caius could almost see the thoughts flitting through that quick mind.

"We need to get you away from the palace compound without anyone knowing. You're under surveillance, I assume?"

"Yes," Caius agreed. "I made a concerted attempt to throw off any shadows on my way here. Whether I succeeded or not is an open question."

The tribuni gave a slow nod. "Subterfuge, then."

Caius raised a hand. "As long as you realize that by taking action to help me, you will be setting yourself against a man who may well be the next emperor. I've placed you in grave danger by even coming here, much less telling you all of this."

Aelio blew out a breath. "Yes, you have. But Kaeto isn't the emperor yet. He isn't even the heir-in-waiting. And who's to say I won't be the next to annoy him, whether I help you or not?"

"A fair point," Caius replied.

"I also take exception to anyone kidnapping old women and holding their families hostage," Aelio added.

"So do I," Caius agreed, his tone going hard and cold.

"Therefore, this is what we're going to do," Aelio said. He raised his voice. "Parsus! Come in here, please."

The servant who'd answered the door entered, dipping his chin in a shallow bow. "Yes, Tribuni?"

Aelio gestured to Caius. "I need you to exchange clothes with this man. Take another set of your own clothes with you, concealed under his cloak. You will go to his house and wait there until morning, when you can leave again, dressed as yourself and pretending to be a tradesman. Return here by a circuitous route—make certain you are not followed. Do you understand?"

Parsus gave his master a speculative look, but he nodded easy agreement. "Yes, Tribuni. Where is the house?"

Caius also shot Aelio a look, but he relayed directions and described how to get in through the back door.

Parsus bowed again. "If I might retrieve some of my clothes for you to wear, sir? That's probably a bit more dignified than the two of us stripping off right here in the kitchen."

"Agreed," Caius said dryly.

The manservant left, and Aelio regarded Caius.

"Next question," he said. "Are you in any condition to go on the run? The last time I saw you, they were scraping you off the floor of the council chamber."

Caius scowled at him. "I made it here, didn't I? I'll be fine." That was probably a lie, but since Caius needed to get away regardless, it hardly mattered at this point. "Just get me into the city, and I'll take it from there."

He had a vague notion of getting a room at the least reputable inn he could find, where he could ride out the course of the poison. After which... well, that was a good question, actually. He supposed he could try to get word to the empress in secret. The worst part was, after today's carnage in the council chamber it was entirely possible that treason by one of the emperor's sons no longer constituted the biggest threat to the empire.

"Do I want to know how things are faring after the attack on the council?" he asked.

Aelio's grim expression grew even grimmer. "No. You *emphatically* do not want to know."

Caius winced. "That bad?"

"*Worse.*" Aelio visibly recalled himself. "With all due respect, Caius, I think you'd do well to focus on your own troubles for the moment. All that can be done regarding the attack—and the massacre the day before—is being done. Just… watch yourself in the city. Things are volatile."

Caius could only imagine. "As you say. I can't say I envy you when it comes to dealing with the mess."

Aelio snorted. "When a man being targeted for assassination isn't even willing to change places with you, things are definitely bad." He glanced toward the door. "Ah. speaking of changing places…"

Parsus entered with a pile of folded clothing and proffered it to Caius. "Sir," he said.

Caius took it and nodded his thanks. Master and servant retreated, giving him privacy to change. He managed to do so without fainting or falling over, though he might've sat down in the chair rather abruptly on a couple of occasions during the process. When the others returned, he handed his rumpled and sweat-staining clothing to Parsus, trying not to feel self-conscious about it.

You've worn worse on the battlefield, he reminded himself. And what was this, if not another battle?

Parsus didn't comment—merely took the clothes with him and reappeared a few minutes later dressed as Caius. Happily, there were similar in terms of height and build. Parsus was younger and broader shouldered, but the cloak would hide both of those facts nicely.

"If you can play up being weak and unsteady on your feet, that might be useful," Caius counseled. "It would be best if anyone watching got the idea that I'm at death's door."

Parsus twitched the hood forward, throwing his features into shadow. "I'll endeavor to give that impression, sir."

"Off you go, in that case," Aelio told him. "Watch your back, but don't let on that you're watching it."

"Of course, Tribuni," Parsus replied stoically, and headed outside, into the night.

Caius watched him go with a sense of foreboding. "What time is it, anyway?"

"Shortly after midnight, I expect." Aelio had returned with his sword belt in hand, and he buckled it on before retrieving a cloak from a peg on the wall. This one was rougher and far less ostentatious than the one now decorating Parsus' shoulders — suitable for a servant.

He handed it to Caius, who put it on, shrugging it awkwardly over his bad shoulder. Caius pulled the hood up one-handed, and Aelio raked him with a head to foot gaze.

"You'll do," he said. "Let's go before it gets any later. If we're followed, we'll lose them in the city."

The echo of Caius' similar words not so very long ago rang in his memory. "Do not, under any circumstances, try to lose them in the alleys and backstreets," he warned. "I made that mistake and ended up underestimating them, much to my detriment."

"Noted," Aelio replied. "However, you were attacked by half a dozen men. If we're followed, it's likely to be nothing more than surveillance, since as a tribuni and his servant, we are not their real targets."

"True," Caius allowed. "Though I shouldn't like to bet your life on it."

Aelio shot him a tight smile and led him toward the front door of the house. "It wouldn't be the first bet I've made with my life. Definitely not the one with the longest odds, either."

They made their way to the stables, and Caius tried not to let on how badly his weakened body was betraying him. Despite his many misadventures, he'd somehow managed to avoid any serious gut wounds during his decades in the military. Tonight, however, he had an obscene amount of empathy for every soldier he'd ever seen crying and babbling for his mother as he cradled his spilled intestines in his hands.

He somehow managed to make it onto the back of the ill-tempered mule that the groom led out for him. The beast was hard-mouthed, and Caius had to wrestle it forcefully around by the reins to fall in step with Aelio's fine bay courser. Even if he'd been in the mood for conversation, he would have stayed quiet. He was the lowly servant, for one thing; and for another, neither of them could risk his voice being recognized.

Relying so totally on another person after years of closing himself off from the backstabbing courtiers and advisors in the palace was... odd. Once, he'd have given no thought at all to trusting his life to a fellow soldier. On reflection, losing that piece of himself had not been a good thing.

As the pair approached one of the gates leading out of the imperial quarter, Caius swallowed an ache at the memory of riding through this same gate with Decian at his side, the evening that everything had gone to hell.

"Late night, Tribuni?" said one of the guards.

"Long day, more like," Aelio replied.

"So I heard," the man said, not without sympathy. He gestured to his companions at the gate crank, and the mechanism groaned into motion.

The massive portcullis rose, and the two of them rode through it. As ever, there were advantages to having an unimpeachable reputation, as Aelio most certainly did. There were also advantages to the anonymity of servants. With no reason to expect treachery from the commander of the imperial security forces, the guards at the gate didn't give Caius a second look.

They left the high wall surrounding the emperor's sanctum behind, entering the quiet government district, empty at this late hour. Caius' body fought itself, trying to maintain high alert, even as his vision swam, and his muscles trembled with weakness. Aelio was right, though. While they might have been followed, there was no reason to expect another attack like the one a few days ago.

He let the mule follow alongside Aelio's horse, distantly aware that he was losing chunks of time. A blink, and when his eyelids opened, city blocks had passed without him noticing. This, he knew, was a very bad sign. His hands and feet felt distant and numb—still under his nominal control but operating on a significant lag. The pain in his gut was becoming all-encompassing.

He blinked again, dragging his heavy eyelids open to find they had entered the central business district in the southern quarter. "This will work," he said, taking care not to let the words slur. "I'll take my leave of you here."

Aelio nodded and gestured toward a livery one block down. "If you're certain. I'll leave the mule stabled there in case you need her again."

"Thank you," Caius told him.

The tribuni waved the words away. "Thank me if the empire is still in one piece in a few days." He glanced up and down the street, which seemed unusually quiet even for such a late hour. "Take care. We weren't able to organize a proper curfew because the city forces are spread too thin—but what guards are available will be stopping people and asking questions."

Caius pulled the mule to a halt at the entrance to the livery and slid carefully down from the saddle, not letting go until he was certain his legs would hold him. "Understood. You take care as well. Watch your back."

"I've been doing that for years," Aelio replied dryly. "Fair winds, my friend."

The tribuni took the mule's reins and led the animal into the livery, calling for service. Caius steadied himself against the stable wall for the space of a few breaths, looking around to get his bearings. This was a road with several shops and drinking establishments, but there were only a handful of people out. The intersection with the Vaia Meretricia lay half a block from him, and beyond that was an inn that would probably serve his purposes, assuming they hadn't barred the doors to new customers after the recent troubles.

The building suddenly seemed very far away. Gritting his teeth, he pushed off from the wall and started walking, keeping the inn centered in his wavering vision. He made it a few steps past the Vaia Meretricia when the stomach cramps that had been plaguing him suddenly became a burning poker shoved into an open wound.

With a gasp, he doubled over helplessly, barely catching himself against the nearest building as his vision tunneled. He heaved, tasting iron and bile, and when he wiped at his chin, his hand came away red with blood. Consciousness flickered out, then back in again. Staggering, he got his feet under him and moved, knowing in a distant and detached sort of way that he needed help, and fast, or he was going to collapse and die right here on the street.

The light from the street lamps loomed strangely in his vision, disorienting him further. He kept putting one foot in front of the other, aware that if he stopped, he probably wouldn't be able to start moving again.

Time flickered in and out. A familiar door appeared in front of him. He pushed it open. Inside lay a hallway and a second, equally familiar door. He pushed that one open, too. The movement unbalanced him, sending him to his knees with the door handle still clutched in one hand.

"*Hey!*" a voice protested.

Caius rocked back, following motion in his field of vision. Saleene's pretty boy swam in and out of focus, bearing down on him. A second figure appeared behind him, its outline wavering—and then Saleene herself was hurrying forward, looking down at him with shocked gray eyes.

"Caius?" she asked, reaching a hand toward him.

"Sorry," he slurred. "I've been poisoned. I didn't know where else to go."

Her hand closed on his shoulder, and he slumped into the grip as consciousness deserted him for the second time in the course of a day.

TEN

What followed was a nightmarish patchwork of dream and hallucination, the whole thing sewn together with thread made of bad memories and regret.

That, and pain. Caius woke to agony in his head and stomach, surrounded by faceless, shadowy figures speaking words he couldn't understand. Sometimes they held him down, pouring noxious potions down his throat even as he cursed, begged, and fought weakly, trying to throw them off.

As time wore on in endless torment, he caught flashes of faces. His father. His mother. Soldiers under his command that he hadn't been able to save. Serah—his poor, doomed wife—and the tiny corpse that should have been their child.

Decian.

Caius could almost swear that *this* familiar face was more real than the rest. Concern warred with wariness in the deep brown eyes looking down at him. A cool cloth mopped at his brow. Decian's presence was exquisite torture in a world already composed of little else besides pain and confusion. His mind tried to play tricks on him, convincing him all the terrible things that had happened in a darkened alley had been the dream, and the reality was the happy stretch of days which had come before.

Day followed night, followed day, until Caius woke into something that felt more like coherence and less like a twisted fantasy world. His stomach still hurt, but not with the same gut-shredding force as before. The ache of it was overpowered by his thirst. It took him three attempts to unstick his tongue from the roof of his mouth, and his eyelids were glued shut by something with roughly the same consistency as the sand in the Great Southern Desert.

He groaned, only to subside into raspy coughing when the sound caught in his bone-dry throat.

Eventually, he managed to pry his eyes open and blink some moisture into them. His vision cleared enough to make out a nondescript room with one small window set high in the wall above the bed on which he was lying. It was daylight. A weak ray of sunshine cut through the dimness surrounding him. His gaze followed its path idly, tracing the yellow beam full of dancing dust motes to where it met the edge of the mattress…

… and illuminated the head of a massive black dog like a giant mastiff, its muzzle resting on the edge of the bed. Soulful brown eyes watched him unblinkingly, and sudden realization jolted through Caius' weakened body like a sword blow. He tried to scramble away, only to discover in quick succession that his arms and legs had lost all strength, and anyway, the bed was situated right against the wall, leaving him trapped.

The dog continued to watch him impassively.

After several endless moments, the air around the animal twisted in a way Caius' mind didn't want to focus on. In the next heartbeat, Decian crouched at his bedside, chin resting on his hands at the edge of the mattress. They stared at each other—Caius tense as a drawn bow, Decian seemingly at ease despite his expression of faint puzzlement.

Just when Caius began to worry that they'd be frozen in this tableau permanently, Decian sat up.

"You're awake properly, then?" he asked.

Caius drew breath to speak, only to swallow dryly instead, his throat clicking.

"Sorry," Decian said. "You must be parched." He reached for a bundle of cloth resting on the small bedside table and shrugged it over his shoulders, the simple toga sliding down to cover tawny skin and lean muscle. Next, he poured something from a pitcher into a cup, proffering it. "Here. It's just water."

Caius accepted the cup with a hand that trembled. His heart hammered against his chest, but he lifted it to his lips and drank. Cool liquid spilled down his chin, but at least what he successfully managed to swallow soothed his throat. His stomach protested, but it quieted after a few deep breaths.

Decian took the empty cup and set it aside before returning his full attention to Caius. His brow furrowed.

"You've been really out of it. I realize that." He paused. "But... why did you keep shouting that I killed your father?"

Caius blinked up at him, feeling sick now from more than just the poison. "What?" he rasped, dreading the answer.

Decian sat down on the edge of the bed, and Caius managed not to cringe away from him.

"While you were delirious," Decian clarified. "You kept calling me a filthy shapeshifter and saying your father was dead because of me. Even though I'm quite certain I've never met your father."

Caius licked his lips, too stripped bare by this point to offer anything but the truth. "I know you haven't. There was a pagan magician who could take the form of a stag. He gored my father to death when I was eight."

"Oh," Decian said.

Footsteps approached from outside the room.

"And was your father also trying to kill this shapeshifter when it happened?" asked a new voice.

Caius looked past Decian to the doorway, where Saleene stood with one forearm braced against the frame. "Yes," he whispered. "As it happens, he was."

"Hmm." Saleene straightened and sauntered into the room, closing the door behind her. "It's amazing how that works, isn't it?" she said. Her tone became tart. "Well done for managing not to follow in dear old dad's footsteps. So far, at least."

"What... happened?" Caius asked helplessly, trying and failing to piece together the recent past.

"What's the last thing you remember?" Saleene countered.

Caius cast his mind back, searching for the point where memory met confusion. "My house slave poisoned me," he began.

Decian's spine stiffened abruptly. "What? *Tertia* poisoned you? You're joking!"

Caius shook his head, overcome by exhaustion. "It's complicated. They forced her to do it. They're holding her daughters hostage."

"*They*," Saleene echoed. "Who's 'they'?"

"Whoever it is that's been trying to kill me for the past several weeks," he replied.

Decian was staring at him in astonishment—as well he might. "Excuse me, *what*?"

"It's true." Caius let his head flop back, staring at a cobweb hanging from the rough plaster ceiling. "The assassins weren't after you. I found out recently that they were after me the entire time. In the woods after the royal hunt. In the alley. Someone in the palace wants me dead, and they don't seem ready to accept failure as an option."

Saleene let out an irritated sigh. "Caius, you *idiot*. You might have mentioned that part when you showed up here to harangue me the other day."

He did his best to glare at her, aware that it probably wasn't a very effective attempt. "Forgive me. It didn't seem as though telling the unvarnished truth was high on the agenda at the time. '*Decian isn't here, Legatus,*'" he mocked. "'*He came, but I sent him away.*'"

"You didn't exactly give me much choice about coming here," Decian pointed out, with less anger than might have been expected. "Where else was I supposed to go with no money, and my clothing in tatters?"

Caius opened his mouth to reply, but there wasn't a good answer to the question.

Decian cut him off before he could come up with anything that might have constituted an explanation. "I wasn't lying to you, you know. Inside the royal kennels was the first time I'd ever shifted—and afterward, I had absolutely no idea what had happened to me. The attack in the alley was only the second time."

Caius looked at the man perched next to him on the mattress. Sweet, uncomplicated Decian, who'd brought joy to his life… and then ripped two men's souls out with his slavering jaws.

"I believe you," he said slowly, feeling a band of cold metal tightening around his chest like a vise. "But I've also seen you with human blood running down your chin, Decian."

Frustration creased Decian's features. "Yeah. You're right. You did. And out of curiosity, how much blood splashed across your face when you were torturing an injured man in that same alley, *Legatus*?" he demanded. "Tell me, did you leave him alive afterward?"

The sand shifted alarmingly under Caius' metaphorical boots, leaving him no solid ground on which to stand.

"No," he said hoarsely. "I cut his throat and left him to bleed out."

"Then what, exactly, makes us so different?" Decian asked.

"I'm a soldier," Caius said, trying to ignore the sickening voice of self-reflection whispering that Decian had killed in defense of Caius' life, whereas Caius had killed men in cold blood—both on the battlefield and off.

Saleene had been watching the exchange with folded arms and a stony expression. "You haven't been a soldier in years, Caius. You're a fucking *palace advisor*. And now it sounds like you're a stuffed straw target, just sitting around and waiting for the next arrow to land."

Caius ignored her, even though the barb hit home. "That night in the alley, I was in control of my actions, whether you approve of them or not," he told Decian. "Whereas you have a monster living inside you. That's what makes us different."

Decian's jaw clenched. "A monster, is it? You think I can't control it?"

A mental image of the hellhound's massive head resting on the edge of the mattress slid across his mind's eye, and he blinked it away.

"Can you?" he challenged.

Eyes flaring red, Decian unhooked the clasp holding his simple clothing closed at the shoulder. Before it hit the ground, the hellhound had returned, resting its front paws on the bed as it stared at him. In his peripheral vision,

Caius caught Saleene's violent flinch as Decian shifted, but he was too busy contemplating whether this would end up being how he died to comment on her reaction.

The hound leapt effortlessly onto the bed with him, prowling forward until its front legs caged Caius' torso—his weakness preventing him from doing anything other than lying flat on his back, waiting for his soul to be ripped free and flung into the void. He stared up at that glowing red gaze, unwilling to go to his death with his eyes clenched shut in terror.

"Saleene," he choked out. "Get out of this room. Lock the door and don't let anyone inside until he changes back."

"Caius," Saleene said. "Your head is so far up your own arse, I'm surprised you don't have to eat every meal twice."

Caius couldn't look away from the slavering jaws poised barely a hand's breadth from his face. The hound leaned down, sniffing at him—its breath warm and humid against his skin. The red eyes faded back to earthy brown. An instant later, Decian leaned over his trembling body—naked, and with a frown creasing his human features.

"You are... genuinely terrified of me," he said, sounding thoroughly taken aback.

"As you can see, he can control it just fine now," Saleene said. "So, the question becomes, are you ready to accept this, or do you intend to leave your head in your arse while the city burns and the empire crumbles around you?" Her gaze sharpened. "Because in case this part has escaped your notice, the emperor's bastard son is a *fucking shapeshifter*. Do you have any idea what that means?"

Caius' head was already swimming, his breath coming in short, unsteady gasps. When Saleene's words registered, the world shifted sideways abruptly. Decian's eyes narrowed in concern.

"Caius?" he asked.

But Caius could only shake his head, his thoughts crushed beneath the weight of the implications. The room darkened around him, his vision tunneling.

"I," he wheezed. "Sorry, I think I'm about to..."

...*pass out again*, he thought, but it was already too late.

ELEVEN

The next time Caius awoke, it was dark. An oil lamp illuminated a circle around the bedside table. To his surprise, Decian was still there, seated in a wooden chair in the corner of the room.

The younger man looked up when Caius shifted position in the bed.

"There's broth thickened with bread," he said, sounding a bit distant. "You should have it if you think you can keep it down. We've barely been able to get water and medicine into you these past two days without it coming right back up."

Caius blinked at him as the latest round of revelations reassembled themselves into some sort of coherent narrative inside his skull. The emperor's son was a shapeshifter. Apparently, he could control it, and perhaps he wasn't as dangerous to innocent people as Caius had originally assumed. The Council had been attacked. The capital was poised on the cusp of large-scale violence, assuming it hadn't tipped over already.

He turned his attention inward, feeling out the shape of his body's pain. It was bad, but not as bad as before. Reluctantly, he reached for the bowl sitting on the table. He had to steady it with both hands to get it to his lips without spilling it. As expected, the first tentative sips landed on his stomach like molten lead… but the broth stayed down. After drinking a little less than half the bowl, he set it aside.

"Has there been more violence in the city?" he asked.

Decian didn't move from his chair. "Yes. The riots are getting worse every night," he replied in a low monotone.

Caius closed his eyes, then opened them again a moment later. Uncertainty compelled him to meet the other man's gaze and ask, "The shift—you're sure you can really control it?"

Decian shrugged. "I've been practicing. You saw earlier, I can control it just fine. When I'm in that form, it's more like... a negotiation, I guess you'd say. But if I rip someone's throat out, it's going to be because they're trying to kill me—or Zuri, or Saleene, or one of the girls working here. Not because I like the sound of screaming. I assure you, I *really don't.*"

A shiver of something cold washed through Caius. He'd been... *practicing.* Decian, the emperor's bastard son, had been practicing pagan magic in the center of the Alyrion capital. The Alyrion capital, where anyone thought to possess unnatural powers was summarily beheaded or burned at the stake. He was risking death if he was so much as *seen* by the wrong person.

God.

Saleene knew about him. Zuri too, it sounded like. Could they be trusted with holding Decian's life in their hands?

"What? You look like someone just kicked your pet cat," Decian said.

With a jolt, Caius realized in quick succession that first, he was worried about Decian's safety because he still cared for him, and second, he himself had held a sword to Decian's throat and threatened to kill him less than a week ago.

"I owe you an apology," he whispered.

Decian raised an eyebrow. "For nearly slicing my throat open after I saved your sorry arse from getting skewered? Yeah, no kidding."

"I'm sorry," Caius told him. "I am truly sorry for the way I reacted." He swallowed convulsively. "On the two other occasions in my life when shapeshifters were involved, people died. And both times, my world was thrown into chaos in the aftermath."

Decian was quiet for a long moment. "A shapeshifter really killed your father?"

"Yes." Caius took a slow breath and let it out. "I was only a boy. He was sent out with two other guardsmen to kill a stag, after several people accused one of the villagers of being a shifter and using dark magic to take animal form. I snuck into the woods that day, following the three of them—thinking it was going to be some grand adventure. Instead, I got lost among the trees. I followed the sound of screaming, and I eventually found their corpses bleeding out in a clearing. The shapeshifter's, as well. Its eyes were glowing red... exactly like yours do."

Silence fell over the room.

"That explains quite a bit," Decian said eventually. "What about the other time? You said there were two occasions."

Caius thought back to a desolate beach on a barbarian island. "After I joined the military, I was deployed as part of the naval force sent to pacify the island of Eburos. I was on the beach when the Wolf Priest of Draebard led an army of wolves to repel us. My comrades were dying all around me, savaged by ravenous beasts while the villagers rained flaming arrows down on us from the clifftops. I barely escaped with my life."

"I suppose I can see why that would put a person off," Decian said.

The words sounded perfectly sincere. Caius rubbed at his eyes, feeling tired to the bone. "Deimok's hairy balls, Decian. You wouldn't know a grudge if it bit you on the arse, would you?" he asked.

Still, there was a new wariness clouding the younger man's normally open features. It broke Caius' heart to realize that he'd been the one to put it there.

"You saved my life," Decian said, with no softening of that guarded expression. "As long as you're no longer planning on running me through or slicing my throat open, we're good."

Only, they weren't. And Caius suspected they never would be—not ever again.

"If you aren't a danger to others, I'm not a danger to you," he replied, hating that he needed to qualify his answer in such a way.

"That's a matter of opinion," Decian retorted, and Caius couldn't begrudge him the sentiment.

Rather than continue down the same path, he changed the subject to something else that had been bothering him. "Why in the name of sanity were you out among the pagans the other day? The street was crawling with guards, and as far as you knew, you were a wanted fugitive from the palace."

Decian's expression darkened. "People were injured. Buildings were burning. Should I have huddled in here doing nothing?"

Yes, Caius wanted to say—but he was aware of exactly how bad that sounded, even in his own head. Before he could come up with anything better, the door opened, and two figures darkened the room's doorway.

Zuri and Saleene entered with the air of being on a mission.

"Is he coherent?" Saleene asked Decian, and Caius tried not to bristle at being spoken of as though he weren't present. Under the circumstances, it wasn't an irrational concern for her to have.

"I am," he said flatly.

"He is," Decian agreed. "As much as ever, anyway."

"Time for a serious talk, in that case." Saleene did not sound happy, and Caius hoped with something approaching desperation that there wasn't some new crisis brewing, of which he was as yet unaware.

"Someone bring me a chamberpot, and then you can talk as much as you like," he said. He tried and failed to roll into a sitting position while Decian pulled the pot out from behind a discreet screen in the corner. "Fuck," he muttered, taken by surprise at the complete lack of strength in his limbs.

Saleene gave a put-upon sigh and wrestled him into an upright position, seated on the edge of the bed. "Let's have you, then," she snapped. "It's not like I haven't handled your cock a hundred times before."

"Just don't expect payment this time," Caius retorted, fumbling at his laces.

When he was done, Saleene helped him tie his laces and shoved a cup of water into his hands. "Here, drink this. Maybe if you drink enough water, we can do this again sometime."

Caius drank the water, aware that his body had suffered one too many insults over the past few weeks... and that he would likely need to be on his feet soon regardless. When he was finished, Zuri dragged a chair over and sat down in it, facing him.

"Time for that talk," she began. "We have a rather large problem, and as of now, we're making it your problem as well."

He met her dark gaze. "From where I'm sitting, we have several problems. But go on."

"The pagans are being blamed for the attack on the Council," she said. "But pagans were not behind it."

Caius frowned at her. "Who the hell else would be behind it?" he asked, only for something unpleasant to occur to him. "And how could you possibly know whether they were or weren't, unless..."

He trailed off.

Saleene was watching him closely. "Ah. Now he's getting it."

"Unless you're part of the underground," he realized, thinking of all the pointed remarks Saleene had made to him over the past several months... of the way Zuri had defended the pagans' right to live and worship as they wished. "Oh, *bloody*..."

But Saleene wasn't interested in his cursing. "Yes, congratulations—you've uncovered our secret, how clever of you. Now, are you going to help us, or are you going to try something stupid, even though you're too damned weak to so much as sit up without help?"

All the ways in which this situation was potentially disastrous flashed through Caius' mind in an instant. Decian stood against the wall with his arms folded tight across his chest, looking like someone who expected the worst possible reaction from him. Of course, Caius had brought that expectation on himself, by the simple virtue of having exhibited the worst possible reaction the *last* time he'd been confronted by something he'd have been happier not knowing.

He took a deep breath and slotted this newest revelation into the growing puzzle that was the last few weeks. Putting aside any emotional response he might have had to finding out two people he considered friends were actually nominal enemies of the state, he focused on the most important question instead.

"How certain are you that your lot wasn't behind the attack?"

"Very," Zuri said.

He shook his head. "It could have been a splinter group, couldn't it?

She scoffed. "An operation like that? Come now, Legatus. That attack took planning. And it wasn't planned by any of ours."

"Planning… not to mention state-of-the-art crossbows if the reports are accurate," Saleene said. "Do you think we've got an armory full of cutting-edge weapons squirreled away somewhere?"

He met her gaze squarely. "I don't know. Do you?"

She let out a derisive snort. "There's probably someone hoarding pitchforks and pointed sticks in a shed somewhere. Beyond that, no. Our only power is in numbers."

"And occasionally, arson," Caius shot back.

Saleene's lips tightened in anger. "People are getting desperate. Being threatened with execution by burning—not to mention being randomly massacred in the street—will have that effect, oddly enough."

Zuri raised a quelling hand, and Saleene broke off, turning away with a frustrated noise.

"Do we have your support when it comes to finding out what really happened?" Zuri asked. "Because it's not what they're saying happened."

Caius lifted a hand to pinch the bridge of his nose, feeling infinitely weary. "I did mention the part where someone high up in the imperial hierarchy is actively trying to kill me, yes? As potential allies go, let's just say you could do better."

"I'm not sure we could right now," Decian said quietly.

With a sigh, Caius let his hand fall back to the bed. "I'm already well aware that something is rotten in the heart of the empire." The admission sickened him, even though he'd known it for years now. "I can't say if all of it is connected or not, but... there are a couple of loose threads that might be pulled to see what unravels."

God. If only he weren't so tired.

Saleene gave him a cautious nod. "Well, it seems you have surprised me, Caius. I won't lie—I argued against telling you any of this."

"Too bad I argued harder in favor," Zuri retorted, visibly smug. "So, what are these threads of which you speak?"

Caius leaned forward, resting his elbows on his knees and ignoring the way his various injuries twinged a warning. "One of them will have to wait until I can stand up without falling over," he said. "The other requires getting a message to the commander of the palace guard in secret." He raised a challenging eyebrow at Saleene. "Assuming you trust me not to betray you and bring the wrath of the magistrate down on your heads."

"I do trust you, even if it pains me," Saleene said evenly. "You are many things, Caius—but disloyal isn't one of them."

"The commander of the palace guard," Decian echoed. "That's the tribuni who helped you limp out of the forest after you were shot during the royal hunt, yes?"

"Yes, that's him," Caius said. "His name's Aelio, and he'll have the most useful information regarding the attack on the Council."

"He seemed like a good man," Decian said.

"He is," Caius agreed, painfully aware that Decian only held that opinion because Aelio had lent Caius a shoulder for support when he'd had a crossbow bolt sticking out of his leg. That simplistic and trusting worldview terrified him. By rights, Decian should doubt the intentions of every single person he came across—Caius included. But instead, he still assumed the best of everyone, and Caius couldn't help the sick certainty that continuing to do so would get him killed one day.

He forced himself to focus on the matter at hand. "Do you have someone you can trust to deliver a message discreetly?"

"Yes, we can arrange that," Zuri said.

"Good," Caius said. "In that case, I'll need to set up a private meeting, away from prying eyes in the palace."

TWELVE

By the time the meeting was scheduled the following day, Caius was at least strong enough to hobble downstairs to one of the back rooms in the Cock's Crow. After the discussion with Saleene and Zuri, Decian had made himself scarce without a word. Since then, Caius' simple meals of broth, bread, and water had mostly been delivered by one of the young prostitutes, whose face he vaguely recognized from previous visits. Once, it had been Saleene's pretty boy, Tullio.

Decian's absence was a painful disappointment and an even more painful relief. Out of this whole ungodly mess, Caius found that his greatest regrets revolved around the young man who'd brought him a glimpse of such happiness before everything went to shit.

How ironic that if he'd only sent Decian home as normal on that fateful night after he'd been followed, instead of trying to smuggle him out of the city, he might have been perfectly safe. Meanwhile, Caius could have died in blissful ignorance at the end of an assassin's sword or Tertia's poison, unaware of the terrifying beast hidden inside his kind and genial lover.

He set the thoughts aside as the door opened, admitting Aelio.

"Still alive, then?" the tribuni greeted. "Glad to see that."

"It was touch and go for a bit, admittedly," Caius replied. "But that's not why I asked you to come. I've been talking to some people, and I need to get your take on the attack in the Council chamber. How is the investigation faring?"

Aelio's expression soured. "Ah, yes. The investigation. Funny you should ask…"

Caius regarded him. "I don't suppose you've come across evidence that the assassins were not, in fact, pagans?"

The tribuni looked up at him sharply. "What makes you say that?"

"Like I said," Caius told him, "I've been talking to people."

Aelio leaned forward, resting his elbows on the table. "I don't suppose you'd care to introduce me to these *people*, so I could have a little chat with them?"

"Not at the moment, I'm afraid," Caius replied implacably. "Regardless, that sounded very much like a *yes*. So, tell me."

Blowing out a sharp breath, Aelio flopped back in his chair. "Here's the thing. You remember that pair with the crossbows after the royal hunt?"

Caius lifted an eyebrow, still sporting the half-healed scars from that particular fight. "It does ring a vague bell, yes."

Aelio snorted. "Right. But do you recall the men themselves—how they were dressed, how they were armed?"

He frowned. "Dark clothing, masked faces. Very expensive crossbows." The connection solidified in his mind, and he paused, taken aback. "*Oh.*"

"*Oh*, indeed," Aelio echoed. "How very odd that the assassins killed in the Council chamber were also masked, wearing dark clothing, and wielding crossbows. It's quite a coincidence, don't you think?"

Now it was Caius' turn to sit back in his chair rather abruptly. "Good god. The men who've been shadowing me inside the imperial quarter have also been dressed in black. And... the ones that attacked us in the alley. Just as well that group wasn't armed with ranged weapons, or the fight would have been over very quickly."

Aelio nodded thoughtfully, offering a half-shrug. "If they were pincering you from both ends, crossbows wouldn't have been the right choice of weapon for the situation," he pointed out. "Silly of them—but they probably assumed throwing six armed and mounted men at you would be sufficient to get the job done."

"It would have been," Caius muttered without thinking, "if not for Decian."

Aelio sobered, still believing Decian to be dead. "That was a real tragedy, all right—the poor sod. My condolences, by the way—I know you and he were friendly."

Caius nodded vaguely and steered the conversation onward. "So, since I think we can safely say that random pagans aren't trying to kill me, that still leaves the question of who's pulling the strings."

"You told me you suspected Kaeto of being behind the attempts on your life," Aelio said. "If we're working on the assumption that the attack on the Council is related..."

Caius thought about that for a moment, but something about it niggled. "Yes, but what's the endgame, if so? Kaeto has been arguing for the moderates to prevail in the Church. This attack certainly hasn't furthered those aims."

Aelio's brow creased in thought. "No, it hasn't, has it?" He took a deep breath and let it out slowly. "There's something else you should probably know, since I doubt you will have heard the news yet."

Caius' braced himself for another revelation that he didn't have the time or energy to deal with. "That doesn't sound good."

"The empress has been implicated in a plot."

A groan of disgust rumbled up from Caius' chest. "Of course she fucking has."

"She's been credibly accused of attempting to bribe one of the surviving Council members to change his vote," Aelio continued.

"Wonderful," Caius muttered. "Do you know which direction the alleged bribe was supposed to sway him?"

"According to the rumors, she was attempting to get one of the moderates to throw his lot in with the *burn everyone* group." Aelio rubbed at his forehead. "I'm just tossing this out there for consideration—but is there any possibility *she's* the one behind all of this? It would at least be consistent."

Caius thought back to his two meetings with the woman. "Would it, though? Why engage me to spy for her if she was simultaneously trying to kill me? Besides, what would she gain from seeing the pagans hunted down and executed… or from seeing the capital descend into chaos?"

Aelio threw up his hands and slapped them palm-down on the table. "I don't *know*. None of it makes sense. Nothing hangs together under closer scrutiny." He scrubbed at his face with both hands and let them fall again. "*Fuck.*"

Caius tried to recall if he'd ever heard the man curse before. "I'll admit your idea seems plausible when viewed from certain angles, but it doesn't feel like the right answer."

With a vague gesture of agreement, Aelio sighed. "All right. What about the other two?"

"Proclus and Bruccias, you mean?" Caius asked. "It sounds like an unusual degree of initiative for Bruccias, and as for Proclus—"

"Neither of us would trust Proclus to lace up his own tunic after a night of drinking," Aelio finished. "Much less mastermind a political plot."

"Conversations like this are so much more straightforward now that we're both saying the quiet parts out loud," Caius observed.

Aelio let out a silent huff that might have been amusement under different circumstances. "There's also the small matter of Proclus already being the heir apparent. Even if he weren't a drunkard, he has no need to plot. The power's already his for the taking."

"Another good point," Caius said.

"We're really rather thoroughly screwed right now, aren't we?" Aelio replied.

"Welcome to my life," Caius told him.

An hour later, after seeing Aelio off with a mutual promise to keep in touch, Caius was back in his room, relaying the news he'd learned to Saleene, Zuri, and Decian. The latter stood hovering just inside the doorway with the air of someone who would have preferred not to be there at all.

Under the circumstances, Caius couldn't really blame him.

"So, you believe us now, when we say this isn't the doing of anyone in the underground," Saleene summarized. "But you still have no idea who *is* behind it. I suppose that's progress of a sort."

"And whoever it is, it's the same person—or people—who want you dead," Decian added. "That seems like kind of an important point, doesn't it?"

Zuri tapped her chin. "If there's one thing that ties all of these goals together, it's destabilization, correct?"

Caius couldn't stop a derisive snort from escaping. "While that's flattering, I think you vastly overestimate the impact if I were to shuffle off this mortal coil. There are maybe half a dozen people in the capital who'd miss me for a day or two before shrugging and moving on with their lives."

From the corner of his eye, he could have sworn Decian gave a slight flinch.

"That will be thanks to your winning personality, I suspect," Saleene told him, without a hint of irony. "Now, the question becomes, what are we to do with this information? I'm going to assume your pet tribuni won't be able to convince the powers-that-be of the pagans' innocence in this attack?"

Caius—who'd been asking himself that very question since Aelio left—didn't have a good answer. "Anyone willing to be swayed by facts would at least have to consider it. Unfortunately, it depends very much on who's behind the plot in the first place. No doubt they'll be doing their best to obfuscate and muddy the waters however they can." He paused. "That said, I don't doubt Aelio will do his best to get to the truth."

"Unless the same person decides to poison him, too," Saleene added.

"Yes," Caius agreed heavily. "Just so."

Decian jerked his head sharply toward the door, and Caius frowned at him.

"What—" he began, only to be cut off when Decian abruptly raised a hand for silence. A sudden suspicion entered his mind, and he cleared his throat, continuing in a more normal tone. "What we need to do now is consider our next steps."

He made a circular *'come on, say something normal'* gesture toward Saleene and Zuri, who shared a concerned glance.

"Well... I don't see that there's much to be done," Saleene replied slowly, her sharp gaze falling on Decian as he moved silently into position beside the closed door and yanked it open without warning.

The male figure crouched on the other side surged to his feet, but Decian was already moving. Caius silently cursed his own physical incapacity as Decian tackled the eavesdropper before he could run. A flash of high cheekbones and attractive, boyish features was enough to identify the man, confirmed when Saleene exclaimed, "Tullio!" in a voice caught halfway between outrage and betrayal.

"*Get off!*" Tullio snarled, kicking and struggling to get free.

Caius itched with the need to stride across the room and grab the youth by the scruff, knowing he was still so weak that any interference on his part would be more of a hindrance than a help. He needn't have worried, though— Decian had spent years in a prison full of dangerous men, and Caius had already seen his skill at wrestling firsthand. In seconds, he had Tullio wrapped in a grappling hold, pinned facedown on the ground.

Saleene and Zuri were already halfway to the door. Caius rose on shaky feet to join them.

"Listening at doors, laaitie?" Zuri said in disbelief. "This is how you repay us for taking you in and giving you a job?"

"Get him on his feet." Saleene sounded absolutely livid.

The potential implications of this alarming discovery flashed through Caius' head in an instant. "This is no coincidence," he said. "We need to search his room and question him. If he's working for the same person who's after me…"

"I'm way ahead of you," Saleene said grimly. "Zuri, get ropes or cuffs to bind him. It's a fucking brothel — there ought to be something useful within easy reach."

Zuri hurried out and returned barely a minute later with a pair of honest-to-god iron shackles. Caius… really didn't want to know. Decian eyed the ugly metal cuffs and chains with distaste, probably because he'd had personal experience with such things in a way that the rest of them hadn't. Nevertheless, he manhandled Tullio into the room and held him restrained while Zuri snapped the shackles around his wrists and locked them, running the chain through the frame of the heavy bed.

"This isn't what it looks like," Tullio said, a bit desperately.

"For your sake, you'd better hope it's not," Saleene retorted. "Decian, will you stay here with Zuri and keep an eye on him?"

Decian gave a tight nod. Saleene's eyes found Caius, and he joined her as she headed down the hallway.

"This is potentially very bad," Caius said, already out of breath.

"I fucking *know that*, thanks," Saleene snapped at him. She gestured at an unremarkable door. "Here. This is his room."

Caius gave the small space a calculating onceover after they entered, before concluding that there were very few places to hide anything. By unspoken agreement, he headed for the plain wooden trunk in the corner while Saleene tore the blankets and sheets off the bed and started feeling around under the straw-filled mattress.

The trunk contained nothing but clothing and a few unremarkable toiletry items. In less than a minute, however, Saleene made a noise of triumph and pulled a cloth bag free of the bedding. It clinked as she tugged it free. Loosening the drawstring holding it closed, she dumped the contents onto the leather mattress cover.

An impressive pile of silver coins poured out, glinting in the room's low light.

THIRTEEN

"I'm guessing you don't pay your employees quite this well," Caius said, eyeing the pile of money. "In which case, we need to go scare some answers out of your pretty boy before Decian loses his temper and rips his throat out."

"Or his soul," Saleene muttered.

Caius did a double take, surprised to discover that she knew about that particular piece of nightmare fodder. "Or that, yes."

"I won't lie—when it comes to ripping that little shit to pieces, Decian might have to stand in line to get his turn," she said, gray eyes blazing with outrage. "I'm going to plant my foot so far up his arse that he'll choke on it. God only knows how long he's been spying on us."

"Let's find out what he knows first, shall we?" Caius suggested. "But, as I said, this doesn't smell like a coincidence."

"Are you suggesting that he was planted to spy on *you*, simply because you come here sometimes to get your cock sucked?" Saleene demanded.

"Either that, or he was planted here because someone knows you're neck-deep in the pagan protests," Caius shot back. "I'm not entirely certain which option I like the least."

Saleene made a noise of angry frustration and marched out of the room, spine stiff with outrage. Caius gathered the damning pile of coins back into the cloth bag and picked it up, following her. He returned to find a tense standoff, with Tullio looking every inch a trapped animal, while the other three glared daggers at him.

Girding himself, Caius strode to the bed and used his slight advantage of height to gaze down at the younger man. He tossed the bag of coins onto the bedside table with a heavy, metallic clink.

"Right. This is the part where you tell us who you're spying for, and what information they're after," he said calmly, not allowing a single hint of weakness to color his tone.

Tullio sneered. "Old man, you can barely walk without falling over. I'm not afraid of you."

"Well," Caius said, grabbing him by the hair and kicking the boy's leg out from under him so he collapsed onto his knees with a yelp, "I never did get the impression you were all that smart."

Decian made a choked noise that sounded suspiciously like a stifled snort of amusement.

Saleene crouched in front of Tullio, whose wrists jerked helplessly against the chains looped through the bed frame as Caius fisted his dark hair, holding him in place. "Tell us what we want to know," she said, "or so help me, I'll gut you myself."

"I don't know what you're talking about," he said, rather unconvincingly. "I'm not a spy!"

Saleene turned to Zuri. "Right. Go find me a knife, will you? Make sure it's a dull one. Those are so much more painful."

Tullio's eyes grew very wide, but Zuri only shook her head. "No need. I'll save you some time." She glanced at Caius. "Keep him on the floor for me, will you?"

Caius gave her a terse nod, tightening his grip on Tullio's wavy locks. Zuri shot the lad a truly disconcerting smile and crouched on his other side, out of range of any potential flailing limbs.

On the far side of the room, Decian appeared more than a little uncomfortable with the proceedings. He spoke up in a tentative tone. "What are you going to do to—"

Tullio's high-pitched cry of pain as Zuri grabbed him by the balls and twisted cut him off, mid-question. Decian and Caius winced in unison.

"I didn't hear anything, I swear!" Tullio yelped, trying and failing to squirm out of Caius' grip.

Zuri twisted harder until he howled.

Decian had the look of a man whose testicles were trying to climb into his abdominal cavity and hide. "Is this likely to bring everyone in the building running to see what's wrong?" he asked.

"It won't exactly be the first time a man has been reduced to screaming and begging in this brothel," Saleene said without a hint of sympathy. "But if you like, go stand outside and tell anyone who shows up that the situation is under control."

Decian nodded quickly and escaped through the door, closing it behind him.

When he was gone, Caius turned his attention back to the squealing captive. "Let's try this again," he said. "Who are you working for? Who paid you those silver pieces?"

"Just a man!" Tullio gasped, once Zuri loosened her grip. "I don't know who he is!" She gave a warning squeeze, and his voice crept up in pitch. "He didn't give his name! He just told me a time and a place to meet and pass on anything I'd heard!"

Caius had to swallow a snarl of frustration. "I'm getting sick to fucking death of mysterious middlemen with no names."

"He said I didn't need to know who he was, only that I'd be paid!" Tullio said, the words tumbling over each other in their haste.

Caius yanked his hair sharply. "What kind of information did he want? What kind of information did you give him?"

Zuri's fist clenched, and Tullio let out a choked noise as he tried to double over, only to be prevented by Caius' grip on him. "Just... information about people who come here," he squeaked. "Names, and times. And anything else that seemed odd, all right?"

Odd, like a refugee from the palace showing up bloodied and half-naked, then ending up with a job the next day... or an imperial advisor staggering in and collapsing from poison.

"So, you've told him about Decian?" Caius pressed. "About me?"

"Y-yes," Tullio stammered. "Well, yes and no. I told him you're a customer, but I haven't met with him since you showed up here and passed out on the doorstep."

That was something, at least. He shared a grim look with Saleene and swallowed the next question he wanted to ask—*do they know Decian is a shapeshifter?* Asking would be as good as telling him if he didn't already know, and after that, the only option would be to kill the lad. Caius... was not strictly opposed to that option, but he suspected Saleene would be, even as angry as she was right now.

With luck, Decian hadn't been foolish enough to practice shifting where anyone might walk in and see him—especially here in the brothel. When he'd changed form to make a point, the first time Caius had regained consciousness, the door had been closed and the hell-beast hadn't made any noise. There had been no snarling or growling that would have given away the presence of an animal in the room. Though they had spoken about it... used the word.

Shapeshifter.

Regardless, it was a moot point as long as Tullio hadn't met with his puppet master since before Caius' arrival. Also, Caius would have expected the lad to be a lot more flustered by Decian jumping on him and wrestling him to the ground if he knew Decian could turn into a ravenous, unearthly hound.

"What about us?" Saleene asked, jerking her chin to indicate Zuri. "Did you pass on any salacious tidbits about your employers?"

Tullio bared his teeth at her. "I told him you're really a man. But anyone who gets a glance at you could tell that much. It's not exactly a secret."

Saleene gave a derisive snort. "Oh, dear. Forgive me while I weep tears of betrayal. My fragile self-image may never recover."

"Bet he would have *loved* to know that you're pagan sympathizers, though," the lad muttered, sullen.

"No doubt," Caius agreed. "Which implies you've only just learned that part. Good." He glanced at the others. "Do you want to try and get anything else out of him?"

"No, I think that covers it," Saleene said.

"I know some people who can make certain he ends up on a ship headed very far away from here," Zuri suggested.

"Or I could kill him and be done with it," Caius retorted, so they would know the offer was at least on the table.

Tullio blanched, but Saleene only gave Caius a hard look. "I'm not murdering the boy just because he's a backstabbing sack of shit, Caius. Zuri, gag him and have your people pick him up an hour before dawn. I want him gone as soon as possible—we have enough problems as it is."

"Wait, I—" Tullio began, but Zuri grabbed a rag from the table and stuffed it in his mouth, cutting him off.

Caius waited until she had it tied into place around his head before releasing his fist from the lad's hair. "We need to talk somewhere that we can be confident of no eavesdroppers," he told them.

Saleene's lips pressed into a thin line. "If I've got more than one spy in this house, 'cross' isn't going to *begin* to describe my mood." She gestured them out of the room. "Come on. That one's not going anywhere with his wrists shackled to a bed frame."

They exited to find Decian waiting for them. He peered inside before Saleene closed and locked the door, presumably to confirm that Tullio was, in fact, still alive.

"He'll be going on a long ocean trip down the coast, that's all," Saleene assured him. "And, no, that's not a euphemism."

Zuri led the way to Saleene's private office. They squeezed inside, avoiding the ubiquitous ledgers and rolls of vellum covering most of the available surfaces. Saleene closed the door, though not without a cautious look along the hallway first.

"Well," Zuri said. "This is certainly a clusterfuck."

Caius didn't mince words. "You need to find someplace to lie low. Get yourselves a safe bolthole, and get your employees away from here, as well."

Zuri frowned at him. "As reactions go, that sounds a little extreme."

But Caius shook his head. "Listen. If they were after information about me, they've already proven they're willing to attack the people around me, like Tertia and her daughters. If they were after information about your ties to the pagan underground, that's even worse. They're assassinating people, Zuri. They're massacring citizens in the street. If a dozen armed city guardsmen force their way into this building and start leveling accusations of treason or magic or both, what do you think is going to happen?"

He saw the words hit home. Saw Zuri's rich brown complexion take on a gray cast.

"But that's—" she began, only to cut herself off. Her eyes flew to meet her partner's.

Saleene had remained silent as they spoke, her expression grim. "He's right," she said. "Tullio is going to miss his next meeting with his paymaster. And when he does, at the very least, they're likely to send someone to find out what happened to him. It could be another spy, but it could just as easily be a unit of armed men, as Caius said. These people aren't constrained by the law… not that the law has ever been much protection for our sort."

"Do you have anyplace to go?" Decian asked quietly.

Saleene directed a tight smile at him. "Believe it or not, we won't be the first in the underground who've needed to disappear for a bit. There are plans and locations set up for such contingencies. And don't worry, Decian. We'll make room for you there." Her gray gaze swung to Caius. "You, as well—even if I'm still fantasizing about thumping you on the head."

"I suspect you'll need to form an orderly queue and wait your turn," Caius told her, carefully not looking at Decian. "Thank you for the offer, but I think it's past time for me to beard the lion in its den."

"What's that supposed to mean?" Decian asked warily.

"An innocent woman's daughters are being held hostage," he said, "after I expressly assured her that there wasn't any danger. If I can find the daughters, I might also find the next link in this chain made up of men with no names. Though even if that weren't the case, it would still be my responsibility to get them to safety if I'm able to do so."

Decian stared at him for a long moment. "What—you're just going to saunter up to this secret hideout with your sword in your hand and ask them nicely to let Tertia's daughters go?"

"No," Caius said patiently.

"Despite having no idea where they're actually being held?" Decian plowed on.

"No," Caius said again.

But Decian was on a roll. "And then there's the small matter that you couldn't even sit up without assistance yesterday..."

"*Decian.*" Caius waited until he was certain Decian wasn't going to keep talking over him. "No, I'm not going to limp up to the front door, fresh from my sick bed. In fact, I intend to rest for a few more hours first—after which I'll return to the imperial quarter, talk to Tertia, come up with a workable strategy, and implement it."

"How very martial of you," Saleene drawled. "One might almost think you had a history with such things."

"One might," he agreed. "And believe it or not, once upon a time, I was even *good* at strategy."

Decian appeared unconvinced, but he held his peace as Saleene scrubbed a hand over her face.

Zuri still looked a bit ill. "If we're really doing this," she said, "it will take some time to make sure all of the girls have a place to go where no one will think to search for them. Tullio surely must have passed on the names of all the people who work here to his contact. We can't just send them back to their families—someone might go looking for them there."

Saleene flopped down in the heavy chair behind her desk. "We'll need to make sure they have enough money to get by for a few weeks. Gods. This is going to empty out the coffers faster than the emperor's tax man."

"Better poor and alive than dead or imprisoned, haartlam," Zuri said. "But yes, this is going to take some doing."

FOURTEEN

Saleene gave a heavy sigh. "All right, then. While you're arranging for our little traitor to go on a long trip, can you also track down Licinius and let him know we'll need access to a safehouse?"

"I'm on it," Zuri said. "Don't get into trouble while I'm gone."

From the corner of his eye, Caius saw Decian glance away with a faint flush coloring his cheeks when Zuri pressed a brief, filthy kiss to Saleene's lips before slipping away. Saleene glanced after her with worried eyes before turning back to Caius.

"I need to call the girls together and let them know what's going on." She turned to Decian next. "Do me a favor and find this one another room where he can rest tonight, since his old one has a disloyal piece of garbage chained to the bed at the moment. Afterward, you can help me pack up the ledgers and other important documents in here."

"Erm..." Decian gave the explosion of books and sheaves a look of mild trepidation before glancing at Caius. "Right. Come on then. You might as well use my cot since it looks like I won't be getting anywhere near it tonight."

"Smart man," Saleene said.

Caius swallowed his own sense of trepidation at the prospect of being alone with Decian. He was painfully aware that there were more important things than his monumental fuck-up in first letting Decian get too close, and then turning on him. Yet, somehow, even now it was deceptively easy to forget about the presence of the unnatural beast lurking beneath the younger man's uncomplicated exterior.

He followed Decian out of the office, down the stairs, and through the main receiving room to a small storage area off the hallway running behind it. Inside, a simple cot had been set up, along with a wooden box for a makeshift table.

"Home, sweet home," Decian said. "Try not to roll over in your sleep, or you'll fall off. Ask me how I know."

"At least the mattress won't be too soft," Caius replied unthinkingly, only to curse himself for a fool the moment the words passed his lips.

There was no world in which joking about the bed they'd once shared was an appropriate response to being alone with his former lover. Decian was a shapeshifter. Caius had held a blade to his throat with a shaking hand, a hairsbreadth from killing him.

"Can I ask you something?" Decian's voice was flat.

Dread settled heavily in Caius' throat, even as he said, "Of course."

"You thought I was good enough to fuck. Did it never occur to you that it might be a smart idea to tell me I was the emperor's bastard, and not some random nobleman's? Because that seems like it would have been relevant information for me to have."

Caius sat down rather abruptly on the cot, only to curse the sudden weakness in his knees since it meant that Decian now loomed over him rather than standing face to face.

"You were safer not knowing," he managed. "I couldn't see any way in which that knowledge would make your life better."

"And that was your decision to make, was it?" Decian asked, his tone deceptively mild.

The sickening awareness of having failed Decian in this as well as everything else settled heavily across his shoulders. "Probably not," he said. "What would you have done with the information if you'd known?"

"Nothing," Decian said, with an unaccustomed hint of bitterness. "I would have done nothing with the information, because what the hell am I *supposed* to do with that?" He made an abrupt, frustrated gesture with one hand and whirled away, pacing across the small space. "Or maybe I would have left Amarius when I had the chance, like you kept saying I should. I don't know."

Caius' heart ached for the circumstances that had defined their ill-fated relationship, ever since their first inauspicious meeting. Distantly, he wondered if there existed some time and place where they could have just... *been together*, without the swirling undercurrents of the wider world dragging them down into darkness.

"I'm sorry," he said, not entirely sure whether he was apologizing for withholding his knowledge of Decian's parentage, or for the disaster that was everything else surrounding them.

Decian stood at the door with his back to Caius, and scrubbed a hand roughly over his short, black hair.

"All I ever asked for," he began, not turning around. "All I ever wanted was to be left alone to *live my fucking life*. Why is that such an unreasonable desire? I don't care about religion... I don't care about the gods-damned imperial succession. I just want a life someplace safe and quiet, not chained up in a cell, and preferably not starving in the street."

"It's not an unreasonable desire, Decian," Caius said, his heart giving a sharp twinge as his idle dreams of fleeing to some fictional rural paradise together slid across his memory. He swallowed. "You can still get away from here. Go someplace far away and start over."

"Like Tullio, you mean?" Decian asked pointedly.

Caius shook his head. "No. Go anyplace. Go to Utrea. Go to Kulawi, or Eburos. No one has to know wha—" He caught himself an instant too late, wincing. "*Who* you are."

"Right." Decian's shoulders were a tight line as he crossed his arms defensively. "Go live with the barbarians, because they won't care that I'm a shifter."

Exactly, Caius thought, but it was clear the sentiment wasn't welcome.

"You'd be safe there," he said instead.

"Maybe I would," Decian replied, his tense posture not relaxing. "Maybe I *will* go."

"Have you never thought of trying to find your mother?" Caius asked.

"Of course I have," Decian snapped at him. "But how do you find a single woman in the whole of the world? Maybe she went back to Kulawi after I was thrown in prison. Maybe she didn't. Maybe she went somewhere else."

"There are ways," Caius said, wondering if he'd survive long enough that he could start quietly asking after the emperor's former Kulawi mistress. Perhaps this was something he could do for Decian if they both made it through whatever was to come—some small way to make up for the harm he'd caused with his very presence in Decian's life. He resolved to quietly put out some feelers, just as soon as he could do so without bringing more danger down on them.

"I should leave you to get some rest," Decian said abruptly, and left the room, closing the door behind him.

Afterward, Caius sat staring after him in the stuffy, windowless little storage area for a very long time, before he finally lay back on the cot with a sigh and let exhaustion take him.

⁂

The sound of the door opening woke him many hours later. Caius swung into a sitting position as Saleene entered, and he was pleased to find that some of the strength had returned to his battered limbs after the uninterrupted rest.

"You look better," she observed, eyeing him up and down. "At least someone in this house is getting their beauty sleep."

"Are things organized for you to get everyone out of here?" Caius asked.

"Nearly," Saleene said. "And I suppose, since you're already in a position to ruin us, you might as well know that there's a passage leading down to the catacombs in the basement of the building that backs up to this one. We'll be leaving through the underground tunnels and emerging elsewhere in the city. To anyone watching the brothel, we'll appear to have vanished like smoke."

He nodded. "Good. And Tullio?"

Saleene's lips twisted in distaste. "Gone on a nice, long sea voyage toward the Eastern lands."

It was as good an outcome as he could have hoped for, under the circumstances.

"In that case, I should leave now for the imperial quarter," he said.

A new figure darkened the doorway. "You're just going to walk up to the gate, wave hello, and say 'hey, it turns out I'm not dead yet'?" Decian asked, sounding skeptical.

"I hadn't intended to mention the not being dead part, but otherwise, yes," Caius told him.

"After which, you'll hatch your daring plan to rescue the damsels in distress?" Decian pressed.

"I prefer plans that are less daring and more practical," Caius replied.

Decian shot him a look that was one part incredulous and two parts disbelieving. "No offense, but that hasn't been my experience since meeting you."

"I haven't exactly been at my best," Caius said tightly. "Fortunately, you can leave the strategizing to me, since you'll be safely hidden away with Saleene and Zuri—which is as it should be."

A muscle in Decian's jaw ticked. "No."

Caius stared at him. "*No,* what?"

"No, you're not traipsing back into the palace alone when someone is actively trying to kill you," Decian said.

"*Decian…*" Saleene began warningly.

He sent her a look of frustration. "You said I could walk out that door at any time. Has that changed?"

She looked between them, her lips pressing into a thin line of frustration. "You're both idiots," she said, biting off the words. "Work out your relationship bullshit without me, but don't take too long about it. We leave for the safehouse in an hour."

With that, she brushed past Decian and left.

Caius watched her go, feeling somewhat at sea. No doubt Tullio would be able to empathize. Meanwhile, Decian's stubborn jaw was set as though for a fight.

"Go be safe," Caius told him, consciously modulating his voice to something less gruff. "Or as safe as you can be until you're able to get far away from here. Tertia's daughters are my responsibility, not yours."

Decian wore an expression every bit as frustrated as Saleene's had been. "You just don't get it, do you? I *liked* Tertia. She was kind to me. It's not a matter of whose responsibility it is that her daughters were kidnapped—though from where I'm standing, I'd say it was the responsibility of the kidnappers and whoever paid them to do it." He waved a hand, brushing away the tangent. "The point is this. All that matters now is getting them back. And since you're short on allies, the more help you can get with that, the better the chances of success, yes?"

Caius sighed, wondering for the hundredth time how someone who'd lived the life Decian had lived could possibly have ended up with such a straightforward, uncomplicated soul. "Decian, you're an escaped prisoner—one who briefly managed to hide in plain sight in the palace as the master of hounds. And now, everyone there thinks you're dead, killed by brigands in a backstreet alley."

There was a short pause. Then, "Did you tell Pip I'd been killed?"

Caius closed his eyes, remembering his brief trip to the kennels on the morning after the attack that had torn everything apart.

"No," he said. "Lying to him about it seemed cruel. Besides, he already knew the truth about you—or parts of it, anyway. He'd proved himself trustworthy. And... I told him to take over your position with the hounds, just as you wished."

Decian let out a slow breath. "Well, thank you for that much, at least."

He wasn't entirely sure what to say in response to that, so he plowed forward. "The point is, there's no plausible way to get you back into the imperial quarter when you're supposedly dead. Too many of the guards know your face."

"Don't be such a fool," Decian said. "Of course there's a way."

Caius bristled.

Before he could draw breath to speak, Decian continued. "The city's becoming a dangerous place with all the recent unrest, right? I mean, think about it. You've already been attacked twice. Surely, no one could blame you for purchasing a big, intimidating mastiff for protection."

FIFTEEN

Caius stared unblinkingly at Decian for the space of several heartbeats. "Are you insane?" he asked eventually.

"No. Are you?" Decian shot back. "You're the one talking about bearding the lion in its den—and no offense, but your last few clashes with these people haven't gone very well."

"All the more reason for you to stay out of it," Caius told him, not able to deny the accusation without blatantly lying.

"I already tried to ask you this once, so let me put it more bluntly," Decian said. "Are you more worried about saving Tertia's daughters, or are you more worried about restoring your tarnished honor by barging in like a one-man army and getting yourself killed? Because if you get killed, I assume that means the daughters will get killed, too. And that doesn't help anyone."

Caius felt his teeth clench. "You seem to have a very poor opinion of my competence as a tactician."

"It's certainly not being improved by your stubborn insistence on refusing help when it's fucking well offered to you," Decian flared.

His own temper rose to match. "You also seem to have a weak grasp of what constitutes *help*."

"Hmm, yes," Decian replied. "A huge black hound that can tear people's souls out. How could that *possibly* come in useful during a battle?"

"Do you even know what you are?" Caius snapped, hating the trickle of fear that snaked down his spine like icy water at the memory of watching that terrifying hell-beast in action.

Decian's aggressive body language relented a bit. "I do now. Zuri recognized it. I'm a rhitsaaru."

Caius made himself take a deep breath and step back. "I don't know that word."

"It's Kulawi. A creature that serves the gods by shepherding tainted souls to the underworld."

So, a hellhound, Caius thought.

"And yes," Decian continued, calmer now. "I expect I'm about as thrilled as you are to discover the underworld is a real place. As if this life wasn't bad enough..."

Caius didn't think he was in any condition to contend with the philosophical and religious aspects of this mess directly, so he didn't. "And you're suddenly in charge of determining whose soul is tainted, and whose isn't," he said flatly, fighting nausea at the idea.

Decian's eyes slid away. "Not me. My alter. My... other form. Some souls are just rotten. But I told you — we've come to an understanding, the rhitsaaru and I. It isn't a murderer. It's only ever killed in self-defense — or in defense of others. But it's not wandering the streets at night, randomly sending bad people to the underworld for entertainment."

Caius felt a twisted urge to ask if his own soul was as rotten as the ones the hellhound had ripped out. He swallowed the impulse harshly.

"It makes no sense for you to return to the palace. That's the single most dangerous place you could possibly be," he said instead.

Decian's expression turned stony. "Do you want Tertia's daughters back safely or don't you?"

"Of course I do," Caius said — tired of this argument. Tired of all of it.

"Look me in the eye and tell me you'd have fared better in that alley if Fido hadn't come back and finished off two of your opponents," Decian insisted.

Caius opened his mouth. No words came out. He closed it again.

"*Fido?*" he asked, after an increasingly awkward stretch of silence.

Decian only shrugged.

Caius closed his eyes and breathed. "Fine. You know perfectly well that I'd be dead if you hadn't" — he paused —

"if that… *beast*… hadn't come back. Which doesn't change the fact that trying to further involve yourself in my problems would be suicidally dangerous."

"In case you've failed to notice, hanging around with Saleene and Zuri isn't exactly the safest pastime, either," Decian pointed out. "Neither is being in the capital in general, the way things have been going lately."

"There's dangerous, and then there's *dangerous*," Caius said.

"That, and I still owe Tertia for her kindness," Decian replied. "I want her daughters to be safe, just like you do. Therefore, I choose the danger because my being there might help the outcome. This is really simple logic, Caius. Don't be dense about it."

Caius thought about it objectively for a few moments.

"I must be losing my wits to even consider this," he muttered, defeated.

"Being battered and shot at and poisoned will eventually do that for you, I suppose," Decian offered. "You should go get some food before we leave—you've been sick for days."

Caius sighed and went, silently cursing himself for an idiot as he did so.

The brothel seemed oddly quiet and empty, making him think most of the girls must have already been smuggled out. Even so, he followed his nose and found a pot of thick porridge bubbling away in the common room that served as a simple kitchen, dining area, and meeting space for the brothel's employees.

He used a thick rag hanging nearby to swing the pot away from the fire so he could ladle himself a bowl. The room was otherwise unoccupied, so he sat at one end of the nearest trestle table and efficiently spooned the tasteless, steaming mush down his gullet. His stomach barely grumbled before accepting the meager offering without much drama, adding to his sense of returning vigor after his most recent brush with death.

The stiffness in his bad shoulder after so much time spent in bed was unavoidable. But he at least felt confident of his ability to walk to the livery stable, retrieve the damned mule Aelio had left him, and ride back to the imperial quarter without embarrassing himself. When it came to the idea of having a hellhound trotting at his side as he did those things, he felt considerably less confident.

He truly must be going mad.

And yet... the ice-cold military part of him that assessed outcomes and weighed risk without emotion knew full well that the creature would be a formidable weapon in a fight. Between terror at the sight of its glowing gaze and the very real threat of its powerful jaws and unearthly abilities, it might tilt the odds in their favor even if they were badly outnumbered. He just hoped Decian was right about his ability to control its murderous impulses and unnatural red eyes. Otherwise, this was likely to be a very short and ignominious rescue attempt, culminating in a public execution for witchcraft.

Footsteps preceded Zuri's entrance into the large room. "Ah. Thought I heard someone moving around in here. I've just spoken with Saleene—did you end up letting the boy join your one-man campaign against the empire?"

"He's not a boy," Caius said. "He's twenty-six."

"So, that's a yes, then?" Zuri asked. She sighed and shook her head. "Gods, you two are a pair." She rummaged in the bag she was carrying and tossed a strip of dark leather studded with small metal spikes onto the table. "Here. I assume you're smuggling him into the palace compound as a dog, since a lot of them must know his face."

Caius stared at the item with incomprehension. "What... is that?"

"It's a collar, Caius," she said. "What the fuck do you think it is? It should fit his rhitsaaru form on the last hole or two, and I know it won't accidentally choke him when he shifts back, since we normally use it on men."

He didn't ask. Didn't want to know, any more than he wanted to know about the iron shackles. "Somehow I can't imagine he's in a hurry to be collared after a decade spent in prison."

Zuri only shrugged. "Well, I expect you already tried to talk him out of coming in the first place, since you're clearly still scared shitless of him. Maybe you can use this to dissuade him."

Male pride urged him to dispute her assertion of cowardice. Truthfulness held his tongue.

"Anyway," she went on, "I'm supposed to tell you the location of the safehouse in case you need to find us later. I'm also supposed to warn you that if you lead anyone there—accidentally or by design—Saleene will personally tie you down and ensure you're exposed to every venereal disease known to humankind."

"Nice," Caius said.

Nevertheless, he listened and committed the directions to memory, before wishing her luck as she took her leave to join Saleene for their flight into the catacombs. When he was finished eating, he dumped out the remains of the porridge clinging to the pot and scrubbed it clean along with the ladle, bowl, and spoon. Then he poured water over the cooking fire to extinguish it.

Afterward, he stood staring at the spiked leather collar for several moments before reluctantly picking it up and returning to Decian's borrowed room. A sense of impending doom dogged his footsteps the entire way.

When he entered, Decian looked up, only for his gaze to fall instantly on the strip of leather and stick there. "Oh, *ha ha*. Bloody *hilarious*, that is."

Caius raised his hands in a gesture of peace. "Not my idea. Zuri gave it to me. And at this point, between the collar and the damned shackles, I may never come back to this brothel again."

Decian let out an irritable grunt and turned his attention back to the modest bag he was packing. "You'll have to carry this for me," he said, changing the subject. "It's just clothes. I'm not risking having to shift back to human, only to end up shivering naked in the street."

He was wearing a simple draped toga and nothing else—the same one he'd donned after shifting back from his canine form at Caius' bedside, when he'd first awoken from unconsciousness.

"I'd rather you didn't risk shifting at all," Caius said dryly. "Particularly on the street."

Decian shot him a look of irritation. "You know what I mean. Here." He shoved the bag at Caius, who took it. "So, are we walking, then?"

"Well, you are," Caius told him. "Aelio left me a mule at the livery down the street. It's fortunate I have no pride left at this point."

"That's where the pony is being kept, as well," Decian said. "Though I guess he's no use to me when I have four legs just like he does. Are you ready?"

No, Caius thought.

"Yes," he said aloud. "Did one of the others tell you how to find the safehouse?"

"Saleene did," Decian replied. "And then she recited a string of horrible things that she'd do to me if anyone followed me there."

"Venereal diseases," Caius suggested.

"Yes. And leeches," he agreed. "*Diseased* leeches." He paused. "Can leeches even get diseases?"

Caius shouldered the bag. He lifted the collar, holding it gingerly between his thumb and forefinger. "I can toss this in a random drawer somewhere on our way out."

Decian sighed. "No, she's right. If I'm supposed to be your new pet dog, I should look the part. Just... not too tight, if you don't mind."

The unease in Caius' gut twisted tighter. "If you're certain."

A frown creased Decian's pleasant features. "Take a breath, will you? I'm trying really hard not to be offended by the fact that you obviously expect me to leap up and rip your throat out at the first opportunity—despite the effort I've already expended to keep your irritating arse alive."

After a moment of shocked silence, Caius took an objective look at himself, aware that he was, in fact, acting like he expected calamity to erupt at the first appearance of fangs and claws.

"It's not so much that," he said slowly, "as a general sense of impending disaster. I'm honestly not trying to offend you more than I already have done."

"Fine. In that case, stop over-thinking this. People keep trying to skewer you with pointy objects, so you bought a big scary dog to dissuade them," Decian said. "That's it— that's the story. It's not complicated. So... let's just get out of here and get back to your house."

"Very well," Caius said. "I'm ready if you are."

Meanwhile, in the privacy of his own mind, he thought, *I am not remotely ready for this.*

Decian nodded. "All right, then. Saleene said to use the alley door and leave it unlocked when we go. People will notice the place is empty soon enough and start poking around. But they removed everything important or incriminating last night, so it doesn't really matter." He gave the leather strip in Caius' hand a sour glance as he unhooked the clasp at his shoulder, and muttered, "A godsdamned *collar*."

"Fido," Caius reminded him.

A scowl crossed the younger man's face as the length of cream-colored cloth slid to the ground. An instant later, reality twisted in a way Caius' eyes couldn't seem to get a proper grip on. When he blinked, a mythical Kulawi soul-ripper sat on its haunches, watching him. Or perhaps—if he could only convince himself it was the case—a very large, matte-black mastiff.

At least its eyes weren't glowing.

The... *dog* continued to stare at him unblinkingly. It took Caius a few moments to shake himself free of his state of paralysis and remember the collar.

The collar that he was supposed to buckle around the beast's neck.

"I truly have gone mad," he said under his breath, steeling himself to step forward.

SIXTEEN

Caius was a seasoned legatus of the Alyrion military. He'd charged into the maw of armies that outnumbered his own forces ten to one. He would not be afraid of a dog, simply because it had been known to rend men's souls on occasion.

He stepped toward the thing that was no longer Decian, holding the leather collar in front of him like a peace offering. "Can you understand me like this?" he asked, feeling foolish.

The dog cocked its head, its eyes falling to the strip of leather and metal. Its lip curled in clear irritation, baring a viciously sharp ivory canine. Nevertheless, it stretched its head up, baring its neck to Caius' approach.

Aware to the depths of his marrow that the words *'Here lies Caius Oppita, who tried to collar the wrong hound'* would make a spectacularly bad epitaph, he reached forward and looped the strap around the hell-beast's neck. His knuckles brushed fur that was softer than the finest velvet in the emperor's palace. Decian — or rather, the thing that lived inside him — sat unmoving, deep brown eyes pinning his.

Caius flushed, fumbling with the buckle until he managed to push the tongue through the second-to-the-last hole. Awkwardly, he hooked a couple of fingers beneath the leather to check the fit — not too tight. He grabbed the discarded toga from the floor, straightened, and took a hasty step back.

The dog rose to all fours and gave itself a vigorous, full-body shake — eminently doglike.

"I have your things," Caius said, feeling vaguely foolish as he twisted to draw attention to the bag of clothing slung over his shoulder before shoving the toga into it. "Let's go."

The animal took up a position at Caius' left heel, keeping perfect pace as he headed for the door leading from the brothel into the alley. It was oddly reminiscent of the way the royal hounds had followed Decian in perfect harmony whenever he took them out.

The hair at the back of Caius' neck and the skin all down his left side prickled with awareness. Outside, the golden light of a clear, perfect morning illuminated the Vaia Meretricia. He glanced at his animal companion, expecting it to appear alien and out of place in the daylight—a night creature, at home in the depths of shadow.

It looked like a dog.

An exceptionally large dog, to be sure, but still a dog.

Passersby gave the animal wary looks and a wide berth, as well they might. They did not, however, start screaming about pagan witchcraft or stampeding to get away. The tension in Caius' shoulders relaxed marginally. He led the way toward the livery where Aelio had taken the mule, taking note of the signs of unrest from the previous night.

Doors along a section of shops had been forced open; wooden shutters torn off their hinges. The smell of smoke hung in the air, and one building had streaks of black soot staining the facade above an open window. Caius had apparently slept through all of it.

Thankfully, the livery seemed untouched—it would have been just his luck to find it burned to the ground or all the animals stolen during the night.

"Wait here," he commanded the thing that wasn't precisely Decian, remembering the panicked reactions of the horses in the alley when the beast had appeared.

He went inside and found the owner of the livery. "Parsus, here to retrieve the mule belonging to my master, Tribuni Aelio," he said, with what he hoped was an appropriate air of servitude.

The man raised a pointed eyebrow. "Your master owes an extra six copper coins. That mule was only supposed to be here for one night."

Caius paid him without complaint. He saddled the mule and led her out into the daylight. The animal's long ears swept back at the sight of the huge hound waiting patiently outside the entrance. She balked but continued forward nervously at Caius' urging.

"This should be interesting," he muttered, gathering up the reins and swinging into the saddle.

The beast was as hard-mouthed as he remembered. Nevertheless, she settled quickly enough when the hellhound made no aggressive moves. Idly, he thought back to his gray gelding's nervous skepticism on the first few occasions Decian had handled him. He wondered how many other little oddities he'd either dismissed or failed to notice.

The hound trotted along beside him as he wended his way through the city, heading northwest toward the palace at a steady pace. Everywhere there was evidence of unrest and rioting during the night. Not even the stately government district had been spared.

As they covered the last open stretch leading to the gate of the imperial quarter, Caius wondered what sort of reaction his reappearance would garner. At the very least, he would need to move as fast as was feasible to retrieve Tertia's daughters before news of his miraculous survival reached the wrong ears. He had no doubt that whoever was behind the plot would punish the girls for their mother's failure to kill him.

The gate was already open for the day, but the guards manning it stopped him as he approached. Caius pulled the hood of his cloak back, revealing his face.

"Good morning," he said.

Surprise flickered across the head guard's features. "Legatus Oppita?"

"Yes?" he replied pleasantly.

The man, clearly taken aback, fumbled for a moment before saying, "Sir, several people in the palace have been searching for you. You've been declared missing."

"Have I?" Caius asked, as though he had no inkling of any such thing. "Well, as you can see, I'm not."

The guard's eyes fell on the hellhound first, then the mule, and finally moved back to Caius, taking in his plain servant's clothing. "That isn't your usual mount. Or... your usual attire?"

"I lost a bet," he said, deadpan. "Bit of a long story."

"And the dog?" the man asked slowly.

Caius shrugged his good shoulder. "The city is growing more dangerous by the day. I purchased the animal for protection. I'm told he's quite well trained."

Decian plopped his haunches down, pink tongue lolling as he panted in the bright sunlight. Caius had to bite the inside of his cheek as the sheer surreality of the scene hit him like a brick to the head.

"I... see, sir," said the guard. "If I might suggest, perhaps you should speak to the tribuni of the palace guard. As I said, your extended absence has caused a bit of a stir."

"Oh, I intend to," Caius assured him, as the men stepped back, opening the way for him. "Good day."

"Good day..." the guard replied, sounding decidedly off-balance after the brief exchange.

Caius could sympathize.

Thankfully, with his hood raised once more, he was able to make his way through the twisting streets to his home without anyone recognizing or accosting him. He tied the mule up with access to a water trough in case he had need of her later in the morning. No doubt there were still watchers arrayed nearby, but they were at least polite enough to keep to the shadows as he let himself in.

Taking nothing for granted, he began a quick but thorough search of the house to ensure that none of those watchers had decided to take up a post inside, as opposed to outside. As though understanding exactly what he was doing without the need for words, the hellhound headed to the opposite side of the house, poking into rooms and sniffing out corners.

They met in the airy atrium, next to the fountain. The air around the beast shimmered like a heat haze, and Decian rose from his crouch.

"No one's here but us," he said. "I can smell Tertia, you, and a bit of me. There's also a hint of the same scent on those clothes you're wearing, but it's faint."

Caius kept his eyes up and centered, ignoring the unpleasant twist in his stomach caused by the sight of the leather collar combined with Decian's nakedness. "That'll be Aelio's servant. We switched places to confuse anyone watching when I escaped into the city." He slid the bag off his shoulder and started to rummage in it for clothing. "Do you want to—"

Decian waved him off. "Don't bother. I've got nothing you haven't seen before, and I expect it'll only be for a minute or two, anyway." He sounded both tired and faintly bitter.

Caius let the toga slip from his grasp, disappearing into the bag once more. "Are you sure about that collar?" he asked, the words escaping without his conscious choice to speak them.

Head tilted, Decian regarded him for a beat. "Well—it's a bit on the nose, and I'll admit I'm irritated. But honestly, it seems to be bothering you a lot more than it's bothering me." Another pause. "Why is that, exactly?"

Caius let out a sharp breath. "You were a prisoner for years. I saw your reaction to those shackles, back at the brothel. I suppose I don't much like the idea of you being collared."

Particularly while naked and alone with me in my house, he didn't add.

"Ah." Decian appeared to digest that for a few moments. "Well, for what it's worth, they never collared prisoners. So… thanks for that, I guess—but maybe you should let me worry about my reaction to symbolic subjugation, while you worry about this masterpiece of military tactics you're supposedly working on."

"Sorry," Caius said, because apologizing seemed to be his new pastime when it came to interactions with Decian.

Decian rolled his eyes toward the ceiling, as though seeking divine patience. "Besides, the collar seems like a good way to keep any guards who see me from immediately reaching for a blade or a spear. Dogs that clearly belong to someone are much less threatening than ones wandering the streets on their own."

"True enough," Caius allowed, aware that his reaction to the whole thing was irrational. But then, when it came to Decian, he'd been making a habit of irrational reactions since the very first time they met. He regrouped, forcing himself to focus on logistics. "Have you slept?"

"Not a wink," Decian said. "I was up all night helping clear out the brothel."

Caius nodded. "I need to go see Aelio. Why don't you get some rest while I do it?"

"That sounds like a wonderful idea... assuming no one's likely to jump out and try to knock you on the head while you're alone. Are they?"

"No," Caius assured him. "For one thing, it will take a little while for word of my miraculous return to reach whoever's behind all this. And for another, they've shown a definite reluctance to resort to physical violence inside the imperial quarter. They want me dead, but not in a way that's suspicious, or could lead back to them."

Decian's expression turned grim. "So if Tertia had succeeded in killing you with poison..."

Caius' lips thinned. "I have no doubt the authorities would have immediately painted her as a rebellious slave with a grudge against me. They'd have sent her to the executioner's block shortly thereafter."

"This whole situation is sickening," Decian said flatly.

"Yes," he agreed. "It is." He let out a sigh, trying to think ahead. "Speaking of Tertia, I told her before I left to continue showing up for her regular duties, and that I'd contact her here as soon as I could. I expect to be back from meeting with Aelio before she arrives. But on the off chance I'm not, just stay quiet and stay in one of the spare bedrooms with the door closed. She'll doubtless have heard through the gossipmongers that you're dead. Given that fact, I suspect being confronted by either the ghost of a dead man or a giant black hound probably isn't the kind of shock she needs."

"Under the circumstances, I expect you're right about that," Decian agreed. "Fine—I'll just go grab a nice little doggie nap while you're gone. Hurry back and try not to piss off any more powerful people in the meantime."

"Pissing them off is the least I'll do to them once I get to the bottom of this," Caius muttered. "Sleep well. I'll be back."

SEVENTEEN

With the Amarian Council in disarray and an investigation ongoing, Caius wasn't at all sure where Aelio was likely to be found, so he went to the man's house and asked Parsus. The servant directed him to the barracks housing the imperial guard, where he was slated to meet with his city guard counterpart, Laurentin, at mid-morning.

Caius rode there on the blasted mule with his face still shadowed by the hood of his borrowed cloak, and waylaid Aelio on his way out.

"We need to talk," he murmured, tilting his head back to meet Aelio's eye.

Recognition flared in the other man's expression before it quickly turned bland. "Yes. Come inside."

Aelio turned and started back to the barracks he'd just left. Caius followed him, painfully aware that anyone shadowing him would know exactly whom he'd been talking to. The tribuni was in the thick of things now. There would be no turning back for him.

He led the way to a windowless room at the back of the building and closed the door after Caius. Aelio gestured him to a chair and took another across from him.

"May we speak freely here?" Caius asked, not mincing words.

"Yes," Aelio replied without hesitation. "I didn't expect to see you back in the imperial quarter so soon, Caius. You're looking better, at least."

"The people I spoke to you about discovered a spy in their midst," Caius told him. "It seemed wise to go our separate ways. I'm here to beg your help, Aelio. You said you took exception to anyone kidnapping old women and their families to use as hostages."

"That I did," Aelio agreed, his tone going hard.

Caius nodded. "Well, I'm about to do something about that, if I can. Since I've already compromised you merely by meeting with you… are you in?"

Aelio raised an eyebrow. "You intend to rescue the slave's daughters?"

"I do," he said.

"Do you know where they are?" Aelio asked.

"Not yet," Caius told him. "That's actually the next item on my list today. Unfortunately, my return to the palace grounds means I'll only have a short window of time before whoever wants me dead makes another attempt. I'll need to move fast."

Aelio crossed his arms and leaned back in the chair. "You mean 'we.' *We'll* need to move fast."

A deep appreciation for the man sitting across from him warmed Caius' soul. "I'd hoped you'd say that. I'll need access to a wagon with a tarpaulin to cover the bed— a goods wagon, or the like. We'll need to take it into the city. We'll also need a way to leave my dwelling without my shadows following. I have no doubt the house will be watched around the clock now that I've returned." He paused, a hint of heat rising to his face. "Oh, and I've acquired a dog."

Aelio blinked at him. "A… dog?"

"For added protection," Caius said, aware of how ridiculous that 'simple' cover story sounded. "I just didn't want it to take you by surprise. The beast might be useful." He cleared his throat, and muttered, "You'll understand when you see it."

After a moment, Aelio seemed to shake himself free of the oddness of the exchange. "I see."

Caius forged ahead. "I intend to make my move tonight. I want answers, and if I try to leave it any longer, it may be too late—for the girls, and possibly for me."

The tribuni gave a slow nod. "So, a goods wagon with a covered bed, a way to leave the imperial quarter without being followed, and a plausible story to explain everything?"

"That's about the size of it, yes," Caius agreed.

"Very well," Aelio said, because he was evidently just as insane as Caius these days. "Expect me an hour past sunset."

"Thank you." Caius rose to depart, only to hesitate as something else occurred to him. "Oh, and one more thing. That mule of yours has a mouth like forged iron. I'm leaving her here for you. Frankly, half-healed crossbow wound or not, I'd rather walk."

Aelio let out a startled bark of laughter. "I'll mention it to Parsus. I trust you'll be able to ferret out the girls' location before nightfall? Otherwise, this may be a very challenging rescue mission."

That was foremost on Caius' mind as well, but he only said, "Tertia is wilier than she seems. I'll wager she has some ideas on the subject."

"Sounds like we're both wagering on that," Aelio said dryly. "You're fortunate I'm a betting man at heart."

"I'm fortunate, indeed," Caius told him. "Until tonight, Aelio."

"Until tonight," the tribuni replied.

⚜

Caius walked back to his house, using the chance to stretch his legs and work some of the kinks out. He knew he was going to have to marshal his physical resources carefully, so soon after his recovery from a succession of injuries and illness. As he made his way through the streets, hood raised and eyes downcast, he wondered idly what it was going to take to get a few days where he could just *rest*.

Preferably, without the world trying to tear itself apart outside his window while he slept.

The hood made it damnably difficult to determine whether or not he was being followed, but he had to assume he was. With luck, anyone who'd been lurking around his home would at least be deterred from snooping inside after seeing a massive hound enter the house with him earlier.

At this point, there was little to be gained by attempting stealth. Someone had almost certainly followed him to the barracks and witnessed him going inside with

Aelio. This evening, Aelio would show up at his front door with a wagon, and that wasn't exactly the sort of thing you could hide.

Caius wished he had a better idea of the shift structure his spies were using. How often did they replace each other? Did they have a method for sending messages to their secretive employer the moment something of interest happened? Or did they report in daily with a summary of events?

Finding the answers to those questions would have required him to hire his own band of spies to watch the watchers, and it was far too late for that now. All he could do was hope that any response to his return would be too slow to interfere with tonight's plans.

He let himself in through the servants' entrance and called, "It's me."

One of the doors to the seldom-used guest rooms swung open and Decian stepped out in human form—thankfully with the toga draped over him, this time. Unfortunately, the damn thing draped over one shoulder, exposing half his chest, and only covered him to mid-thigh. Caius had to fight the magnetic pull on his gaze toward bare, sinewy arms and muscular thighs.

"How did it go?" Decian asked.

Once, the question would have been delivered in a tone both guileless and eager. Now, it was subtly guarded—the tone of someone who'd been hurt by trusted hands and had no intention of making themselves vulnerable a second time. The change made Caius feel as though some small part of him had died. His hands itched to fix what he'd broken... even though he knew such things could not be fixed.

Irrational though it had been, Caius had taken the revelation of Decian's shapeshifting ability as a personal betrayal. But in the end, he was the one who had done the true betraying.

"Aelio will be here an hour after sundown with a wagon to smuggle us into the city," he said, since perhaps *this*, at least, was something he could still make right. "We have until then to figure out where the girls are being held."

"And how do you plan to do that?" Decian asked.

It was a fair question. "I'm hoping that Tertia—"

The sound of the door to the servant's entrance rattling as someone unlocked it cut him off mid-thought. "Ah. She's here," he said. "Quickly—you're supposed to be dead. She shouldn't see you in human form."

Decian shot him a dark look, but he shrugged out of the toga and tossed it to Caius, who threw it into the guest room and closed the door. When he turned back, the hellhound stood a few paces away, its head cocked and ears pricked toward the rear entrance of the house.

Tertia bustled into view and shrieked as her eyes landed on them, dropping the basket she was carrying. It rolled onto its side, folded linens spilling onto the floor as she scrambled backward.

"Hello, Tertia," Caius said dryly.

"Legatus," she said on a gasp, one hand clutched to her heart. Her eyes fluttered between him and the giant dog, as though unsure where to land. "You're all right?"

Of course, she'd had no way of knowing whether or not he'd succumbed to the poison after limping away to hide in the city. He'd tried to put a reassuring face on things the last time he spoke to her, but—

"Yes," he said gently. "I'm mostly recovered, despite your best efforts. Apparently subjecting myself to your cooking for years has strengthened my stomach lining. Small mercies."

Beside him, the hellhound let out an irritable rumble of a growl at him. Startled, Caius revised his assessment of how much Decian could understand in this form.

In the normal course of things, Tertia would have growled at Caius herself for the slight to her cooking. This was not the normal course of things, and it occurred to him that their usual ill-tempered bantering was perhaps less than appropriate under the circumstances.

"What is that... *thing*?" Tertia asked, her eyes now firmly fixed on Decian.

"It's a dog?" Caius replied, not having intended the words to rise into the pitch of a question. He cleared his throat and tried again. "I, erm, acquired it while I was in the city. For protection."

Decian sniffed the air in Tertia's direction for a moment, and then a long pink tongue lolled out, as he began panting happily.

"You bought a dog," Tertia said slowly, before appearing to consciously relegate the revelation to her employer's growing collection of eccentricities. "It's very… big."

"I'd noticed, yes," he told her. "Now, we need to talk. Did you see anyone watching the house as you arrived?"

She took a deep breath, refocusing. "There's one watching the front entrance and one watching the back entrance."

He nodded. "That was my impression as well. I told you I'd return as soon as I could to try to get your daughters back. Well… it's time. I have an ally coming after dark with a wagon to transport us, but we need to know where they're being held."

They were standing at the edge of the open garden area, beneath the overhang that covered the walkway around the edges. Tertia shuffled forward and sat down heavily on the nearest bench, the basket of linens on the ground forgotten.

"You're going to rescue them?" she whispered hoarsely.

"I'm damned well going to try." He walked forward and would have crouched in front of her, had the half-healed wound on his leg not prevented any such thing. As it was, he ended up looming awkwardly over her. The hellhound padded up and sat down at her feet, looking up at her with its deep brown gaze.

She watched the beast for a moment, wide-eyed, but didn't cringe away in fear. When it made no aggressive moves, she reached out a tentative hand and stroked its blocky head. Her gnarled fingers trailed down one side of its velvety jowls before falling away.

Tertia tangled her hands together in her lap and looked up at Caius with hope and fear twisting her expression. "When they took us, I tried to keep track of the route while we were in the back of the wagon. But I was too frightened, and it was too confusing since I couldn't see anything."

He nodded, urging her to continue.

"When they brought me out of the building afterward, though, they made a mistake," she said. "They didn't put the hood back on until I was already outside. I saw the mountains in front of me, silhouetted in the moonlight, and the spires of the palace in the distance to my left."

"Good," Caius said, mentally mapping out the swath of the city that met those two criteria. It was a disconcertingly large swath. "That's good, Tertia. Was there anything else?"

Her sharp eyes met his and held. "The air. It smelled of rotting fish."

He sucked in a breath. "The docks."

Tertia nodded. "I couldn't go there myself to search, or send anyone else to do it, either—I'm sure they're watching me, and it's not as though I could give exact directions. But I saw the outside of the building before they tied the bag over my head. Trust me when I say I'd recognize it in an instant if I saw it again."

Caius' instincts sharpened with the promise of a real lead. "It was an abandoned building, you told me? Was it a warehouse?"

"Yes, I think so—but not one of the huge ones," she clarified. "It was two stories tall, and most of the windows were boarded up. The siding was very weathered. Some of the boards were warped."

He reached down, covering her restlessly twisting hands with one of his. "We'll find it. There are only so many mid-sized warehouses close enough to the water to stink of fish."

She looked up at him, her soft chin trembling. "You'll get them out?"

"I'll do my very best," Caius promised her.

The hound gazed at both of them, a spark of excitement kindling points of red in its deep brown eyes.

EIGHTEEN

Midday came and went while Caius painstakingly pulled every detail of the abduction that he could from Tertia's memory.

"We should all get some rest," he said, once he was confident that he had a full accounting of everything she'd seen and heard that night.

"Speak for yourself, Legatus," she retorted, with a hint of her old mettle. "If you think I'll be resting before I have my daughters back safe and sound, that poison must have permanently damaged your wits."

He didn't argue. "Fair enough. In that case, you're on guard duty. I don't think our mysterious adversaries would do something as blatant as storming the house, but I also didn't think they'd go after you. Fool me once, and so forth."

"That much, I can most certainly do," she said with relish.

Caius nodded. "I'm going to change into my own clothes first, but I'll rest in the spare bedroom." He jerked his head toward the room behind him, where Decian had been sleeping. If nothing else, that would offer an explanation as to why the bedclothes were rumpled in a room that never saw use. "Wake me if anything seems suspicious. On the off chance that anyone armed breaks in, point them toward my normal room and then get out of the way. Sneak out of the house if you can. Find Tribuni Aelio and tell him everything you told me."

Tertia gave him a solemn nod.

Feeling a bit foolish, Caius turned his attention to the hound. "You—stay with her. Protect her if it comes to that. That's your job now."

Decian—*the dog*—raised its head from its paws and held his gaze. Caius didn't have a hope of deciphering that canine expression, but the animal stayed at Tertia's side when Caius turned and headed for his room to find some clothes he could fight in.

Feeling slightly more like himself once he was no longer dressed as a servant, he collected a small arsenal of blades and secreted them about his person. Suitably armed, he grabbed his sword belt and headed into the garden again.

Tertia had staked out a seat at one of the windows, with the hellhound curled up at her feet. The shutters were closed, but the cracks around the edges were wide enough to use as a peephole. She clearly had one of the watchers in her sights, able to see him even though he wouldn't be able to see her. Caius gave a single, satisfied nod to himself.

He cleared his throat, not wanting to startle her. "I don't suppose there's any chance of some food that hasn't been poisoned?" he asked.

She snorted, a soft, self-deprecating sound. "Avoid the red wine. Everything else is fine."

"Thank you," he said. "What about you? Have you eaten?"

Tertia turned to him. "You want me to eat first? Prove it's not tainted?"

"No," he replied. "I'm genuinely asking. It's going to be a very long day. You should eat if you haven't."

She hesitated, perhaps at the idea of a slave asking an imperial legatus to fetch and carry for her. "I suppose that's true. I'll... take some bread and cheese if you're offering."

He headed into the kitchen, trying not to get lost in the memory of standing here with Decian a few days ago—eating and drinking and teasing each other as the rain pounded down on the roof. Together in their own little insulated world.

With a sigh, he pulled out cold salted meat, cheese, and a loaf of bread that probably would have been better used two days ago. He ate quickly, but cautiously—feeling out his stomach's response to the food. It still churned a bit, but the agonizing pain had faded, seemingly for good.

After washing the simple meal down with water rather than wine, he gathered a plate for Tertia and another for Deci—for *the dog*. With the plates balanced on one arm, a flagon of water held in his other hand, and an empty bowl tucked under that arm, he made his way back to the pair by the window.

Tertia took her plate with an uncertain smile of thanks. He put the other one on the floor, and the beast's ears perked up. The huge animal hefted itself to its feet and dove into the food with enthusiasm—so reminiscent of Decian's first reaction to having unlimited access to decent food that it made Caius' chest ache. He set the empty bowl nearby and dribbled water into it, then gave the rest of the flagon to Tertia.

"I'll be in the north guest room," he said quietly. "Don't hesitate to wake me."

"I will," Tertia told him. She hesitated briefly. "Thank you, Legatus."

He gave her a wan smile. "Don't thank me quite yet." With that, he turned away from the pair and trudged to the spare room, hoping for a few hours' sleep to bolster himself for the night's events.

━ ⚜ ━

Decian's scent was all over the damned sheets. Exhaustion ensured Caius dozed anyway, but every time he woke, there was no warm body next to him as his mind had insisted there must be. He rolled over and let out a quiet groan. In his forty-six years of existence, he'd shared a bed with Decian for a total of one night.

One *fucking* night.

It hadn't even been this bed, for god's sake. He couldn't afford to take comfort from the scent clinging to the linens. He couldn't afford to turn his face into the pillow and inhale, simply because the smell of sweat and spice made the tension in his shoulders ease. It was ridiculous. It wasn't fair to Decian. It wasn't fair to *him*.

Caius had been the one to put the invisible wall of distance behind Decian's warm brown gaze. After what had happened, that wall was undoubtedly permanent. It wasn't going away. He could only imagine Decian's reaction to discovering Caius had been wallowing in his scent, fantasizing about the handful of gilded days they'd spent together before everything fell apart.

He had a job to do tonight. After that, it was an open question how much longer he'd be able to dodge a never-ending string of assassination attempts masterminded by a powerful foe. He also needed to convince Decian to leave and find a way to make it stick this time. It would only take one wrong person discovering that the bastard son of Emperor Constanzus was a shapeshifter, and Decian would end up in the middle of a conflict that would make the drama surrounding the Council of Amarius look like children tussling in the market square.

He stared at the unfamiliar ceiling of the guest room. The light was growing dimmer; sunset was approaching. With an odd jolt, it occurred to him that he'd left his aging house slave alone with a beast that tore the souls from living bodies. He hadn't even given it a second thought. *Protect her,* he'd told the beast, as though assigning a soldier to a guard detail.

He thought of the stag in the forest when he was a boy. He thought about the legendary Wolf Priest of Draebard, leading an army on four legs to defend Eburos from invasion. Had some barbarian ruler ordered him to attack the Alyrion troops when they landed on the beach? Had they purposely trusted a shapeshifter with the safety of their home?

His eyes slid tightly shut and he lifted a hand to his forehead, where the beginning of a headache was trying to break through. How much of what he'd believed for the past four decades about pagans—about *shapeshifters*—was a lie? Zuri was a pagan. Decian's mother had been a pagan. And there was another thought—the emperor of Alyrios had taken a pagan mistress.

Constanzus had been the first emperor to declare Deimonism the true religion of the empire. Had he always believed that? Had he ever believed it at all? Or was it simply a politically expedient move to unify the disparate territories of Alyrios under a common faith?

The deeper he got in this mess, the more Caius was concerned that he'd built his entire life on a foundation of shifting sand. And now, the windstorms had arrived.

Knowing any further rest was a distant dream, Caius rolled into a sitting position and began to stretch his aching body with a series of simple exercises. He was fast approaching the point where he would no longer be able to bluster his way through additional physical injuries with a combination of stubbornness and desperation. However, that point wouldn't be coming tonight. He wouldn't allow it.

He could rest when he was dead — or, at the very least, when Tertia and her daughters were safe, and Decian was away from the capital.

As soon as his joints no longer felt like creaking, rusty hinges, he checked his hidden daggers, strapped on his sword belt, and emerged from the room. Tertia was still seated by the window with the hellhound at her feet, just as he had left them hours ago. They both looked up at his approach.

"I'll take over the watch," he told Tertia. "Go stretch your legs for a bit in the garden. Eat some more if you can, maybe have a small cup of wine to help you relax. Though... you might want to avoid the red."

The light was too low to tell if she flushed in response to the jab, but she pursed her lips and nodded agreement. "I told you when you ordered it that the vintage was too sweet for your tastes," she muttered. "You should've listened."

"Live and learn," Caius told her. "Oh, and would you feed the dog again while you're up?"

"As long as you can promise he won't take my hand off at the wrist while I'm doing it," she said, and Decian gave a small whine of offense.

"I think you're probably safe," Caius retorted, still surprised on some level to realize that he meant it.

Decian was the hellhound. The hellhound was Decian. Tertia was no more in danger from the beast than she was from the man, though Caius wouldn't rate the chances of anyone who tried to harm her while he was guarding her.

It had taken Decian's stubbornness to convince Caius to let him come along, but he acknowledged now that he would have been a fool to turn away the other man's help tonight. Perhaps, between Caius, Aelio, and the hellhound, they had a chance of pulling this off — assuming they could even find the right place.

He settled in the chair his house slave had abandoned. The hellhound — *Decian* — gave him a long look before trotting after Tertia in search of food. Caius turned his attention to the gap at the edge of the shutters, scanning the area across the street until he found the darker shadow amongst the shadows of a building that marked the position of one of his watchers.

Caius kept an eye on him to see if a replacement would come, or if he spoke with anyone. The man slunk further into the shadows when the lamplighter made his rounds, clearly not keen to be noticed. Tertia returned to ask if he wanted food or drink, but he declined on the grounds that he didn't want his stomach weighing him down later.

Decian appeared to be growing restless, and Caius had to remind himself that while the other man might be good in a fight, he had never been a soldier and was not in the habit of involving himself with rescue missions.

Dusk turned to full dark, and eventually the sound of cartwheels creaking and juddering over the cobbles broke the silence of the quiet street. A goods wagon, pulled by two draft horses and driven by a man wearing a hooded cloak, came to a halt near Caius' front door.

He rose and turned to the others. "It's time," he said.

NINETEEN

Aelio dismounted from the wagon and walked up to knock on the front door, bold as brass. Caius let him in with equal disregard for stealth. They were well past that point now.

"Good evening," he greeted. "We've narrowed down our destination to an abandoned two-story, mid-sized warehouse near the docks, with weathered wooden siding and the windows boarded up. Tertia saw the position of the mountains and the palace spires when they brought her outside. She'll be coming with us to identify the building. Tertia, this is Tribuni Aelio of the imperial guard. Aelio, Tertia."

"Madam," Aelio greeted, even as Tertia dropped into a low bow.

A slave's bow.

"Thank you, sir," she said, not looking up at him. "For helping."

"Please, get up," Aelio told her. "There's no need for formalities. I'm simply not prepared to accept abduction, extortion, and ongoing assassination attempts within the imperial quarter. Especially not since keeping order within the palace grounds is in my actual job description."

Tertia straightened. "Even so…"

He waved her off. "You can thank me if we're successful, Tertia. If we're not, I daresay you'll be cursing both our names before the night is over."

Caius stepped in. "We need to move fast. One more thing, though. I did warn you about the dog. He'll be coming with us."

He gestured to Decian, who stalked forward into the light of the lamp illuminating the entryway.

Aelio's eyes widened. "Good god, Caius. When you said, *'protection dog,'* I wasn't quite sure what to picture. How much did you pay for this beast?"

Caius raised a wry eyebrow. "He's cost me a fair amount so far, but I'm fairly confident he's worth it."

Aelio was still staring at the animal. "I... daresay." He visibly refocused on the task at hand. "Right. We need to move quickly. I marked two men lurking in the shadows as I approached. We should try to take them alive."

"Agreed," Caius said. "You take the one watching the front, and I'll take the one watching the servants' entrance in back. Tertia, would you be good enough to assist Aelio with a distraction? We'll need to take them both at once, or else one of them will have enough warning to escape."

"That sounds like a reasonable plan, since I suspect you know the back alleys in this area far better than I do," Aelio agreed. He turned to Tertia. "Shall we, madam?"

"Give me a slow count of one hundred to get in position," Caius said. "Then go outside and make a fuss, Tertia. Start yelling that I've gone mad or something. I'll move on the man in back as soon as I hear you."

Tertia lifted her chin and nodded. Caius beckoned Decian to follow him through the house to the back door. Once there, he said in a low voice, "Aelio can chase his man down if need be. I can't—not with this leg. I need you to circle behind him in the alley and flush him toward me. But for god's sake keep the glowing eyes under control—if we're keeping these two alive, I don't want him seeing anything more unusual than a large, aggressive dog."

Decian blinked up at him, and Caius hoped like hell he'd been right in his assessment of the creature's ability to understand speech. He opened the door, and the huge animal slipped out like a shadow, disappearing into the warren of alleys at a lope. Caius gave him a bit of a head start and stepped out of the house, drawing a dagger from his belt as he started toward the watcher's hiding place.

As expected, the man immediately retreated. Caius kept his pace leisurely until Tertia's shrill cry echoed from the street running in front of the house.

"Please! He's gone stark raving mad! I know you've been watching the house — you have to tell someone what's happening! Quickly, before he kills someone!"

Caius picked up his pace to a jog, favoring his bad leg heavily as he followed his target farther into the darkened alley, ears straining to pick up the faintest noise. From somewhere in front of him, a low snarl rumbled through the alley, followed by a deep, full-throated bark of warning.

A gasp of fear from his target accompanied more growling and barking. Caius came to a stop, listening to the running footsteps heading his way as the man fled the massive hound coming after him. He braced as the spy ran toward him, arms and legs pumping. With his dagger held in his left hand in case it should be needed, Caius cocked his right fist and drove it into the shadowy figure's jaw as he tried to shove past.

The fleeing man dropped like a sack of turnips, and Caius shook out his hand to ease the sting. A second dark shape lumbered toward him. Despite knowing intellectually that he was in no danger, he couldn't help the way his heart rate picked up in alarm.

"Deimok's balls, but you're a terrifying bastard in the dark," he muttered, as the dog came to a halt and bent down to snuffle at the man's unmoving form. "And... now I've just realized that I'm in no condition to drag or carry this piece of offal back to the house." He sighed. "Watch him for me while I go get Aelio, please?"

The hellhound huffed, but he dropped down to sit next to the unconscious man. Caius made his way to the main road, where he found Aelio in a discussion with a flustered housewife across the street whose name Caius probably should know but didn't.

"My apologies, madam," Aelio was saying, in exactly the same respectful tone he'd used with Tertia earlier. "We suspect this man and his compatriot of planning robberies in the area. Since I was already here, it seemed prudent to catch them straight away, rather than waiting for more guardsmen to arrive."

The woman's hands fluttered at her chest and neck. "Oh, my goodness! I'm *sure* I've seen them lurking around here before, but my husband kept insisting it was just my imagination. How dreadful!"

"Definitely not your imagination," Aelio assured her. "We'll take them inside Legatus Oppita's house and restrain them until the authorities arrive."

The woman's hand landed on Aelio's chest as she simpered up at him. "I'm so glad you were here to catch these miscreants. Just imagine if they'd decided to break in while I was here alone…"

Caius narrowly prevented himself from rolling his eyes, even as Aelio took a calculated step back, breaking the contact.

"Think nothing of it," the tribuni said, the picture of professionalism. "I'm pleased I could be of help."

Caius cleared his throat as he approached. "Madam," he greeted stiffly.

Her manner abruptly cooled. "Legatus," she replied. "Such a shocking business. I suppose I should leave you both to it. Thank you again for your *heroic* actions, Tribuni."

She disappeared into her home, the front door closing behind her. Caius raised an eyebrow at Aelio.

"Making new friends?" he asked dryly.

Tertia emerged from the shadows. "I've seen street corner harlots that were subtler," she muttered. "Did you get the other one, Legatus?"

Caius nodded. "He's out cold, but I'm afraid I won't be lugging any unconscious bodies around on my own at the moment."

"Just as well," Aelio said. "I wasn't looking forward to dragging this one inside by myself, either." He jerked his chin toward the crumpled form lying at the mouth of the alley next to his unwanted admirer's home.

"Right. Let's get this one off the street first." Caius moved to the downed man and hunched over awkwardly to grab his feet, while Aelio got his shoulders. "Tertia, would you get the door, please?"

They took him to one of the unused guest bedrooms and dropped him on the bed, placing him on his side so he wouldn't choke to death if he vomited while regaining consciousness.

"I'm sure I've got some rope somewhere in this house—but I've no idea where," Caius admitted. "Oddly enough, binding unconscious men hasn't really come up recently."

"There's some in the wagon," Aelio assured him, and went to get it.

They efficiently tied up the prisoner and went to get the other one from the alley, with Tertia carrying a lamp to light the way. Aelio gave a noticeable flinch when the light reflected off the dog's eyes in the dark, but the momentary glow was just the normal flash of yellow-green from an animal's eyes at night—not an unearthly red.

"Good god above, that beast is *massive*," the tribuni muttered, before following Caius' lead and retrieving the second lookout.

Caius was huffing and puffing, cursing his debilitated state by the time they got the man inside and tied him up in another of the spare bedrooms. He made a quick but thorough check of both rooms to ensure there were no blades or sharp edges that might be used to saw through rope, while Aelio double-checked the security of the bindings.

They couldn't afford to wait around for either of the men to regain consciousness so they could be interrogated. However, it was worth holding onto them, since they might have useful information that could be extracted once they returned from the mission to free Tertia's girls. Or, alternately, Caius and his merry band would be killed during the attempt, and these two poor sods would be left here until they died of thirst. Frankly, he couldn't work up much guilt over the possibility.

"Time to go," he told the others. "Tertia, lock up the back. I'll get the front."

Caius and Aelio both rechecked their weapons. The motley group piled into the wagon, hopefully unseen by anyone else who might be inclined to immediately run off and report what was happening to Kaeto — or whoever sat at the center of this tangled web of intrigue.

Aelio drew the tarp over them in the wagon bed, leaving Caius huddled in the suffocating dark with his nervous house slave and a preternatural shapeshifter in the form of a gigantic hellhound. He had only enough time to contemplate the state of his life before Aelio climbed into the driver's seat and clucked to the horses, sending them lurching into motion.

Tertia's uneven breathing could be heard over the creaking of the wheels and the clatter of hooves on cobbles. She hadn't uttered a single complaint, but it occurred to Caius rather abruptly that the last time she'd been hauled out of the imperial quarter in the back of a goods wagon, it had been with a bag tied over her head after being abducted from her bed in the middle of the night.

Such things didn't come naturally to him, but he reached out anyway, fumbling for her arm in the dark. "Tertia," he said. "It's only for a few minutes. Once we're away from the imperial gate, you'll go sit up front with Aelio so you can look for the right building."

"I know that," she snapped… but one of her gnarled hands covered his where it rested on her forearm, holding tight.

A quiet whine broke through the muffled confines beneath the tarpaulin, and Decian wriggled around until the hellhound's blocky head nudged beneath Tertia's arm.

She let out an unsteady breath. "Some attack dog you've got here. He's more like an attention-starved pup."

But Caius felt her wrap her bony arm over Decian's sleek-muscled shoulders, her breathing growing less frantic as the wagon bumped and juddered along the road.

After a bit, the wagon rolled to a halt, for which he was grateful. Unsurprisingly, the jolting ride combined with the stifling atmosphere and disorienting darkness beneath the tarpaulin wasn't doing wonders for his still sensitive stomach. Voices reached them as Aelio spoke with the guards at the gate.

"You taking up a new job as a tradesman, sir?"

"Mind your tongue, guardsman. I may be stuck playing delivery boy tonight, but I can still have you dredging latrine pits tomorrow. The city guard needs fresh supplies for their extra patrols. In case you hadn't noticed, we're short-staffed — so, since I was headed there anyway, I agreed to take them."

"Of course, sir. Sorry, sir."

Again, Caius reflected that having an unimpeachable reputation came in handy when you were engaged in subterfuge. The clanking sound of the portcullis being raised preceded the wagon jerking into motion again, and soon they were out of the imperial quarter.

Aelio drove them a little distance into the city before stopping on a quiet side road and pulling the cover off. Caius eased into a sitting position, his stiff joints and muscles protesting the movement. Next to him, Tertia sucked in a deep breath of fresh air. The dog popped its head up, looking around with interest.

"It's a bit more comfortable up here, madam," Aelio said, climbing up and offering his hand.

"Enough with the 'madam,' if you please," Tertia said, accepting his help as she climbed to the front of the vehicle. "You can use my name like everyone else, *Tribuni*."

"As you like," Aelio replied easily. "Now, let's start by getting to the port area, and you can tell me when the relative position of the palace spires and the mountains looks right."

Freed from the need for concealment, Caius took up a position sitting against the tarp, crumpled in the front left corner of the wagon bed. Decian flopped down on his belly on the other side of the wagon, resting his head on his front paws. Unwavering brown eyes watched Caius fixedly. It was damned disconcerting, to be honest, but it wasn't as though he could scold his 'dog' for staring at him — not without coming across as even more unhinged than the others already thought him.

He narrowed his gaze, suddenly finding himself locked in a childish game of 'who blinks first' with a fucking *shapeshifter*, and not entirely sure how he got there.

As it turned out, hellhounds could go a very long time without blinking. Caius eventually broke eye contact in favor of watching the city go past. The area they were driving through was uncharacteristically quiet for the time of evening. In the distance, however, he could make out an orange-red glow that spoke of something large on fire.

Aelio was grim and quiet as he directed the horses along the narrow streets. Tertia watched the faraway flames for a few moments before asking, "Riots again?"

"More every night," Aelio replied in a monotone.

They drove north through residential and business districts, until their surroundings began to grow seamier. The area of the city surrounding the docks saw staggering amounts of wealth pass through it, but very little money stayed to make a home there. Warehouses didn't have to be pretty; they only needed to keep the rain off the merchandise they housed until it could be passed on to the buyer. Fish markets didn't have to entice their clientele; they only needed to sell fish.

And, indeed, as he pondered this, Decian raised his head and sniffed the air. Not long after, the first hints of brine and decaying sea creatures tickled Caius' nose.

"There's no moon tonight to see the mountains properly," Tertia said, "but I think we must be close."

"At least the streets around here are mostly on a grid," Caius called up to them. "I think we're just going to have to run through the area on a standard search pattern."

"Agreed," said Aelio.

He began to do exactly that, driving the length of a road before turning at an intersection and going for one block, then turning again to drive the road running parallel to the first. Caius kept an eye out for a warehouse with boarded windows and weathered wood siding, aware that Aelio and Tertia were doing the same.

An hour passed like that, and another. They passed occasional carts laden with crates from whatever trade ship had most recently docked, but those were few and far between. On the occasions when the buildings surrounding them didn't block the view, Caius could see that the fires in the distance were growing larger.

He tore his attention away from the half-seen destruction, and back to searching the surrounding facades. Still, the sense of failure—that he somehow wasn't doing enough to stop this slow slide into chaos—ate at him. He glanced at Decian, only to find the hound watching him with a look that surely could not be one of understanding.

Before he could convince himself that he was being ridiculous, Tertia raised her finger toward a building ahead of them and hissed, "*That's it!*" from the driver's seat.

TWENTY

"Don't point," Aelio muttered. "You'll draw attention."

Immediately, Tertia lowered her hand to her lap. "I'm sure that's the place," she said, excitement and fear swirling together in her voice.

Caius craned to the side to get a look. A moment later, he let out a snort. "Even if you hadn't recognized it, the guards outside the door are a bit of a giveaway."

"Only two of them," Aelio observed. "That's something, at least."

"There might be more inside," Caius said. "Take the next crossroad. We'll tie up the wagon somewhere out of the way and reconnoiter the building perimeter on foot. If there are additional exits—or additional guards posted in the back—I want to know about it before we tackle those two."

"A solid plan." Aelio took the next turning, a block before they would have reached the not-so-abandoned warehouse with its armed sentries.

Even in such a rundown area of the city, the lamplighters had done their job. Aelio pulled the team to a halt in the circle of light beneath a lamppost and set the wagon brake before dismounting. He tied the nearest horse to the pole, then came back to offer Tertia a hand down from the driver's seat.

Caius eased his battered body out of the wagon bed, silently cursing crossbows, mounted assassins, and poison. Decian leapt lightly down beside him. Aelio gave Caius a brief once-over and met his eyes frankly.

"At the risk of giving offense, I can probably move faster and more quietly than you right now—so I volunteer to do a reconnaissance sweep of the building's back and sides while you stay here to guard the others," said the tribuni.

"No offense taken," Caius told him wryly. "They'd probably hear my damned joints creaking a block away."

Aelio nodded. "I'll scout any additional entrances and see if there are any unobstructed views of the inside—windows that weren't properly boarded up, or what have you. Back shortly."

He disappeared around the corner, and Caius turned to Tertia. "Your daughters are here, and still alive. They wouldn't bother with guards otherwise."

Tertia gave him a tight nod. "I know. I just want this to be over, Legatus."

He looked at her evenly. "We haven't talked about afterward, and we need to."

She swallowed, her wrinkled throat bobbing. "You're going to send me away."

An unexpected heaviness settled in his chest. "I can see no other way to keep you and your daughters from further harm, Tertia. Not when I don't even have proof yet of who's behind all this."

His house slave's complexion had grown pale, but she didn't dispute his words. "I understand," she said. "If you're able to get Ennia and Helvii out safely, that will be more than I could have hoped for. As long as I have them—as long as we're together—we'll survive somehow."

Caius didn't have the heart to point out that the girls' safe return was hardly a foregone conclusion. There were too many variables here that he couldn't control, making the entire plan a form of madness. However, it went without saying that the girls' chances were basically nonexistent once word of Tertia's failure to kill him reached the wrong ears. A poor rescue plan was at least better than certain death.

They waited in silence for Aelio to return. Decian's ears pricked several minutes later, and the tribuni appeared shortly thereafter, jogging up to join them.

"The only other entrance is unguarded, but it's also nailed shut," he reported. "There are several windows where the boards have gaps and are partially rotted, but trying to break through them to gain entrance would make enough noise to bring everyone in the area running."

"Were you able to see inside? Did you see the girls?" Caius asked, aware of Tertia leaning forward in anticipation of the answer.

"Yes and no." Aelio shook his head in frustration. "I could see that there were lamps lit inside the warehouse, but it's a good-sized building and I wasn't able to see anything useful through the gaps."

Caius sighed, resigned. "Looks like we're staging a frontal assault and going in blind, then."

"For what it's worth, I'd be shocked if this place is swarming with men," Aelio said. "This is, at best, a side note for whoever is masterminding things. To be honest, I'll be surprised if there are more than one or two guards inside with the girls."

Caius concurred, but he only said, "Let's hope you're right."

Aelio looked to Tertia, his brow furrowing. "It would probably be safer for you to stay here with the wagon, but—"

"I'm coming along," Tertia said, cutting him off.

Aelio nodded as though he'd been expecting that. "There's an alley running along the west side of the building where you can stay out of sight until we've secured the place. One of the windows on that side has several gaps where it's boarded up, so you'll be able to hear what's going on inside."

"By which he means, if one of us yells '*run*,' you fucking run," Caius told her sternly. He looked at Decian. "You'll guard her. Keep her safe if anything goes wrong."

He ignored the odd looks the others gave him, holding the hound's gaze as it blinked up at him. Satisfied, he took a deep breath and squared his shoulders. "Let's do this."

Aelio led the way to the next block and over, heading into the dark gap between two buildings on the street that backed up to the warehouse. Caius herded Tertia and Decian in after him, before taking up the rear. The four moved mostly silently, their stealth betrayed only by the soft sound of Tertia's uneven breathing.

They crossed a larger alley — not quite wide enough to be called a road, but large enough that a cart or wagon might pass as long as it didn't meet anyone coming from the other direction. This, Caius gathered, was the alley that would have served the rear entrance of the warehouse when it was in use.

Aelio continued to guide them along the side of the building until Caius could make out the glow of street lamps ahead — the road at the front of the building, where the guards were stationed. Next to them, slivers of faint light escaped through the gaps of a badly boarded window. Aelio used the pale illumination coming from inside the building to lift his hand and call for a halt.

Caius joined him in the light and turned, placing a hand on Tertia's shoulder. He lifted his other hand to place a finger over his lips in a gesture for silence. Then, he pointed at her, and at the ground. *Stay here.*

She nodded her understanding, tight-lipped.

He moved his gaze to the hound. Decian's eyes reflected the escaping light — luminous, but not unnatural. The beast lowered its haunches to sit at Tertia's side, guarding her as he had requested.

Caius gave Tertia's bony shoulder a final, reassuring squeeze and stepped back, drawing his sword with a hiss of steel. He locked eyes with Aelio, and they moved in unison toward the front of the building.

Aelio called a halt at the corner of the structure, just out of the line of sight of the guards. The pair plastered themselves close against the wall, and Aelio ducked his head out just far enough to get a glance at the front door and confirm that the guards were still there. He retreated into the shadows and nodded at Caius. Still two men; still stationed in the same place as before.

The tribuni pointed to his own chest, then toward the two guards. He pointed at Caius, made a halting, palm-out gesture, and flashed five fingers twice in quick succession. *I'll engage both of them,* the gestures said. *Give me a count of ten before you join the fray and try to take them by surprise.*

It wasn't a terrible strategy under the circumstances — especially given Caius' current physical limitations. As soon as either one of them broke cover, they'd be seen. Better for them if the guards initially thought they were only under attack by a single assailant. Aelio was an experienced soldier. He'd be able to hold two men at bay long enough to draw them into the fight and keep them firmly focused on him. At that point, Caius could sneak up and attempt to jump one of them from behind.

He dipped his chin in agreement with the plan and adjusted his right-handed grip on the sword. With his left hand, he drew one of his many concealed daggers. This fight needed to be quick—even with the sleep he'd gotten earlier, his endurance was still likely to be complete shit. Aelio met his eyes and counted down on his fingers in the poor light.

Three... two... one... now.

The younger man sprang from the mouth of the alley at a dead run, bearing down on the guards stationed some twenty or thirty paces away at the door. Caius remained hidden in the shadows and relied on his ears, resisting the urge to peer around the corner and watch.

"You there—halt!" called one of the guards.

The running footsteps didn't falter as Caius counted down steadily from ten. Steel clashed, and someone let out a heavy grunt. Aelio didn't speak, letting his blade convey the message instead.

Caius reached the end of his countdown and risked a glance at the fight. Aelio was trading blows with both men, giving ground as he did in an attempt to draw them away from the alley as Caius emerged. He kept close to the wall, moving as smoothly and silently as he could with a barely healed crossbow wound in one thigh.

The guards were competent fighters. More than competent, which might end up being a serious issue. He was within a few steps of the nearest one when Aelio flinched and cursed as a blade slashed at his upper arm—not, thankfully, his sword arm. At the same instant, the guard who'd struck him turned just enough to see Caius in the corner of his eye and cried a warning.

Instead of striking unprotected flesh, Caius' blade scraped against a hasty parry as his target spun to face him. In the next heartbeat, he was engaged with a fighter far too well trained to be guarding an abandoned warehouse holding relatively low-value hostages. His weakened muscles burned with effort as he traded a flurry of blows with his opponent. Aelio, meanwhile, appeared to be an alarmingly even match for his attacker — especially now that he was protecting a wounded arm.

Caius spun and managed to drive a knee into his opponent's gut. The man staggered back, but he recovered almost as quickly from receiving the blow as Caius had from landing it.

"Fuck!" the guard cursed. His voice rose to a bellow as he charged toward Caius like an angry bull. "Geord! We're under attack! Kill the two bitches and get out here to help!"

TWENTY-ONE

In the alley, Decian rose to all four feet as the sound of blades clashing echoed through the air. His heightened rhitsaaru senses captured the overwhelming scent of Tertia's terror that something would go wrong, combined with breathless excitement that it might instead go right. He could make out fainter traces of multiple people inside the building, in addition to the lingering sweat-and-steel scents of Caius and Aelio in the alley.

He'd tracked the quiet sounds as the two men made their way to the mouth of the alley and paused there, waiting. Then, the sound of one man running. It was Aelio—the footsteps were too regular to be Caius with his slowly healing limp. Steel met steel in the open street, and within seconds, Caius' familiar gait left the alley at a slower pace.

Grunts, cursing, weapons impacting, and then…

"Geord! We're under attack! Kill the two bitches and get out here to help!"

Tertia sucked in a hissing breath. In the next instant, she was clawing at the half-rotted boards nailed across the window where they were standing, muttering a litany of *"Oh, no… no you don't, damn you—"* as her gnarled hands tugged and strained against the weathered, splintering wood.

Decian gave the situation only a moment's consideration before he shouldered her away from the window with his blocky body. She stumbled a few steps before catching herself against the wall.

"What are you doing?" she pleaded, pushing away and righting herself. "You have to let me—"

But Decian was already backing up to the far side of the alley. Muscles coiled, he launched himself forward from powerful haunches. One stride… two… and he leapt, putting all of the rhitsaaru's considerable strength behind it. His body twisted in midair, his left shoulder impacting the rotten boards across the window. They splintered beneath the assault, sharp edges scraping along his hide. He landed gracelessly among broken bits of wood and scrambled upright, ears pricked.

The sound of movement came from deeper in the echoing building. He gathered himself and charged toward it, eyes adjusting to the relative brightness of lamplight after the darkness of the alley.

Ahead, a man holding a dagger loomed over two girls huddled on the floor. He held the closer one roughly by the hair as she shrieked and clawed at his arm with manacle-bound hands.

"Stop struggling if you want this to be quick, girl," the man growled.

Decian lunged across the distance still separating them. He saw the moment the man registered the movement. Saw his eyes go wide with shock in the instant before thirteen stone of angry shapeshifter plowed into him and bore him to the ground. Decian clamped his jaws around the arm holding the knife. Freed, the girl scrabbled backward as much as her shackles would allow, the two sisters clinging desperately to each other.

The man Decian held gibbered in fear, trying fruitlessly to kick and punch at him in an attempt to free himself. The putrescent smell of his sadism and utter lack of human empathy hung around him like an aura. The scent of it enraged the rhitsaaru.

The human part of Decian was aware, on some level, of what was about to happen. Distantly, he wondered if he should be trying to do something to stop it. Yet… he'd seen the man about to slice open the throats of two innocent, chained girls. He'd seen the bruises on their faces… the way they'd cowered from their would-be murderer in terror.

The rhitsaaru's spirit form lunged forward and grabbed the guard's soul in its teeth. It ripped the insubstantial wisp of life from its moorings and shook it like a terrier with a rat before flinging it into the darkness where it belonged. The man's physical body slumped; its spark extinguished. He let it drop to the ground, where it lay unmoving.

Satisfied, he looked up at the girls, both of whom smelled sweet and uncomplicated beneath the metallic scent of fear. Only then did he realize that his eyes were burning with the intensity that signaled an unearthly red glow. The pair scrambled backward until their shoulders hit the wall behind them and started to scream.

Appalled by their obvious terror, the human part of Decian floundered for some way to reassure them that they were safe... that they weren't about to meet the same fate the guard just had. A moment later, despite not truly having intended it, he found himself crouched naked and human next to the corpse of the guard he'd just killed.

"Oh," he said, feeling the blood rushing to his cheeks. "Erm. Hello. Sorry. That probably hasn't helped much, has it?"

From the way they kept shrieking and clinging to each other, it definitely hadn't.

"Helvii! Ennia!" Tertia's breathless voice had him whipping his head around to find the old woman rushing toward them faster than Decian would have thought she could move. She stumbled to a halt as her gaze caught on him and lit with recognition. "Wh-what?"

Decian sighed. "Bit of a long story. Not dead, obviously. Hello."

He lifted a hand and gave her a weak wave of greeting. She blinked once before tearing her eyes away from the naked and mysteriously resurrected master of hounds in favor of examining her daughters for injury.

At least the girls had stopped screaming.

"Mother!" the one on the right cried, chains clanking as she extended her arms toward Tertia.

Tertia let out a sob of relief and crashed to her knees between the two young women, wrapping them up in an embrace. Decian averted his eyes as the three wept in each other's arms. Idly, he wondered if he could sneak in close enough to grab one of the threadbare blankets lying on the ground without setting off a new round of hysterics.

A loud crash sounded from the front of the building, followed by a second, and a third. It sounded very much like a locked door being kicked in. Since the guards out front would presumably have a less destructive means of entrance to the building, Decian figured it must be Caius and Aelio making the racket. Well... probably Aelio, considering the state of Caius' leg. And his shoulder. And his arm.

He briefly considered the merits of shifting back into animal form, only to decide that it would probably make things worse rather than better at this point. Instead, he took advantage of the distraction to seize the nearest blanket—one of the few creature comforts the girls had been given, from the looks of it. While it hadn't exactly been designed for use as a toga, he was able to wrap it around his waist and over one shoulder, tying the ends together in a way that might have lacked elegance, but at least covered all the embarrassing bits.

No sooner had he done so than Caius and Aelio charged around the corner, swords drawn and murder in their eyes. They slid to a halt upon registering the scene before them. As Tertia had done, Aelio froze and executed an almost comical double take upon recognizing Decian.

"What the *hell*?" the tribuni asked.

After having seen several of Caius' spur-of-the-moment strategies firsthand, Decian would not have chosen him as the best option to come up with an impromptu cover story. Unfortunately, there was no one else for the job.

"Ah," Caius said. "I... may have been a bit economical with the truth when it came to Decian's survival after the attack on us." His gaze landed heavily on Decian. "Though I can say with complete honesty that I didn't expect to see him here tonight."

Decian shot him a flat, unamused look.

"What about the dog?" Aelio asked slowly.

One of the girls lifted a shaky finger to point at him. "It was him! He changed—"

Tertia cut her off with a hand on her arm, speaking over her. "He showed up and the dog ran off. Maybe not such an impressive guard animal after all—eh, Legatus?"

"I'll have a word with the trainer," Caius said grimly.

Aelio was looking between them as though he thought they might all be mad. After a moment, he appeared to shake off his musings in favor of turning to the two girls and their mother. "Are any of you injured?"

"They've been beaten." From Tertia's tone, it was just as well the guard lying near Decian's feet was already dead.

"We'll be all right," said the smaller of the girls. "But what about you, Mama? Your arm is bleeding."

Tertia looked at her arm in surprise, then gave a dismissive shake of the head. "Must have scraped it on the broken boards when I was crawling through the window. I daresay I'll have splinters in my arse, as well."

Aelio nodded. "In that case, we should get the injured guards off the street. You'll be all right here for a few more minutes?"

"Yes, of course," Tertia said. "Decian, are there any keys on that man's belt?"

Decian, who hadn't thought to check, crouched and began rummaging around the dead man's clothing. The other two left to drag the injured guards inside.

"Yes!" Decian exclaimed, unhooking a heavy iron ring and lifting it triumphantly. Most of the keys were large, obviously meant for doors or gates. Two smaller ones nestled among the others, however—but when he started forward to see if they fit the girls' shackles, they cringed away from him. He froze, then took a step back.

Tertia grumbled, hauling herself to her feet to take the key ring from him. Decian let her.

For the first time, the possible implications of his slip began to truly penetrate through the heady buzz of battle and a successful conclusion. The authorities in Alyrios killed shapeshifters. They burned them. They beheaded them. And the two girls chained to the wall had seen him shift. He might have helped save their lives, but they were still terrified of him.

The older of the two shot him a furtive glance as Tertia fumbled with the keys, trying to release the metal cuffs.

"Mother," she began. "That man—he's a shapeshifter. He killed the guard…"

"Hush," Tertia said harshly, tugging one of the iron shackles free and tossing it aside before moving to the next one. "*That man* saved your lives. You will not breathe a word of what you saw."

Decian held his breath, waiting.

"Yes, Mama," said the younger sister. After a tense moment, the older sister nodded her agreement as well.

The others returned, Aelio dragging his unconscious opponent by the ankles. Caius' prisoner was on his feet, at least until Caius shoved him onto the ground in a heap and held him there at sword point. Freed now, the girls scrambled upright and backed away, putting space between themselves and their former abusers.

"Which one of you is in charge?" Caius demanded, his sword point hovering over the conscious man's heart.

The guard clenched his jaw, saying nothing. Aelio came over to join them, staring down at the prisoner coldly.

Caius' blade slid down to rest over the man's groin instead. "Shall I ask you again?"

"I am." The guard spit out the words like a curse.

"Well, that's convenient, at least," Caius said conversationally. "Decian, would you take the women outside, please? We'll meet you back at the wagon in a few minutes."

Remembering the sound of screams and begging emanating from a dark alley, Decian swallowed his nausea and glanced at Tertia and her daughters. "Trust me… you're not going to want to be here for the next part. Come on. We'll try for a door this time, rather than a boarded-up window."

He waited for Tertia to gather up her girls and herd them toward the front of the building, giving Caius a long look before joining them. One of the wide double doors was twisted on its hinges, hanging half-open at an angle. Decian forced it further open and led them outside. He looked both ways cautiously, only to find the street deserted.

They didn't make it all the way back to the wagon before the screaming started.

The girls flinched at the tortured sound.

"Will they kill him?" the younger daughter asked.

"I'm not sure," Decian said. "Probably."

"Good," spat the older one.

They backtracked through the alley and onto the next street over, where the wagon team stood patiently tied to the lamppost.

Decian let out a long, slow breath. "What will you do now?" he asked. "You can't go back to the palace any more than I can, Tertia. Not after this."

"I don't know yet," Tertia said. "We'll have to leave the city. We might have been forced out in fear of our lives, but in the magistrate's eyes, we'll still be escaped slaves."

He nodded, sick to death of contemplating the way the ruling classes played games with the lives of common people. Buying and selling them. Decreeing who would live and who would die.

"What about you, Decian?" Tertia asked. "Does Caius know you're a shapeshifter?"

TWENTY-TWO

Decian closed his eyes, weary beyond belief of all of this. After a moment, he opened them again. "Caius? Yes. He knows."

The look she gave him was not without compassion. "That's good. I'm glad he does." She hugged her daughters to her sides. "Thank you, Decian. Thank you for saving my girls' lives back there." She took a deep breath. "When those men captured us and forced me to use the poison, I thought I'd been buried in a hole so deep I'd never see the light of day again."

The younger daughter looked up at her, stricken. "You didn't really poison anyone, did you? Say you didn't, Mama!"

"Oh, I most certainly did," Tertia replied heavily. "And yet he's inside that building right now, carving up one of the men who hurt you, from the sound of things."

"Caius masterminded this whole rescue," Decian added, suddenly struck by what that fact said about the gruff, foul-tempered ex-soldier he'd been sleeping with up until not so long ago.

Tertia let out a harsh breath that sounded like a laugh, but probably wasn't. "He promised me he would. He was lying on his back, half-dead, and I'd just confessed what I'd done to him. I told him they were holding both of my girls hostage; that they'd threatened to kill them if I didn't kill him. *Leave it to me,* he said... and damned if he didn't come through in the end."

She took a step away from her daughters and scraped a shaky hand down her face.

"Will you be all right?" Decian asked quietly. "Starting over, I mean?"

He knew the feeling of staring into an empty future that loomed ahead of you like a void. He'd been doing quite a bit of that lately, in fact. How different it had been, back when that nebulous future meant a new life as master of hounds, sharing a bed with a grumpy bear of a man who looked at Decian like he'd hung the stars in the sky. How different now with a bleak future ahead, as a nameless fugitive in some distant city with no friends or acquaintances.

"We'll have to be, won't we?" Tertia said. "We'll make it through somehow, as long as we're together."

The daughters looked at their mother, expressions full of both love and trepidation. Would the girls be leaving friends behind? Sweethearts? All for an uncertain future with no money and few prospects…

An idea came to Decian, fully formed. Before he could open his mouth to speak it, movement from the alley across the road caught his eye. He stiffened reflexively, but it was only Aelio. Caius trudged behind him—exhaustion clear in his slumped shoulders and exaggerated limp.

"Did you get the information you wanted?" Decian asked warily, noting the splatter of blood across Caius' collar and the side of his neck.

"Yes and no," Caius replied.

"They didn't know who's been pulling the strings from the top," Aelio said, and paused to tie off a makeshift bandage around his upper arm with his teeth. "But we at least have the name of the next person up the chain."

Decian nodded. "And… did you kill them afterward?"

"Obviously," Caius said. "No witnesses."

His tired gray gaze moved to Tertia and her daughters. With a jolt, Decian realized that Caius wasn't thinking solely about witnesses to the rescue mission. The girls had seen Decian shift form, and Caius must have realized that.

Tertia met his gaze frankly. "You've nothing to worry about from us." She glanced at Decian, and then back to her former employer. "I hope you already know that."

Caius nodded. "I know. Just don't expect me to accept any red wine from you in the future."

"I imagine you'll be pouring your own wine from now on, Legatus," she said.

"Doubtless I will be," he agreed.

Decian turned to Aelio, breaking the moment. "We need to go to the livery where you stabled the mule. Can you take us there? All of us?"

"Do we really?" Caius asked.

"Yes. We do," Decian told him.

Aelio shrugged. "If you like. Normally, I'd warn you again about the curfew patrols. But given the size of that fire burning in the eastern quarter, I expect the city guard will be otherwise occupied tonight."

They piled into the wagon, and Aelio untied the team. Before long, they were trundling down the road again, leaving a broken warehouse full of dead bodies behind them. The six of them were silent for the most part, each lost in their own thoughts as the horses' hooves clattered against the road, drawing them away from the northern quarter and into the familiar business district.

Here, too, the streets were quieter than normal, only a few people out and about as evening deepened into night. Eventually, Aelio pulled up in front of the livery.

"I'll leave you here, if that's all right," said the tribuni. "For one thing, I should be getting back to those lookouts we left tied up at your house, Caius." He hesitated. "I... assume you won't be returning to the imperial quarter right away."

"You assume correctly," Caius told him. "I'll be in touch when it's safe to do so. Thank you again for your assistance. I'm sure you're well aware that it's put you in additional danger."

"Danger?" Aelio let out a derisive snort. "*Danger* is a madman trying to destabilize the imperial succession. Or, for that matter, a city hurtling toward open rebellion."

"I can't argue the point," Caius said. "But you should still watch your back."

The five of them clambered down from the wagon bed with varying degrees of grace.

"I do mean it though, Aelio," Caius continued. "Your help made all the difference tonight."

Aelio gave him a wan smile. "Don't mention it. I hope your dog comes back, by the way." His incisive blue gaze fell on Decian. "And, uh—you might not want to be wearing its collar when you speak to the livery staff."

Decian's hand flew to his neck, where his fingers encountered the thrice-damned dog collar. Before either he or Caius could say anything, Aelio had flicked the reins against the draft horses' haunches, and the wagon trundled away.

"Damn," Decian muttered, low and heartfelt. "Is that likely to become a problem?" he asked Caius, fumbling with the buckle and jerking the blasted thing off his neck.

"I sincerely hope not," Caius replied, watching as the wagon disappeared around a corner. He turned and eyed the livery. "Now—why are we here, exactly?"

Decian handed him the studded leather strap and checked to ensure his makeshift toga was still tied properly. "I have a gift for Tertia," he said. "Stay here—I'll be back in a few minutes."

He went inside, relying on bluster to get past the fact that he was basically wearing someone else's dirty bed sheet as clothing. After confirming that Saleene and Zuri had continued to pay board money for his stolen pony, he retrieved the little beast and awkwardly tacked it up with the saddle and bridle. Sending a nod of thanks to the livery owner on his way out, he led it outside to where the others were waiting.

"Here," he said, passing the reins to Tertia. "He's yours. You can use him to carry supplies, or take turns riding him so you don't have to walk the entire way to wherever you end up going."

Tertia stared at him. "I can't accept your horse, Decian."

"Yes, you can," he told her. "Besides, he's not mine. He belongs to the emperor. You might as well take him, since I expect this pony is the only thing you'll be getting from his royal high-and-mightiness. You could even sell him if you end up needing the money more than the transportation."

"That won't be necessary," Caius said, rummaging at his belt. He came up with a fat coin purse and tossed it to Tertia, who fumbled to catch it with her free hand. She drew breath to speak, but Caius cut her off. "Don't bother. We were always evenly matched in stubbornness, so making a fuss will just waste time."

Tertia snapped her mouth shut, visibly flummoxed.

"Thank you," said the younger daughter. She moved forward and stroked the pony's forehead. Decian raised an eyebrow as the foul-tempered little demonspawn closed its eyes and leaned into the touch with every indication of enjoyment.

"Yes," the older daughter echoed. "Thank you both." She tried to smile at them, but her eyes were still haunted.

Tertia drew in a heavy breath. "Goodbye, Legatus. Don't let anyone else finish the job I tried to start." She turned to meet Decian's eyes. "Goodbye, Decian. Watch out for him, and make sure he watches out for you, as well."

Objectively, Decian barely knew Tertia. But that didn't stop his throat from closing up, with the feeling of long-established constants shifting and fading away.

"Goodbye, Tertia," he said, the words emerging hoarse.

"Fair journey," Caius told her. "I'm sorry I ever let you and your family get caught up in this mess."

"You don't control nearly as many things as you think you do, Caius," Tertia said. "For now, maybe you should focus on the things you really *can* change."

Without waiting for him to come up with a response to that, Tertia gestured for her daughters to join her, and led the pony down the road, heading in the opposite direction from the one Aelio had taken back to the imperial quarter. Decian watched them go, aware of Caius next to him, doing the same.

The silence lingered, growing heavy after the little family disappeared from sight. There were a hundred different things that needed to be said.

"We should get off the streets," was what Caius eventually offered. "I wonder if Saleene's offer of safe harbor is still open?"

"I expect it probably is," Decian replied, suddenly wanting nothing more than to find someplace dark and sheltered to lick his metaphorical wounds.

They made their way on foot to the unremarkable neighborhood that played host to one of the pagan underground's many safehouses, moving at Caius' slow, hitching pace. It hadn't escaped Decian's notice that the roads they traveled were very close to the same ones Caius had used in his attempt to evade their pursuers, before the two of them were eventually cornered by six men in a fateful dark alley.

A faint shiver went through him, and he rubbed absently at his arms.

Caius gave him a sidelong glance. "I didn't think to bring the bag with your clothes along when Aelio picked us up this evening. I'm sorry." He sighed heavily. "And all that, after you specifically said you didn't want to be caught naked in the street if you had to shift."

"I'm not naked," Decian muttered.

"No," Caius said, "but I imagine your feet will be scraped all to hell after walking a couple of miles barefoot."

Decian huffed irritably. "It's not as though they wasted sandals on us in the prison work crews. My feet are used to it." A partial truth—he'd been used to it once upon a time, but his feet had already started to soften after weeks of wearing boots.

"I'm still sorry," Caius said.

Decian shot him a look. "You seem to be saying that an awful lot lately."

"That's because I've spent an awful lot of time regretting things recently."

Conversation trailed off as they took the final few turnings through the warren of twisting streets that made up the oldest part of the city. Decian fought a silent battle with himself over his emotions toward the exhausted man walking next to him and lost, cursing himself for a fool the entire time.

You wouldn't know a grudge if it bit you on the arse, would you? Caius had asked him, not so very long ago.

The truth was, Decian was perfectly capable of recognizing grudges, along with the circumstances that should reasonably evoke them. He just… wasn't very good at executing them. Especially when he was tired and disheartened, and the object of the grudge looked so utterly beaten down by life and his own readily acknowledged failings.

The pair approached a sagging two-story structure at the end of the road. They exchanged a glance, silently confirming with each other that this must be the place. It looked long deserted, which was reassuring in its way. No one without prior knowledge would see this house and think, '*Hey, there are probably a bunch of pagan fugitives hiding here.*'

After a final check to ensure that no one had magically managed to follow them on their twisting route, they went around to the back and banged on the small door next to the cellar entrance. After a lengthy wait, they heard the muffled sound of a heavy bar being removed. The door opened a crack, and a wary eye peered out of the gap, raking them up and down.

"Saleene and Zuri said we might find refuge here," Caius told the eye's owner.

"Wait here," said the man, and the door shut in their faces. The heavy bar thunked into place a moment later.

"Charming," Caius drawled, directing the word at the locked door in his face.

More time passed, and the door opened again, this time framing a rather disgruntled looking Saleene. She was dressed in a thigh-length tunic and trousers, her long hair gathered in a single messy plait. For the first time in their acquaintance, Decian could detect the shadow of a day's stubble darkening her jaw.

She eyed them for a beat. "Right. I suppose you'd better come in," she said, turning and walking away. "Bar the door behind you."

TWENTY-THREE

They came in and barred the door before following Saleene deeper into the tumbledown house. The place had the air of a hastily assembled camp, like something a traveling caravan might have thrown together inside a convenient cave to avoid the rain. There didn't appear to be any proper furniture to speak of. Rather, people were using whatever they could find—crates for seats and tables…makeshift palliasses made of sheets or cloaks draped over piles of straw… blankets hanging from rafters to form doors or walls where there otherwise were none.

A large room with a cooking hearth at one end smelled faintly of some kind of simple legume stew, the scent hours old, but still lingering. The other side of the room was packed with more people sleeping on the floor, and even a couple of tents.

Saleene kept walking, not slowing at any of the doorways. She led them up a flight of stairs with several of the treads missing, to the questionable architectural soundness of the second floor. On the positive side, many of the upstairs rooms had real doors. Decian could make out the sound of quiet talking behind some of them and snoring from others.

Saleene knocked lightly on the door at the end—a complicated series of taps that Decian suspected was probably a code. A metallic click came from within, and Zuri opened the door. The room beyond was tiny, basically a closet. But it was lit by an oil lamp set in a sconce on the wall, and the entire floor was taken up by an actual mattress—a mostly intact leather pad, big enough for two people, sprouting occasional tufts of straw or hay where some of the stitching had gone bad.

Zuri looked… not quite as rumpled and out of place as Saleene, but still not great.

"Oh, it's you," she said. "That's good. Did you rescue your damsels?"

"Yes," Caius said. "My colleague in the palace also has the name of someone a little further up the chain of command of this conspiracy, along with two additional prisoners who might know more. Now, though, we need a safe place to land for a day or two until I can figure out the next step."

Saleene gestured at the building around them with a sweep of one hand. "This house — and all the others like it in the city — are full to bursting. You'll have to take the room at night, and we'll take it during the day. We're up most nights in meetings anyway."

Her tone was brusque, even more so than usual. Decian got the distinct impression that roughing it didn't agree with the elegant brothel owner.

Caius glanced past Zuri at the tight quarters... the single mattress. "Erm..." he said. "There's only one —"

Saleene rounded on him, eyes snapping fire. "Oh my god, you sanctimonious prick. You can either grovel your way back into your lover's good graces and share the damned bed, or you can sleep on the bare floor in the hallway until someone trips over you, and the organizers kick you out for being a *bloody pain in the arse*. At this point, I don't honestly give two fucks which option you choose."

Caius looked mildly alarmed in the face of Saleene's towering bad temper. It was honestly rather impressive.

"It's fine," Decian said tiredly. "For the gods' sake, Caius — just... don't make a fuss."

The moment stretched, before Caius visibly deflated, the tension flowing out of his body as he scrubbed a hand down his face, pulling at the skin. "Yes. Of course it's fine. Thank you Saleene. Zuri."

Zuri nodded. "You both look like you could use some rest." She gestured at a bag tucked in the corner. "Mind our things for us until morning?"

"We will," Caius told her. "Thank you again."

Moving to the bag, Zuri fished around in it and pulled out a knife sheath, which she strapped to her right thigh before straightening and joining her partner in the hallway.

"All yours," she said, sweeping an arm out to indicate the tiny room. "Your kingdom awaits."

The pair turned and headed toward the stairwell without a backward glance, leaving Caius and Decian alone outside the door. Caius looked at Decian, looked at the room, and entered it with the air of someone about to lock himself in a very small cage with a very hungry wolf. After a slight hesitation, Decian joined him and closed the door, flipping the small metal locking bar into its bracket to keep it shut.

The rapid flicker of the flame from the oil lamp threw odd shadows around the room. A small window was set high in the wall opposite the door. Caius stood stiffly to one side, his boots making heavy imprints on the edge of the thin mattress, since there was quite literally nowhere else in the room to stand.

Decian eyed him. "Are you still afraid of me?" he asked, with something like resignation.

"Bloody terrified," Caius replied, his voice lowering to a mutter as he added, "Though probably not for the reasons you'd assume."

That was a bit cryptic, which was unfortunate since Decian didn't really feel up to deciphering opaque language after the day he'd had.

"All right," he said. "Well, you look like you're about to pass out from exhaustion, so lie down and you can be bloody terrified while you're horizontal instead of vertical."

He was rewarded by a surprised huff of self-deprecating amusement.

"At least the mattress isn't stuffed with feathers," Caius offered, and indeed, they were hardly going to be sleeping on eiderdown tonight. There were no pillows. There were no bedclothes except for the pathetic prisoner's blanket Decian was wearing as clothing.

"Guess you'll feel right at home," he said. "Now, go on. I'm going to put out the lamp so we can both be terrified in the dark instead of wasting our hosts' supplies of oil."

Caius slowly unbuckled his sword belt and placed it in the narrow space between the mattress and the wall, within easy reach. His heavy brow furrowed as he looked up at Decian. "Both of us, eh? What have you got to be terrified about tonight?"

My own questionable instincts of self-preservation, he thought.

Aloud, he said, "Exactly the sort of things you'd assume." Which wasn't an answer, any more than Caius' earlier cryptic mutterings.

He waited until Caius had stiffly lowered himself to lie on his back on the very edge of the bedding, then directed a brief prayer for strength at the same gods his mother had always prayed to. Inside him, the rhitsaaru shifted restlessly for a moment before settling. Decian licked his thumb and forefinger, snuffing out the wick on the simple clay oil lamp.

Instead of throwing them into pitch blackness, a faint orange glow from the high window painted the room a murky gray. That wall of the house must face east, where part of the city was still burning.

"That's a bit of a grim reminder," Caius observed gruffly.

Decian didn't answer since there was really nothing to say. He arranged himself on the other half of the worn buckskin mattress cover, lying on his side facing Caius in the dark because apparently he really was too much of an idiot to ever learn from his own mistakes.

Silence stretched between them. Despite Caius' clear fatigue so soon after recovering from poison, the other man's breathing showed no sign of deepening into sleep. On the contrary, an aura of tense wariness radiated from that side of the bed.

Eventually, Decian gave in and asked the question that had been sitting on the tip of his tongue. "Why did you risk so much to help Tertia today?"

There was no answer for a long moment. Then, "What do you mean?"

Decian shook his head, frustrated. He could just make out the faint reflection of light in Caius' pale eyes as the other man rolled onto his side to mirror him, leaving them facing each other.

"She poisoned you," Decian said. "I don't know how much you remember, but you nearly died. Saleene was certain you were going to, that first night. Tertia turned on you. Betrayed you. But you still put your life—and Aelio's—in jeopardy to help her."

This time, there was barely any hesitation before the reply. "Tertia acted in the only way she could, to try and protect her daughters' lives. What kind of loyalty would you expect her to hold toward the man whose food she cooked and floors she scrubbed, compared to her own family? I don't blame her for the choice she made."

It… wasn't quite the answer Decian had expected.

"Besides," Caius went on after a short pause. "We've all hurt people we shouldn't, at one time or another. Betrayed their trust… acted without thinking." He swallowed; the sound clearly audible in the small room. "All we can do is hope that those we've wronged might someday give us a second chance."

Decian's lungs abruptly stopped working. Before he could second-guess himself, he lunged across the space separating them and gathered Caius' face in his hands, crushing their lips together.

Caius made a muffled noise of shock, and Decian remembered with a hint of trepidation that the man's sword was still lying within easy reach. Then one of Caius' rough-callused hands wrapped around the nape of Decian's neck, and they were tangled together in a desperate kiss.

"This," Caius panted into their shared air, as he allowed Decian to roll him onto his back, poised above him. "This is the part that terrifies me."

"Yeah, actually I'm right there with you," Decian murmured, and went back to plundering his mouth.

Caius pushed him away with a hand on his chest—just far enough to speak. "I don't know that I can protect you. Hell, I have doubts about keeping *myself* alive much longer."

"I don't care about the first part," Decian said. "I never asked you to protect me. I *do* care about the second part, but unless you're planning on expiring in this room tonight, it will have to wait until morning."

Caius' reply was hoarse. "If you think you can refrain from shifting and ripping my throat out, I expect I'll muddle through until daylight somehow."

The pressure of the hand against his chest fell away. Decian fumbled for the knot holding his makeshift toga together and let the scratchy cloth fall. Immediately, he turned his attention to Caius' clothing—layer upon frustrating layer of buckles and hooks and ties. Thankfully, Caius put his own hands to use and started helping, until somehow, they managed to get everything off him and toss it out of the way.

"I'm sorry," Caius said, clutching at Decian's shoulder and hip as Decian climbed on top of him and started kissing his way along Caius' collarbone. "I'm so sorry for all of this…"

His touch was like a brand, lighting up Decian's skin with heat wherever it landed.

"Stop being sorry for one night and just let me fuck you," Decian begged. "I don't *want* to hate you. I don't *want* to hold a grudge. I'm *terrible* at grudges."

A choked noise escaped the man beneath him. It might have been laughter. It might have been something darker. "You really are, you know," Caius said. "I've never met anyone as bad at grudges as you. You have all the emotional self-preservation skills of a fence post."

"Shut up," Decian retorted, his own voice none too steady. "If you can't say anything nice, then just lie back and be fucked."

He dove for Caius' mouth again—teeth clashing, tongues tangling. He wasn't quite sure if the desperate noises filling the little room were coming from him, or from Caius, or from both of them. But after a few moments, Caius' body sagged into the lumpy leather mattress, melting under Decian's hands and mouth. Ceding control, in a way that he never really had before, when they were together like this.

Gentling his movements, Decian lowered himself until they were pressed together from chest to ankle. Caius was half-hard, his cock nestled in the crease of Decian's hip. Decian was fully hard, and he knew exactly what he wanted. He kissed Caius until the older man drew back, breathless, chest heaving for air.

Decian lifted his weight away with reluctance. "Roll over for me," he said, and took advantage of Caius' compliance to regain his feet. He fumbled for the oil lamp, removing it from its sconce, and folded to his knees next to Caius' hip. The belly of the little clay container was still faintly warm against the palm of his hand.

As though fully aware of what Decian intended, Caius hitched his good leg to the side, exposing himself for easier access. The red glow coming from the window illuminated the exhausted line of his back, now that Decian's eyes had adjusted more fully to the low light. Decian placed a flat palm over the dip at the base of his spine and slid it slowly upward, over knotted muscle and sinew.

A line of shadow marred the smoothness of Caius' left shoulder, the muscles there twisted and asymmetrical. Hypnotized, Decian's fingers explored the dips and whorls of what had to have been a horrific wound. *Battle axe,* Decian remembered him saying. A blow taken to protect an emperor who probably didn't give two shits about the man who'd saved his life.

An emperor… who just so happened to be Decian's father. Caius had saved his father's life. The realization jolted through him like a lightning bolt, even though he couldn't have said exactly why.

His fingers curled over the old scar. Caius hissed out a breath, and Decian jerked his hand back as though burned.

"Did I hurt you?" he asked.

Caius craned around, trying to look at him over his good shoulder. "Hurt? No. Scars like that one don't hurt. Usually, I can't feel anything at all there."

TWENTY-FOUR

Tentatively, Decian replaced his hand on Caius' damaged flesh. "You saved my father's life." He wasn't even sure why he'd said the words aloud. It wasn't as though Caius was unaware of the fact. After all, he was the one who'd taken the wound.

"He was never a father to you," Caius said. "Besides, it was years after the fact. Decades, even. You were already languishing in prison by the time that axe fell."

"I know," Decian said, stroking the uneven scar tissue. "I... it's just..." He faltered for a moment. "Never mind. It's hard to explain."

"Let's not focus on the past. Not tonight, Decian — please."

Decian splayed his fingers over Caius' shoulder and leaned down to press a kiss to the back of his neck. "Sorry."

Caius exhaled a puff of air through his nose. "Now who's apologizing?"

"Well, I'd say 'sorry' again, but I suppose that wouldn't help, would it?"

"Not really," Caius agreed. "Besides, you've got oil, and I can think of better things we could be doing than expressing endless regrets at each other."

"True." Decian let out a sigh that was mostly for show. "So much for rationing our hosts' valuable oil supplies."

"I won't tell if you don't."

An ache of impossible fondness tightened Decian's chest, despite everything that had transpired between them. This was what he'd missed... what he'd thought lost forever. The instinctual understanding. The easy way of fitting together.

"Fair enough," he said, and picked up the lamp, tilting it to drizzle oil through the wick-hole and onto his fingers. "I trust you'll let me know if I'm getting it wrong."

Caius relaxed onto the mattress once more. "I don't honestly think you could, at this point."

Our history together says otherwise, Decian thought, but he applied himself to seeking out Caius' opening and working an oiled finger inside. Caius let out a quiet grunt, though he didn't tense up or otherwise complain. The inside of his body was tight, and hot, and impossibly soft against Decian's skin. His cock throbbed its eagerness at the idea of being in that warm, grasping place.

"More," Caius said, as Decian continued to work him.

Decian dribbled more oil and worked a second finger inside. Remembering how long Caius had spent preparing him on the one other occasion they'd done something like this, Decian was surprised when he said, "That's enough," after only a minute or two.

"Are you sure?" Decian asked, sliding his fingers out carefully.

Caius rolled over so he was lying on his back once more. "I need the burn tonight. Just make sure to waste a bit more of that valuable oil on yourself first."

Taking him at his word, Decian slicked up his cock and lowered himself into the cradle of Caius' hips. Between his inexperience and the lack of light, it took a bit of shuffling around to get himself lined up. Even then, it felt like trying to thread a sewing needle with a length of rope. He hesitated, but Caius flexed his hips, sending sparks across his vision.

"Just do it," Caius ground out. "Take what you want—it's yours anyway."

Something animal and possessive rose inside Decian. He hooked a hand under Caius' knee and pulled it up, pressing into the man beneath him with unyielding pressure at the same time. Caius' defenses gave way, and Decian sank into that impossibly tight heat. Caius arched with a stifled cry, his head falling back.

Decian pushed deeper until he couldn't go any farther, the sensation squeezing around him like a tight fist. It grasped at him even as he pulled back, and he couldn't help driving forward again in an attempt to recreate that first, impossibly perfect slide of flesh on flesh.

Caius thrust his hips upward, meeting him, and before long Decian was pounding into him, balls slapping rhythmically. His hand gripped Caius' thigh above the knee, fingers sliding across a divot in the flesh where a crossbow bolt had left a fresh scar.

There was something disturbingly cathartic about pinning Caius to the lumpy mattress and driving into him without restraint or mercy—even more so when Caius groaned and reached between them to get a fist around his cock, pumping himself in time with Decian's thrusts.

It was never going to last long. Not like this. Even so, it took Decian by surprise when Caius went rigid beneath him, his arse clamping around Decian's cock as he jerked through his release, painting both their stomachs with hot seed.

That was too much for Decian, who followed him down into a pit of ecstasy, balls drawing up tight as he pulsed deep inside Caius' body. It seemed to last for an age, until at last he pulled out with a wince, spent and oversensitive. Caius shuddered beneath him at the sudden loss.

"Sorry," Decian rasped, their temporary moratorium on endless apologizing apparently at an end already. He rolled off, flopping onto his back next to his companion. A moment later, it occurred to him that there was no convenient ewer of water in the room. No rags, either.

"Erm, I've just realized there's nothing here we can use to clean up," he said. "I guess I could tear a strip off the blanket I'm using for clothes…"

Caius lay limp and unmoving, completely wrung out. "I've got a kerchief here somewhere, I think."

Since it didn't seem like he was going to be moving anytime soon, Decian hitched himself over to the pile of Caius' discarded clothing and began going through it until he found a square of soft cotton cloth. He scrubbed at his oily hand, the spunk on his stomach, the spunk on Caius' stomach, and finally, the mess leaking onto Caius' thighs.

"Thank you," Caius said, sounding barely awake.

Decian set the soiled rag next to Caius' sword belt and replaced the abused oil lamp in its place on the wall. The small, stuffy room was redolent with the scent of sweat and musk. "I've just realized that we're sharing this room with other people, and it's going to be blatantly obvious to anyone who walks in what we got up to in here."

"They're brothel owners," Caius replied. "If they're not used to the smell of sex by now, I don't know what to say."

Decian lowered himself onto the mattress, only to hesitate—suddenly unsure if his presence in Caius' arms would be welcome, or even if it were appropriate under the circumstances.

Caius rolled his head to the side to look at him. "Come here," he said, only to hesitate as well. "Unless... you're having regrets?"

Decian unfroze, shuffling close enough to lie down with his head pillowed on Caius' good shoulder. "Not regrets. Uncertainties, I suppose."

He felt Caius' nod. "Understandable." His chest rose and fell beneath Decian's cheek, even as his arm circled Decian's shoulders. "My greatest regret out of this entire disaster is the knowledge that I was the one to put that new look of wariness in your eyes."

Decian couldn't think of a way to respond to that. The silence grew deeper, settling around them until it threatened to grow even more stifling than the stuffy, sex-soaked atmosphere of the room.

"People are still trying to kill you," he blurted. "What are you going to do now?"

"I dunno yet," Caius replied. "It'll depend to some extent on what Aelio can get from those two lookouts we took prisoner... and the name we got from the guard at the warehouse."

In reality, Caius appeared to hold no confidence in his ability to stay ahead of the assassins forever. He'd basically said as much, earlier.

Decian lay against Caius' side, his mind restlessly worrying over what the future would bring, despite his body's heavy, post-coital lassitude. He kept expecting Caius' breathing to even out into the deep rhythm of exhausted sleep, but his companion remained as awake as he did.

A long time passed like that. Long enough that Decian's mind had finally begun to wind down toward slumber when Caius drew breath as though to speak, only to hold it.

"What is it?" Decian murmured.

A moment's hesitation, before Caius said, "It's… well, I'm not really sure how to ask."

"Just ask," Decian told him. "After everything else, how bad can it be?"

Caius swallowed. "Your other form. The… what did you call it, again?"

"The rhitsaaru?" Decian rolled onto an elbow, not sure where this was going.

"Yes, the rhitsaaru. You said it could… *smell* the evil in souls?" He sounded nervous. Uncharacteristically so.

"For lack of a better way of describing it," Decian said carefully. "Everyone's soul is a mixture of good and bad. But some are just… tainted. Sadistic. Putrescent with evil."

"Rotten, you said earlier." Something in his voice sounded hollow.

"Yes, that's another word for it," Decian agreed. "Caius, what are you trying to ask?"

"My soul," Caius said softly. "You must have smelled it. Am I… irredeemable?"

The question hit Decian like a punch to the gut.

"What would make you ask something like that?" he asked, bewildered.

"Answer the question." The tone was gentler than Decian might have expected. "Is my soul rotten?"

Decian reached out, cupping Caius' jaw. "Caius, no. Your soul is…" He reached for a description that could adequately convey the reality. "Fire and blood."

"I can't tell if that's better or worse," Caius said after a moment.

"It's… *you*," Decian tried to explain, still struggling to get his ideas across. "Fire can burn a city, but it can also warm a family's hearth. Blood can mean the blood of your enemies, or your own, shed for the protection of others."

Caius slowly closed his eyes, tension still evident in his body.

"Have you ever seen a lunar eclipse?" Decian asked. "Your soul is the moon, luminous, but cast in shadow." His tone hardened. "You are not... *rotten.*" He practically spat the last word.

"I am a killer," Caius said evenly. "A torturer when it's called for. That's what you're in bed with, Decian."

"And do you enjoy it?" Decian shot back. "Do the screams of your victims twist pleasure in the pit of your stomach?"

"Of course not," Caius snapped, his eyes flying open again. "But in the end, does that truly matter?"

"*It does to me,*" Decian snapped back. He took a deep breath, trying to center his emotions. "And it does to the rhitsaaru. The souls it's reaped... those men *did* take pleasure in their cruelty. They reveled in it. *Wallowed* in the pain they caused. That's the difference."

Caius turned his face away, releasing a bitter exhalation of laughter. Decian reluctantly let his hand fall.

"Well," Caius said, "I suppose if I can't escape whoever wants me dead, I'll find out for myself soon enough. I wonder what the afterlife is truly like? Because I won't lie—I'd been looking forward to the option of stark non-existence. It always sounded positively restful."

Decian huffed out a puff of frustration and lowered himself to lie half-sprawled over Caius once more. "Maybe it will be a series of endless imperial galas with dancing and gold flakes floating in the wine. I know how much you adore things like that."

Caius groaned. "Good god above, don't even *think* such things. I wonder if you can commit suicide when you're already dead?"

Decian couldn't help it—he snorted. "It seems like that would probably break some kind of rule. Then again, who knows?" He slung a leg across both of Caius' and gathered him close. "Now, would you please stop obsessing over deep, existential questions and get some damned sleep? You're exhausted, and come to that, so am I."

Caius' good arm tightened around him. "Sorry," he said, which at least made them even when it came to stupid, post-sex apologies.

"You're forgiven," Decian told him.

He lay there until sleep finally claimed Caius a few minutes later, letting the soothing sound of his companion's breathing lure him down into dreams, as well.

TWENTY-FIVE

The sound of a quick, complicated knock against the door jerked Decian awake an unknown amount of time later. Morning light was pouring through the east-facing window. He was still naked, sprawled across Caius, who was also naked.

"Erm… just a minute?" he called, tossing Caius' rumpled cloak over the lower half of his body before scrambling for his repurposed blanket and wrapping it around himself.

Caius slept on, unmoved by any of this. Apparently, even soldiers' reflexes had their limits.

Decian moved to the door and unlocked it, positioning his body in such a way as to block it from opening more than a couple of inches as he peered out cautiously into the hallway.

"Oh," he said in relief, opening it to Saleene and Zuri. "Good, it's just you."

There was no question of the others entering while Decian and Caius were still inside; there simply wasn't room in the cramped space. Saleene gave a delicate sniff and raised a pointed eyebrow.

"Well, that certainly didn't take long," she said. "Please tell me you cleaned up the spunk afterward and left some oil in the lamp."

Decian felt his face heat. "Yes, and… I think there's a bit left. Probably."

Zuri eyed Caius' unmoving form curiously. "You didn't accidentally kill him with sex, did you? Maybe you should check for a pulse."

"He's just tired," Decian said.

"Aren't we all?" Saleene replied in a tart tone. "Get him up. We need to talk, and he's hogging my bed."

She'd managed to procure a razor for a shave at some point during the night, but she still had the air of a nervy, finely bred racehorse that had been turned out to forage for itself in a rocky field full of brambles.

"Give me a minute," Decian told her, and closed the door to give Caius privacy so he could dress without being ogled. Or at least, without being ogled by anyone who wasn't Decian.

Decian crouched next to him and stroked his stubbled cheek with the backs of his fingers, then traced a gentle thumb over the bottom of the scar that ran vertically over his left eye, bisecting the eyebrow and the cheekbone below it. When that didn't elicit any response, he clasped Caius' good shoulder. At that, Caius finally blinked awake with a groan.

"Hey," Decian said quietly. "Time to vacate the room. I assume you'll probably want clothes for that."

Caius looked up at the daylight visible through the window, and down at his naked body under the cloak.

"Blast," he muttered succinctly.

"I gather Saleene and Zuri want a word this morning," Decian told him.

"I'm up," Caius grumbled, rolling into a sitting position with a wince.

"You all right?" Decian asked. "After last night, I mean."

"Which part of last night?" Caius asked with a rueful half-smile, as he rummaged through his pile of clothes for stockings and smallclothes. "The fighting, or the fucking?"

Decian managed to swallow the swell of comfortable warmth that washed over him in response to that small, self-effacing twitch of the lips.

"Both," he replied. "Well, mostly the fucking, actually. You seemed fine after the fighting."

The smile grew, crinkling the corners of Caius' gray eyes for a moment before his expression sobered. "I expect I'll survive playing host to your prick, yes. But thank you for the concern. Any idea what the other two want to discuss?"

"Not really," Decian said. "Next steps, at a guess."

Caius nodded, and continued pulling on clothes. When he was done, he picked up the soiled kerchief, balled it up, and stuck it inside his jerkin rather than leaving it lying in Zuri and Saleene's sleeping area.

"Here's hoping they have some better ideas than I do right now," he said, and opened the door. "Good morning."

"If you say so," Saleene greeted. "Come downstairs. There's something simmering in the kitchen that's allegedly edible, and we need to have a frank discussion."

Decian followed the others down the rickety, terrifying staircase and accepted a bowl of something gray and watery. It tasted of nothing—oddly reminiscent of one of the staples in the prison where Decian had languished for a decade. He and Caius both sipped from their bowls without comment.

When they were finished, Saleene led them to the back door, stopping to speak with the man guarding it on the way out.

"We're borrowing the cellar for a bit, Luka," she said.

Luka nodded, and they climbed down the claustrophobic stone staircase leading underground. The cellar smelled faintly of damp and mildew. Zuri remained at the door, holding it open to admit a bit of light while Saleene bustled around and lit a rush, which she then used to ignite a couple of lamps.

Decian looked around as Zuri closed the door and joined them. The place was larger than he might have guessed, and surprisingly well kept given the state of most of the house. The walls were covered with shelves and stocked with a respectable collection of simple foodstuffs—including bags of rye that had probably contributed to the tasteless gruel in the kitchen.

The space in the center had been furnished with an actual table and chairs, which must have posed an interesting challenge, given the narrow door and staircase. A pile of vellum sheaves lay on one corner of the table, along with a selection of quills and a bottle of ink. A map lay half-unrolled on the other side. Decian thought it might be of Amarius.

Saleene set one of the lamps on the table, safely away from the documents. "Sit," she said, gesturing at a couple of chairs across from the ones she and Zuri took.

They did, and Caius leaned forward intently, resting his elbows on the table. "Has there been any word on the fire last night?" he asked.

"Several words, in fact," Saleene said curtly. "Most of them either curses or prayers for divine intervention."

"At least four city blocks burned to the ground in the temple district," Zuri clarified. "And there's no indication that any of our people were behind it."

"Just like the attack on the council chamber," Caius said heavily.

"Precisely," Saleene bit out. "Someone is still dead-set on framing the pagans for murder and mayhem. And so far, the strategy seems to be working quite well."

"The Council halted their meetings after the attack, right?" Decian asked. "Have they started up again?"

"Not yet, but soon," Saleene said. "And at this point, I think the end result is almost a foregone conclusion."

"Maybe not," Caius said, though he didn't sound convinced even as he said it. "Aelio is working on proof of the pagans' innocence in the council attack. If he can convince them, there may be backlash against the radical wing."

"Or there may not be," Zuri snapped. "In which case, this city is going to split down the middle."

Saleene's gaze fell heavily on Decian. "The point right now is that you need to decide what you're going to do before Amarius fractures."

Something cold slithered through Decian's chest. "What do you mean?"

She shook her head in frustration. "Decian. If anyone outside of this room finds out what you are, half of the city is going to want you burned at the stake, and the other half is going to want to use you as a figurehead."

Caius had gone very still next to him. "Then we need to make sure no one finds out."

"Caius, you're a fool!" Saleene flared. "Did he or did he not go out as a fucking dog yesterday, and come back as a human? You're not exactly being the picture of discretion!"

Decian thought of Aelio... of Tertia and her two daughters. Four more people who knew about his shapeshifting abilities. He could see exactly the same thought darkening Caius' expression.

"All three of you should leave the city," Caius said in a monotone. "It's the only way you'll be safe."

"*Safe* is relative," Saleene growled. "Do you really think the rest of the empire is going to be any more welcoming?"

"I think it's not a tinderbox waiting for a spark, like the capital is," he retorted. "Not yet, anyway."

"And what about you?" Decian demanded. "Do you think you're any safer here? *You're* the one with an assassination order on his head."

Caius laced his fingers together so tightly that the knuckles went white. "I dragged Aelio into this morass. I can't just throw him into the muck and then leave him to flounder."

"Still bound and determined to do your duty, are you?" Decian snapped, surprised by the sudden bitterness welling up in response to the realization that Caius could fall apart in his arms at night, and then send him away without a second thought the very next morning.

"The empire is falling apart," Caius said. "Someone has to fight for it, or there will be chaos."

Saleene raised her eyebrows. "And you walking to the gallows to voluntarily stick your neck in a noose is going to save the empire, is it? How does that work, exactly?"

Caius wore the stony expression that said he knew everything was about to go straight to shit, but he wasn't willing to admit it openly. "I have to try," he said.

Why? Decian wanted to demand. *Why do you have to try?*

Caius continued before he could. "Decian, you should see if you can find your mother. Visit the village where you grew up. Ask around—find out if she returned to her home in Kulawi. If so, follow her. You'll both be safe there.

Alyrios has too many problems of its own to turn outward toward conquest like it used to. Those days are over."

Decian stood up abruptly, his chair legs juddering across the dirt floor as his frustration boiled over into anger. "You know, my mother was right about Alyrions. She told me over and over when I was growing up—one day, they act as though they own you... as though you belong solely to them. And the next day, they'll discard you like a piece of old trash."

Caius' eyes flew to his. "That's not—"

"I'm good enough to fuck," Decian said viciously. "But not good enough to keep. Just like my mother was good enough for the emperor to fuck but not to keep. Funny how that works."

The blood had drained from Caius' face under Decian's verbal assault. He was distantly aware of Zuri watching them, wide-eyed, while Saleene leaned back in her chair and crossed her arms with the air of someone settling in to watch an exceedingly tiresome sporting event. None of it touched Decian's abrupt, incandescent rage over the circumstances of the last several weeks.

"Your mother became the mistress of an emperor," Caius said hoarsely. "That's an inherently unstable position. But I'm only trying to keep you safe. Those are entirely different situations."

"Maybe they would have been entirely different situations, *if she'd had any understanding whatsoever* that she was disposable in his eyes!" he snapped. "Instead, he gave her a ring and promised her that in exchange for pledging herself solely to him, she would enjoy his protection forever. She's Kulawi—she had no idea what being a mistress was supposed to mean!"

Caius' jaw snapped shut. His eyes bored into Decian's, and Decian wasn't sure why.

"He... what?" Caius asked slowly.

"None of this is the point!" Decian said. "The point is that... you... *Alyrions* act like love is some unbreakable contract that binds two people together. But as soon as it stops being *convenient*"—he spat the word out—"it's as though that contract never existed!"

Beside him, Caius appeared frozen in shock.

"Decian," Saleene said, very deliberately, "are you saying that your father gave your mother a ring?"

"Yes," he said, frustrated that everyone seemed to be fixating on the least important parts of what he was saying. "She wore it on a necklace all the time I was growing up. She said it was to remind her that northern men couldn't be trusted. She never told me who my father was—only that he promised her the world at his side, and then a few months later she was an outcast, hiding out in a tiny village after he discarded her."

"This ring," Caius whispered hoarsely. "What did it look like?"

Derailed, Decian stared at him for a long moment before replying. "It was a… signet ring, I think they're called? With a flat face on top. Why?"

"Was the top carved with an image?" Saleene asked. She appeared to be wearing a very odd expression. Next to her, Zuri was looking between them with a look of confusion that probably mirrored Decian's own.

"Yes," he said. "With a hound and a lion."

"Oh, dear god above," Caius breathed.

Saleene grabbed a sheet of vellum from the pile next to her and shoved the inkpot toward Decian. "Sketch it. As much as you can remember."

He looked at her, bewildered.

"Please," Caius said. "Decian, it's important."

Feeling as though he'd fallen into some surreal dream world, Decian took up a quill and dipped it in the pot. As a child, he'd drawn the image of the stylized lion and hound many times, facing each other on their hind legs with their front legs entwined. His artistic skills, such as they were, had grown rusty over the years, but he sketched out the sigil as best he could. When he was finished, Saleene practically snatched the page out from under him.

"The imperial lion," she said, holding it up for Caius to examine. "And I presume the hound represents his mother's house. How very apropos."

"I don't understand," Decian said, irrational dread pooling in his stomach.

"The emperor didn't just take your mother as a mistress and give her a pretty trinket, Decian," Saleene told him. "He married her."

Decian blinked. "He... what? What are you saying?"

Caius had gone as gray as a wraith. "That's an imperial union signet, given to your mother long before Constanzus wed the Empress Stasia. You're twenty-six years old. That makes you the emperor's oldest son conceived in wedlock." His voice was absolutely flat.

Decian stared at him. "But... I... I'm..."

Saleene, too, looked like all the blood had drained from her face. "Decian, don't you see? You aren't a bastard. God help us all... you're the legitimate heir to the Alyrion Empire."

End of Book 2

MASTER OF HOUNDS: BOOK 3

ONE

Caius Oppita, late of His Imperial Majesty's armed forces, was certain there had once been a time when his life didn't feel like a runaway goods wagon careening toward the edge of a cliff. He listened with a feeling of both sinking dread and painful inevitability as a breathless street urchin relayed the latest news from the capital, aware of the groans and winces of the people gathered around him.

He and his lover Decian were still sheltering in one of the pagan safehouses scattered throughout the city of Amarius. His lover... who also happened to be the *bloody heir apparent to the Alyrion Empire.*

God above, how had he ended up here?

The answer, of course, was that he had done something foolish because he'd thought it was the right thing to do. He'd saved one of the emperor's bastard sons from being executed for no other reason than the circumstances of his birth. And that had all been well and good, right up until Decian revealed that his Kulawi mother possessed an imperial signet ring proving her lawful marriage to the Emperor Constanzus. A marriage, mind you, that predated his union to the current empress—the mother of Constanzus' three so-called legitimate sons.

This would have been enough of a crisis to be going on with. Unfortunately, the revelation had occurred against the backdrop of an ecumenical council convened to determine the empire's stance on pagan heretics. Decian, his mother, and two of Caius' closest friends were pagans. Additionally, Decian was a shapeshifter—the worst possible kind of heretic in the eyes of the Deimonist Church. All of them would face the prospect of being burned at the stake if the radical wing of the church held sway.

"There's been *another* attack on the council?" someone asked. "*Seriously*? Are they blaming this one on pagans as well?"

The urchin nodded rapidly, as though his slightly too-large head was on a swivel. "Yes, sir. They're saying half a dozen churchmen died this time, including one of the head muckety-mucks. There's talk of closing down the meetings for good!"

Caius resisted the urge to cover his face with his hand in utter dismay. Someone high up in the imperial hierarchy—and he had a good idea who it was—had already arranged an attack on the council chamber once, making it look like the work of pagan sympathizers. After a hiatus of several days, the council had reconvened, allegedly with tighter security.

But he'd seen the venue where the debates were taking place. The building was a security nightmare, and no amount of overworked Amarian guards stationed around it would be able to change that fact.

He cleared his throat. "If the Amarian Council disbands without making a formal decision," he said, pitching his voice to be heard over the babble of voices, "radical deimonists will take that as an excuse to start hunting down pagans in the streets. If that happens, all of you need to be somewhere far away from here."

Saleene, the owner of a brothel Caius had long frequented, added her voice to his. "He's right. There's already rioting every night. How much longer until organized mobs start dragging suspected pagans out of their homes and burning them in the public square? We need to think strategically."

"How does one strategize against an angry mob?" Zuri, Saleene's Kulawi partner, mused aloud.

The hubbub swelled again as everyone began talking at once. A warm shoulder pressed against Caius', as Decian stretched over to speak in his ear.

"This is going to be bad, isn't it?" said the younger man.

Even if Caius were inclined to offer meaningless platitudes in the face of this new disaster, he would have been hard-pressed to come up with any.

"Yes," he replied quietly. "This is going to be bad."

When it became clear that the urchin didn't have any other news of import to relay, Saleene caught Caius' eye and jerked her chin toward the door at the back of the large room.

"Come on," Caius told Decian, and started pushing his way through the crush of bodies.

They'd been gathered with the other residents in a communal area of the tumbledown old safehouse—one used for cooking and dining as well as meetings. With Zuri at her heels, Saleene led the way deeper into the structure, to a terrifyingly rickety staircase that led to the second story. After several days here, it was becoming second nature to step over the missing and broken treads, although the sound of wood supports creaking with strain would never be anything other than disconcerting.

The room that the four of them had been using in shifts for sleeping was too small to hold all of them at once. Fortunately, with everyone else downstairs, the hallway was empty and quiet except for the sound of the building settling and groaning around them.

"This is turning into a clusterfuck," Saleene said bluntly. "We need to begin thinking about exit strategies."

Zuri scowled. "So… what, then? Are we to flee and leave the rest of Amarius' pagan population to the wolves?"

Saleene crossed her arms. "Unless you'd prefer to stay here and burn at the stake with them, I'm not certain there's much of a choice. What would be the benefit of our continued presence here? How would us staying in Amarius help?"

Zuri opened her mouth as though she might reply, only to close it again a moment later and shake her head angrily.

Caius took a breath, feeling as though a heavy weight was pressing down on his shoulders from above. "There might be one more thing to try."

Immediately, Decian's brown gaze landed on him with enough force to bore a hole through his skull. "No," he said.

"You haven't even heard what I was about to suggest," Caius pointed out tiredly.

"I don't have to," Decian shot back. "Because whatever it is, it's going to be reckless, poorly thought out, prone to unforeseen complications—and you're going to tell us that you have to do it alone."

"I'll definitely have to do it alone," Caius agreed. "So that means you won't need to worry about the rest of it, will you?"

Decian stared at him. Saleene and Zuri wisely didn't comment.

"You... *bastard*," Decian said, at length. "Gods*damn* you, will you just *listen* to yourself for once?"

"My parents were lawfully wed," Caius told him in an even tone. "Same as yours, apparently."

Saleene held up a hand. "Could we not drag that part up right now? Caius, what exactly are you proposing?"

Caius leaned back against the wall, covering a wince as his bad shoulder twinged in protest. "There is still one thing that could head off open pagan persecution in the city."

"What's that?" Zuri asked with clear skepticism.

"An imperial decree."

They were all looking at him like he was mad now—not just Decian.

"Keep talking," Saleene said, after an uncomfortable beat.

"As a first step, I need to get a message to the tribuni of the palace guard," he replied.

"You mean Tribuni Aelio?" Decian asked. "Is that wise, since he knows about—" He waved a hand at himself, presumably indicating his shapeshifting abilities.

Aelio had surmised Decian's secret after accompanying them on a recent mission to rescue two girls taken hostage by whoever was pulling the strings of this political plot. Decian had started the mission in animal form, but unexpectedly shifted back to human form after attacking the guards holding the girls prisoner. Aelio had seen him wearing the ridiculous leather dog collar that Zuri had given him to make his giant black hellhound alter ego seem less threatening.

By rights, Aelio should have arrested both of them on the spot—and honestly, no one would have questioned it if he'd struck Decian down with his sword in the middle of the street. But Aelio had always been a man of honor—as well as one who apparently thought for himself, rather than blindly following dogma.

"I don't propose to parade you around in front of him," Caius said. "Mostly, though, I imagine if he were going to raise a fuss, he would have done it before now."

"How would one even go about getting a message to someone inside the palace, under the circumstances?" Zuri asked. She was still frowning, but she hadn't dismissed Caius' tentative plan out of hand.

"And why do you need to get him a message?" Decian pressed. "What does that have to do with getting a mad emperor to issue a decree telling people to be nice to pagans?"

"I need to meet with Aelio in person," Caius said. "He still has freedom to come and go from the imperial quarter. I don't."

Decian narrowed his eyes. "That doesn't answer my question. If Aelio could secretly control the emperor from behind the scenes, we'd know about it, wouldn't we?"

"If Aelio could secretly control Constanzus from behind the scenes, it's doubtful we'd be in this mess in the first place," Caius replied dryly. "I don't need him to put a word in the emperor's ear. I need him to put a word in a particular pageboy's ear. That, at least, should be well within his purview."

Decian subsided—still obviously unhappy, but no longer openly rebellious. "A pageboy. Right. You're scheming something crazy, but I don't suppose a simple meeting is likely to devolve into total chaos. So, you need to get a message to someone inside the palace? Someone who can, in turn, get a message to Aelio without it being traced back to a pagan safehouse?"

"Ideally, yes."

Decian's lips twisted into something that wasn't a smile. "Fine. I can do that for you."

Caius regarded him suspiciously. "How?"

Decian ignored him, turning to the others. "Saleene, do you know if I could borrow that boy from the meeting for a private errand?"

Saleene, too, seemed dubious. "Probably, though I expect it depends on the nature of the errand."

"Message delivery," Decian said, his gaze returning to Caius. "It's market day today. Pip will visit his mother and little sister in the city tomorrow evening. He goes there every week, and I know where they live."

Pip was the apprentice who'd inherited Decian's short-lived—and shamelessly fraudulent—position as the royal master of hounds. Caius stared at Decian in bewilderment. "How in sanity's name could you know such a thing?"

Decian stared back. "How do you *think* I know it? He told me about them."

Caius shook off his momentary bafflement at the idea of people who'd worked together sharing such personal details, apparently for no other reason than the sheer hell of it. "Fine. Yes. That could work. He'd need to get a return message to us somehow, detailing a time and place for the meeting. I imagine Aelio is stretched a bit thin at the moment, what with everything else that's been going on."

"I certainly wouldn't want to trade places with the man," Saleene muttered. "And I say that as an out-of-work brothel owner huddling in an overcrowded tenement."

"I don't think anyone in the empire is lining up for the tribuni's job right now, no," Caius agreed.

"Someone will need to give me a few coins to hire the boy to take the message," Decian said. "And Caius, you should know that I'm only doing this because if I don't, I know you'll come up with an even worse plan."

Caius raised an eyebrow. "I fail to understand your continuing lack of faith in my tactical planning abilities. We're both still alive, aren't we?"

Decian let out a harsh bark of a sound. It might have been ironic laughter. "Yes, with the exception of you being shot twice with crossbows, poisoned, and both of us currently being in hiding in a city tearing itself apart at the seams, I'd say everything has gone swimmingly."

"It could be worse," Caius told him.

"It can *always* be worse," Saleene said, with the air of someone who had extensive personal experience in the matter. "Come on, let's go catch the boy before he leaves. At this point, I'll take even a bad plan over no plan at all."

Caius bit back the sarcastic retort that wanted to escape. "Fine. We're agreed, then. After you."

Later that night, he and Decian lay on the lumpy mattress in the cramped, closet-like space that they'd been assigned for sleeping. With so many pagans in hiding as conditions in Amarius worsened, the old house was bursting at the seams with refugees. Decian and Caius had use of this room from dusk till dawn, while Saleene and Zuri attended late-night planning sessions. Then they returned to take possession of the straw-stuffed bedding from dawn until dusk.

It made sense, given that brothel owners were used to late hours. And it was far from the worst place Caius had slept. Unfortunately, it also included the presence of the shapeshifter who'd somehow wormed his way past Caius' hardened defenses, and who wouldn't stop slamming him in the face with unwanted revelations.

After an initial period of gilded happiness where Caius had wandered around like a callow youth obsessed by his first romantic crush, Decian had revealed his unnatural gift in the course of saving Caius' worthless skin during an assassination attempt.

When Caius was a boy of eight, his father had been gored to death by a pagan shapeshifter who took the form of a giant stag. Early in his career as a soldier, Caius himself had nearly been killed by an army of wolves under the control of a shapeshifting pagan priest on the island of Eburos. So, when Decian had unexpectedly turned into a massive, jet-black hellhound with the rather disconcerting ability to rip out men's souls and fling them into the void, Caius… hadn't taken it well.

In retrospect, he wasn't proud of his reaction, which had included holding a sword to his lover's throat and threatening to kill him if he ever so much as entered Caius' presence again. Fortunately, or perhaps unfortunately, Decian wouldn't know a grudge if he tripped over one. Days later, when Caius had ended up at Saleene's door, poisoned and weak to the point of helplessness, Decian had foregone the very sensible reaction of bashing Caius over the head in favor of giving him a second chance.

They'd reconciled in this very room, on the first night after they'd sought shelter here. And by 'reconciled,' Caius meant that he'd invited Decian to pound his arse until neither of them could remember their own names. Then, the following day, Caius had discovered that he'd just been buggered by the presumptive heir to the Alyrion Empire.

If he could somehow travel back to the hours before that revelation…

But perhaps that was shortsighted of him. Hadn't he been lamenting the empire's future under the rule of any of Constanzus' three sons by the Empress Stasia? The oldest, Proclus, was a drunken fool. The middle son, Kaeto, was a sadistic viper clad in human flesh. The youngest, Bruccias, was so slippery and backstabbing it was a wonder someone hadn't put a knife through his ribs long before now.

And here was Decian—a genuinely kind and good man. The eldest son of the emperor, by his lawfully married Kulawi wife. Not to mention, a pagan shapeshifter with royal Alyrion blood running in his veins.

God. The imperial court would eat him alive and pick their teeth with his bones.

The aforementioned heir presumptive was currently curled against Caius' left side. Caius was painfully aware that he was lying on the ancient palliasse like a plank of wood, stiff and unbending in Decian's loose embrace. He was also painfully aware that he himself hadn't made any sort of move toward physical intimacy since the most recent revelation, and that the atmosphere in the cramped space was growing heavy with unspoken words.

Eventually, Decian sighed and rolled onto his back. "Right. I'll be the one to say something, shall I?"

Caius only grunted, already dreading the next few moments.

Decian rolled up on an elbow, looking down at him even though he would barely be able to see a thing in the darkness of the stuffy little room. Or perhaps Decian could see in the dark, as a shapeshifter. Caius had never thought to ask.

His lover sighed. "I can't tell if you're angry at me, or if you're assuming you're going to die in whatever mad plan you're going to concoct with Aelio, or if I'm completely misreading this and you've simply got a bad case of indigestion. Would you care to enlighten me?"

In point of fact, Caius would have been perfectly content to remain in the stifling darkness, both unenlightened and unenlightening. However, that wouldn't be fair to the man next to him, and he knew it. He'd known it all along—he was simply a coward. He cleared his throat, which seemed to do very little to ease its tightness.

"Decian. *Think*. You're the heir to the Alyrion Empire. You can't keep fucking a used-up soldier twice your age." He'd been right. The words hurt to say aloud.

There was another heavy pause.

Finally, Decian spoke. "First, I'm not the heir of anything. I'm the same fugitive prisoner I was yesterday, and the day before, and the day before that. Secondly, I think we've established that I can fuck a used-up soldier twice my age very effectively if I want to." He hesitated. "Also, I have to say this—I weep for all your previous opponents on the battlefield if your current state is one of relative ineptitude. Because I'm sorry, but you're a bloody *menace* with a sword."

Caius huffed. "I used to be far more of one, believe me. My point still stands, though. You *are* the heir, whether you want to be or not. The last thing you need is to court the kind of scandal that could be used against you by your enemies in the future."

Decian placed a hand flat on Caius' chest, warmth radiating outward from the contact. "The only thing I want between me and my enemies is distance, Caius."

Caius closed his eyes against the darker gray silhouette looming over him. It didn't help. When he spoke, his voice was hoarse. "I don't think it's going to be that simple, Decian."

The fingers splayed over his heart twitched. "Then maybe this will be simple enough for you." There was a degree of unsteadiness hiding beneath the words. "Damn you, Caius—I'm terrified. And—" His voice broke. "I don't think I can do this alone."

TWO

Caius clenched his jaw, silently cursing himself for both a fool and a cad. He knew very well how much the revelation of Decian's parentage had rocked him. What must Decian be going through—the uncomplicated young man who'd only ever asked to be left alone to live and love as he wanted?

"Damn it, Decian," he said, covering his lover's hand with his and using the grip to pull him down so he was lying half on top of Caius' body. "Come here."

Decian collapsed without argument and clung. Caius wrapped both arms around him, ignoring the ache as the muscles in his damaged shoulder pulled.

"I don't want to be the emperor of Alyrios," Decian said against his neck. "I don't want to be the *anything* 'of Alyrios.' I just want to go somewhere people aren't trying to kill us. At this point, I'd even go live with the blasted barbarians on Eburos if it meant this would all just *stop!*"

"I know." Caius slid his right hand up to stroke over Decian's short, springy curls. "I *know.* I'm so sorry."

Decian buried his face against Caius' shoulder for a long moment. Eventually, he took a deep, centering breath, some of the tension in his slender, hard-muscled body loosening as he exhaled. "Please help me make all of this go away for a little while," he murmured, the words puffing warm and damp against Caius' skin. "I don't want to think tonight."

Caius was still cursing himself for a fool as he rolled Decian onto his back and kissed him.

Days after their arrival here, Decian was still wearing a makeshift toga fashioned from bedclothes. It was all he'd been left with after Caius lost the bag of clothing he'd been carrying for his lover while Decian was in hellhound form. There was nothing else—they had only the meager possessions they'd carried with them when they walked in the door. Caius had at least washed the dirty sheet that was all Decian had to wear — leaving him alone in the room with Caius' shirt and smallclothes, while he went out back to scrub and rinse the grimy length of cloth by moonlight.

The only positive side to this particular situation was that togas were exceptionally simple to unwrap, even for an old soldier with one bad arm. It didn't take much work before Decian was laid out bare beneath him, his lean form nothing more than a darker blur against the undifferentiated gray of the palliasse.

Caius returned to kissing him, recalling with aching fondness the day that he'd first pulled Decian onto his bed and pinned him there with hands and mouth, while he delivered exacting retribution for the younger man's earlier sexual teasing.

Word to the wise, Caius had told him. *Never tease a soldier — even a wounded one.*

Decian had immediately come back with, *Oh... I dunno — I feel as though it's working out rather well for me so far*, and Caius had been lost, there and then.

But the simple and straightforward nature of that first brief encounter wouldn't do tonight.

"Cross your wrists over your head and keep them there, no matter what... or else I'll make you keep them there," he said, pulling back from the kiss. He ran a possessive hand over Decian's hairless chest, exploring by touch and wishing there was enough light to see what he was doing properly. His meanderings led to the discovery of a flat nipple, the flesh softer and with more give than the skin around it. Decian hissed and arched, always so beautifully responsive to his touch. Caius rubbed the small nub as it pebbled beneath the rough skin of his thumb.

"Oh, gods," Decian managed.

Stilling his movements, Caius shook off the frisson of disquiet he always felt when Decian slipped up, his unconventional religious upbringing peeking through.

"I won't even chide you for that tonight," he said. "Seeing as how we're hiding out in a pagan safehouse, I suppose invoking the pagan gods is appropriate."

"Stop talking and touch me, *please*," Decian begged.

Caius shook his head, marveling for the hundredth time at what fate had brought into his life. Stress, worry, and nagging, half-healed injuries had drained him these last several weeks. Yet he was already half-hard in his breeches, after only a kiss and a few fleeting touches to a body he couldn't even see in the darkness.

"I'll touch you," he promised, "but tonight, you won't come until I let you. And I won't be letting you for a very long time indeed."

Decian choked on a strangled sound, but he obediently kept his hands over his head while Caius mapped every square inch of his body with lips and fingers. He was shaking by the time Caius finally closed a hand around his prick and stroked, only to let go when Decian's hard flesh began to swell and throb in his hand.

"You're a monster," Decian accused.

"Says the man who turns into a slavering hellhound," Caius shot back.

"*Rhitsaaru*," Decian corrected mulishly, using the Kulawi term for the legendary beast. "And I do *not* slaver."

"Hellhound," Caius insisted. "Big black beast of a dog. Slobber everywhere — worst I've ever seen."

"Oh my gods, *fuck you*," Decian said, and Caius couldn't help the laughter that wanted to bubble up in his chest, despite all the horrors surrounding them.

"Not tonight," he said. "I think if we used the last of the oil in the lamp, Saleene and Zuri really would murder us."

Decian grumbled something unintelligible under his breath, and Caius set himself to the task of teasing him to the edge and leaving him there, over and over, until he was confident that there wasn't a single thought rattling around inside Decian's head beyond his desperation to come.

"*I hate you*," Decian ground out. "I hate you, I hate you, *oh gods…*"

"No, you don't," Caius told him, silently adding, *though you definitely should.* Finally having pity on his victim, he firmed his grip and drove Decian over the edge.

Decian grunted; the sound wrenched from somewhere low in his chest. His spine arched, his prick spurting over Caius' hand — and probably his own chest and belly, based on the amount of force that seemed to be behind it. Caius gentled him through his release, until the spasms became shudders, and the shudders, stillness. He felt around next to the mattress for the freshly washed handkerchief tucked in an inner pocket of his discarded jerkin.

Before he could return to make a clumsy effort at cleaning Decian up in the dark, his lover groaned and rolled bonelessly toward him, fumbling at the lacing of Caius' breeches. He'd loosened them earlier to give himself some relief as Decian writhed and begged beneath his hands — so it didn't take long for Decian to get the clothing out of his way and free his rock-hard cock.

The jolt of his lover's hand closing around the sensitive flesh was nothing compared to the hot pleasure of lips closing over the tip. Caius drew an unsteady breath and fell back, bracing himself on one elbow as his need rose insistently.

"So good," he murmured, as Decian took him deep. His technique was sloppy with post-coital fogginess, and Caius couldn't imagine anything better. The speed of his own climax would have been embarrassing, had he not been waiting every bit as long as he'd made Decian wait. Ecstasy rose up and swamped him like a warm wave, drawing every bit of tension from his body and expelling it as he spilled into Decian's willing mouth.

His partner hummed and swallowed around him, and Caius had a moment's regret that he hadn't thought to do the same for Decian earlier — it would have eliminated the mess, for one thing. Thankfully, he still held the kerchief clutched loosely in his hand, so he made a clumsy attempt at wiping down Decian's chest when he crawled up Caius' body to lie next to him.

"Better now?" Caius asked quietly, once he was done. But Decian was already fast asleep.

For Caius, the nights spent with Decian in this strange limbo were a study in tortured conflict—he was painfully aware of exactly what he shouldn't be doing, and yet he did it anyway. Daylight brought clarity, thank heavens. In the light of the sun, Caius knew what needed to happen. And while he was less than confident of his ability to accomplish his goal, the steps involved in moving toward it were straightforward enough.

In due course, Pip returned a message from Aelio with a time and a meeting place. The tavern Aelio named was such a questionable establishment that Caius was frankly impressed he'd even known of its existence. Certainly, it was a safe bet that no one in his right mind would expect to find the prim and proper tribuni drinking there.

Caius entered alone and pulled down the hood of his cloak, running hard eyes over the disreputable crowd until he found a figure with familiar sandy hair and a spine too straight to truly fit in with his surroundings. He pushed his way through the crush of bodies, snatching at a hand that tried to worm its way beneath his cloak, presumably in search of a coin purse.

There was no point in telling the man he'd be sorely disappointed with the results of his efforts. Caius twisted the would-be thief's wrist until he squeaked, and then shoved him away. Aelio, who'd watched the brief exchange, lifted a brow.

"Hello, Caius. That little scamp Pip wasn't exaggerating about this place, was he?" he said, by way of greeting—which at least explained how the tribuni had learned about this tavern.

"Hello, Aelio," Caius replied, seating himself on a wooden chair that exhibited more stickiness than was strictly welcome. "I take it he's doing well these days?"

"Our new master of hounds?" Aelio's smile was a bit lopsided. "Yes, he appears to be. I'm glad to see you still in one piece, my friend—though I'll confess an unhealthy amount of curiosity regarding what this summons is about. Meeting with me openly, even in a place like this, isn't really the best idea."

"I'm well aware," Caius told him. "It's important, though. This involves Constanzus."

Aelio appeared startled. His brow creased, and he glanced around in an uncharacteristic show of nervousness. Around them, the clamor and buzz of drunken conversation covered their low exchange. No one was paying them the slightest attention.

"You've heard, then?" Aelio leaned forward, his frown deepening. "But… no. You couldn't have."

The familiar stomach-swooping sensation of yet another thing about to go wrong assaulted him. "Heard what?" he asked with a resigned sort of dread.

Aelio appeared to debate with himself for a long moment. "You're placing me in a difficult position, Caius."

"Yes. I am. Now, what is it I haven't heard?" Caius demanded, more forcefully. "Is he worse?"

A muscle in Aelio's jaw twitched. "Blast it all," he muttered. Then, in a quiet voice, "Yes, you could say that. Constanzus is acutely ill. He is not expected to survive more than a few days." He hesitated. "His symptoms are remarkably similar to yours after your house slave attempted to poison you."

Caius' stomach fell like a rock. "Hell and perdition."

"Quite," Aelio agreed.

With a deep breath, Caius put his elbows on the table and leaned in. "Is it true that the council intends to disband after the latest attack?"

The tribuni nodded. "It is. And no, you don't have to tell me what that will mean for the city. Or for the empire as a whole."

Caius itched to relay the news of Constanzus' previous marriage… of his unknown heir, who might conceivably salvage Alyrios from ruin. Or who, more likely, would end up getting stabbed through the heart before he ever set foot in the palace.

He held his tongue. It was Decian's decision to make, and he'd been quite clear that he wanted no part of his birthright.

"How is the empress faring?" he asked instead.

Aelio shot him a look of surprise, evidently not having expected the question. "She is holding her own against the accusations against her—so far, at least. It probably helps that His Imperial Majesty has softened toward her as his end nears. She often sits with him at his bedside."

A spark of hope kindled in Caius' chest. That was more than he'd hoped for.

"That's good," he said. "I need you to relay a message for me."

"Caius…" Aelio began.

"Not to the empress. To a particular pageboy of hers, that's all."

Aelio looked decidedly unreassured.

"The lad's name is Jules," Caius continued. "He's trustworthy, as much as can be said of anyone within the palace walls."

The head of the palace guard looked at him, unblinkingly.

Caius huffed. "Present company excepted, of course."

"Of course," Aelio echoed.

"Tell him I need an audience with Her Majesty, and that he can relay her answer through Pip."

Aelio continued to stare at him for an exceptionally long time.

"To what possible purpose, Caius?" he asked, at length. "You must know what kind of danger you'd be in, even attempting to enter the imperial quarter."

"As opposed to the danger of hiding away in a city tearing itself apart by tooth and claw, you mean?" Caius retorted. "I need to see the empress because I need access to Constanzus, and she's my only means of entry."

"You need to see the—" Aelio cut himself off, shaking his head. "This is madness, Caius. You must realize that. You're not a fool. Again, what can you possibly hope to accomplish with this gambit?"

Caius held the tribuni's pale blue gaze unflinchingly. "I hope to save the empire from civil war, before it's too late."

THREE

"I knew it." Decian scrubbed his hands through his close-cropped hair as he paced back and forth in the dingy outdoor area behind the safehouse. "I *knew* it would be something crazy."

He paused, pointing an accusing finger at Caius' face. "You're doing exactly what I said you were going to do. Risking your life, and for *what*?"

"Other lives," Caius told him without hesitation, and Decian threw up his hands.

"Why does it have to be you?" Decian demanded angrily, a red glow kindling behind his frustrated gaze.

"Decian," Caius said quietly. "Your eyes."

With a snarl of frustration, Decian closed them, and when he opened them, they were once more the deep, rich brown of fertile earth.

"It has to be me, because I don't know who else could — or would — do it," he continued. "People will die, and the chaos we're seeing now will seem like a gentle summer breeze compared to what's coming. There will be no safe place in the empire for you — or for Zuri, or Saleene, or anyone else suspected of pagan sympathies."

Decian drew breath as though he wanted to argue more, but then he made a sharp gesture of anger and whirled away, resuming his pacing. Caius reached out a hand and tugged him to a stop the next time he stormed past.

Words stuck in his throat. He wanted to tell Decian that he needed to fight for his birthright — to find his mother and get proof of the marriage, then bring it to the imperial court and demand a hearing. He wanted to beg him not to let Proclus or Kaeto get their hands on the Alyrion throne.

"If I'm not back within a day, get out of the city," he said instead. "Go to Eburos and live with the Wolf Priest. Go with Saleene and Zuri to Zuri's village in Kulawi. Go someplace—anyplace—where no one will hate you simply because of what you are."

Decian wouldn't meet his eyes. "Why do you have to be like this?"

He cupped the younger man's cheek and tipped his head up until Decian had no choice but to look at him.

"It's the only way I know how to be," he said, because there was no other answer. "But with luck, I'll be back by the end of the day, after convincing the emperor to issue a deathbed decree protecting the pagans from persecution."

"A deathbed decree." Decian's eyes closed again. "My father's dying. What in sanity's name am I supposed to feel about that?"

Caius tugged him forward into an embrace, despite the possibility of watching eyes inside the house. "Whatever you want to feel," he said. "Or perhaps you should feel nothing at all. He was never a real father to you."

Decian leaned against him for a long moment before pulling back. "I'm not sure that helps." He let out a pained breath of self-deprecating laughter. "You know, all I can think right now is that I really want to see my mother."

"You should look for her," Caius told him firmly. "In fact, after I finish this, we should go and do exactly that."

"Promise me you're coming back," Decian demanded.

Caius hesitated for only a moment. "I promise you that I will expend the last ounce of strength in my body and the last breath in my lungs trying."

"You're so bad at this," Decian said. "Why do you have to be so bad at this? Just say, '*Yes, Decian, I promise I'll be back within a day.*' Is that really so hard?"

"I can't promise you that." Caius reached up again, stroking the backs of his gnarled fingers over Decian's jaw. "But I'll do my best. With luck, you'll see me soon."

"Damn you," Decian said, and surged forward, pressing a desperate kiss to his lips.

The down-at heel tavern where he'd met Aelio two days previously had probably never hosted an armed honor guard of palace soldiers before. At the sight of them, Caius spent a nervous few moments wondering if he was about to be arrested rather than escorted.

Aelio's presence went some way toward reassuring him, even though he'd fully expected to be smuggled into the imperial quarter in secrecy. Instead, the empress had apparently exercised her power and was intending to bring him into her presence openly. Caius conceded that this approach might confer some possible benefits... in addition to the possible risks.

After all, Caius was only an enemy to whoever had tried to assassinate him. He *had* committed treason, it was true — when he'd saved Decian's life, after he was sentenced to execution. But as far as Caius was aware, Pip was the only person who knew Decian's identity as an escaped imperial prisoner, while he and Aelio were the only ones who knew that Decian was still alive.

Aside from that one mutinous act, the most Caius could be accused of was dereliction of duty. He'd run off after rescuing his house slave's daughters from the men holding them hostage. However, it wouldn't be hard to argue that he'd merely been indisposed for an extended period after his very public collapse in the council chamber.

The Empress Stasia was no fool. If she were, she wouldn't have been able to hold onto power after the latest attempt to discredit her. Caius trusted that she knew what she was doing by bringing him here under the gaze of everyone in the palace. It was, however, rather unfortunate that he would be parading past the palace servants and courtiers while wearing torn and stained street clothes in dire need of a thorough cleaning.

Or perhaps, a thorough burning.

To Caius' surprise, Aelio had even brought along his horse. That was an unexpected bit of thoughtfulness, and Caius patted the gray gelding's neck before stiffly hauling himself into the saddle. It felt strange to ride through the streets surrounded by so many men. Stranger still to approach the gate to the imperial quarter, and the palace compound beyond.

A part of him had wondered if he would ever see this place again. His home of several years—a richly appointed four-bedroom insulae—lay tucked away in one of the many winding streets. There, he'd bedded Decian for the first time. He'd bantered with Tertia, the acerbic house slave who'd later attempted to poison him. Most of his possessions would still be inside, unless someone had broken in and helped themselves to the building's contents.

It was likely there were things inside that would be of use to him, and he briefly wondered how practical it might be to visit the place after his meeting in the palace. He supposed that would depend heavily on how well or poorly the meeting went.

He and his escort of armed soldiers approached the opulent palace, stopping several times while Aelio entered into increasingly lengthy exchanges with guards stationed around the heart of the emperor's stronghold. Eventually, the group reached the main entrance and dismounted. Caius was painfully aware of the stares he was garnering in his battered cloak and battle-stained breeches.

The royal escorts formed up around him. Caius marched through the massive marble entrance into the lofty building where he'd spent so much of the last four years. Most of the memories here weren't fond ones. Looking back, he wondered at his own ability to ignore the obvious signs of rot at the heart of the empire for as long as he had. It wasn't as though he'd been unaware of things slowly going bad around him. Quite the opposite. The subject had weighed heavily on his mind.

And yet, he'd done nothing… until the day a random imperial bastard had been thrown to the royal hounds, only to miraculously survive his own execution. Caius could never have conceived where his spur-of-the-moment decision to save Decian would lead. And even now, he wouldn't dare guess at what path the future might take. He could only walk forward, one limping step at a time, and hope that his current desperate gamble would pay off.

"Good lord," muttered one crusty old courtier, as he recognized Caius walking at the heart of the honor guard.

Caius swept past him without making eye contact, all his attention focused on the upcoming meeting. They reached the wing that housed the imperial family without incident, heading for a seldom-used reception room rather than the private gardens where Caius had met with the empress twice before.

Jules, the empress' trusted pageboy, awaited them outside the room's double doors. He bowed low as the group came to a halt before him, the front guards stepping aside to allow Caius passage.

"Legatus Oppita," Jules said. "You are expected. The palace tribuni may accompany you inside, but the rest must stay behind."

Aelio gave Caius a piercing look before dismissing the rest of his men. Caius wondered if he were rethinking this whole thing. If so, it was a bit late now. After a moment, the tribuni shook his head wordlessly and followed Caius inside the room. There, the empress was waiting for them, seated at the head of the long meeting table.

"Legatus Oppita and Tribuni Aelio to see you, Your Imperial Majesty," Jules said, bowing low. Caius and Aelio followed suit.

"Approach," the Empress Stasia commanded, not rising to greet them. "Legatus Oppita, what is the reason for your request to speak with me?"

Caius straightened from his bow and crossed to the table with Aelio at his side, while Jules faded back to stand by the door. Recent events had weighed heavily on the empress, it seemed. She had always been a delicate woman, but new lines of strain were visible around her eyes and mouth.

"Your Majesty," Caius said. "Events beyond the palace walls are reaching a crisis point."

"So are events *within* the palace walls," Stasia said sharply. "What would you have me do regarding rabble burning and looting in the city, while my husband lies ill?"

Caius hid his surprise that she would bring up her husband's deteriorating condition unprompted. This was no time for mollycoddling, though.

"I need an audience with His Imperial Majesty," he said. "The same person who has been plotting against you is also plotting to plunge Alyrios into civil war. Your husband is the only person who can stop this madness before it goes any further than it already has." He sank to one knee at her feet, his injured body barking a protest. "Your Majesty, I desperately need your help. The *empire* needs your help. I humbly beg this of you."

At that, Stasia rose, her chair legs scraping against the inlaid stone tile. "My husband is dying," she snapped. "Poisoned by someone inside his own household!"

Caius didn't glance up from his supplicant position. "Then time is of the essence, Your Majesty."

Even without looking, he could feel the waves of tension sliding off the empress as she mastered her emotions. He didn't know enough about her to hazard a guess at what sort of weight she would place on saving the empire. She had always been a diffident and accommodating figure on her husband's arm—he knew very little about her as a person in her own right.

Did she resent the lofty title of empress, which confined her as much as it elevated her? Once Constanzus died, her delicate position would become even less tenable. If whichever of her sons had chosen to turn on her succeeded in ruining her, she would have nothing to show for half a lifetime of devotion to her husband except exile into obscurity... or, perhaps, execution.

"Very well, " she said, after what felt like a small eternity. "But you will see for yourself. The emperor is but a shell of a once-great man. Whatever you hope to gain from him, you are unlikely to get it."

Caius desperately hoped that wasn't the case. He needed a signature and a royal seal, and he would be relying solely on whatever dregs of goodwill Constanzus retained for a soldier who had once saved his life on the field of battle.

"Thank you, Your Majesty," he said. "All I ask is a chance."

One last chance for peace in the empire.

FOUR

Unlike the empress' receiving room, the emperor's chambers were heavily guarded. Apparently, it hadn't kept someone from poisoning the man—which was a rather good trick, given that he'd used food tasters for years to prevent exactly such an occurrence.

"How in heaven's name did anyone manage to get poison into him?" Caius asked Aelio, in a tone too low to be overheard.

Aelio's pleasant features twisted into a scowl. "We suspect the physician," he replied in a voice equally as low. "But the blasted man is nowhere to be found."

That made sense. Medicines wouldn't go through the testers, since they were formulated individually for the patient and might well cause symptoms of their own. Certainly, Caius had been subjected to enough noxious tinctures and herbal drafts in his younger days—concoctions he wouldn't have wished on his worst enemy, much less an innocent food taster.

"Even so," he murmured, "it seems a bit sloppy on the part of our conspirator, using the same method of attack twice."

Aelio made a wordless noise of acknowledgement.

In front of them, Stasia was engaged in a quiet argument with the one of the guards.

"No one is allowed in except yourself, the new physician, and the head of the palace guard, Your Imperial Majesty," the guard was saying. "Those were the emperor's explicit orders." The man looked exceptionally discomfited—as well one might when attempting to deny the command of an emperor's wife.

Caius raised an eyebrow, struck by the exclusion of the emperor's sons from that very short list of allowed visitors.

"I am your empress," Stasia snapped. "And the head of the palace guard stands right behind me, in case it's escaped your notice. Legatus Oppita is a trusted palace advisor who has saved my husband's life on the battlefield. You *will* obey my orders and open this door."

The guard shot Aelio a look bordering on panic.

"I'll take full responsibility, guardsman," Aelio said, not sounding overwhelmingly thrilled at the prospect. "Let us in, and if His Imperial Majesty is in any condition to shout at someone, he can shout at me."

Face pale, the guard ducked his head in a shallow bow and opened the door. Caius had never been inside Constanzus' private sanctum before. He suspected very few people had been. As one might expect, the main room was a study in opulence. Caius appreciated the martial flair to the decor—a reminder of the brilliant military man the emperor had once been.

Exotic weaponry lined the walls—blades, spears, and axes from faraway lands. The remaining bare spaces were hung with art, mostly depicting great battles. The furniture was richly embroidered and deeply cushioned. None of it was enough to distract from the overwhelming stench of illness in the room.

The smell of shit, piss, and vomit hung heavy in the air. Caius could relate all too well to the sad figure lying on the massive bed. If this was, in fact, the same poison that Tertia had used on him, the emperor was likely to be in agony.

The door closed behind them. Caius and Aelio exchanged a look as Stasia crossed to her husband's bedside. A wooden chair with a red velvet cushion on the seat sat next to the bed, and she sank into it, taking Constanzus' hand.

"My husband," said the empress. "You have a new visitor."

At first, Caius wasn't sure the emperor was even conscious. But after a moment, Constanzus stirred and groaned.

"No visitors," he rasped. "Told th' guards..."

Caius stepped forward without being asked, his errand here too important to stand on ceremony. He came to stand on the opposite side of the bed from Stasia, looking down at this man who had once commanded legions on the battlefield.

"It's Caius, Your Majesty," he said. "I need to speak with you urgently on a matter of grave importance to the empire."

Stasia had been right—the Emperor Constanzus was a mere shell of his former self. He'd been in decline for some time, but this gaunt creature with fever-bright cheeks and gray, chapped lips could *not* be the same person who'd swept across half of a continent, conquering and pacifying nation after nation.

Grizzled brows drew together like confused caterpillars above rheumy, unfocused eyes. "The empire?" he echoed, as though the words held no meaning for him.

"Your Majesty," Caius said, with increasing desperation. "Please—your people are on the brink of tearing Alyrios apart. You must make a proclamation declaring tolerance toward the pagans and ordering the end of the violence on both sides. I have a decree written—it needs only your signature and official seal."

He reached beneath his cloak and pulled out the sheet of vellum. There would be ink and a quill somewhere in the room, he was certain—a quick look around identified a heavy desk in the corner, made of some dark, exotic wood.

When he turned back to the bed, Constanzus was looking up at him quizzically. His features cleared, recognition flaring in that confused gaze.

"Caius!" A faint smile lifted the emperor's lips, only to disappear an instant later beneath a convulsive twitch of pain. "I know you. Of course I do. You were assigned to my private guard on the eastern front. Took a blow from a battle axe for me once, didn't you?"

"Yes, Your Majesty," Caius said, his stomach twisting in an unpleasant knot composed of equal parts nostalgia and desperation. Those had been simpler times, but he needed Constanzus' mind on the present, not the past.

The emperor patted Caius' hand where it rested on top of the sheet of vellum on the edge of the bed. "You were always my most loyal legatus," he murmured.

Nausea roiled in Caius' gut. *Loyalty, indeed.* He wondered how the emperor's opinion of him would change if he knew that Caius had spent the past few nights fucking his estranged half-Kulawi son inside a pagan safehouse, while secretly plotting ways to ensure none of Constanzus' acknowledged sons gained the Alyrion throne.

"The decree, Your Majesty," he said, a bit desperately. "If you would only sign it—"

But Constanzus was no longer looking at him. He'd rolled his head away, his faraway gaze landing on Stasia instead. He lifted their joined hands to his cracked lips. A shudder went through his frail body as he lowered her hand back to the bed. His lips pulled back as fresh pain wracked him, revealing yellowed teeth.

"Ishumi?" he asked. "Is that you?"

Stasia went very still.

Constanzus' eyes had once more grown unfocused, and Caius experienced a sensation of deep foreboding.

The emperor stared straight through his wife. "Ishumi. I'm so sorry, my love. I should never have let my advisors talk me into forsaking our marriage. Can you ever forgive me, dearest?"

Stasia dropped her husband's hand as though it had transformed into a red-hot coal. She rose abruptly from the chair, nearly stumbling against it in her haste.

Constanzus barely seemed to notice. His head rolled back in Caius' direction, though his eyes appeared totally unseeing. "Are you still here, Caius?"

Heart in throat, Caius took his emperor's hand. "I'm here, Your Majesty. Please, I beg of you—you must sign this paper. Aelio, bring a quill and ink, hurry!"

Constanzus' head moved weakly back and forth. "No. No... I need you to serve me one more time, Caius. It's my sons, Proclus and Kaeto. You must... you... must..."

The words trailed off. His body convulsed, the hand wrapped in Caius' own clenching in a death grip as a gout of blood erupted from his mouth, spilling down his cheeks and onto the bedclothes. The clatter of pottery breaking across the room dragged Caius' appalled gaze to Aelio, who had just dropped the pot of ink.

"The physician," Caius said hoarsely. "Your Majesty — summon the physician here immediately!"

Stasia didn't move, staring at the grisly spectacle of her husband coughing up blood with a sort of sick, detached fascination.

"Aelio!" Caius snapped — but the body on the bed had already subsided into weak twitching. Moments later, it went still.

Aelio's face was white as a sheet. "I fear it's too late."

Caius looked down at the carefully penned imperial decree — unsigned and worthless now. Even had he been fool enough to attempt to forge the emperor's signature and unearth the official seal from wherever it might be stored in these chambers, a spray of Constanzus' arterial blood marked the vellum like a silent accusation.

Too late.

It was too late.

He'd failed.

The empress resembled nothing so much as a doll carved in ivory, as she stared fixedly at her dead husband's staring eyes.

"You will not speak of this matter to anyone," she said, a telling quaver hiding beneath the words. "If either of you ever utter the name *Ishumi*, I will see your heads roll."

"Of course, Your Majesty," Aelio said. He grasped Caius' arm. "Come away, Caius. *Move.*"

Caius barely had the presence of mind to grab the sheet of vellum from the bed and stuff it inside his jerkin. Rather than pulling him toward the door through which they'd entered, Aelio dragged him deeper into the maze of private chambers.

"What are you doing?" Caius asked, trying with limited success to drag his wits back into some kind of order. The task was made more difficult by the series of realizations that seemed to be crashing into him like battering rams.

The emperor was dead. Proclus would ascend to the throne. The pagans in Amarius would be in imminent danger as the news spread.

Aelio was fumbling around with something on the wall of what appeared to be a private bathing chamber. A heavy clunk sounded from behind the decorative frieze, and a concealed panel swung open.

"It's a hidden passage," Aelio said. "Turn left at the junction, and it will take you to the empress' quarters. Find Jules. Tell him he's to smuggle you out through the sewers. I do *not* want you discovered standing over the emperor's blood-soaked corpse. This is going to be complicated enough as it is."

The fact that it would now be the empress who was found standing over Constanzus' body went unspoken. There was every possibility that Kaeto would be able to twist that fact against her somehow, if he thought it was to his advantage to do so.

"What about you?" Caius asked.

"What *about* me?" Aelio snapped. "I'm the tribuni of the palace guard. The emperor is dead. Long live the next *bloody* emperor, even if he's a drunken fool."

The horrifically surreal nature of contemplating Proclus on the throne was enough to make Caius retch.

"*Just go*," Aelio said. "Don't make this worse than it already is."

Feeling the situation crumbling around him, Caius went.

The secret passage was dark and narrow, hung with cobwebs and smelling of age and mustiness. When Aelio closed the panel behind him, he was reduced to feeling his way along the walls until his hand eventually slipped into nothingness—the promised junction. He turned left, following the cramped corridor to its terminus.

Momentary panic gripped him as he came up against the apparent dead end, but this had to be the back of another panel. The one in the emperor's quarters had swung inward; this one probably did as well. He forced himself to feel around the edges methodically, looking for some sort of mechanism. At shoulder height on the right side, his fingers encountered a recessed square that gave beneath his touch with a dull *thunk*.

The panel swung open, and he breathed a sigh of relief. That lasted until he slipped inside a bathing chamber that appeared to be a mirror image of the one in the emperor's suite, startling a shrill yelp out of the mousy little maid who was hauling buckets of heated water to the sunken pool in the center of the room. The girl froze, staring at him in obvious terror.

Rather than attempt to reassure her—since that would probably only make the situation worse—he adopted a matter-of-fact tone.

"There's been an emergency in the emperor's chambers. Where is Jules?"

The maid gaped at him, wide-eyed. Caius prayed that she wouldn't panic and throw the bucket of scalding water at him.

"H-he's stationed in the corridor," she stammered. "Outside the main door."

"Thank you," Caius told her, and headed in what he sincerely hoped was the right direction.

As it turned out, the architect had designed the emperor and empress' chambers to be precise mirror images of each other, so he was able to find the entrance without any missteps. Jules was, as promised, standing outside. He frowned when Caius appeared in the doorway, but covered his expression of surprise almost instantly.

"Legatus Oppita," he said. "I did not expect to see you here, sir."

It was time to put Jules' supposed loyalty to the test.

"The emperor is dead," he told the boy. "Tribuni Aelio and the Empress Stasia are still in his chambers, but it wouldn't be prudent for me to be inside the palace when the news spreads. The tribuni requests that you escort me out in secret through the sewers—assuming such a thing is, in fact, possible."

The lad looked deeply troubled, but he nodded quickly. "Of course it is, sir. There have always been plans in place for the evacuation of Their Majesties in the event of the palace being overrun by enemy forces. You came into Her Majesty's quarters through the secret passage, I take it?"

"I did," Caius informed him.

Jules nodded. "Back the way you came, then, sir," he said, and ushered Caius into the empress' rooms once more. After a quick glance up and down the corridor, the pageboy closed the double doors behind them. Not before Caius heard the distant echo of shouting, however.

It appeared the emperor's death was no longer a secret.

Jules led Caius to the bathing chamber, and lifted a finger to his lips as the maid started to say something. "Not a word about this to anyone except the empress herself, Maisie. Understand?"

"Yes, Jules," the girl said meekly.

The panel hadn't closed properly after Caius came through. Jules ducked into the main room and returned with an oil lamp. Its tiny flame smoked and sputtered as the lad urged him back inside the cramped passage. He closed the entrance and checked that it was sealed properly this time. When he turned, the flickering lamplight threw strange shadows across his young features.

"The escape route involves a very steep spiral staircase, sir," he warned. "The sewers are quite far below us."

"I'll manage," Caius assured him, hoping like hell that his leg would be up to the task.

Jules nodded. "Follow me. I'll light your way."

He squeezed past Caius in the narrow space and started walking, continuing straight past the intersection with the spur leading to the emperor's quarters. There were other junctions beyond that one—perhaps leading to the princeps' chambers. Caius didn't ask. He was too focused on his footing, as the stone floor of the corridor grew slippery and uneven.

Eventually, they reached the promised stairs. Jules slowed his quick tread when it became clear that Caius wasn't able to match his speed. Caius leaned heavily on the rough masonry wall, gritting his teeth and favoring his bad leg. He lost count of the number of steps in the staircase fairly early on. It took a good quarter of an hour to reach the bottom, by which time Caius' muscles were screaming—and not just on the left side, where he still carried the fresh scar of a crossbow bolt in his thigh.

He was shaky with exhaustion as they emerged into a larger open space. It looked like an underground waterway with banks made of brick and stone. It smelled like a two-month-old latrine pit.

Jules handed him the sputtering lamp and pointed. "Follow the tunnel and don't take any side turnings, sir. It leads to an outlet on the far side of the river gate. There's an iron grate across the exit, but it's loose. You can push it out of the way enough to squeeze through, but please replace it afterward. It's the only unguarded way out of the imperial compound, and it mustn't become general knowledge."

"I understand," Caius told him. "Thank you."

With that, he turned and limped away in the direction the lad had indicated, knowing he was in for a long and unpleasant slog. Almost worse was the prospect of being alone with his thoughts after his abject failure to salvage the situation.

The next three hours were, in fact, terrible. The metal bars across the sewer outlet were heavy, and nearly impossible for one man with a bad shoulder to move. When he finally succeeded, he had to wade through a morass of foul-smelling mud that enveloped him nearly to the knees, trying to suck him down and trap him.

When he finally dragged himself free of the muddy riverbank, there was still a trek halfway across the city awaiting him. Darkness had fallen by the time he finally limped up to the door of the safehouse, having taken a circuitous route to ensure that no one could possibly have followed him.

Luka was manning the entrance—a massive man with a crooked nose and the flattened features of a professional boxer. He raked Caius with a head-to-toe gaze and jerked his head to invite him inside.

"Saleene!" he bellowed toward the interior of the house. "Your soldier is back! He don't look so good, either!"

Caius unobtrusively steadied himself against the wall as his balance wavered. Saleene appeared in due course, gave Caius a quick look, and cursed sharply under her breath. Caius' legs chose that moment to give out on him, and he slid to the floor with a grimace.

"How badly did things go wrong?" Saleene demanded. Her features were pale and pinched.

Caius shook his head, scrubbing a hand over his face. "I'm sorry," he said. "But we're *all* in the shit now. The emperor is dead."

FIVE

Half an hour later, the entire house knew about the emperor's passing, and Caius was sitting on the ground in the back yard in his smallclothes.

Decian, who'd set himself to scraping the dried mud off Caius' breeches and boots, kept shooting him worried sidelong glances. Saleene had stayed inside to meet with the others regarding the latest calamity, but Zuri was here, watching both of them with her arms crossed.

"Your mother's name," Caius said. "What was it, Decian?"

"Ishumi," Decian told him. His tone was wary. "Why?"

Caius nodded to himself. "Because Constanzus confessed to the marriage in front of the empress right before he died."

Decian's hands stilled for a moment before he returned to his work on Caius' ruined clothing. "Huh," he said, studiously conversational. "How'd she take it?"

Caius snorted and rubbed at his face. "About like you'd expect."

"Well, it means she's not really the empress, doesn't it?" Zuri observed. "Not like she was going to be happy about having it bandied about. I wonder if she already knew?"

"I doubt we'll have the chance to ask her." Caius shifted on his rump, silently cursing the rocky ground, but too exhausted to rise until he had to. "We need to leave. In fact, everyone who can do so needs to leave. And the ones who can't, or won't, should find someplace to hide."

Decian glanced up at Zuri. "The catacombs?"

Zuri nodded. "I expect so, yes." Her dark eyes landed on Caius, incisive as ever. "I'm guessing that's not what you have in mind, though."

"No," Caius said. "Decian, I was serious before. I think we should search for your mother."

Zuri's expression perked up with interest.

Decian frowned. "You... do?"

"Of course he does." Saleene joined them in the barren plot, ringed by a high stone wall. "I expect he's already plotting to install you as the new emperor. But to make a credible claim, you'll need that signet ring you told us about."

Caius scowled, glancing around quickly to double check that no one else was within hearing range.

Decian's expression closed off. "I already told all of you, I don't want to be within a hundred miles of the Alyrion throne."

"That's not why we should search for her," Caius said. "And while I desperately wish someone else besides Proclus and Kaeto would inherit the title, I also know damned well that anyone who tried would have a target painted on their back the moment they crawled out of the woodwork."

"Then why are you so eager to go after my mother?" Decian asked.

Caius closed his eyes. "Because if you're wrong about her having returned to Kulawi, and she's still in Alyrios, she's in as much peril as any other pagan practitioner."

Decian hesitated. "And if I'm right? If she's back in her home village beyond the Southern Desert?"

"Then that's an excellent place for you to be, as well."

Caius prodded at his emotions, wondering if he was truly so ready to discard Decian's claim to his title. He was conflicted—there was no denying it. But he was also cognizant of the danger involved. Additionally, he wasn't certain how one would even go about installing an emperor who continued to repeatedly and vehemently renounce the position.

And... it was *Decian*. His lover. His generous, uncomplicated lover who occasionally turned into a slavering hellhound and ripped people's souls out by the roots. The entire situation was such an impossible tangle that shunting Decian off to safety in Kulawi seemed like the only potential strategy not doomed to end in utter disaster.

For his part, Decian appeared a bit wrong-footed in response to Caius' declaration. "I assumed you'd try to talk me into making a claim."

"It's not my decision to make," Caius told him.

They locked eyes for a moment, as though Decian were trying to ferret out any dishonesty on Caius' part. After a long pause, he tore his brown gaze away.

"What about you two?" Decian asked Zuri and Saleene.

Saleene's complexion was pale. Dark circles underlined her catlike eyes. Ever since she'd been ripped from her brothel—the place she'd made her own after building it up from nothing—she'd been struggling.

Zuri rested a hand on her shoulder. "It sounds like we might be heading in the same direction."

Saleene covered her hand and squeezed. "Yes, I suppose we might be, at that." She sighed. "I've always been curious about a place that doesn't believe in marriage, and doesn't bat an eyelash at people like me."

"You mean sarcastic hard-asses?" Decian asked, deadpan.

"Very funny," Saleene said.

Zuri snorted. "I think she means two-spirit people."

It made sense, and it went some way toward putting Caius' mind at ease. Saleene had been born into a male body, and forced to live that way against her will for a good part of her life. In Alyrios, she was able to live as she liked, but only in the shadows. In Kulawi, she would be unremarkable—at least in the sense of her gender.

"So you want to stick together?" Decian said. "Even if it means searching for information about my mother in our old village first?"

The pair exchanged a speaking look.

"I will admit, I'd like to know more about your mother and her story," Saleene said slowly.

"Plus, I gather Caius is pretty good with a sword," Zuri said, with every indication of seriousness. "Could come in handy on the road."

"Once a respected legatus, now reduced to hired sword," Caius grumbled, thinking that he'd be lucky to even lift a sword in his current condition.

"Well, I don't know about *hired*," Saleene said, giving him a critical onceover. "I'm used to money flowing in the other direction when it comes to our relationship."

"Yes. Money," Caius said. "I'm sorry to say—if you've still got any, you'll likely be the one funding this expedition."

"I'd rather assumed that would be the case," Saleene replied, dry as dust.

"One thing about being a pair of whores," Zuri added, "there's always a market for our business."

Caius cringed internally at the implication, only to mentally berate himself for a hypocrite an instant later. As Saleene had said, he'd certainly paid enough coin for her services over the years.

"Has anything been decided inside?" he asked, redirecting the conversation.

Saleene's expression turned sour. "Typical waffling. Some people plan to leave the city. Others want to stay and fight, because they're apparently idiots with a death wish. Some want to leave, but can't, for whatever reason. They'll hide out as best they can, I would assume."

"We should arrange to leave as soon as possible," Caius said. "Conditions are unlikely to improve in the coming days, to put it mildly."

Internally, he dreaded the thought of tackling such a journey on foot—exhaustion, nagging wounds and all. He would have to talk to Decian about traveling on four legs instead of two. Depending on how tight the money was, even the added expense of acquiring boots and proper clothing for him might be prohibitive, assuming they also wanted to eat.

"Yes," Saleene agreed, sounding as tired as Caius felt. "Shall we aim for two days hence? Getting supplies is going to be a real challenge as things stand now."

"Two days it is," Caius agreed, hoping like hell that he could at least get some decent rest before then.

Rest was something of a hit-or-miss proposition, but Caius did receive a message from the familiar errand boy the following afternoon. It was cryptic—a mere two words. *Livery stable.*

But it had come via Pip, which made Caius think it had probably originated with Aelio. Whatever the case, it seemed too vague to be a trap. Caius roused himself for the walk to the livery where Aelio had once left his servant's mule for Caius' use. If that wasn't the livery in question, then the message was as good as useless. It could mean anything.

Decian insisted on accompanying him in canine form. Caius tamped down his instinctive resistance to the idea, knowing anything that might dissuade angry people in the streets from accosting him was likely to be helpful in the current circumstances.

In some ways, the presence of the hellhound—the *rhitsaaru*—at Caius' side would never grow less surreal. In others, it was becoming almost a familiar ritual. Once again, Decian donned the blasted leather collar that Zuri had provided from some obscure corner of the brothel that Caius didn't want to know about.

With luck, this time he would at least refrain from shifting form in front of witnesses. If he didn't, this was likely to be a journey with a very abrupt and ignominious ending. But in the meantime, people were giving them a wide berth, even in areas packed with men and women chanting angry slogans.

He wondered if Proclus had been crowned yet. It felt odd to be so detached from the goings-on at the palace. No doubt he could have asked someone in the angry mob and received news that might or might not be accurate—but for now, his goal was the livery.

When he arrived, he was greeted with a wary reception by the man inside. With a gesture, Caius indicated Decian should stay just inside the door, where he wouldn't startle the horses. The massive hellhound plopped its haunches down to wait. On a hunch, Caius introduced himself as Parsus—the name of Aelio's servant—and said his master had sent him.

The mistrustful expression on the man's face eased. "Oh, right. I remember you. You're here for the gelding and the mule, then? The saddles and bridles are in the tack room. There's a set of saddlebags, too."

Aelio, you beauty, Caius thought. *I'll add this to my running debt to you.*

"Thank you," he replied, holding his rampant speculation regarding the saddlebags in check with difficulty.

The man conveyed him to a pair of tie stalls, where Caius found his familiar gray gelding standing next to the hard-mouthed molly mule belonging to Parsus. As promised, tack awaited him as well. The saddlebags held a promising heft, but he resisted the urge to open them and look at the contents.

"Everything's as your master left it," the man said quickly. "I run a professional establishment."

"I'm sure you do," Caius agreed.

The livery's proprietor relaxed. "You're looking a lot better than last time, if I may say so. Terrible ague going around this year."

"Yes. Worst I've ever had—I definitely don't recommend it," Caius replied gravely, and went to saddle the animals.

After confirming that the bill was paid up—which was just as well, since he only had a handful of copper coins to his name at the moment—he led the gelding and the mule toward the stable doors. The mule cocked her long ears at Decian's canine form, only to lose interest almost immediately. She'd been exposed to him once before and seemed to have concluded that he was harmless. Caius' gelding snorted and balked, sniffing the air for long moments. After giving a mighty shake, the horse consented to approach the huge dog.

Idly, Caius wondered if the gelding remembered Decian's human scent and was somehow able to connect the two. The gelding had been oddly skeptical of Decian from the start—long before Caius had discovered the truth of Decian's other nature. Whatever the case, both animals accepted the beast's presence without too much drama, which was a relief.

"Careful out there, mate," the proprietor called after him. "It's getting crazier by the day."

"Same to you, friend," Caius replied.

Gathering up the reins, he hauled himself inelegantly into the saddle. Wistfully, he spared a thought for his youth, when he'd vaulted onto horses' backs without a second thought, saddle or no.

Decian gazed up at him as he settled into place, arranging the gelding's reins in one hand, and the mule's in the other.

"Come on," Caius said, and headed once more into the confusion and chaos of a city rife with unrest. "Let's get back to the others."

SIX

Saleene and Zuri were nowhere to be found when Caius and Decian returned to the old house. Caius had stopped in a deserted alley a block away to allow Decian to shift form, remove the dog collar, and don his makeshift toga out of sight of any onlookers.

When they arrived, Caius sent Decian inside rather than ask him to help with the animals while barefoot. For lack of any better options, he picketed the horse and mule in a corner of the rocky, enclosed yard that still had some tufts of dry grass clinging to life. After hanging water buckets for the animals, he returned to the house with the saddlebags to see what, if any, news had arrived in their absence.

There was nothing of particular interest or relevance. Evidently, Proclus had insisted on a full ceremony with all the trimmings for his coronation, even as Amarius burned around him.

"What an arsehole," Decian muttered, and Caius couldn't bring himself to disagree.

On the positive side, when Caius retreated to their shared room to investigate the saddlebags, he found that they contained money in the amount that a palace tribuni might be able to spare on short notice. There was also enough dried meat and hard cheese to feed four people for a couple of days, along with a short letter.

When Zuri and Saleene finally showed up, it was full dark. Caius was loath to admit that he'd stayed up waiting for them like an anxious father awaiting a pair of daughters out past curfew... but the city was becoming a dangerous place.

As the two women approached the house, Caius took in the smear of gray walking between them in the moonlight. It had once been a horse—presumably. Now, it appeared to be little more than sagging skin draped over jutting bones.

"Don't judge," Saleene snapped at him, as Zuri closed the gate to the yard behind them. "I got it from the knackers. It can at least carry supplies for us until it drops dead of extreme old age and decrepitude."

Decian approached the elderly animal, which sniffed at his fingers for a moment and then sneezed all over him.

"I used to have a pony that would have got on well with you," he told it, wiping his face.

"Put it with the others," Caius said. "Aelio came through for us—we have my gelding and a good mule, as well. Also, a bit more food and additional coin."

"Well, well," Saleene mused. "Your pet tribuni is turning out to be a useful ally."

"Mostly, he just wants me far away from here," Caius told her. "He also sent a note to the effect that his life would be a lot simpler if I didn't keep popping up to cause trouble."

"Well, we were going anyway, so I suppose he'll get his wish," Zuri said, patting the aged horse gingerly on the neck.

"I suppose he will," Caius agreed.

"So, we're leaving first thing in the morning?" Decian asked. "I think this poor beast might collapse if someone tried to sit on it—but if I walk and Caius rides his horse, the two of you could switch off riding the mule."

"I can walk part of the time, as well," Caius said, not liking the implication that he was an invalid who needed coddling.

"You could, yes," Saleene agreed tartly. "Assuming we care to move at a snail's pace."

That stung, mostly because it was true.

"To be fair, I think the pace will be determined by this relic," Decian said, scratching the horse's forehead.

"Whatever the case, we should all try to get some rest tonight," Caius offered, wondering when it was that he'd become the person for whom accommodations needed to be made. "If someone can scare up a blanket, I'll sleep out here to make sure no one gets any ideas about stealing the horses or saddles."

"I'll keep you company," Decian said. "I get the impression several people have already left. There should be some spare bedding we can drag out here to use."

"That's a plan, then." Zuri yawned and stretched as Saleene led the horse off to tie it with the others. "Can't say I'm really looking forward to becoming an early riser after so long spent sleeping during the day."

"Occupational hazard," Caius suggested. "For what it's worth, we may be better off traveling at night as long as there's a moon to see by. But I think it would be prudent to get out of the city as soon as possible. We can worry about details later."

"The village where I grew up is less than a day's travel from Amarius," Decian said. "We can get that far by tomorrow night, and plan the rest from there."

"Yes," Saleene agreed, rejoining them. "One step at a time. Well, goodnight, you two. One of you will probably have to wake us in the morning when it's time to leave."

"I'll go find us a couple of blankets," Decian said, and joined them as they headed for the back door of the safehouse.

Caius limped over to a convenient section of fence near where the animals were tethered and started clearing it of rocks.

⁕

The moon had grown low in the sky when a commotion at the front of the house jolted Caius from sleep. Raised voices were coming from that direction, shrill in the nighttime darkness. Decian jerked upright from where he'd been slumped against Caius' side with a groggy, "*Wha—?*"

Caius was already climbing to his feet. "Stay here. I'll see what's going on. Can Fido jump this fence if need be?"

Decian, still half asleep, eyed the stone fence. "Er… probably?"

"Watch over the horses. If anyone armed comes in here and you're not completely confident you can take them on, get away and go to the catacombs. It sounds like there should be other people you can join up with hiding there."

"What? Caius, *wait!*" Decian called after him.

But Caius was almost to the house and didn't answer.

Inside, almost everyone who still remained was awake and rushing toward the front door. The sound of people talking over each other was more pronounced than it had been outside, but there were no screams or sounds of battle. Caius pushed past the people clustered in the hall, revealing a gray-haired man sitting on the floor of the entryway. The newcomer was clutching his bleeding arm. Luka and a woman Caius didn't know by name crouched next to him.

"They set fire to the house and attacked us when we fled outside!" The injured man's voice was high and quavering. His face was bruised, one eye nearly swollen shut.

"And this happened at another safehouse?" Luka asked. "How did they even know where it was?"

"I don't know," the newcomer said. "There were dozens of them, armed with pitchforks and clubs. I don't know how they found us!"

Caius strode forward, sheathing his sword. "Let me get this straight. Civilians attacked the pagan safehouse where you were staying? You're certain they weren't Amarian guards?"

The man looked up at him with his one good eye, tears running down his swollen face. "No, they were just regular people. Men and boys; a couple of women."

Caius exchanged a glance with Luka. "And you came straight here after you got away from them?"

The man nodded.

"Were you followed?" Caius asked, even though the answer wouldn't change what needed to happen next.

"I..." the man began. "I... don't think so?"

"Fucking brilliant," Luka muttered.

Zuri shoved her way through the small crowd of gawpers to reach them. Saleene followed a moment later.

"Problem," Caius told them, rather unnecessarily. "Another safehouse was just attacked, and this one might also be compromised. Everyone needs to leave. *Now*. Us included."

Saleene cursed, short and filthy. Zuri scrubbed at her face. Around them, the others started talking over each other again.

"*Quiet!*" Luka bellowed, startling everyone silent. "He's right. If someone followed this man to see where he went, they might be going back to get reinforcements. Wake up everyone who's still asleep. Anyone who's got nowhere else to go can follow me to the catacombs."

Reassured that the wider situation was under control—as much as it could be, under the circumstances—Caius turned to his companions. "Decian's still out back, watching the horses. Get whatever supplies you were able to gather today. I'll go and start saddling up."

The two women's faces settled into grim lines.

"We'll meet you outside," Zuri said.

Caius returned to the yard, where he found Decian pacing restlessly, one of the blankets wrapped around his shoulders against the nighttime chill. He stopped abruptly as Caius approached.

"What's happened, what's going on?" he demanded.

"It was a refugee from another safehouse that was attacked by a mob," Caius told him. "The fool's not sure if anyone followed him here or not. Saleene and Zuri are getting our supplies. Everyone's leaving before a torch-wielding mob shows up here, too."

"*Balls*," Decian said succinctly.

Caius headed for the saddles and grabbed one, steadying his gelding with a word and swinging it onto the animal's back. By the time Saleene and Zuri appeared, carrying saddlebags and bedrolls, he'd cinched up the mule's girth as well and was about to bridle her.

"Caius, can your horse carry Zuri double with me, for long enough for us to get out of the city?" Saleene asked. "The sooner we manage that, the happier I'll be."

"Yes," he said. "I can take the mule, god help me. Decian, I hate to ask, but—"

"I'll shift," Decian replied. "Where's the damned dog collar?"

Caius jerked his head toward Saleene's flea-bitten gray nag. "Does that thing trot?" he asked, and went to rummage for the collar.

"It will if it knows what's good for it," Saleene said.

The nag flickered an ear at her and went back to chewing on its mouthful of grass.

"The village we're heading for is southwest of the city," Decian said, accepting the strip of leather and buckling it around his neck with an expression of distaste.

"We'll leave by the southern vaia," Caius said. "It shouldn't be heavily guarded."

"It may not be guarded at all, if all the soldiers are busy trying to keep the peace inside the city itself," Saleene said.

She and Zuri finished strapping the extra packs and bedrolls onto the nag. Caius rolled up the blankets he and Decian had appropriated for their earlier vigil and tied them onto the back of the mule's saddle, since more blankets were usually better when traveling. Lastly, he accepted Decian's toga. The air twisted, and the mastiff-like hellhound once more stood where a man had been an instant earlier.

The nag snorted, looking more alert than it had at any point previously.

"Let's go," Caius said, taking up the mule's reins and the nag's lead.

He opened the gate, turning back in time to see Saleene settle into the gelding's saddle. Before he could ask if Zuri needed a leg up, the dark-skinned woman hooked an elbow through Saleene's and vaulted up behind her, neat as you like.

Caius contented himself with clambering onto the thankfully shorter mule, at which point he was quickly reminded of the beast's abominably hard mouth. As he wrestled it around and got the nag sidled up next to it, he spared a moment to wonder if Aelio's choice of donated mount was a jest at his expense... or perhaps a subtle bit of revenge on Caius for making the tribuni's life even more difficult that it already was.

Caius nudged the mule through the gate, tugging the nag along with him. The hellhound took up position on the mule's other side, and Saleene guided Caius' gelding through after them. As soon as they reached the darkened roadway, Caius urged the mule into an amble, praying the nag would be able to keep up.

The aged creature let out a couple of bone-rattling coughs, sneezed explosively, and took up a steady trot. Somewhat amazingly, it appeared to be more or less sound.

Saleene trotted up until the gelding was abreast of the mule, riding on the far side of the nag so they could talk without having to shout at each other. Zuri sat easily behind her, an arm wrapped around Saleene's middle for balance.

"If we keep to the residential areas, we'll be less likely to run into trouble," Saleene said.

"Unless we run into the mob that's burning safehouses," Zuri added, rather unhelpfully in Caius' opinion.

"Agreed on both counts," he said. "We've got maybe an hour before we lose the moon, and another hour after that until predawn."

After being cornered by assassins in an unremarkable alley in this part of the city, Caius would never again assume that he knew Amarius' backstreets better than anyone who might be following him. But with a bit of luck, no one would be following this time.

He sincerely hoped that the other refugees from the safehouse made it into the catacombs unmolested. This wasn't quite the exit he would have chosen, but as long as they got out of the city safely, he supposed the details were unimportant.

The knowledge that he was well and truly abandoning his post—if you could even call it that, anymore—was a sobering one. He'd been trying not to think about it too closely.

It was an open question whether Constanzus' death made Caius' decision easier or harder. The idea of Proclus in power was... unimaginable. Not that he would wish Kaeto in power either, but somehow that prospect seemed, if nothing else, a bit less surreal.

He told himself that he would ensure the others got to safety, help find Decian's mother if it was possible to do so, and then return to see out his duty to the empire. What form that duty might take remained something of an open question.

"I trust you can multitask well enough to brood while also keeping an eye out for danger," Saleene said.

He shot her a sidelong glance in the waning moonlight. "Saleene, I've raised brooding to an art form. Have a bit of faith."

The acerbic grunt he received in reply wasn't precisely a ringing endorsement. Nevertheless, they continued along the meandering backstreets, the silence broken by the clop-clop of hooves on cobblestone and the faint, rhythmic wheeze of the nag's breathing. In the distance, new fires lit the sky orange as the people burned their own city. When they slowed to let the nag catch its breath, the sound of faraway crowds shouting and chanting filtered to them.

Eventually, they reached the main vaia leading south out of Amarius. They were not the only ones fleeing the city tonight. A steady stream of people on foot, on horseback, and in carts lined the road, all heading in the same direction—*away*. As it had the previous afternoon, the presence of the massive black dog at Caius' side discouraged anyone who might have been tempted to go after their horses or supplies.

As Saleene had suspected, there was no sign of the Amarian guard. Either they were, in fact, stretched too thin to spare the manpower, or the new emperor-to-be didn't care who came into or out of the city.

The closely crowded buildings of the central capital gradually thinned out to nothing, until they were riding through open country. The number of people on the road with them grew smaller at every crossroads.

Eventually, Saleene indicated a road going west. "This should take us in the direction we need to go, yes?"

"I think so," Caius agreed.

"I can barely see my hand in front of my face," Zuri said. "We'll have to stop for a bit until the sun gives us some light."

It was true. The moon was barely above the western horizon, and while Decian might still be able to see, the last thing they needed was to lame a horse by stepping in a hole in the dark.

Decian glanced up at Caius with glowing eyes and darted off the road, toward a blur of deeper black that was probably trees. They followed him, crouching low in their saddles to avoid overhanging branches, and dismounted in the clearing Decian led them to.

With the hellhound to keep watch for anyone approaching, they settled in to wait for enough predawn light to see by. When blackness turned to gray, they emerged once more from the trees, rejoining the handful of early morning travelers on the wide dirt road. It would be a full day's journey to reach the tiny village of Lucera, and then they would see if any answers might be found there.

SEVEN

"This is surreal," Decian said, as they approached the huddled collection of buildings surrounding a modest Deimonist temple. Once more in human form, he was wearing his toga, along with a pair of sandals Saleene had acquired for him in the course of gathering supplies for their journey.

He hadn't been to this place in more than a decade. In all honesty, he hadn't expected to ever walk these streets again. He'd been barely more than a boy when the emperor's soldiers—his *father's* soldiers—arrived to haul him away to prison.

With a small shiver, he recalled his mother's screams as he was taken away. She'd grabbed a kitchen knife and tried to rush one of the uniformed men. The soldier had knocked the pitiful weapon out of her grasp and shoved her hard, sending her stumbling.

Why hadn't the rhitsaaru appeared then? All he'd been able to do was kick and bite, his struggles ineffectual as the armored soldiers restrained his arms and dragged him off.

"All right?" Caius asked quietly, from the back of his gray gelding.

He and Zuri were riding, while Decian and Saleene walked. The old nag ambled along with its head at the level of its knees, laden with their packs and bedrolls, but it had kept up the pace throughout the day.

"I'm not sure," Decian replied truthfully. "The last time I saw this place, I was being dragged away to a jail near the Utrean border."

Caius grunted—a wordless noise that still managed to convey understanding.

"Where should we start asking around for information?" Saleene asked. "Were there any people here that you and your mother were particularly close to?"

Decian sighed. "Not really. We were different, and folks in these parts tend not to cozy up to people who are different."

"This ought to be fun, in that case." The words were sour. Saleene was dressed in practical riding clothes, as she had been at the safehouse. But her tunic was cut for a woman, and her long hair was tied back in a tight braid. The overall effect made her gender appear ambiguous, and it was indeed possible that the fact would cause problems in a place like this.

"What did you and your mother do for money when you lived here?" Zuri asked, reining in the mule.

"My mother took in sewing," Decian told her. "I worked odd jobs as a laborer, once I was big enough."

"Then we should look for people who did business with her and were happy with the work she did for them," Zuri said.

"That seems reasonable," Caius offered. He looked around. "Is there a pub or a tavern?"

Decian snorted. "No, nothing like that. Look around you."

"Village green?" Caius asked.

"Sort of. Though it wasn't usually very green." He glanced around to get his bearings. Some buildings had been torn down in the intervening years, while new ones had been erected. It was disorienting. "Here, follow me."

Decian set off toward the little shack that was the only real home he'd ever known. But when he turned the familiar corner, there was only a fenced pen full of pigs. He came to an abrupt halt.

"Our hut," he said blankly. "It's... *gone.*"

Feet hit gravel a short distance from him as someone dismounted, and a moment later a hand fell on his shoulder. He turned, meeting Caius' dappled hazel eyes.

"Nothing ever stays the same, Decian," Caius said, not without sympathy. "Even if the building were still there, it wouldn't be the place you remember."

And that was true, but somehow it didn't make the hut's absence any less jarring.

"I suppose it isn't as though I was going to move back in," he muttered, trying to put a brave face on it. He cleared his throat. "Right. Maybe we should —"

A new voice cut across him before he could articulate what it was he thought they should do next.

"Oy. Strangers. Help you with something?"

Decian turned, startled. A man was approaching — broad shouldered and dark haired, with the gnarled hands of a laborer. He knew that face, though it had been less lined and careworn when he'd last seen it.

"Gavinn?" he asked.

Gavinn stopped cold, staring at him. "Decian?"

Sheepishly, Decian raised his hand in an awkward wave of greeting. "That's me. Hello."

The man whose turnip field Decian used to weed in exchange for a few copper coins stood blinking at him in surprise. Then, Gavinn's gaze played over Decian's companions with clear misgivings.

"What are you doing back here?" Gavinn asked. "Thought you were in prison."

Somehow, he didn't think that telling Gavinn he'd survived attempted execution by turning into a mythological creature that could reap souls would help matters.

"Ten years is a long enough sentence for most things," Caius said, before Decian could come up with anything better. "Especially being born to the wrong father. He's out of prison now, as you see."

Gavinn's attention fell on Caius' hand clasping Decian's shoulder. Decian stepped away from the contact, hating the unwanted flush of embarrassment that heated his cheeks.

"Ten years is a long time, aye," Gavinn agreed, his tone neutral. "Hope you weren't planning on moving back in. A storm blew the roof off your hut. Neighbors had to tear down the rest."

One of the pigs oinked, setting off a brief cacophony of porcine squealing inside the pen.

"So I see," Decian said. "No, I wasn't planning on moving back in. I was hoping someone could tell me where to find my mother."

Gavinn shrugged. "She left. Dunno where she went."

"Oh." Decian wracked his brain for half-forgotten names. "I don't suppose Aileen still lives here? Or Yenna?"

Gavinn scratched his chin. "Yenna died two winters ago. Aileen's still around, though."

"Is there anywhere we could purchase oats and hay to feed our mounts?" Caius asked. "It's been a long day's journey."

Apparently, Gavinn's wariness about their group didn't extend to letting animals go hungry. He grunted and pointed. "Go to the house at the end of that road. Ask for Bren and tell him I sent you. He'll put the beasts up for the night, assuming you can pay."

"Thanks," Decian said, without much enthusiasm.

His life here hadn't been miserable. Far from it. But even as a boy, his skin color and the circumstances of his mother's arrival in the village had made them outsiders. Evidently, having been summarily arrested at the age of sixteen for unspecified offenses and thrown into prison hadn't further endeared him to the townsfolk.

Gavinn shrugged. "It's nothing. Glad you finally got out, mate. Good luck finding your ma." He gave the others a final mistrustful look and headed off to whatever he'd been doing before.

"Charming," Saleene murmured, hopefully too low to be overheard.

"We should get the horses and mule seen to," Caius said. "Decian, do you know where this woman Aileen lives?"

"I know where she lived ten years ago," he replied. "Hopefully she's still there."

They continued to the end of the road and arranged for the animals to be stabled overnight. Carrying everything with them that was too valuable to risk leaving in Bren's care, the others followed Decian wordlessly. He led them to a cottage that was slightly larger and nicer than many of the other homes in the village.

Aileen had been one of his mother's customers, and Decian remembered her as being a kind enough woman. He took a deep breath and approached the front door, noting that it needed a new coat of paint rather desperately. In fact, the entire front of the cottage was looking a bit ragged. Decian frowned and knocked against the rough wood.

A full minute passed before the door opened, revealing a stooped, elderly woman. Her eyes were milky with cataracts, and she clutched a stout walking stick in one hand.

"Yes, what is it?" she asked. "Who's there?"

"Aileen? It's Decian. Ishumi's son." Decian took in the changes that age had wrought in the old woman, mourning anew the lost decade of his life.

"Ishumi?" Aileen echoed. "Now there's a name I haven't heard in some time. Who's there with you, boy?"

"Friends," Decian said. "They've come along to help me find her."

Aileen made a considering noise. "Well, it's good to have such friends, I suppose. You'd all better come inside. Come, come!" She gestured with the stick for them to enter.

Decian relaxed a little, relieved that someone in the village would at least invite them over the threshold. "Thank you. My companions are called Caius, Saleene, and Zuri."

"Good to meet you," Aileen said, leading them into a cozy front room that had seen better days. "Can't say I get many visitors these days. Pardon the mess."

"Your hospitality is most welcome, madam," Caius said.

"Indeed it is," Zuri agreed, setting down the saddlebags she'd been carrying.

"Ah!" Aileen crowed. "I recognize that accent. If I could still see through these old eyes, I imagine I'd see skin as black as Ishumi's, yes?"

"We are countrywomen, both from Kulawi," Zuri replied. "Though we've never met personally."

"May we help by lighting a fire in your hearth?" Saleene asked. "There's a chill in the air this evening."

"Please do," Aileen said. "I'm not one to turn down assistance when it's offered. Things have been hard since my dear old Corinn passed. One of the boys from the village comes 'round to chop wood and fetch water for me, but it's still difficult. You listen to me, Zuri—you're still young. Have yourself a whole passel of children before it's too late, so you'll have someone to look after you when you're old."

"I will certainly keep your advice in mind," Zuri said, deadpan.

Caius and Saleene set about laying a fire and coaxing it into life. Meanwhile, Aileen moved to the kitchen area and started rummaging, muttering to herself as she did so. Before long, the five of them were clustered around the crackling hearth fire, eating bread and cheese, and washing it down with sour-tasting ale.

"So, you're looking for Ishumi, are you, boy?" Aileen said, once they'd finished the simple meal and expressed appreciation for their host's hospitality.

"Yes, that's right," Decian said, trying to keep a lid on the burgeoning hope in his chest. "Gavinn said she'd gone, but he didn't know where."

"She did go—that's true," Aileen confirmed. "And you won't find anyone here who can say for certain where she ended up."

Decian's bubble of hope deflated as quickly as it had appeared.

"But I can tell you this," Aileen went on. "She left the same day you were dragged off by those soldiers. She was going after *you*, Decian."

Decian's breath caught; his throat closing up and cutting off any words he might have wanted to say. A faint, choked noise emerged instead.

"She followed the men who took Decian away?" Caius asked, since he couldn't. "You're certain?"

"That's right, young man," Aileen said. "And I ain't never seen a woman more determined. Wherever they took you, that's where I'd start looking, Decian."

"Where were you kept prisoner?" Zuri asked. "Could you find the place again?"

Decian had to swallow a couple of times before speaking, and even then his voice emerged hoarse. "I know the name of the town nearby."

"Then surely that's a promising lead," Zuri said.

"Yet your mother never visited you in prison," Saleene added. "Or I assume you would have mentioned it. That argues against her having successfully followed you there."

Decian wet his lips. "Not... necessarily. Getting in as a visitor at that place required a substantial bribe. I doubt she could have come up with that kind of money. The guards didn't exactly let people in out of the goodness of their hearts."

To think that she might have been right there in the village, trying again and again to see him, only to be repeatedly rebuffed at the gates...

"Men can be so cruel," Aileen murmured, poking at the crackling flames with a rusted old fire iron.

"They can indeed," Caius agreed gravely.

"This was extremely helpful, Aileen," Zuri said. "Thank you—for both the information and your hospitality."

Aileen smiled, her deeply lined cheeks wrinkling. "As I said, I don't have visitors often. All I have to offer is what you see before you, but you're welcome to stay the night if you care to. It's too late to go gallivanting across the countryside to wherever you're going."

Decian set aside his excitement and trepidation at the idea that his mother might be within his reach after all. He settled in with the others, and spent the next couple of hours quizzing Aileen about the goings on in Lucera over the past several years. Aileen seemed happy to have an audience for her gossip and grievances; she passed the evening bringing him up to date on anyone she thought he might remember.

The others were quiet except for the occasional interjection. Decian could feel Caius' eyes on him... could feel the worry and protectiveness rolling off the other man.

At some point, they would have to talk—about Decian's legacy, and about the empire Caius loved so much, that seemed to be sliding into ruin before their eyes.

But not tonight.

Eventually, Aileen excused herself, saying that an old woman needed her sleep. She bade them make themselves comfortable in the main room near the fire, and disappeared into a small room at the back. Zuri and Saleene settled on one side of the hearth. Caius and Decian placed their bedrolls next to each other on the far side.

Decian lay down, reflecting on what kind of world they lived in—a place where he didn't even dare roll sideways into his lover's comforting embrace while staying in a blind woman's house. Caius' hand found Decian's forearm and gripped it, leaving Decian to close his eyes and focus on that single point of contact.

Tonight, they would rest. Tomorrow, they would begin their journey back to the place where Decian had spent the worst ten years of his life.

EIGHT

Caius had spent surprisingly little time near the Utrean border during his decades in military service. Constanzus had set his military sights on the barbarian lands to the north and east, rather than the rich coastal land to the southwest.

Once, Utrea had boasted an army of dragonriders that would have made any attempt at conquest an expensive proposition, even for an empire. Sometime before Caius was born, Utrea's king had entered into an agreement with Constanzus' grandfather—peace and economic cooperation with Alyrios, in exchange for the slaughter of all the Utrean dragons.

While Caius personally considered the long-dead Utrean king a fool for agreeing to such a treaty, in truth, it had successfully kept the peace between Alyrios and its powerful neighbor for decades. It might have done so indefinitely, but the bounty on dragons and dragon eggs hadn't quite succeeded in eradicating the beasts. Several years ago, the disinherited eldest son of the Utrean king had discovered a cache of dragon eggs and successfully hatched them, using the powerful beasts to wrest control of the kingdom from his younger brother.

It hadn't taken long for dragons to repopulate the skies—not only over Utrea, but also over the barbarian isle of Eburos, with whom the Utreans had an alliance forged through marriage. By that time, Alyrios was already so fraught by its own internal and external pressures that no aggressive action had been taken regarding the broken treaty.

Utrea and Alyrios retained a wary peace, and the borderlands between the two countries were more porous than most in the empire. The village that abutted the prison where Decian had been held for ten long, miserable years was firmly on the Alyrion side of the border, but in addition to the official language of the empire, the people here also spoke a sort of mongrel patois incorporating Utrean words and grammar. Many of them had the dark-haired, golden-skinned look of southerners rather than the paler complexions typical of Alyrios.

After some discussion, everyone had agreed that it would be safer for Decian to stay in animal form, rather than risk being seen by a prison guard who might recognize him. The settlement here appeared to exist mostly in service of the prison, with the residents working as guards or in other support positions.

Unlike Decian's childhood village, the place boasted taverns and whorehouses to keep its disgruntled men from focusing on the unpleasantness of their employment—and to separate them from as much of their hard-earned coin as possible. It rankled, but Caius had agreed to stay behind with Decian, waiting in the forested area outside the town with the horses and mule, while Zuri and Saleene paid a visit to the local prostitutes in hopes of gathering information.

"Either the place is tight-knit enough that they'll know about a Kulawi woman who used to hang around the prison looking for her son," Saleene said, "or it's not, but they'll know about places where pagans go to gather, and we can try there next."

Not to say Caius wasn't still worried, but it wouldn't surprise him overmuch to learn that there was honor among whores, even out here in the borderlands.

The place where he and Decian were sheltering wasn't far from the eastern edge of the town. He'd hobbled the horses and mule so they could graze in a small clearing set among the trees, surprised as always that the old flea-bitten nag had enough teeth left to do so. The rhitsaaru lolled beneath the shade of a large tree with its tongue hanging out.

Caius eased himself down to sit next to the beast, back resting against the tree trunk. He rather wished Decian would shift back so they could talk, but understood why he might find it appealing not to do so. What must it be like for him to be back here?

"I don't envy you, you know," Caius said. "It's probably not much different than me returning to the beach on Eburos where the Wolf Priest's army massacred my regiment."

The hellhound scooted over until its shoulders were pressed against Caius' thigh. Tentatively, he stretched a hand out and stroked fingertips over the blocky skull with its velvet-soft black fur. Decian sighed in contentment and rested his head on Caius' knee.

The light was beginning to fail when the rhitsaaru lifted its head, short ears pricked in the direction of the settlement. Caius rose, but Decian's lack of alarm told him clearly enough that it was only Saleene and Zuri's return.

"Well, that was certainly informative," Saleene said, by way of greeting. She grabbed a canteen from one of the saddles and drank, then handed it to Zuri.

Caius pulled out Decian's toga and proffered it at the giant dog. "Come on. Sounds like you'll want to be human for this."

Reality twisted, and Decian reached for the length of cloth, covering himself. "What did you learn?" he asked, sounding torn between excitement and trepidation.

"Your mother doesn't reside in this village any longer, but it turns out that she's become something of a local legend." Saleene's tone turned dry. "Congratulations. You, Decian, are the son of not only the former emperor of Alyrios, but also the notorious Black Oracle of Osca."

Decian blinked. "Excuse me?"

Zuri took up the tale. "Apparently, your mother became something of a regular fixture around the prison for the first year or so after she followed you here. When it became obvious that the guards were never going to let her in to see you, she put a curse on the place and moved up the coast to a fishing village."

"Where she has since made a name for herself as the focus for pagans and pagan sympathizers in this part of the world," Saleene finished.

"Good lord," Caius said faintly, not sure whether to be impressed or appalled.

"And this fishing village?" Decian asked, hope shining in every word. "It's called Osca? How far away is it?"

"Not far," Zuri said. "We can be there tomorrow—though actually getting an audience with your mother may be a bit more complicated."

"What do you mean?" Decian asked.

"This isn't Amarius," Saleene said. "But that doesn't mean a prominent fixture in the pagan underground won't have protections in place. If random people could just walk in and see her, she probably would have been arrested long before now."

"I propose we travel to this village and start asking around," Zuri said. "If we say that I'm her sister and Decian is her son, it might bolster our case for getting an audience."

"It's worth a try," Caius agreed.

Saleene raised an eyebrow at him. "Interesting how the loyal imperial advisor keeps getting dragged deeper and deeper into the pagan underworld isn't it?"

"I'm not sure the word 'loyal' really applies anymore," Caius replied. "And some of my best friends are pagans."

She snorted. "Some of your best friends are idiots for agreeing to come along on this insane quest."

"I dunno," Zuri said. "I'm more intrigued than ever to meet this woman."

"I'm glad you both came." Decian's words were barely more than a whisper.

"Well," Saleene offered, "it was certainly easier for the two of us to get this information than it would have been for you or Caius. I won't argue that."

"If you got it in a brothel, then I daresay you're right," Caius agreed. He glanced up through the tree branches. "Clouds are rolling in, so there won't be a useful moon tonight. We should camp here until dawn. Decian, can the rhitsaaru keep watch?"

"Yes," Decian replied. "Not like I was going to get much sleep anyway, after hearing that news. Get some rest, all of you. The beast will sense anyone approaching during the night."

They made the journey the following day, as planned. Osca was larger and busier than Caius might have expected. It appeared to be a thriving fishing village situated on an active trade route, bustling and happy compared to the settlement that served the prison.

That made a certain amount of sense, since it would have been difficult for a pagan woman with a widespread reputation to stay hidden and safe from arrest in a tiny hamlet. Mind you, Caius still found it rather impressive that she'd been living here more or less openly for years, apparently unmolested.

They found an inn with a stable attached for the animals, and used an uncomfortably large portion of their remaining money to pay for a room. Belongings safely stowed, they headed out to explore the area. Fisherfolk were a superstitious lot, as Caius' mother had always insisted. So it wasn't too much of a surprise to find, in addition to the expected Deimonist temple, a space near the docks filled with the trappings of the old gods.

Offerings of food, wine, and flowers lay on makeshift altars arrayed along a section of wall. Caius and the others stayed back while Zuri approached a raised plinth overflowing with simple gifts. A young woman with a baby on her hip stood in front of it, dashing a few drops of something from an ornate glass vial—perfume, perhaps, or blessed water.

Zuri took a few copper coins from her purse and placed them among the other offerings, bowing over the gifts and touching first her head, then her heart. When she straightened, the woman with the baby was watching her.

"Good afternoon," Zuri said pleasantly.

The woman seemed to realize she was staring and cleared her throat quickly. "Good afternoon," she replied. "You must be a visitor—welcome to Osca."

"Thank you." Zuri looked around, gesturing at the altars full of bounty. "My friends and I have just arrived. I must say, I'm pleasantly surprised to find… all of this."

The woman laughed nervously. "Oh, yes. Well, many of us here still follow the old ways as well as the new. It helps keep our men safe when they're out to sea."

"Indeed," Zuri agreed. "I don't suppose you could help me—I'm searching for my sister, Ishumi. In fact, I'm here with her son." She indicated Decian.

The woman's eyes grew rather wide. Her baby began to fuss, and she jounced it gently against her hip to quiet it. "Y-your sister?"

"That's right." Zuri gestured at herself, indicating her dark skin with a smile. "We figured it shouldn't be too difficult to find her in a sea of pale faces."

"Oh," said the woman. "Yes, I see. I think maybe you should talk to the Brotherhood. They might be able to help you."

"Thank you," Zuri told her. "We will. Where might we find this Brotherhood?"

The woman's eyes darted around before she refocused on Zuri. "You, uh… you could ask for Wes. He runs the tavern on the far side of the docks."

"That's very helpful. Thank you again," Zuri said.

The woman gave her an uncertain smile. "Good luck," she offered, and hurried off.

"That was a bit of an odd conversation," Decian said, when Zuri returned to them.

"Perhaps not so odd, if the villagers are protective of their oracle," Zuri replied.

"Right." Saleene gave a sigh. "Tavern?"

"Tavern," Caius agreed, and headed in the indicated direction.

Wes turned out to be a grizzled man somewhat older than Caius, but built like a bull. "Ishumi?" he echoed. "Nope. Don't know anyone by that name."

If Caius was any judge of expression, Wes apparently didn't care that it was obvious he was lying through his teeth.

"How about the Black Oracle of Osca, in that case?" Saleene said. "Perhaps *that* name rings a vague bell?"

Wes' smile wasn't a nice expression, and it made Caius' right hand itch to move to the hilt of his sword.

"Wouldn't know anything about that, either," he said. "Sounds like you've been listening to fairy stories."

Decian leaned forward, his hands slapping the wooden countertop separating them. "Not fairy stories."

The proprietor's expression went slack with shock, and Caius shot a glance at Decian just in time to see his eyes fading from glowing red back to brown. His hand *did* move to his sword then, as he silently cursed the younger man for his recklessness.

But Wes snapped his slack jaw shut, and didn't immediately yell for help or dive for a hidden weapon behind the counter. "Well, I'll be..." he said.

"As Zuri said, I'm her son," Decian snapped, still leaning forward on his palms. "*And I want to see my mother.*"

"Huh. Who'd've thought?" Wes murmured, as though to himself. He shook his head briskly, freeing himself from his reverie. "It's not quite that easy, lad. But I believe you — or at least, I believe you have a good case for seeing her. I'll relay the message. Where are you staying?"

Caius told him the name of the inn.

Wes nodded. "Someone'll be around in the morning to collect you, if she agrees to see you. If they don't show up, that means the answer is no — and in that case, I'd advise you to travel on. Osca protects our own."

"Understood," Caius said, placing a hand on Decian's arm when it seemed the younger man might protest. "Thank you for passing on the request for us."

Their host shrugged. "If you're telling the truth, it's a bit of a thing, innit? We've all heard the stories about her son."

"Believe me — the stories don't tell the half of it," Caius told him, and herded the others out of the tavern.

NINE

Decian was beginning to worry that he'd never sleep again. He paced the small available area inside their rented room in the inn restlessly, pausing now and then to stare out the window at the back of the building across the narrow alley.

His mother was here. He might see her in the morning, after years spent thinking that she'd gone back to her tribe in Kulawi, forever beyond his reach. She'd followed him. She'd spent a *whole year* trying to get access to him, inside the prison. And now, apparently, she was the Black Oracle of Osca.

That part, he could admit he hadn't seen coming.

She'd spoken of the old ways when Decian was growing up; taught him about the gods, and magic. Like many in the river tribes, she revered the goddess Danesti as a particular patron—Lady of the Sun, Lady of Fire. But Decian never had the sense as a boy that his mother was fanatical about religion. She made daily offerings at the small altar in the back of the hut. She prayed when times were particularly hard. She tried to embody the virtues of a good person. That was about it, really.

Somehow, trying to translate those memories of casual faith into 'becoming a pagan figurehead' was making his brain hurt.

"Come to bed," Caius rumbled from his spot on the floor.

Saleene and Zuri were crammed onto the room's single bed. Saleene muttered something unintelligible—but clearly uncomplimentary—and rolled over, pressing her face against Zuri's shoulder.

Decian sighed and crossed to the pair of bedrolls on the floor with reluctance, knowing he'd be no closer to sleep if he lay down. Caius lifted a hand to him, beckoning, the gesture aimed very slightly in the wrong direction since it was black as pitch in here, and he lacked a rhitsaaru's senses. Decian took the offered hand, because he was powerless to do otherwise, and let himself be drawn down.

"Better," Caius whispered, when Decian was draped half across his upper body.

Navigating by touch, sword-callused fingers wrapped around the nape of Decian's neck and guided him into a kiss. He fell into it with abandon, relief flooding him in response to the offered distraction.

It wasn't a kiss that seemed particularly designed to lead to anything else — probably just as well, with Zuri and Saleene lying in the bed barely an arm's length away. That didn't stop Decian from rutting gently against Caius' hip as the slide of lips on lips deepened, but Caius gave no indication that he intended things to go further.

There was something freeing about the simple lack of expectation, along with the need to stay quiet. Decian found it possible to lose himself in this little slice of *now*, letting tomorrow float free to be dealt with whenever it arrived. They might have kissed for ten minutes or two hours, but eventually, the stillness of Decian's mind let exhaustion trickle through.

Still held snugly against Caius' body, he slept. And when he opened his eyes, it was dawn outside.

"Up." Caius nudged him. "Have a quick wash and eat something. No telling when our visitors might arrive."

Decian levered himself off his lover's chest to find Saleene eyeing the gray light beyond the window as though it had personally offended her, while Zuri lay on her back on the bed with an arm thrown over her face. Caius rose and stretched cautiously, joints popping. The four of them moved around each other in an awkward dance, preparing for the day.

They were chewing on strips of dried meat from their travel rations when a knock came at the door. Decian opened it to reveal the inn's owner, a thin-faced man with pox scars and a receding hairline.

"People downstairs asking after you," he said.

"We're expecting them," Decian told him. "Send them up, please."

The man nodded and left. After a short wait, two sets of boot steps came up the stairs. Decian held the door open, waiting as a pair of armed men wearing the garb of common fishermen approached.

"Hello," he said. "The space is a bit tight, but please come in."

Caius and the others made room, pressing against the far wall. Decian saw his lover cataloguing the newcomers' weapons, his shoulders a tense line. He closed the door anyway, giving them relative privacy in which to speak.

The taller man's eyes fell heavily on Decian, assessing. "Colleague of ours says you claim to be the oracle's son. That true?"

"It is," Decian said. "We were separated when I was sixteen, some ten years ago now. Soldiers came to our village and hauled me off to the prison down the coast, on charges of being a nobleman's bastard."

The man nodded, offering no opinion on the fairness or unfairness of such an occurrence. "Is that right? Prove it."

Decian paused. "I'm not certain what proof you're after. My mother's name is Ishumi. She's from the N'Ganda river tribe in Kulawi. She has a pale scar on the back of her right hand where she scalded it in the kitchen when I was ten. She'd be... forty-one this year, I think?"

The man appeared unmoved. "Wes says you showed magic."

"Oh, that. Yes," Decian said. "Er... did you want to see?"

"Show us," said the man.

"*Decian.*" Caius' tone was a warning.

"They already know," Decian replied, feeling suddenly tired despite his earlier uninterrupted sleep. "My mother is a *pagan oracle*, Caius." *Whatever that even meant.*

He reached for the knot holding his toga closed and loosened it. The cloth fluttered to the floor, but he was already shifting, his other nature coming to the fore. His forelegs hit the ground, his senses changing along with his body. The scent of the men's fear hit him, along with the complex tangle of good and bad that defined every person in the room.

The shorter of the two visitors stepped back with a gasp, grabbing for a dagger from his belt. Decian immediately shifted back, crouching on the floor as he reached for the discarded toga and wrapped it around himself.

"Easy," he said. "I won't hurt you. I thought that's what you wanted to see."

"Bugger me blind," muttered the shorter one, sheathing his blade.

"I mean, you *did* ask," Saleene observed dryly.

The taller man had gone pale in the face, but he cleared his throat as Decian rose from the floor, tying his simple clothing back in place. "That I did. Well, then—I suppose you'd better come with us. We'll take you to her."

This was it. He was going to see her. His heart beat strong and fast against his ribcage.

"Thank you," he told them. "Is it far? Should we bring our horses?"

"It's a fair ways off," said the tall man. "But the horses won't help you. Come on. Let's get going."

They collected what they weren't willing to leave behind in the room and left. Their nameless escorts led them toward the same part of the city they'd visited yesterday, continuing past the open area with the altars set along the wall of a warehouse. This time, they went to the docks themselves, where fishing boats of all sizes floated next to weathered wooden piers.

Caius came to a halt, staring at the collection of vessels. "What is this? Where are you taking us, exactly?" His expression didn't look pleased.

"Told you," said the more talkative of the two men. "Horses won't help you get to the oracle."

Zuri frowned. "Is she living on an island or something?"

"Not an island," the man replied.

"A ship," said his companion. "Safer that way. No imperial guardsmen are gonna find our oracle unless she wants to be found."

"Oh," Decian said, picturing it. If the wrong people came poking around Osca, looking for her, she could simply sail away.

"That's both tactically brilliant... and rather unsettling," Caius said.

The tall man raised an eyebrow. "Missing your sea legs, soldier?"

"I left them on a beach on Eburos almost forty years ago," Caius replied, his tone one of mild self-deprecation. "If I ever had them at all, that is."

The shorter man snorted. "You can always stay behind, landlubber."

"Not a chance," Caius told him. "Just show me which railing to puke over."

"'Railing,' he says," mocked the tall man. "That's funny. Let's go, then."

They ended up at an open boat perhaps three times as long as a man was tall. It had a tall post sticking up near the center that Decian vaguely thought was called a mast. Four benches made of planks spanned the width of the unassuming craft—two in front of the mast and two behind. There were no railings. Caius eyed it dubiously.

"All right?" Decian asked him quietly, not overwhelmingly enthusiastic about the idea of sailing into the sea on this flimsy bit of wood himself.

"Never better," Caius said, in a tone of heavy irony.

By comparison, Zuri and Saleene appeared relatively unfazed.

"If you two are going to spend the whole trip throwing up, you can get your own bench," Saleene told them.

Decian followed the women's example, stepping cautiously from the dock into the unsteady boat. It was probably too big to capsize from the clumsy entry of a single person, but the unexpected swaying was still disconcerting. He clambered past Saleene and Zuri to take an empty bench at the front.

Caius joined him a moment later. "At least we won't have to row."

"Nah," said the tall man. "The wind's on our side this morning."

Decian craned around, to find him and his companion matter-of-factly untying the rope tethering them to the pier, tossing the heavy coils into bottom of the boat. The tall man went to stand at the very back, where some sort of device appeared to require his attention, while the shorter one started hauling on the ropes that lifted the sailcloth up the mast. Decian's human senses found the boat's movement highly disconcerting, though the rhitsaaru didn't seem much bothered.

"Bloody perdition," Caius grumbled, clamping a hand on the side of the boat as they turned away from land and began to pick up speed. All the color had drained from his face, leaving it a pasty shade of gray. He swallowed hard a couple of times.

Decian's stomach felt a bit queasy for the first few minutes, but it settled as he became more accustomed to the swaying movement. There did seem to be an awful lot of *nothing* stretched out before them, though. He wasn't at all confident that his long ago experience swimming in the river that ran past Lucera would be enough to get him back to shore if this fragile construction of wood and iron tipped over.

"Can you swim?" he asked, out of morbid curiosity.

"After a fashion," Caius replied. "And before my shoulder was mangled. On the positive side, the last time I did this, I was wearing metal battle armor, and people were hurling flaming arrows at me."

Decian winced.

Around them lay several distant specks on the sea — other boats. Or ships, perhaps, since he wasn't at all certain of the difference. One in particular grew larger as the wind pushed them ever forward, until Decian could make out more of the details. It was, he realized, a massive craft — bearing as much resemblance to the boat they were on as Caius' huge, four-bedroom house in the imperial quarter bore to the tiny two-room hut where he and his mother had grown up.

Where their boat had one sail, the boat—*ship?*—ahead had at least four. Its wooden sides rose above the surface of the water far enough that a person would have to climb to get aboard. And, as Caius would no doubt appreciate, it had railings all along the edges of the deck.

It was also their destination, evidently. Decian leaned forward, as though drawn by some invisible rope connecting him to his mother. Impatience thrummed in his veins.

The ship grew closer, and closer still. He could make out figures standing on the deck, including one with dark skin, her hands crossed over her mouth as though to keep a cry of excitement inside. His heart skipped a beat, and he waved frantically.

"Mother!" he called, but he couldn't see if she reacted because their little boat had passed so close to the towering hull that it blocked his view.

The two vessels knocked together gently, and Decian steadied himself, aware of Caius doing the same next to him with a white-knuckled grip. Their escorts efficiently docked the small boat to the huge one, tethering it to a metal ring protruding from the ship's tarred wooden side. A male voice shouted down, and a rope ladder uncoiled from above, falling nearly into Decian's lap.

"Up you get," said the tall man, gesturing at him. "Looks like someone up there's waiting for you."

Decian reached for the ladder and paused, looking at Caius with a question in his eyes. Caius met his gaze with an expression softer than Decian had ever seen him wear.

"I'll scramble up somehow," he said. "Don't worry about me. Just go." His callused hand cupped Decian's face for a bare moment before falling away.

Heart in throat, Decian nodded. He grasped the rope rungs in both hands and started climbing. The ladder terminated at a gap in the ship's railing, and he had to fumble around a bit to get his body off the ladder and safely through the open space.

His mother was waiting for him. *"Maaytú,"* he cried, and fell into her arms.

"My son, my son," she sobbed, over and over, rocking him back and forth in time with the sway of the waves. "Oh, by the goddess, I didn't think I'd ever see you again."

She felt small in his arms, if only because he was a grown man now. He clung to her, pressing his face against her shoulder to hide the tears.

The sound of a throat being cleared jerked him upright. He turned to find Saleene at the top of the ladder, giving him a meaningful look. Sheepishly, he shuffled them both out of the way so she had room to get through the gap and onto the deck. Zuri followed a moment later.

She turned and looked down. "Caius is coming," she said, by way of reassurance. "Might be a minute or two."

"These are your friends?" his mother asked, in the sweet voice he'd missed so much.

"They are," he said, still hugging her. "My friends, and my lover—once he makes it up."

She pressed her forehead to his. "I have so many questions. But my son… oh, it feels good to hold you in my arms once more."

He tightened his grip on her shoulders and lifted his face enough to press a kiss to her forehead. "I've missed you so much. So, *so* much. And to find you here? Let's just say, I have questions, too."

A pained grunt announced Caius' arrival. Decian gave his mother a final squeeze before letting her go so he could help Saleene haul Caius over the edge of the hull and onto the deck, where he steadied himself with a wince before waving them off.

The two escorts from Osca followed with considerably more grace, taking in the scene. "Ma'am," said the shorter one, with clear deference. "Is everything as it should be here?"

His mother's smile was like the sun coming out. "Yes, everything is wonderful. Thank you, my brothers. The captain is in his cabin. You should go speak with him."

"Yes, ma'am," said the taller man with a shallow bow. "We'll be belowdecks whenever your guests need a ride back to shore."

Decian took a deep breath, feeling as though some unseen weight had lifted from his chest. "Maaytú, this is Zuri. She's also from Kulawi. This is Saleene, her partner. They've both helped me so much since I got out of prison." He reached a hand out to grasp Caius by the arm. "And this is Caius. He's the reason I'm still alive, even if he's occasionally infuriating. Everyone, this is my mother Ishumi."

His mother nodded solemnly to each of them in turn, though Decian thought she gave Caius a particularly piercing look first. "Friends of my son—thank you for bringing him back to me. Please, come inside and accept what hospitality I have to offer. We have much to discuss, I think."

Decian offered her his arm. She took it, leading them across the long deck to a structure in the middle, like a little house built right on the ship. A cramped stairwell lay next to it, leading down into the belly of the ship.

"This is the captain's cabin," she said, indicating the raised structure. "My cabin is belowdecks. This way."

They trooped down the narrow stairs after her. Decian was pleased to discover that the swaying of the ocean wasn't so noticeable on this larger ship, though Caius still looked a bit green around the gills. The stairway continued down to yet another level, but his mother stepped off at the first landing and headed toward the back of the vessel.

Barrels and crates filled much of the space, but beyond lay a solid wall with a door set in the middle. Lanterns hung on either side, providing illumination as they approached. His mother opened the door and gestured them inside with a smile. Decian looked around in fascination. The room was a generous size and pleasantly furnished. He recognized a handful of objects of Kulawi origin—a few small statues, a water gourd, a woven wall hanging.

She turned to face them, and Decian took a moment to truly drink in the sight of her. She was dressed in plain

Alyrion clothing, with the exception of her colorful headscarf and the dozens of heavy, beaded bracelets hanging from her arms.

"Home, sweet home," she said, sweeping her hands wide to indicate the comfortable cabin. "Now, my son—tell me how you came to be free... and how you were able to find me here."

TEN

Caius watched Ishumi as Decian ran through a slightly disjointed synopsis of the last several weeks, aware that she was also watching him from the corner of her eye. He could only imagine what Decian's mother made of him.

That her son's lover was a man would apparently not be shocking to a native of Kulawi. That he was older than she was... might be. Caius wasn't certain where the perverse desire to tell her what he'd almost done to her son in an Amarian alley came from. But when Decian started to gloss over Caius' initial reaction to the rhitsaaru, Caius stopped him.

"Your son is being too generous," he said. "A shapeshifter killed my father, and another one almost killed me, some years later. When I was confronted with Decian's... *other nature*, I didn't respond well. Instead of trying to understand, I threatened him and sent him away. I don't claim to understand why he forgave me."

She held his gaze, unblinking. Her eyes were black—the irises so dark that he couldn't see where they ended and the pupils began. "That's how he is. That is how he has always been. The question is whether you will give him more reasons in the future to have to forgive you."

"I'm afraid I probably will," he told her. "But I hope it will never again be because of ignorance or narrow-mindedness."

Decian watched the exchange with an expression of disquiet. "Maybe both of you should let me worry about what I'm willing to forgive. Anyway, we found out later that it was actually Caius who was the target of the assassination attempts, not me. We went into hiding with the pagans in Amarius, but then the emperor died—probably of poison—and we had to flee. So we came looking for you, and instead, we found the Oracle of Osca."

Ishumi's expression stilled. "So the reports are true, then? Constanzus is dead? I wasn't certain whether to believe it."

"It's true," Caius said grimly, remembering blood spattering across parchment.

"Yes," Saleene agreed. "And about that…"

"We know that Constanzus was Decian's father," Zuri said. "Decian said he once gave you a signet ring inscribed with the images of a hound and a lion. Do you still have it?"

Expression hardening into granite, Ishumi tugged a chain free of the high neck of her dress. A gold ring dangled from the necklace, and Caius caught his breath.

"Do you know what that ring supposedly signifies?" Decian asked, his voice thin.

She snorted. "His vow of fidelity? Of *marriage*?" Ishumi's tone turned as hard as her face, and she spat out the final word as though it tasted bad. "So I have since been informed."

"It means that in the eyes of the law, you are the Dowager Empress of Alyrios," Saleene said, "And Decian is the true heir to the empire."

"Yes." Ishumi settled the necklace back beneath her clothing. "There is a reason the people here protect me. Those who practice the old ways might not rally behind some random bereaved mother, wailing her pain in the streets. But when that bereaved mother also happens to be the rightful empress of the land, shunned and exiled for her pagan beliefs? *That* woman, they will follow."

"Bereaved?" Decian asked, as though he wasn't certain he wanted to hear the answer.

"I went to the prison every day, trying to see you," Ishumi said. "Several months passed with the guards either laughing at me or demanding more money than I would be able to amass in a lifetime as a bribe. One morning, I went to the gate as usual, and the guards told me you had been whipped to death as punishment for helping a prisoner escape."

Decian sat down heavily on the nearest chair. His hand flew to cover his mouth.

Caius answered for him. "He did try to help someone escape, and he *was* flogged. It left him feverish and weak, but he eventually recovered."

There was a spark in Ishumi's eyes that didn't bode well for the guards who had lied to her. "I continued to go there every day, demanding more details... demanding my son's body for burial. They laughed and laughed at me — perhaps the whole thing was a great joke to them. After a month of this, I gave up. I left that horrible place and came here, to begin plotting revenge against the man responsible for all of my tribulations. *Constanzus.*"

Decian let his hand fall. "All this time, you thought I was dead?"

Ishumi crouched in front of his chair, gathering his hands in hers. "The first I knew otherwise was when the message came last night, saying that someone with dusky skin and magic in his gaze had arrived in Osca, claiming to be my son. I only truly believed it when I saw you with my own eyes."

Decian crumpled forward, falling into his mother's embrace and holding her tight. "I'm so sorry," he whispered. "Maaytú, I am *so sorry.*"

She patted his back, where the skin was marred by twisted scar tissue from that long-ago flogging. "You've nothing to apologize for, my son. You found me. You never gave up, even when I did. It's in the past. Now, the goddess has brought you back to me, and together we can lead our people to justice. We can finally take back what is ours."

Caius' neck prickled at the words, an instant before Decian's shoulders stiffened. He pulled back, uncertainty writ large across his face.

"What do you mean?" he asked.

Ishumi straightened, looking down at him and cupping his cheek. "Decian. My son. You have been blessed by the old gods — given powers of magic that most could never dream of. You are also the rightful emperor of this land. I have the proof." Her free hand moved to cover her heart, where the ring hung beneath her clothing. "I also have an army — one that grows larger and stronger every day. Now that you have returned to me, we can put right what has gone wrong in Alyrios. We can ensure that the pagans on this continent never have to fear for their safety again."

ELEVEN

That afternoon, Caius stood on the deck of the great ship, eyes fixed firmly on the distant shore as he tried not to remember the terrible look on Decian's face. *This is not my decision to make*, he repeated silently, over and over. If Decian came to him for advice, he would give it. Otherwise, it was not a matter in which Caius should have a say.

At the same time, a tiny, competing voice whispered, *this is it… this is the chance to save the empire from Proclus and Kaeto.* He quashed that voice ruthlessly, because such a chance would only come at the expense of Decian's safety. Of his future.

I already told you, Decian had said. *I don't want to be within a hundred miles of the Alyrion throne.*

Footsteps approached. Saleene fetched up next to him, leaning her forearms against the sturdy railing and following Caius' gaze to the shoreline.

"I'm not at all certain how I should be feeling about this newest wrinkle," she said, by way of greeting. "There's a bloody *pagan army* that none of us in Amarius knew anything about."

Caius grunted, having nothing more insightful to offer.

Saleene cut him a sharp, sidelong glance. "I must say, I thought you'd have more concrete opinions on the matter, *Legatus.*"

"I'm not the commander of anything now, Saleene," Caius said. "Least of all Decian… or his mother. I don't want to see any of Stasia's sons sitting on the Alyrion throne. I also don't want to see the man I love cut down in battle… or stabbed in the back… or poisoned… or any of the other terrible things that could happen to him."

Saleene turned to face him, eyebrows raised.

Caius paused, realizing what he'd just said, and deflated. "*Shit.*"

"Hmm." Saleene returned her attention to the distant smear of brown that signified land. "Well, I'm glad to hear that what's obvious to everyone else here is also obvious to you. I don't suppose you've told him."

He drew breath to answer, but she waved off the words before he could form them.

"No. Don't answer that," she said. "Caius, the woman has a *literal army*. Maybe not with uniforms and ranks and barracks... but they have weapons. They have a structure of command. They've even been implementing bloody *supply lines*."

It was easy to forget that Saleene had been a soldier, during her life before.

"And will you be joining that army, if Ishumi decides to march on the capital?" he asked.

"If Zuri joins the cause," Saleene said, in an absolutely flat tone. "Then, yes, I will."

He nodded.

"What about you?" Saleene pressed. "Will you be joining, assuming she succeeds in talking Decian into becoming the figurehead around which we all rally?"

"Of course I will," he snapped. "Blast it all."

Silence fell over the deck for a long moment.

"Well," Saleene said at length, "I daresay our odds would be better with you than without you."

He scowled at her. "Did you really think I'd say, 'No, *Saleene — I plan to let Decian march into that pit of vipers and take his chances in Amarius without me*'?"

She didn't back down. "Not really. But I might have laid odds on you abducting him away to some out-of-the-way backwater and hiding him in obscurity, before he has the chance to do anything as foolish as what's being proposed."

The words slid between his ribs like the thinnest and sharpest of blades.

"Not my decision to make," he muttered.

"No," she agreed after another pause. "I don't suppose it is."

The next person to find him was Decian, and Caius' heart clenched.

"Why did you leave?" Decian asked. His complexion was gray with strain beneath his dusky skin.

Guilt seeped through Caius' veins, every bit as insipid as the poison Tertia had slipped him. "I didn't trust myself not to offer opinions."

Decian leaned against the railing, looking out across the water much as Saleene had done. "Maybe I wanted to hear those opinions," he said. "What would they have been?"

Caius shook his head. "That's the worst part—I'm not certain."

"*You*? Indecisive?" Decian shot back. "I don't believe it."

"I don't want Stasia's sons on the throne," Caius said. "I also don't want you in danger, or forced into a role you're not willing to play."

Decian rested his weight on his elbows and scrubbed his hands down the length of his face. "Well, that's certainly helpful."

"Hence my decision not to stay behind and add to the ambient level of noise."

They were quiet for a bit.

Caius took a slow breath. "I think the opinion that matters here is yours. I know what you thought about this yesterday. I'm less sure how you feel about it today."

Decian chewed on his lower lip for a moment before letting it slip free. "My mother—the woman who used to take in sewing to keep food on the table—followed me halfway across the country and spent a year trying to get into a prison so she could see me. She kept trying for a full month after she thought I was dead. Then she raised a secret army to attack an emperor and avenge the wrongs done against our family."

Caius nodded.

"An *army*, Caius," Decian repeated. "My mother... *has an army*."

"And now she wants you to march at the front of it," Caius said heavily.

"Yes."

"If you decide to do that, I'll be marching at your side. Please tell me you already knew that." Caius swallowed. "And if you decide not to do it, I'll still be at your side."

Decian made a small, involuntary noise as though someone had rabbit-punched him. "Will you, though?"

Caius frowned. "Of course."

Their eyes locked. "You're talking about shuffling me off to safety somewhere."

"Well, yes," Caius said, frowning.

"After which you'll turn around and march right back to Amarius so you can feel like an honorable man… until someone there finally succeeds in killing you." The words were bitter.

Caius hesitated, caught out by the sharp accusation.

"Say it," Decian snapped. "We're right back to where we were before. I'm good enough to fuck. I'm good enough to hide away somewhere, to keep me out of trouble. But I'm not good enough for you to *stay*."

The flat statement flayed his skin like a butcher's knife.

If you finally had the life of safety and security you always wanted, why would you still need me? The question pressed at Caius' lips, but he swallowed it down. *Hard.* And with that hesitation, he'd left his answer too long. Decian's expression closed off.

"My duty—" he began instead, but Decian cut across him.

"Fuck your duty!" Brown eyes blazed. "You think you're the only one with a duty to other people? *Argh!* Why am I even trying to have this conversation with you?"

They stared at each other across a gulf of age and life experience—Decian with clenched fists, Caius with a clenched heart.

"Fine," Decian said at last. "You want to know what I think about this, after finding out about my mother? I think she wants me to be the heir to the bloody Alyrion Empire. I think everyone's been telling me I'm already the heir to the bloody Alyrion Empire whether I want to be or not. So, I guess they're all right and I'm the heir. *Lucky me.*"

Caius took him by the shoulders, turning him so they were facing each other directly. "No. This isn't what you want. Say the word, and I'll get you away, Decian."

"I just said the word, and that word was *yes*," Decian spat. "Weren't you listening?"

Something cold and constricting took root in Caius' chest. He let Decian's shoulders go with reluctance, consciously unpeeling his fingers.

"I was listening," he said. "And I wasn't lying earlier. If you're marching on the capital, I'll be at your side."

"Brilliant," Decian said, without so much as a hint of enthusiasm. "In that case, you'd probably better invite yourself to the strategy meetings. You're the only legatus I know, and it's all gibberish to me."

He turned and left. Caius stared after him, ice crystallizing around his heart.

TWELVE

The pagan army's plans rolled forward like a boulder dislodged from the top of a mountain, unstoppable and gaining speed with every moment that passed. On one level, Caius was reluctantly impressed with what Ishumi and her informal commanders had managed to build under the noses of the empire. On the other hand, he knew exactly what happened when a large, relatively untrained and untested army went up against a smaller, more advanced one.

He'd seen it firsthand, after all. And he wasn't the only one.

"The bloodshed on both sides will be extensive," Saleene said, during one of the meetings. "And I do mean *extensive*."

They were still on the ship, which was acting as a base of operations—but it was now docked in Osca's port. Zuri looked up from the maps spread across the table.

"Is this not an improvement over the other option, where all of the bloodshed is on the pagan side, haartlam?" she asked.

Zuri and Ishumi seemed to have hit things off, a fact Caius ascribed to the deep anger toward injustice they both shared. Decian—who had remained largely quiet during the strategy meetings—looked ill in a way that had nothing to do with the gentle swaying of the anchored ship.

One of Ishumi's military leaders spoke up—a man named Traban, whom Caius grudgingly acknowledged was not a fool when it came to planning campaigns.

"Aye, it's true enough," he said. "We might have the advantage on the way to Amarius, simply by virtue of numbers. But the imperial quarter is a fortress. Numbers won't help us once we get that far."

"A siege," Caius suggested. "Messier in some ways, cleaner in others."

Traban gave a thoughtful nod. "There's an idea. Depends to some degree on how robust our supply lines turn out to be, once they're put to a real test."

Some might have expected Caius to have qualms about suggesting the best way to overthrow the regime he'd served for so long. They would have been misguided in that expectation. It was an immense relief to finally place his support behind the true heir to the throne. At least, it *should* have been an immense relief. It definitely *would* have been, if the true heir to the throne didn't perpetually look like he wanted to throw up during these meetings.

As the days slipped by, the ship became a hub for countless messages sent and received. And every night, Caius cornered Decian.

"Are you sure about this?" he'd ask. "There's still time to change your mind."

"Of course I'm sure," Decian would snap. "Stop asking."

After which, Decian would mutter something about being too restless to sleep, and Caius would retire to a bunk alone, waking alone hours later when morning came.

Things progressed far more quickly than Caius would have credited. It reinforced his suspicion that these plans had been in place for a long time, and only required a bit of tweaking to incorporate Decian's presence as the army's new figurehead. Meanwhile, news from the capital reached them in fits and starts, since Osca was so far from the center of power.

Proclus had—so far, at least—managed to avoid succumbing to any assassination plots by his brother. His war against the pagan population was apparently proceeding apace. Informal tribunals were beginning to pop up in and around Amarius, sentencing suspected pagans to public execution. The descriptions were gruesome enough to make Caius hope the stories had been exaggerated in the telling. But then again, he'd rescued Decian from execution by a pack of starving hounds.

Troops—dressed in the garb of peasants and bearing weapons of wildly varying quality—were amassing in Osca. Before Caius was ready for it, the morning of their departure arrived. Caius joined the group at the head of the column, mounted on his gray gelding. Suitable horses had been found for the others. Aelio's mule had been relegated to the pack train, while the surprisingly plucky knackers' nag had been left behind—gifted to a family who might get some use from the unlikely beast.

All of Caius' interactions with Decian these days seemed to end in friction, but the younger man's expression had been one of abject relief when Caius informed Ishumi and her generals that he was, and would remain, Decian's personal bodyguard. Decian looked ridiculously ill at ease in his newly acquired fine clothes, riding a black stallion that was, frankly, too spirited for his level of competence on horseback.

Ishumi rode on Decian's other side, with Saleene and Zuri also at the front. The five of them were swept along by the weight of the masses marching behind them, and they picked up even more fighters at every town along the way.

If any proof were needed that the empire was descending into chaos and dysfunctionality, it would be the lack of any coordinated military response to a private army marching toward the heart of the empire. Had news of their presence reached anyone who might be in a position to muster a force to confront them? It should have, by now. And yet, they marched onward, unopposed.

With the exception of some small issues, the supply line held. Caius had been surprised to learn that it had Utrean connections—but perhaps he shouldn't have been. With the treaty in tatters, he supposed Utrea's king would be more than happy to sow discord in Alyrios. It was a gamble on the part of King Rathanii, but if Decian successfully took the throne, he would be heavily beholden to Utrea from the very first day of his reign. As strategy went, Caius had seen far worse.

The army had covered just over three-quarters of the distance between Osca and Amarius when they ran headfirst into a small party on horseback, riding at speed along the winding, wooded road they'd been traversing. The riders, who had apparently not been expecting to find a massive fighting force descending on them, pulled up violently and tried to wheel away.

A jolt of surprise hit Caius as something about the color of the horse and the posture of the lead rider prickled at his instincts. "Capture those men!" he bellowed. "Take them alive!"

He spurred his gelding into a gallop, aware of several of the other mounted men doing the same. Caius focused on the familiar figure riding a distinctive buckskin stallion, chasing the man down before his horse could recover from the abrupt maneuver and gain speed.

The stallion reared as Caius' gelding bore down on it. Caius leaned over dangerously and grabbed for the horse's reins, yanking as hard as he could. Further unbalanced, the stallion staggered, its shoulder knocking heavily against the gelding's. Its rider, who'd been clinging to the saddle, slid sideways with a curse and fell, landing hard.

Caius was out of the saddle in a flash, the rush of battle lending strength to his aching body as his feet hit the ground. He drew steel and kicked the man as he tried to roll upright, sending him sprawling onto his back again. The point of Caius' sword was at his captive's throat before the man could make another attempt.

Princep Kaeto, emperor Constanzus' middle son, glared up at Caius, panting and beaten.

THIRTEEN

Saleene had already ridden down another of the men and managed to unhorse him. She shoved her captive at a pair of nearby soldiers, and they grabbed the man by both arms, restraining him. Around them, the other members of the small riding party were also being caught and bound.

When Saleene joined Caius, looking down at the figure lying on the ground, her gray eyes grew very wide.

"Wait. Is that who I think it is?" she asked. "It can't be, can it?"

"If you think it's the man who ordered Decian's execution—and tried to have me assassinated on at least three separate occasions—then yes, it is." Caius' sword never wavered.

Decian chose that moment to join them, still mounted on his nervous stallion. "Oh, you have *got* to be joking. My half-brother's here? What in perdition's name is going on?"

Kaeto, who had been watching the exchange with a wary gaze, hissed, "*What did he just say?*"

Caius took more pleasure than he probably should have in the princep's obvious wrong-footedness. "He said he's your half-brother," he repeated with relish. "You've met twice before, of course—but I suppose you weren't properly introduced on either occasion. Kaeto... this is Decian, the eldest son of emperor Constanzus, by his lawfully wedded first wife. You may remember him as the man you tried to have torn apart by the royal hounds, not so very long ago."

The slack look of shock on Kaeto's face was incredibly satisfying.

"Forget about all that for a moment," Saleene said. "Right now, I'm much more interested in why an imperial princep would be fleeing Amarius with no banner flying.

And injured, too. That shoulder wound didn't come from falling off a horse."

Kaeto's shirt was torn and dirty, revealing a glimpse of bandages wrapped around his left shoulder. They were stained rusty where blood had soaked through.

He ignored Saleene as though she didn't exist, focusing his glare on Caius. "Turning traitor, *legatus*? I suppose it's comforting to know I was right about you all along."

"It isn't treason when you're supporting the rightful heir to the throne," Caius said. "*Soldiers*—tie this man securely and get him on a horse. If he tries to talk to anyone, gag him." He barked the order at the men milling around, never looking away from the snake he held pinned at the end of his sword.

Caius waited while Kaeto was bound with his wrists behind him. The princep grunted in pain as his arms were pulled back, shooting Caius a murderous look. Only when he was thoroughly secured did Caius sheath his sword, allowing himself to ponder what in the actual hell was going on here.

Ishumi, Traban, and Zuri rode up, joining them as the prisoners were taken away.

"What's happening?" Ishumi asked, frowning. "Who were those riders?"

"We've just captured one of Constanzus' sons fleeing Amarius with a small party of guards," Caius told them.

"You're joking," Zuri said.

"That's what I thought, but apparently not," Decian replied. "I recognize him, too. So does Saleene. It really is Princep Kaeto."

Traban looked thoughtful. "You said there was infighting among the three sons, Caius?"

"To put it mildly," Caius replied.

"It occurs to me that this road is the most direct route leading to Utrea, outside of the main roads used for trade," Traban said. "If he's running from something, he'd want to avoid any routes with regular patrols."

"That occurred to me as well." Caius craned around to ensure that Kaeto was being watched closely. It had barely been two minutes, and one of his guards had already felt the need to gag him. "I'll lay odds that Proclus went after Kaeto before he had a chance to go after Proclus… but it's all speculation at the moment. We'll need to question him and his men, but not here. We should keep moving."

"They were riding fast," Ishumi said. "If anyone is chasing them, they'll run straight into our forces, too."

"Yes." Caius locked eyes with Traban, who shrugged.

"You could remove the gag long enough to ask him if anyone's after him," Traban said.

"He'd only lie," Caius replied. "We should put Decian and Ishumi farther back in the column, though, as a precaution. As much as I hate to say it, we're going to run into another army sooner or later. At least any forces sent to chase after Kaeto are likely to be small—organized with speed in mind, rather than brute force."

"Sounds like we might get some practice targets, in that case," Traban suggested.

"Something like that," Caius agreed.

Saleene went to retrieve her horse from the soldier who'd caught it. "Being surrounded by the army rather than marching at the front of it suits me very well," she said, swinging into the saddle. "Come along, you lot. Let's go lead from the middle."

Caius retrieved his gelding and ensured the animal was uninjured after the collision with Kaeto's horse. Instinct urged him to stay at the front of the column, where his experience and expertise might be of more use. Emotion urged him to stick to Decian's side, because he didn't trust Kaeto to be within a league of his lover, whether the princep was bound and gagged or not.

Traban had been watching him. "Go on. Keep Decian safe. Without him and his mother, this army is nothing."

Caius wasn't entirely certain when he'd become so transparent. He had a sneaking suspicion it had been at approximately the same time he'd first seen a naked prisoner crouched inside the royal kennels.

"Right," he said, feeling suddenly tired. "I'll send another group of mounted fighters up front to you."

Traban's expression turned wry. "Very good. And look at it this way, legatus—if we can't trounce a small force while we still hold the element of surprise, we're not going to get very far once we reach Amarius."

That was true enough, and yet it did little to ease Caius' worries.

"If anyone does come, try to capture at least one of them alive," he said, and headed back to reorganize the mounted men.

~⚜~

Proclus' pursuing forces came barely an hour behind Kaeto and his men. Caius itched to force his way back to the front of the column and fight, but he resisted the urge. The skirmish was brief and bloody—over before he would have been able to make any difference.

It had only been a dozen men, and they were quickly overrun by the pagans' vastly superior numbers. Three of Ishumi's soldiers were injured badly enough to require moving them to the supply wagons for transport to the next village. Two of Proclus' men survived, but one was unconscious after a blow to the head that had probably addled his wits permanently. The other was bleeding heavily from a sword slash to the leg. They bound him up and dumped him with Kaeto's men in another of the wagons for later questioning, if he survived.

The patchwork army continued on, meeting only the occasional farmer or tradesman—all of whom gave them a very wide berth indeed. After making camp in the river valley that evening, Caius and Traban went to talk to Kaeto.

Decian hurried after them. "I'm coming, too. Though I do hope you're not planning on cutting off his fingers or anything equally terrible."

"Tempting," Caius said. "But unfortunately, it's probably a bit premature to start maiming one of the presumptive heirs to the empire."

"You'd better not let Ishumi hear you call him that," Traban observed.

In truth, Caius was almost as interested in what lies Kaeto might try to tell as what truths he might try to tell. The princep had been bound with his back resting against a sturdy tree, his arms stretched around the trunk and wrists tied behind it. He was still gagged, Caius noted.

"Leave us," Caius told the man guarding him.

Kaeto's eyes were shrewd in the firelight as Caius untied the gag and pulled the wad of material from his mouth. He worked his jaw for a few moments before speaking.

"Water," he rasped.

Caius gestured to Traban to bring him some. "You know, if we'd nabbed your older brother, I expect he'd be begging for wine rather than water," he observed.

The princep didn't rise to the bait. He drank from the skin Traban lifted to his lips, rivulets of liquid dribbling down his chin. Eventually, he turned his head to indicate he'd had enough, and Traban pulled back, standing up.

Caius sat down on a section of log a few feet away, facing the princep. He leaned forward, resting an elbow on his knee as he regarded the disheveled figure in front of him. Decian and Traban flanked him on either side, still standing.

"I ask myself why you might be fleeing Amarius with a hole in your shoulder," Caius began, "and the only answer I can come up with is that you lost a battle of wits against a drunken idiot. If so, I must say I'm a bit disappointed in you. I expected better."

Kaeto continued to watch him wordlessly, his haughty features impassive.

"It does also make me wonder what the point was of all of your scheming and killing," Caius continued. "Your father's bastards... the council members... random pagan protesters in the streets... your own mother" — his eyes narrowed dangerously — "... and, of course, *me.*"

"I've never lifted a finger against you, legatus. Much less against the Amarian Council." Kaeto lifted an eyebrow. "I'm surprised you haven't figured that out yet — but then, you always were more of a blunt instrument than a physician's scalpel."

Decian crossed his arms. "You lifted a finger against *me*, brother—and a dozen or so of our other half-siblings, I gather. There's no wiggling out of that."

Kaeto eyed him with clear distaste. "Of course I did. I already had one stubborn obstacle to remove on my way to the throne. The last thing I needed were more of them popping up." He jerked his chin to indicate the camp around them. "Case in point."

"And the accusations against your mother?" Caius pressed. "That was also your work?"

"Obviously. She supports Proclus."

Caius made a considering noise. "She also proved more resistant to removal than you expected, I'm guessing."

Kaeto gave a bitter laugh. "She'll fall from grace soon enough, now that Father is dead. Not that it matters now."

"And you claim you aren't behind any of the attempts on my life?" Caius asked.

"Good lord, no," Kaeto said. "What would have been the point?"

Caius pondered that for a moment. "I'd assumed it was because you thought I'd support Stasia's eldest son in his claim to the throne."

"*Please*," Kaeto said dismissively. "Look around you. I think I'm a better judge of character than that. Your horror at the idea of Proclus becoming emperor has always been palpable."

"If you know that, then I imagine you also have an idea of my horror at the prospect of *you* becoming emperor," Caius told him.

Kaeto scoffed. "Would you have chosen to throw your lot in with that bootlicker Bruccias? Somehow I think not."

"Bruccias seems happy enough to support Proclus," Caius said.

"My youngest brother thought he could bide his time until Proclus killed me, and then kill him in his turn." Kaeto let his head fall back against the tree, looking up at the branches above him in the flickering firelight. "He's a fool. In fact, it wouldn't surprise me if he's a dead fool, by now."

Caius nodded. "Once, I might have supported him as the least appalling of the three options. Fortunately, you're all illegitimate pretenders to the throne, so now I don't have to." He tilted his head, considering. "Let's return to the previous subject, though. You've been plotting to remove obstacles in your way—but you say you're not involved in the scheme to undermine the council and turn the Church against the pagans."

"Obviously not," Kaeto said. "What benefit would there be to tearing Alyrios apart at the seams?"

"And yet, I have a difficult time picturing Proclus masterminding the assassination of a single man, much less plotting to bring on a civil war inside the empire." Frankly, Caius had a difficult time picturing Proclus tying his own bootlaces.

Kaeto's lips twisted into an expression too bitter to be a smile. "Ah. You've underestimated him, I see. Well, don't feel too bad. Most people do."

If it was true, this revelation was going to require some considerable reshuffling of Caius' preconceived notions about what had been going on in the imperial palace for the past several years.

"You said it yourself," Caius said. "What benefit is there to fomenting civil war?"

Kaeto sobered. "That depends entirely on what one's goals are."

"What do you mean?" Decian asked.

The princep's cool gaze raked over his half-brother. "Proclus has visions of turning the empire's ambitions outward once more. And, drunkard though he is, he knows perfectly well that in order to unite a populace under one banner, you first have to unite them *against* something."

A chill of unease trickled down Caius' spine. "You believe he intends to turn the people against paganism inside the empire's borders, and then turn them outward against other nations?"

Kaeto's lip curled. "Think about it. Utrea. Kulawi. Even that benighted island to the north. All populated by heathens who deny the One God. Once the pagans inside the empire have been put down, what's more natural than to turn to the stain of paganism lurking outside our borders?"

"Alyrios no longer has the resources for that kind of conquest," Caius said. Somehow, his confidence that the statement was true did nothing to alleviate the chill growing inside him.

"Yes," Kaeto said. "You are absolutely correct. And that is why my brother must be stopped at all costs."

FOURTEEN

Traban gestured at the camp around them. "Got an army here ready to do exactly that, mate. Which, to my mind, makes you surplus to requirements."

The cool, calculating distance returned to Kaeto's gaze.

"No," Caius said. "He may be strategically useful. We need to hold onto him."

"Oh, good," Kaeto said, not breaking expression. "In that case, I require food and a physician."

Caius snorted. "Yes to the first. No to the second. Apparently, you haven't spent enough time on the battlefield to learn that physicians are more of a hindrance than a help, in most cases. Besides, I'm happy enough to ensure you stay too weak to try anything foolish."

"Waste of good food if you ask me," Traban muttered, before heading off to find the guard Caius had dismissed.

Ishumi chose that moment to arrive, with Zuri walking at her side. The rightful empress of Alyrios crossed her arms, looking down at her captive from safely outside of kicking range.

"So," she said. "This is one of Constanzus' illegitimate whelps?"

Kaeto straightened against the tree, puffing up like an offended rooster. "*How dare you.*"

"Kaeto," Caius began, taking vicious satisfaction in the words, "may I present Empress Ishumi, late of the N'Ganda tribe in Kulawi—and your father's first wife."

"*Only* wife, I think you'll find," Ishumi said, tone flat. "At least, that's how I'm told it works."

"Ridiculous!" Kaeto snapped. "My father has had no other wife besides my mother."

Ishumi raised an eyebrow and tugged on the chain at her neck, freeing the signet ring from her high collar. "Constanzus took me from my village when I was fifteen, *boy.* I was a gift to him, meant to ensure that the empire didn't descend on Kulawi and enslave us, like he enslaved so many others."

She turned the ring in her hand, letting the light play over the engravings on its flat upper surface.

"He tore me away from everything I'd ever known and brought me to his court in Amarius. There was an immediate uproar, of course. His advisors wouldn't hear of it. They convinced him to send me away and pretend I'd never existed—but I was already pregnant."

Decian stepped up beside her.

"I was abandoned. Tossed aside," Ishumi continued, her voice like steel. "All I had was my son. The son *you* tried to take him from me."

Kaeto's jaw clenched. His breath came in harsh, angry rasps as Ishumi systematically dismantled the foundations of his life and identity.

"But now your father is dead, while my son is still alive." A harsh smile tugged at Ishumi's lips. "So together, we will return to Amarius and finally take back what is ours. After which, you may enjoy languishing in your treacherous father's dungeons, as my son languished for ten long years in one of his many prisons."

Kaeto looked as though an apoplectic seizure was a real possibility. Face twisting, he hawked and spat a gob of saliva at Ishumi, hitting the hem of her dress. Decian growled and took a single, aggressive step toward the bound man before Caius grabbed him by the arm and pulled him to a halt. Decian's eyes glowed eerie red in the low light. Caius cursed sharply, but it was too late. Kaeto jerked back against the tree trunk as though he'd been kicked in the chest, all of the blood draining from his face.

"Holy *God*," he said.

Decian jerked against Caius' grip. "Not even close," he snarled. "*Brother.*"

"*Enough*," Caius said—a parade ground bark. "We're done here. Let's leave the prisoner to his gruel." *And his fresh nightmares*, he didn't add.

"Yes," Ishumi agreed. "Let's."

Caius kept a hand on Decian's arm as they turned and headed for the section of camp where their tents were set up. Decian was shaking beneath Caius' grip—with rage or reaction, he wasn't sure.

"That certainly went well," Zuri muttered.

"It hardly matters," Ishumi said. "Soon, all of Alyrios will know that the emperor's true heir has magic."

Caius tamped down his deep-seated misgivings, and resolved to have a serious talk with Decian at the first opportunity.

⚜

That opportunity didn't come as soon as he would have liked. Ishumi took Decian into her tent to discuss matters, letting the flap fall closed very firmly in Caius' face. After eating something and readying his supplies for an early morning departure, Caius let himself be talked into sparring with Saleene as a way to pass the time and take the edge off.

It had been a number of years since *Saleene the brothel owner* had been *Saliari the mercenary fighter*. She'd been good—there was no question about that—but she was also out of practice. Caius danced forward and back with her in a clear area near the campfire, running through basic sword forms.

"Your cause of treasonous justice looks like he's about to come apart at the seams, Caius," Saleene observed, thrusting and parrying neatly. "You should probably try to do something about that before we reach the capital."

"Not treasonous," Caius retorted, feinting and lunging.

"Nor particularly just." Saleene's counterattack was clumsy, and Caius swiped it aside without effort. She huffed. "Since I wouldn't wish his position on my worst enemy."

"It's his choice," Caius said, nearly choking on the wrongness of the words.

"Is it?" Saleene lifted a hand, calling a halt as she wiped sweat from her brow. "How, exactly, was he supposed to turn all of this down?"

That was the crux of Caius' qualms regarding the situation, and he had no answer worth a damn.

"He's going to be an emperor," Zuri said, looking up. "There are worse fates."

"Or else he's going to be dead," Saleene shot back. "Along with the rest of us, if this crazy quest goes tits up."

"The old gods sent Decian to us for a reason." Zuri's tone was serene. "This was meant to be."

"I think you'll find it was Caius that sent Decian to us," Saleene said. "But I sincerely hope you're right."

The exchange did nothing to quell Caius' queasy sense of impending doom.

When Decian finally emerged from Ishumi's tent, Caius was waiting for him. "We're talking," he said. "*Now.*"

Decian glanced around with the air of someone searching for an avenue of escape — but the camp stretched endlessly around them, offering no useful cover. His shoulders sagged. "The answer's still no," he said.

Caius frowned. "What's the question?"

"The question is, will I let down my mother — not to mention, all of these people relying on me for the pagans' survival — by turning tail and running."

The bald statement churned in Caius' gut. There was no angle, no way of phrasing things that didn't boil down to exactly that. And if it had been anyone other than the gentle, impossible young man that Caius loved, he would have been at the front of the line offering rousing speeches about the need for honor and personal sacrifice when innocent lives were at stake.

His hesitation brought a bitter smile to Decian's face. It wasn't a pleasant expression. "For what it's worth, none of it's your fault," Decian said. "So you can stop looking so guilty about it."

Caius had been the one to suggest searching for Decian's mother, so that seemed like a generous assessment of the situation. "I'm still sorry."

"For what?" Decian asked. "I've got my mother back, when I never thought I'd see her again. I'm supposed to rule a bloody empire and live in a palace, for the gods' sake."

Caius wanted to drag the younger man into his arms and hold him until he stopped looking like he was heading for the executioner's block. And he didn't dare, because they were standing in the open surrounded by soldiers who saw Decian as an emperor in waiting—a paragon to be held on a pedestal above other men.

"We should go to your tent," he said.

"No. We really shouldn't," Decian replied. "You're the one who said I couldn't afford to be seen in a relationship with a soldier, if I was also going to play at being the emperor."

And you're the one who told me you couldn't do this alone, Caius thought, feeling his chest tighten. *Unfortunately, we were both right.*

"I understand," he said. "I'll be on guard outside your tent if you need me."

Decian's brown gaze was tortured, the man behind it unraveling before Caius' eyes.

"I won't," Decian said. "Good night, Caius."

FIFTEEN

This was hell—the shadowy land of torment where the deimonists believed bad people went to suffer after death. At this moment, if someone had offered Decian a magic way to return to his prison cell in the time before any of this insanity had happened, he would have taken it without a second thought.

The pagan army continued its steady march toward the capital, keeping to the smaller roads and out of the way villages. Every evening, his mother brought him to her tent to remind him of the importance of what they were attempting, and discuss what he would need to do once he gained the throne.

"The courtiers are poisonous vipers," she was saying. "They will resist your direction at every turn when it comes to the pagans. We will need to surround you with guards who are absolutely loyal to you, and you alone. Only then will you be able to cow the imperial advisors into following your commands."

With a pang, Decian thought of his most loyal protector, sleeping outside his tent every night because Decian refused to let him sleep inside it. The first night, he'd nearly tripped over Caius' prone body when he stepped through the tent flap to go relieve himself behind a tree. The message had been clear—*no one gets to you without first going through me.*

If Decian allowed Caius inside the tent, he'd end up sobbing in his lover's arms and begging to be rescued from this nightmare. But there was no rescue. How could there be? Without him at its head, his mother's army was nothing. Her only claim to power and recognition was through his blood. Being the emperor's true wife meant very little on its own. By contrast, being the mother of the emperor's eldest—and *only*—legitimate son meant everything.

"What about the Church?" he asked. "Even if the imperial court falls in line, the Church Elders could break with the throne rather than agree to recognize pagan rights."

His mother's face might have been carved from ice. "Let them try. Constanzus was the one to recognize deimonism as the official religion of Alyrios. His son can be the one to abolish it, if necessary."

In Decian's mind, all the words conjured up was the prospect of more bloodshed.

"I hate this, Maaytú," he said wretchedly. "No matter what happens, people are going to die."

"People are already dying, my son," his mother said. Her tone was as hard as her expression.

Yes, he thought. *But before, it wasn't directly because of me.*

They were two days out from Amarius at most. Decian dreaded with every fiber of his being the moment when Proclus' forces would meet them to defend the city. It could happen at any time. The fact that it hadn't already was a testament to the upheaval that must be happening inside the capital.

He returned to his tent, exhausted and skittish, to find Caius waiting. A callused hand closed around his arm as it did every night, warm and steadying.

"Decian," Caius began.

"Don't," Decian said. "Don't ask me if I'm sure. Don't tell me I can still back out. Just... don't."

"I was going to ask if you'd eaten," Caius said mildly.

Decian paused, caught out. "Oh. Yes, sorry. I'm just tired."

It was a lie, on both counts. He couldn't face the prospect of dumping tasteless camp rations on his roiling stomach, and he was so jittery he'd probably be awake half the night. He thought with longing of the peace and oblivion that came with sleeping in Caius' arms after a good, hard fuck.

"Then get some rest," Caius said. "I'll be outside if you need me."

You have no idea how badly I need you, he thought, and ducked through the flap, letting it fall closed behind him with a curt, "Good night."

A cry of alarm from elsewhere in the camp jerked him upright from his bedroll, several hours later. He scrambled for the entrance, only to nearly run into a broad back.

"Stay in the tent," Caius said, sounding cool and competent. "Let the guards and lookouts do their job."

His sword wasn't drawn. Decian let himself be barred inside by Caius' raised arm as shouts echoed back and forth in the distance.

"It'll be a scouting party from Amarius, if I had to guess," Caius said after a few minutes. "We'll have to wait and see if any of them got away."

"And if they did get away?" Decian asked, dreading the answer.

"Then we can expect imperial forces sometime later today," Caius told him matter-of-factly. "But of course, we were expecting imperial forces today or tomorrow anyway."

"And then, people start dying," Decian said, feeling sick to his stomach.

"I'm afraid so, yes," Caius replied. "The people here have chosen to risk their own lives in hopes of securing a better future for others. This is a volunteer army. They had far more of a choice in the decision to be here than you did."

It might as well have been a punch to the stomach. He didn't answer, because what kind of answer *could* he give to that?

The shouting from the far edge of the camp subsided. "Let's go to your mother's tent," Caius said. "It's likely that Traban will head there to report on what's happened."

They went. As Caius had guessed, lookouts had spotted a small group of scouts skulking around the edges of the camp. The riders had kept their distance, and they'd managed to get away clean. Proclus would know the whereabouts and general size of their force within hours.

And yet, it changed nothing, because they already knew they were going to have to fight their way into the city. There would be no attempt at altering the army's route to the capital; no digging in to mount a defense against the oncoming imperial soldiers. The bulk of their forces would continue to march toward the city outskirts, and Proclus' army would march out to meet them.

Caius stopped Decian as they were returning to his tent, turning him by the arm so they faced each other.

"Decian," he said. "I have a request for you. I want you to travel as the rhitsaaru today. When these two armies clash, I want the hellhound for that battle, rather than the man. Will you do that for me?"

Decian looked at him, heart in throat. "You want me to fight?"

Because Caius, of all people, knew that Decian was no soldier. Wrestling? Yes. Fistfight? Sure, if it was absolutely necessary. Swords and pikes and crossbows? Not a chance.

Caius placed his free hand on Decian's other arm, ensuring he couldn't look away. "No. I don't want you to fight. I want you to survive, and I want your mother to survive. No one in the capital knows you're a shapeshifter except Aelio, and he'll be defending the palace, not the city. The opposing army won't be searching for a mastiff among a sea of mounted soldiers and infantry."

Decian swallowed hard. "All right."

If he allowed the rhitsaaru to take control, he'd be better able to defend his mother. He'd be better able to defend *Caius*, if it came to it.

Caius squeezed his arms. "Thank you."

He almost gave in to the compulsion to crumple forward and hide against Caius' hard-muscled chest. *Almost.*

"We'll be leaving at first light?" he asked instead.

His companion nodded. "Yes, the quicker, the better. We'll want to be as close to the city as possible for this battle."

When Decian padded up to the command tent on silent paws, his mother's gaze was full of both pride and awe. Murky pre-dawn light was just beginning to spill through the forest. Caius walked at his side, a protective shadow — leading his gray horse by the reins.

"Truly, the goddess has blessed me with such a son," his mother murmured, touching her fingers to her heart and forehead in a ritual benediction.

In hindsight, Decian should have done this sooner. He'd been so wrapped up in his impossible situation that he'd forgotten how much simpler his emotions felt in shifted form. He nuzzled his head against his mother's hand, and she stroked his blocky skull the same way she used to stroke his wild spirals of hair when he was small. A rumble of contentment vibrated his wide chest.

In a surprisingly short amount of time, the men had the tents down and packed, ready to leave. Many of the men on horseback had already left. He could only smell a few of the animals left in the camp, compared to the dozens upon dozens of horses that led the column on most days.

Caius and Traban had talked late into the night, collaborating over strategy. Decian knew the pagan army was likely to have the advantage of numbers, although most were infantry, traveling and fighting on foot. Meanwhile, the imperial troops would have the advantage when it came to weapons and training. No one seemed willing to make a prediction regarding which side would ultimately prevail.

The column formed up and marched out. Decian and his mother were, as had become the usual arrangement, situated in the middle of the army. Decian trotted between Caius' gray gelding and his mother's snow-white mare, with Zuri riding on her far side and Saleene riding on Caius' other side. The remaining mounted riders were arrayed in front of and behind them. Their horses danced nervously for the first few leagues, in response to his unfamiliar shifted presence among them.

The scents of human anticipation, excitement, fear, and barely hidden bloodlust wafted around him, mixed with the more mundane odors of sweat and equine musk. Decian's mother smelled of resolve and a metallic tang that felt uncomfortably like obsession. Caius was worry and watchfulness. Zuri, determination and faith. Saleene, by contrast, reeked of uncertainty.

There were soldiers in the column whose souls smelled far too pure for the bloodshed that was to come. Others made the rhitsaaru's hackles rise with the need to send them to the underworld for the darkness that lay within their hearts. Most were somewhere in the middle — a mix of good and evil, passion and apathy, kindness and cruelty.

The sun rose slowly in the sky, cresting overhead and beginning its downward arc toward the western horizon. It was well behind them, casting long shadows on the dusty road, when the first warning cries sounded from the front of the column.

The imperial forces had arrived.

"Halt!" Caius called to the mounted men around them. "Form up!"

The mounted ranks closed in around Decian and his mother, with Caius holding point. Men on foot continued to flow around them like a river current rushing past boulders, as the sound of clashing metal and screams of pain echoed from the front. Decian's human mind scrabbled at the constraints of the rhitsaaru's impassivity, appalled by what his presence here had wrought.

"How close are we to the city?" his mother shouted over the growing din.

"Close," Caius said grimly.

The foot soldiers ground to a halt around them, unable to make forward progress as the leading edges of the two armies collided. The smell of fear swelled through the ranks, as the reality of combat forced itself on men who'd never experienced it firsthand before.

"Steady," Caius called, his battlefield voice wrapping around the untried troops, holding them in place and bolstering them for the fight. "Hold the line — wait for the enemy to come to you!"

And the enemy *was* coming to them—smashing through the pagan army's leading lines. A hail of arrows rained down from the sky, finding targets perhaps fifty paces in front of their little knot of horses and riders. Shrieks and screams rent the air.

"Damn it!" Caius cursed. "Riders—fall back! Get closer to the rear of the column!"

"Where's the bloody cavalry?" Saleene snapped.

"Probably still figuring out that the battle has started," Caius said. "Right now, we need to worry about keeping these two out of longbow range. *Move!*"

Another storm of arrows descended, the leading edge closer to them this time. Decian nipped at the heels of his mother's horse when it didn't move fast enough. The groans and cries of injured men grew deafening, battering against Decian's rhitsaaru senses.

"*Capture the leaders!*" came a cry from the center of the melee ahead of them.

Decian growled, sending the horses around him skittering nervously. The onslaught of arrows had stopped, but the sound of metal clashing was getting ever closer. Caius had heard it, too. In an instant, his gray gelding was blocking the path leading to Decian and his mother, turned sideways in the road to give Caius freedom to use his sword against the oncoming soldiers.

The other mounted guards formed a tight, protective cluster. The next thing Decian knew, enemies were breaking through the last lines of men on foot to reach them. Caius roared a wordless battle cry and started hacking. The rhitsaaru didn't think. It darted past the legs of the horses surrounding them and made for the enemy mounts, snarling and snapping.

Horses reared, eyes rolling in fear as they tried to wheel and bolt away from the massive predator. Riders cursed, wrenching at their reins. The pagan soldiers' horses had at least had more exposure to Decian's altered form, and were less panicked. They held the line, protecting his mother behind them.

"*Cavalry's here!*" someone bellowed. "*They're moving in from the flanks! Keep fighting!*"

That had been Caius and Traban's grand strategic plan to keep them from getting crushed when they finally encountered Proclus' forces. Most of the mounted riders had been sent off early that morning, heading north and south before turning to ride parallel to the main force. As soon as the imperial army was thoroughly committed to the frontal assault, they were supposed to attack from both sides, pincering the enemy column between them.

They were late, but maybe not too late.

Decian snapped his jaws at an enemy horse's belly. It scrambled away in terror, its rider slewing in the saddle and nearly falling. He heard Saleene cry out in pain and whirled just in time to see an enemy rider dart past her, toward his mother. The white mare his mother was riding reared in alarm, and she fell from its back.

The rhitsaaru was already in motion. Decian snapped jaws around the enemy horse's hock, tearing at skin and tendon, narrowly avoiding the animal's panicky kick. The horse staggered away and went down hard, pagan soldiers on foot descending on it to dispatch its unlucky rider.

Decian lunged across the remaining distance to his mother, who was lying huddled on the trampled dirt of the road where she'd fallen. He set himself protectively over her, ready to rip out the throat of anyone who got within reach. The familiar dark legs of Caius' gray horse appeared in front of him — another layer of protection.

From the sound of things, the crush of their cavalry pressing in from both sides had broken the enemy column, cutting off some and sending the rest scurrying back toward Amarius.

"They're retreating!" Traban's voice bellowed. *"Press them back and finish off the stragglers!"*

Decian stood tense and wary, but barely fifteen minutes later, the sound of battle faded entirely. His mother had rolled into a kneeling position, one arm wrapped around the rhitsaaru's broad shoulders. She was trembling.

"That's it," Caius said. "It's over."

Around them lay a scene of desolation, cut through with the moans of the injured — untold carnage composed of both pagan and imperial casualties littering the road as far ahead as Decian could see.

SIXTEEN

Decian hadn't wanted to shift back to human form. The rhitsaaru was in some ways indifferent to death—happy to mete it out when required, and to see the souls of those who deserved it cast into the void. But, as a human, all Decian saw was the river of blood that had been spilled unnecessarily… *in his name.*

Ignoring the toga Caius held out for him to cover himself, he staggered to an empty patch of road and fell to his knees, retching uncontrollably. A strong arm came around his shoulders, lifting him to his feet when he was done.

"Your mother will be all right," Caius said in his ear. "She's just bruised. No broken bones."

"Saleene?" Decian choked. "I heard her cry out—"

"Took a slice to the thigh," Caius told him. "She wasn't unhorsed, and it doesn't seem to be bleeding too badly. One of the pagan healers is looking at it. Here, put this on." He helped Decian shrug into the toga, and then steadied him again with an arm around him—support that Decian needed more than he needed air.

"We should get off the road and make camp," Caius continued, leading him toward the stream of exhausted and battered people heading into the woods nearby. "Let the healers and physicians work on the survivors—poor sods. Then we'll figure out where this battle has left us."

Decian found his mind blanking in and out, awareness of his surroundings coming and going in fits and starts. When he came fully back to himself, he was seated on a downed log, staring at a campfire. His mother was beside him, her face buried in her hands.

He blinked several times. "Maaytú?" he asked, his voice sounding terribly young to his own ears.

She looked up. Her eyes were dry, but red-rimmed. "My son. I've failed you. Our army was not strong enough."

Decian stared at her uncomprehendingly. Movement caught the corner of his eye and he looked up to find Caius assisting a hobbling Saleene to the campfire, with Zuri hovering at her other side. Between them, they eased her down to sit with one leg stretched out before her, the thigh bandaged tightly in strips of linen. Saleene hissed in irritation and settled back, accepting the cup Zuri handed her.

Caius lowered himself stiffly to sit across from them.

"How bad is it?" Decian's mother asked.

"We lost at least four hundred, with another five hundred or more injured," Caius said in an even tone. "It's Traban's opinion that we don't have enough forces remaining to attempt a siege of the imperial quarter, much less the city as a whole. I concur."

She closed her eyes, tilting her head away as though to hide her expression from view.

"Please, Maaytú," Decian said hoarsely. "We can't continue this. You have to give it up."

"We can't stop now," she said, still not looking at them. "If we do, we'll lose everything."

Decian rose to his feet, his hands shaking as they clenched into fists at his sides. "Almost a thousand dead and injured in the space of an hour or two," he said. "And that's just on our side!" His voice shook as badly as his limbs. "This is my fault. I should never have agreed to be your figurehead. I won't play this role anymore. If you want to throw the rest of these people off of your personal cliff, you'll be doing it without me!"

"You're the rightful heir!" his mother cried. "We can't let them get away with this!"

"*Stop.*" Caius' voice sounded like gravel grinding. He rose to his feet, taking Decian's arm and hauling him gently backward until he was bodily shielding him from his mother. "Tell me, Ishumi—do you truly want to help the pagans? Or are you more concerned with personal revenge, even at the cost of your life, your son's life, and your followers' lives?"

His mother drew breath to speak, but no words formed.

Saleene shifted uncomfortably. "Don't take this the wrong way, Caius, but from where I'm sitting, the pagans look to be pretty well fucked at this point, regardless of what we do next."

But Caius didn't look away, still staring down Decian's mother with an unyielding battlefield glare.

"Please, mother," Decian murmured. "Please don't turn this into some kind of twisted suicide mission over *honor*." He spat the last word out, wishing he never had to hear it again.

"What else can we *do*?" she asked. "There is no way out but forward. If we turn tail and run, Proclus' army will hound us to the edge of the sea. He will never allow an attack by pagans to go unanswered—more will die, and not just our soldiers."

Caius was still looking down at her with granite stillness. "If I could offer you a way out..." he began. "If I could give you a way to extricate your son from this mess, while also protecting the pagans from Proclus' cruelty—would you take it?"

Ishumi stared at him. "Such a way out does not exist."

Caius' hand tightened on Decian's arm. "That's not an answer."

Zuri frowned. "What do you have in mind, Caius? What are you plotting?"

"Something you're all going to hate," he said. "Give me half an hour, and you can tell me exactly how much."

He turned and stalked off. Decian stared at his retreating back for the space of several heartbeats before hurrying after him. He fell in at Caius' shoulder, keeping pace with the familiar, hitching stride.

Caius shot him a sidelong glance. "Let's talk privately."

He led the way to a different part of camp. It was far from deserted, but the men surrounding them were too focused on what they were doing to worry about a low-voiced conversation taking place nearby.

Decian reached out, bringing him to a halt. "I'm so sorry I didn't stop this when you asked me."

Caius covered his hand. "Decian, none of this is your doing. I might have a solution—for a given definition of the word, anyway. But it will almost certainly require both of us to leave Alyrios."

Decian's breath caught. "Both of us?" he echoed.

"Assuming we both survive that long, yes," Caius said. "Maybe I can salvage some of this mess, but if so, I'll be burning the bridge behind us in the process."

"What about my mother?" he whispered.

"I sincerely hope you can convince her to be on our side of the bridge when it falls," Caius told him. "This isn't going to be pretty, and it isn't going to be neat. I intend to offer Kaeto the throne in exchange for his promise of protection for the pagans. I'm about to offer an empire to the man who tried to have you killed, because I don't see any other way for us to escape this mess unscathed."

Shock froze Decian's wits to ice. "*Kaeto?*"

"Yes."

Kaeto, his conniving half-brother—who'd arranged brutal executions for his father's bastards, and tried to destroy his own mother simply because she was in his way. A man who was currently a prisoner of one army, after being chased out of Amarius by another... and who'd expressed disdain for Proclus' plans to foment unrest inside the empire, before turning the hatred and intolerance outward, beyond its borders.

"I don't know how I'm supposed to respond to that," Decian said, at length.

Caius wrapped a callused hand around the nape of his neck. "Respond however you like, Decian. I'm still going to do it."

Heedless of the soldiers bustling around them, Caius tugged him forward and pressed his lips to Decian's temple. Tears burned at the backs of Decian's eyes, and he resisted the urge to fall forward into Caius' arms. In the absence of words, he nodded.

Please, he thought. *Just get us out of this, and I'll do* anything.

SEVENTEEN

Caius gave the nape of Decian's neck a final stroke, and left him behind as he went to make a bargain with a venomous snake.

It took a bit of walking to find the area where the prisoners were being kept. The princep's wrists had been bound behind his back with rope. A second length looped around his neck, the other end tethered to a sturdy tree branch.

"Kaeto," Caius said, approaching. "We need to talk."

He dismissed the guards with a sharp gesture and pulled out a dagger, cutting the princep free of his bonds. Kaeto winced and rubbed his freed wrists, turning to lean dramatically against the tree trunk, as though he needed the support.

"Legatus," he said. "How lovely to see you. Aren't you worried I'll try to overpower you and make a run for it?"

"Not particularly," Caius said. "Though feel free to try. I'd enjoy the excuse to punch you in the jaw a few times before beginning our conversation."

"Goodness," Kaeto said mildly. "I don't believe I fully appreciated the degree to which you've been reining yourself in at court over the years."

"I'm a plain-spoken man, *princep*," Caius said, placing heavy irony on the title. "So allow me to speak plainly. Your legitimate half-brother was press-ganged into this disastrous attempt at a military coup, and I'm partly to blame for that. What's left of his mother's ragtag army won't be enough to get the job done, and even if it was, the Amarian court would eat Decian for breakfast as soon as he took the throne."

"An admirably concise assessment." Kaeto continued to watch him warily.

"This is my proposal for you. I will attempt to get Proclus out of the way," Caius told him. "I will hand you the Alyrion empire on a platter... but only in return for your agreement to issue officially sanctioned protections to the pagan population. No more witch hunts. No more trials for heresy. No more executions. No interference with their right to worship as they see fit."

"Done," Kaeto said, without a second's hesitation.

Caius paused, scowling at his easy capitulation.

Kaeto looked at him blandly. "What? You expect me to turn down such an offer in favor of being tied to a tree by a rope around my neck?"

Which... fair point.

"I'm not finished," Caius said.

Kaeto waved an airy hand, every bit the languid royal son. "Yes, yes. Do go on."

"Safe passage out of Alyrios for Decian and his mother."

The bland expression flickered, but only for an instant. "I would have to be a fool to allow that harpy and her son to go free. I might as well exile Proclus to a nice cottage in the countryside rather than killing him."

"Too bad. That's the deal," Caius said. "Take it or leave it. Besides—there's a fundamental difference. Proclus *wants* the throne. Decian wants to be on the other side of the world from it."

Kaeto was silent for a long moment. "Then I suppose I shall accept your *deal*, since the alternative certainly leaves much to be desired. There is, however, one small problem. Namely, the fact that you have no earthly way to make good on your side of the bargain."

Caius snorted. "Who says I don't? Honestly, Kaeto—if you were as smart as you believe yourself to be, you'd have already thought of it, too."

The princep's brows drew together in consternation.

"Time isn't on our side," Caius continued. "We're going to need a small force of fighters chosen for speed, stealth, and a willingness to trudge through sewers."

Kaeto's eyes widened in sudden understanding. "*Oh*. I *see*. Very bold indeed, legatus. I'll confess myself mildly impressed."

"You can be impressed if we manage to pull it off without dying in the process," Caius said. "For now, we need to break this news to a group of people who are going to be deeply unenthusiastic about it. I would strongly suggest laying the courtly charm on thick, because your life and your fortunes now rest in the hands of some exceptionally pissed off pagans bearing weapons."

Kaeto smiled a slow smile that wasn't precisely reassuring. "Why, *legatus*. I'm not these people's enemy. You of all men should know that I've been lobbying on their behalf since that benighted ecumenical council began."

"For purely altruistic philosophical reasons, of course," Caius said, deadpan.

"Come, legatus. We are not children." The princep held his gaze, openly challenging. "If we acted for purely altruistic philosophical reasons, you would have turned traitor years earlier than you did."

That barb struck uncomfortably close to home, as Caius remembered the growing corruption and injustices he'd forced himself to ignore during his time at court.

"Once again—supporting the lawful heir to the empire isn't treason," he said. "Though I suppose you're right, in the sense that putting *your* obnoxious arse on the throne will be a treasonous act."

"Only if you fail," Kaeto retorted.

"Come on," Caius said. "Let's go face the chorus of angry people. I'll have someone change those bandages for you, too."

"Lovely," Kaeto said, sarcasm dripping from every pore.

"How did Proclus get you, anyway?" Caius asked, gesturing at the wound.

"An assassin with a crossbow," Kaeto replied.

"Oh, the irony," Caius muttered.

"Yes, well," Kaeto said, as they began to walk. "At least I didn't end up bedridden for days afterward."

"The advantages of youth—nothing more," Caius told him. "At least *I* didn't end up captured by enemy troops and tied to a tree. Are you going to be able to keep up when we break into the palace? Only, this plan does rather fall apart if we need to carry you the entire way on a litter."

Kaeto's lip curled. "You'll find there's very little I won't do to get my drunken fool of a brother off the throne, whether I have a hole in my shoulder or not."

"Good," Caius told him. "I hope that extends to groveling in front of the woman you recently spat on."

"I prefer to think of it as engaging in slightly belated diplomacy." The princep shot him a sidelong look. "Speaking of which, would you care to enlighten me regarding what sort of misbegotten creature this half-brother of mine is?"

Caius remembered Decian's glowing eyes as he'd held the younger man back from attacking Kaeto. "Your father sired a shapeshifter. Another reason you'll be well-served to work with the pagans in the empire, rather than against them."

Kaeto stopped. "You're serious?"

"Feel free to test it by irritating him again," Caius said. "It would rather complicate my cunning plan to fix this mess, but it might still be worth it, if only for the entertainment value."

The princep paused for a moment before resuming walking again. "Clearly the magical taint comes from his mother's barbarian bloodlines, not my father's."

"Keep telling yourself that," Caius told him.

⤐ ♕ ⤏

The grand reveal of Caius' plan went about as well as one might expect.

"Are you insane?" Ishumi asked. "This creature tried to kill my son!"

"As long as he protects the pagans, he can have the throne, as far as I'm concerned," Decian said in a monotone. "And much joy may it bring him."

"Madame," Kaeto said, bowing to Ishumi with courtly grace. "It's possible we got off on the wrong foot during our first meeting."

Ishumi spat at him. The gob landed squarely on his right cheek before sliding down his jaw. He wiped it away with his good hand.

Caius frowned. "You can grab this lifeline, or you can stick with the scenario where all of your people die horribly in a doomed attempt to take the palace by force."

"After which, you'll have no one to sit on the throne anyway—because I still can't play this role for you, Maaytú," Decian added. He stood with his arms wrapped tightly around his own chest, his shoulders a tense line as he regarded his murderous half-brother in the firelight.

"Decian," Ishumi began.

"No," Decian said, cutting her off. "I'm not a leader. I can't accomplish what you want me to accomplish for our people."

"You can't force this boy to be your emperor." Saleene's voice was low, but the words cut through the air like a knife. "Seriously—what would that even look like, Ishumi?"

Zuri had been quiet during the discussion, her expression deeply troubled. "Perhaps the gods are showing us a new way to enact the changes we seek."

Ishumi shot her a look of betrayal, evidently not having expected support for Caius' plan from that quarter.

Traban, who had also been keeping his own counsel, shifted his weight from foot to foot. "What guarantee would we have that this bastard pretender wouldn't simply renege the moment he has a crown on his head?"

"Simple enough," Kaeto said dryly. "There's the small matter of a pagan army camped outside the capital, combined with a pagan mob marching the streets and setting fire to things *inside* the capital."

"Your brother Proclus has got those problems as well," Traban pointed out. "Doesn't seem to be slowing him down all that much."

"True," Kaeto said. "But there's a significant difference, in that I'm not a drunken fool."

Silence descended. Caius let it stretch.

Traban broke it, but when he spoke, it was to Ishumi, not Kaeto. "Oracle, I'm sorry to say that left to our own devices, we're going to fail. The force Proclus sent out to meet us was easily twice as large as what we expected, and his army fared far better in the battle than ours did."

Ishumi stared at him. "So you want to surrender to this upstart pretender."

"We want pagans to stop dying," Saleene said. "If this is the best way to accomplish that, count me in."

"I agree," Zuri said. "I'm sorry, Ishumi."

Ishumi looked around the campfire; all of her support eroded in the course of a single day. Her dark-eyed gaze fell heavily on Kaeto. "Even if you take the throne away from my son, you will not be rid of me so easily. I will be always standing in the shadows behind you, ready to ensure that your word remains good."

It sounded as though Ishumi was angling for a position as palace advisor, or at least, palace gadfly. Caius covered a wince, trying to picture a world in which *that* plan would go well.

"If you wish a role at court, Madame, we can certainly discuss it," Kaeto said, with brittle charm. "For now, though, perhaps we should concentrate on the details of prying my brother away from his grasp on power, and worry about the details of everything else once that lofty goal is accomplished."

A glance around the assembled group showed no open signs of rebellion against the plan. "We're all agreed, then?" Caius asked. "In that case, it's time to talk strategy. This needs to happen tonight, before Proclus' forces regroup enough to attack again."

EIGHTEEN

There was only a sliver of moon in the sky above the Alyrion capital. Caius hadn't intended Decian to come along on this last-ditch mission to sneak into the heart of the empire's power base.

You should stay with the army, he'd suggested, hoping to keep Decian out of the thick of things. *Stay with your mother. It will be safer.*

I said I didn't want to be emperor. I didn't say I wouldn't fight alongside you to fix this horrible mess, Decian had replied, in a tone that didn't invite further debate.

In the end, the cold, calculating part of Caius' mind had accepted the presence of the rhitsaaru on the mission. That unfeeling military strategist was an aspect of himself Caius was coming to like less and less—but Decian's hell-beast could see in the dark without torches or lanterns, and had more than proven its value in a fight.

In the end, it had been worth it simply to see Kaeto's reaction to the rhitsaaru firsthand. 'Regal' wasn't the first description that came to mind when the haughty princep had stumbled backward in terror and landed flat on his arse in the dirt.

Caius got the impression Decian had taken a certain amount of satisfaction in it as well. He'd shifted back as Kaeto gaped at him, crouching before the fallen princep. *It's only me, brother*, he'd said mildly, and his slow smile in the instant before his body twisted into animal form again had been truly terrifying.

To Kaeto's credit, he'd at least avoided pissing himself. He'd also regained control of his emotions relatively quickly, and hadn't voiced any objections to his half-brother's presence within the small strike force. To round out their merry band, Caius had also brought Traban, along with four strapping men that Traban assured him were among his best fighters.

It was a pity Ishumi's army didn't have access to advanced weapons, such as the crossbows Proclus' assassins were so fond of. The human members of Caius' team were armed heavily with blades, both long and short—but they had no ranged weapons.

Caius sincerely hoped this wouldn't put them at a noticeable disadvantage. They weren't going up against Proclus' mercenaries in black, after all. Instead, they would be pitting themselves against the palace guards. In the normal course of things, those guards would be armed much the same as they were, with swords and daggers. Mind you, this was hardly *the normal course of things*, with an army camped outside Amarius. However, Caius was banking on Proclus feeling secure within the imperial quarter.

They'd waited until well after dark to sneak away from the pagan army camp, and skirted far out of their way to avoid detection. While the imperial quarter inside the city was completely walled for defense, the same couldn't be said of Amarius as a whole. It was simply too large. Some approaches to the city were fortified, but others simply transitioned by degrees into the surrounding countryside.

Caius had chosen to take advantage of one such approach to the city. He was viscerally aware that they were passing through the same stretch of rolling pasture and hills where he'd once ridden out with Decian to exercise the royal hounds. The two of them had passed an idyllic afternoon picnicking on the banks of a babbling stream, surrounded by trees and birdsong.

There would be no such enjoyment to be found tonight. Now, his goal was a stretch of the river some distance west of the unimaginatively named 'river gate.' This particular stretch of the city's main waterway boasted nothing of interest beyond a particularly unpleasant stench of sewage, along with a particularly deep and clinging variety of mud.

That, and an unremarkable iron grill covering a sewage outlet, which just happened to have a couple of the hinges broken.

Kaeto had assured Caius that it was doubtful his brother would have posted guards at the sewage outlet. The network of secret passages inside was, in fact, quite a well-kept secret. The number of trusted servants and guardsmen who even knew about its existence numbered less than a dozen. Additionally, the sewer outlet was well beyond the boundary of the imperial quarter. In order to avoid raised eyebrows, Proclus would have to post city guards there, rather than palace guards.

Since no one who knew about the passages would be in a hurry to explain why a city guardsman should have to stand in the stinking mud of a sewer day and night, it would likely remain unguarded.

They lost the moon shortly before reaching the river, and one of Traban's men lit a dark lantern for the final approach. After his first experience with the place, Caius had insisted that the party carry several lengths of wooden plank along with them, repurposed from one of the army's many supply wagons.

It was awkward, but they laid two planks down on the muddy riverbank, forming a sort of movable walkway that allowed them to make their way to the sewage outlet without having to struggle through knee-deep, stinking muck. As they moved forward, the men at the back passed the boards up to the front to extend it.

Two of Traban's men wrenched the iron grate free from the stonework, making enough of a gap that they could slip through into the sewer one at a time. The inside was a manmade river—filthy water running in a brick-lined channel with room on either side for them to walk in single file. The passage was empty and echoing, with no signs of life beyond the rats.

"How well do you know these passages?" Caius asked Kaeto.

"Inside the palace? Quite well indeed," Kaeto said. "I spent a fair amount of time exploring and hiding away there as a boy."

"And the sewers?" Caius pressed.

The princep shrugged his uninjured shoulder in the wavering light cast by the lantern. "Not at all, I'm afraid. I always turned back when the stench in the stairwell grew too noxious."

That left it entirely up to Caius' memory when it came to finding the entrance to the staircase leading up to the palace.

"We continue straight," he said. "No turnings. Decian, I need you to ensure we don't accidentally pass the opening leading to the spiral staircase. It will be on our right."

It felt odd to acknowledge Decian's terrifying canine form in front of other people. Evidently, Kaeto agreed.

"Good lord," Kaeto said. "Can that foul creature really understand human speech?"

Decian growled at him, and Kaeto wisely shut up.

It was a long trek through the sewer, and Caius was fairly certain he would, in fact, have missed the stairwell without Decian's assistance. The rhitsaaru darted into every right-hand opening to check it. Eventually, they reached the one containing a spiral staircase, and the rhitsaaru gave a short yip.

Climbing up the seemingly endless twisting stairs was no more enjoyable than climbing down them had been. Happily, traveling on horseback with an army and engaging in a single, short battle had been positively restful compared to the previous few weeks. Caius' leg was noticeably improved since the last time he'd come this way. If anything, he fared better than Kaeto—with his fresh wound and days spent as a prisoner.

Just as Caius was thinking they must surely be near the top, Decian snarled and lunged ahead, disappearing from view around the corner. A choked cry reached them, followed by a shout of alarm.

"Guards," Caius snapped, rallying a burst of strength as he charged up the remaining steps, sword drawn.

He reached the top to find one palace guardsman on the ground, and a second trying desperately to free his sword from its scabbard while also being bitten by a massive black hound. Caius crossed the few steps separating them and slashed his blade across the man's throat. He fell to the ground next to his fellow, gurgling.

Caius packed away the knowledge that these were Aelio's men they were slaughtering. That fact would be something to deal with later, in the privacy of his nightmares. Right now, whether they were Aelio's men or not, they were also Proclus' men… and that made them the enemy.

"It appears my brother is taking *some* precautions, at least," Kaeto said clinically, looking down at the men without expression. "Good for him."

"Give the lantern to the princep," Caius ordered Traban's soldier.

The man looked to Traban, hesitating before obeying the command.

"Do it," Traban confirmed. "We're all allies here, lad."

Kaeto accepted the metal lantern with its flickering flame. "Follow me," he said. "With luck, the sound of these two fools expiring won't have carried through the walls. Stay quiet from here on."

They followed, taking side corridors Caius had passed by during his earlier escape from the palace, in the aftermath of Constanzus' death. After some debate, they'd decided to check Proclus' private quarters first, on the basis that his bedroom would be the simplest place to dispatch him without having to engage in a major battle.

Unfortunately, though perhaps not all that surprisingly, his chambers were empty. They tried Constanzus' quarters next, since Proclus could have taken them over once he'd become emperor. That yielded a single, very startled servant, but no sign of Proclus. They left the man bound and gagged so he wouldn't raise the alarm.

When they'd been discussing their strategy back at the camp, Kaeto had argued for trying the throne room first. That, he'd said, would be the most likely place to find Proclus while there was an army camped on his doorstep. Apparently, his instincts had been correct. The sound of muffled voices in animated discussion could be heard beyond the concealed panel, despite the late hour.

Kaeto glanced at Caius and Traban, one eyebrow raised as if to say *I told you so.*

"Cover the lantern," Caius murmured, too low to carry through the hidden door. "We'll go in on a count of three."

Kaeto nodded, grim-faced. The rasp of blades being drawn filled the cramped corridor. The princep lowered the panel on the dark lantern before setting it out of the way, with a clink of metal against stone.

Caius took up the count, his voice a bare murmur. "One... two... *three.*"

The panel swung outward. They rushed through, with the rhitsaaru leading the way. Shouts of alarm erupted within the echoing space of the throne room. Caius caught movement to his left and whirled, blocking a slash from a guard who'd been stationed next to the secret passage. Traban and his men swarmed past him, one of them turning to bury a dagger in the guard's ribs. Caius shoved the unlucky man out of the way. He fell to the floor with a groan.

With a quick whirl, Caius took in the scene. Traban's men were sprinting across the open space, ready to engage the palace guards who rushed to meet them.

A familiar voice called out, and Caius' heart sank.

"Your Majesty!" Aelio cried. "Get out of this room, and send us more guards! I'll cover your escape!"

Before Proclus could comply, a dark blur lunged toward the heavy double doors, darting past both him and Aelio — cutting off Proclus' exit. He slid to a halt, staggering back with a gasp as the rhitsaaru growled at him in warning, its eyes glowing red.

Quick as a flash, Decian shifted form. He dropped the heavy locking bar across the doors, barricading them inside and any additional guards outside. Then he was once more a snarling beast, holding Proclus at bay as Aelio stood protectively between his emperor and the rest of the room with his sword drawn.

Traban's men were doing an effective job of keeping the handful of palace guards busy. There were a few other courtiers huddling along the wall as the small battle raged, but Caius discounted them when it came to the fight. He and Kaeto stalked toward Aelio. Kaeto's full attention lay with Proclus, who was pinned between the tribuni protecting him and the rhitsaaru guarding the door.

Caius saw the moment Aelio recognized him as more than an anonymous attacker. The tip of the tribuni's sword dipped for an instant before he raised it again.

"Oh, Caius... *no*," Aelio said, in the tone of one desperately wishing he could make something not be true by denying it with sufficient vehemence.

"Aelio," Caius said. "Step aside, and there may still be a chance to save the empire from ruin. Kaeto has agreed to take a moderate stance with the pagans. He's committed to fixing things inside our borders. Proclus will happily watch everything burn to the ground in pursuit of fresh conquest that Alyrios can no longer sustain."

Aelio's expression was tortured. "I can't do that, Caius. I swore an oath. Please don't make me kill you in the course of upholding it."

The problem with honorable men was that they were honorable. For the first time, Caius felt he had a true understanding of Decian's disgust with the whole concept of honor and nobility.

"Very well. In that case, I'm truly sorry for this, my friend," Caius said, and lunged.

Aelio parried, caught momentarily by surprise—as though he hadn't actually expected Caius to attack. In the corner of his eye, Caius saw Kaeto dart past them and make for Proclus, with his dagger in hand.

Aelio attacked Caius with a flurry of blows, a highly competent assault that showed no sign of being intended as anything other than disabling or deadly. Caius, by contrast, felt constrained not to kill the man who'd helped him again and again... who'd protected Decian's secret despite the untenable position in which it put him.

The part of Caius that gloried in battle relished this chance to pit himself against a younger, highly skilled opponent… if only it had been for any other reason. Aelio was a soldier at the top of his game. Meanwhile, Caius' only advantage came from decades of battle experience, combined with a berserker mentality that he couldn't afford to unleash—not against an opponent he didn't want to kill.

The pair traded blows, blades clashing. Caius snatched glances past Aelio's shoulder between volleys, trying to gauge the progress of the fight between Kaeto and Proclus. Proclus had pulled a dagger as well, and appeared to be utilizing his slight advantage of height and reach against his already injured younger brother.

Kaeto cried out and went down, his brother's dagger protruding from his thigh. Caius, momentarily distracted, barely managed to dodge the boot that would have landed in his gut as Aelio ducked and kicked out at him. The blow rolled off Caius' hip instead, and he used the momentum of his spin to slam his sword hilt against Aelio's supporting knee, sending them both to the ground in a tangle.

Proclus screamed, and Aelio jerked his head around to look. Caius took the momentary advantage, pinning Aelio's sword arm to the floor. He dug his fingers brutally into the tribuni's wrist, until Aelio's grip slackened and Caius could knock his opponent's weapon across the floor, out of reach.

He rolled off the younger man and staggered upright, holding Aelio at sword point. The tribuni craned to check on Proclus, his jaw going slack as he took in the ghostly outline of the rhitsaaru lunging forward to tear out the emperor's soul. The wisp of diaphanous gray disappeared screaming into the void, and the beast's ghostly echo snapped back into its prosaic, earthly form.

An instant later, Kaeto dragged himself over to his brother's body, gritted his teeth, and plunged a dagger into the corpse's heart.

Utter silence fell over the room.

NINETEEN

Kaeto flopped back to sit on the floor, clutching his bleeding thigh. "The emperor of Alyrios is dead. *Again.*" He pitched the pronouncement to be audible to the gawping courtiers huddled at the edges of the room. His voice faded to a mutter as he added, "Long live *me.*"

Caius risked looking around to assess the situation. Two of the imperial guards appeared to be dead, as did one of Traban's men. Another one of the pagan fighters was on the ground, wounded, with Traban leaning over him. The other two pagan fighters were holding the remaining pair of imperial guards at sword point, much as Caius was holding Aelio. The courtiers were still cowering.

The rhitsaaru stared at Kaeto as though considering whether or not to make him its next soul-snack. Caius caught the beast's unearthly red gaze. *For god's sake, don't kill him, or you'll end up as emperor after all.* He tried to convey the message silently, via the medium of a severe frown.

When Decian's low growl subsided into a grumble, Caius dragged his attention back to the man at his feet. "Do you yield, Aelio?"

Aelio stared back at him. "Of course I yield, you bloody terrifying old bastard. You've just taken the Alyrion throne with seven men *and a goddamned dog.*"

"Execute him," Kaeto ordered hoarsely. "The guards, as well."

"No," Caius said. "I'm not killing your palace tribuni, Kaeto. Stop and think, will you? The man hated Proclus as much as everyone else does, and he was still willing to die for him. Prove you're committed to ruling well and salvaging this fiasco with the pagans, and you'll have earned the respect of the most loyal commander an emperor could ask for."

The princep huffed. "*Fine.* Tribuni Aelio, do you swear fealty to your new emperor?" When Aelio hesitated, Kaeto scowled at him. "In case you're wondering, the answer that keeps your head attached to your shoulders is *yes, Your Majesty.*"

Aelio shot Caius a helpless glance. Caius took the sword away from his throat and offered him an eyebrow shrug.

The tribuni cautiously rolled upright and took a knee with a wince of pain. He lowered his eyes, dipping his chin to his chest in a bow of respect. "If your intention is to rule for the good of all your subjects, then I humbly pledge myself to your service… Your Majesty."

"How terribly virtuous of you," Kaeto said, still clutching his wound. "Your service is accepted. I expect your pledge to extend to your men. Any who object to the change of regime will be turned away without wages. Any who lift a weapon against me will be summarily executed."

"I understand, Your Majesty," Aelio said. "May I ask, with the greatest respect, what exactly is happening here?" He paused. "Beyond the obvious, I mean."

Caius had pity on him. "There's… a respected pagan oracle from Osca. She's been quietly raising an army for several years now. That army started marching toward the capital after news reached them that Proclus had taken power, legitimizing sham trials and executions of pagans in Amarius. Decian and I were with them. We ran into Kaeto, fleeing an assassination attempt by his brother, and realized that we're all after more or less the same thing."

"And that is?" Aelio asked slowly.

"Peace within the empire," Kaeto told him. "An end to this madness."

Aelio nodded. "Then it seems we truly *are* on the same side."

The new emperor climbed to his feet with a heartfelt curse and hobbled to the throne, just as the first sounds of battering at the heavy double doors broke the tentative peace.

"Get your guards under control, tribuni," Kaeto snapped, falling into the ornate seat with a grunt. "And someone bring me a physician." Then, something seemed to occur to him, and he leaned forward. "But first, tell me what happened to Bruccias. Is he dead? Did Proclus have him killed?"

Aelio hesitated. "Not to my knowledge, Your Majesty. Bruccias and the Empress Stasia fled during the night, shortly after you disappeared. They haven't been seen or heard from since."

Kaeto leaned back. "Interesting. Perhaps I underestimated my younger brother's sense of self-preservation." He waved an airy hand at the tribuni, as the sound of crashing against the doors intensified. "Now see to that ruckus, before a small army breaks in and stumbles over the corpses."

Caius approached the throne, beckoning Decian to join him. Meanwhile, Aelio limped to the door to explain the situation to his guards.

"I think it would be best if Decian and the pagans were gone before the Aelio's men enter," Caius said quietly.

"I couldn't agree more," Kaeto replied waspishly. "In fact, why don't you go with them?"

"I'll stay," Caius said, in a tone that brooked no argument. "To ensure you uphold your end of our bargain."

"My *dear* legatus." Kaeto's voice was nearly a purr. "One might almost think you didn't trust me."

⤞⟊⫷ ♛ ⤝⟊

The rhitsaaru stared long and hard at Caius before agreeing to take the others back to rejoin Ishumi's forces. Traban's injured man was able to walk, thankfully. The dead pagan's body was placed in the secret passage to wait for later removal and burial.

The courtiers fell in line with surprisingly little fuss. Or perhaps it shouldn't have been surprising, given they already knew Kaeto and probably feared for their heads if they failed to support him. The imperial guards were loyal to Aelio, and weren't likely to defy their tribuni's orders.

It also helped that pretty much everyone in the palace had hated Proclus with a deep-seated sense of visceral loathing.

Within twenty-four hours, Kaeto had been formally crowned as emperor. He issued decrees protecting the pagans and criminalizing their persecution as his first imperial act. Aelio sent palace troops to escort Ishumi's army into the city under a flag of truce. This neatly avoided the prospect of city guards who'd fought hand to hand against the pagan forces being expected to welcome them into Amarius with open arms.

Caius watched in mild amazement as outraged Church leaders descended on the palace to berate Kaeto over his new policies, only to be verbally eviscerated, one by one, and sent scurrying away with their tails between their legs.

Your lack of even the most basic intelligence regarding political reality is making me rethink my father's decision to declare Deimonism the official religion of the empire, Kaeto told one doddering old episkopos. *Please, continue to test me, and see what happens next.*

Was I unclear? he asked another—this one a young firebrand of the hell-and-damnation variety. *The attacks on the Amarian Council were a plot by my brother to destabilize Alyrios. The pagans are not, and have never been, your enemy. I'm certain Deimok is more than capable of smiting them Himself if He wants them dead so badly. Now go away and don't cause trouble.*

Kaeto was still pale and wan, nursing two serious injuries beneath his imperial finery. Yet his eyes glowed with a nearly fanatical light. Caius was beginning to harbor a fragile sense of hope that his fanaticism truly did lie in undoing the damage his feeble father and power-hungry brother had wrought on Alyrios.

When Ishumi was duly welcomed to court as an old friend of his father's—and the new liaison between pagans and the crown—a handful of the oldest courtiers looked as though their eyes might pop out of their heads. Yet, when no major eruptions occurred in the palace landscape after her arrival, Caius started to relax a tiny bit. Kaeto and

Ishumi's interactions remained frosty and painfully formal, but the peace held—both inside and outside of the palace.

On the third day without any new crises erupting, Caius paid a visit to the royal kennels.

"Legatus," Pip greeted, sounding surprised. "Didn't really expect to see you here again."

"Pip," Caius replied warmly. "I won't be at court very much longer, but I wanted to thank you for all you've done, both on my own behalf, and on Decian's."

Pip nodded, not attempting to downplay the risks he'd taken for them. "You're welcome. You two been staying out of trouble lately?"

"Not even remotely," Caius told him. "But we'll be taking our trouble elsewhere before long."

"Huh. I'm sorry to hear that," said the lad. "You and him are all right, even if you're both making me old before my time. I found a gray hair the other day, and I blame you."

"What are you, thirteen?" Caius asked skeptically. "If that?"

"Oy! I'm fourteen," Pip replied in a tone of deep offense. "What are you, sixty?"

"It certainly feels like it sometimes," Caius told him.

On the fourth day, he returned to Decian. The members of Ishumi's pagan army had scattered throughout the city. Decian was staying at the safehouse where he and Caius had sheltered before, along with Saleene, Zuri, Traban, and several others.

Caius walked into his lover's arms with abject relief, burying his face against Decian's shoulder and taking a moment to soak in the fact that they were both, *somehow*, still alive.

"Hello," Decian murmured against his ear. "Missed you."

"So much," Caius agreed, the exhaustion of the past few hectic days crashing over him like a wave. "Tell me — do they still make that horrible lentil stew here?"

"Mm-hmm," Decian said. "What's the matter? Are you tired of pies made with sparrow's tongues and wine with gold flakes in it?"

"Unutterably," Caius told him, not moving from Decian's arms. Eventually, he dragged himself away. "Let me go get a bowl, and then we're going to need to talk about what comes next."

TWENTY

Caius sat at a rickety table with Saleene, Zuri, and Decian, shoveling grayish green slop into his mouth as the others threw ideas back and forth.

"A lot of people in the southern part of Eburos speak Alyrion as a second language," Saleene was saying.

"Maybe so," Zuri put in, "but the priests in the temples also turn little boys into eunuchs. At least, that's what people say."

Caius had resolved to stay out of the decision regarding their future home as much as possible, wanting Decian to have the freedom to choose. Even so, he couldn't help the way his stomach flipped at the idea of returning to that wild and magical place where he'd nearly died as a young soldier.

"You're looking a bit pale there, Caius," Saleene observed critically. "Is the stew not to your liking?"

"I'm fine," he said. "Long week, that's all."

"My mother thinks we should go to Kulawi." Decian had been fiddling with something under the table. He lifted it, revealing that he'd been turning a very familiar signet ring over and over in his fingers.

Zuri frowned. "Isn't that—"

"Yes," Decian said. "She gave it to me to keep, and then told Kaeto she'd thrown it into the river."

"Your mother does like to live dangerously," Saleene murmured.

Decian shrugged. "I'm leaving, so it's not as though Kaeto will ever find out she lied about it."

"Ishumi may be onto something when it comes to choosing Kulawi," Zuri said. "Think about it. After growing up with it, Decian knows enough of the language to get by, even if he's rusty. Caius, you can pick it up as you go along. And if you go to her tribe for help, you'll have kin who can help you get settled. Plus, no one there will bat an eye at you two being lovers."

"I expect they might also be better disposed toward your hellhound, Decian," Saleene said. "At least they'll know what it is, and I assume they'll have respect for it."

Decian nodded. "I suppose so. My mother's probably right about Kulawi being the best option. What do you think, Caius? You've been awfully quiet."

"I think Kulawi would be fine," Caius said. He was unable to drum up much enthusiasm for the prospect of leaving Alyrios, but at least no one in Kulawi had tried to kill him... *yet*.

"In that case, you should start thinking about the best way to travel," Zuri said. "You can get there by traveling along the river, but I really wouldn't suggest it. The mosquitoes are terrible in the lowlands. Do you have money?"

Caius grunted. "Kaeto offered me a very generous pension as a lump sum. The unspoken message of *'here, take this and get out of my way'* was fairly clear."

"Then you should travel down the coast by sea," Zuri stated firmly. "That's the best way to make the journey."

"My stomach would tend to disagree with that assessment," Caius muttered.

"You'll be stuck on a boat either way," Saleene told him.

"*Ship*," Zuri corrected. "There's a difference, haartlam."

"Yes, your point is taken," Caius told them.

"You know, it won't be the same here without you," Saleene said. "I mean, with you two gone, who's going to show up and collapse on my receiving room floor in the middle of the night?"

Caius frowned. "Are you planning on having a receiving room again soon?"

Zuri nodded. "We're reopening the brothel in a few days, yes."

"That's wonderful!" Decian said.

"It will be a relief, certainly," Saleene agreed. "The last few weeks have reminded me quite effectively of all the things I despise about army life."

"You think it will be safe to open again?" Caius asked, remembering Tullio, the spy who'd been planted in their midst.

"Well, Proclus is dead, and you two will be in an entirely different country," Saleene replied caustically. "So I figure that's most of our problems sorted."

Decian winced. "Ouch."

"She means it affectionately," Zuri assured him. She paused. "Well, except for the part about Proclus."

Silence settled over the room, as Caius returned to his stew.

"I'll miss you both," Decian blurted. He jerked his chin at Caius. "He will, too — even if he won't say it aloud."

"I'll say it." Caius tried on a smile for the pair. "We'll both miss you. I'm entirely unsure what I did to earn your friendship in the first place, but it's been an honor."

"Mostly, you paid on time and didn't abuse the girls," Saleene said, deadpan.

Zuri elbowed her. "*Stop*. It's not every day you get to have lunch with someone who deposed an emperor and saved countless innocent people from execution."

"Or suck their cock," Saleene added unrepentantly. "Though that's a job I'm more than happy to foist on someone else from now on."

Decian choked, looking as though he was either desperately attempting not to collapse into laughter, or about to pass out from mortification.

"You overcharge," Caius retorted. "Four years of my life, and it was highway robbery the entire time."

Saleene leaned back and crossed her arms, raising one haughty eyebrow. "*I* am worth every single copper, my dear Caius."

Caius' lips twitched, and he hid it behind a spoonful of the noxious lentil stew.

A week later, Kaeto's new regime still hadn't crumbled beneath the weight of his ambitions. The tentative detente between the pagans and the deimonists in the capital seemed to be holding. Meanwhile, diplomats from neighboring territories were beginning to trickle in, paying homage to the new emperor and attempting to curry favor.

Caius had returned to his house in the imperial quarter to find it dusty, but otherwise undisturbed. Being there was unpleasant. It reminded him of the many compromises he'd made over the years, while he'd watched the empire sliding toward ruin from the comfort of his position as imperial advisor. On top of that, Tertia's cranky ghost haunted the shadows. He could hear her spectral voice complaining about the dust and the mess — never mind that the insufferable woman wasn't actually dead.

He stayed only long enough to sort out the few belongings he cared enough to bring with him, and arranged to have the rest auctioned off to the highest bidder. Between the proceeds from selling most of his worldly goods and the so-called pension from the imperial coffers, he possessed more than enough coin to outfit himself and Decian for a one-way trip to an unfamiliar land.

They each had a set of trunks for traveling, along with clothing, toiletries, weapons, and enough gold to — hopefully — fund the start of a new life. Caius visited Aelio one last time to thank the man and reassure himself that Kaeto was still holding the line. Before leaving, he gave the tribuni his gray gelding.

"Payback for the use of the mule," he said dryly. They clasped forearms, and Caius added Aelio to the mental list of people who might like him well enough on a personal level, but still seemed rather relieved to see the back of him.

On the morning of their departure, Ishumi met them with a cart and a driver to take them to the docks. Caius had already paid to have their trunks transported ahead and loaded on their ship, so they had very little to carry with them—but it still would have been a very long walk to get there on foot.

Decian sat with his mother in the rear-facing passenger seat of the cart, and Caius sat facing them in the seat at the back. Ishumi had her son's arm twined with hers, holding his hand tightly.

"You're absolutely certain you won't change your mind and come with us, Maaytú?" Decian asked, and Caius heard the faint hint of unsteadiness behind the words.

They hadn't spoken of it, but Caius could only imagine how difficult it must be for him to leave Ishumi behind after finally reuniting with her.

"No, my son," Ishumi said. "Someone needs to stay here and ensure that crazy half-brother of yours doesn't turn on our people."

"I know." Decian sighed heavily. "I'm going to miss you, though. I don't want to say goodbye."

She patted his hand. "Then don't. Stay in my village, and I will come and see you as soon as I can. It's only a week's journey from here by ship and oxcart."

Decian brightened. "Promise it will be soon," he said. "Don't leave it for ages."

"I won't. I promise, my son. We won't say goodbye, only farewell for now." Ishumi lifted one hand to the chain at Decian's neck. "You still have my gift, yes?"

He nodded, and pulled the signet ring from beneath his shirt to show her, before letting it slide down again, hidden from view. "I'm not sure why you wanted me to have it, though. It's yours, not mine."

"Insurance," was all she said.

Caius doubted the Kulawi villagers would be terribly impressed by an embossed ring, but he could appreciate the desire to hedge one's bets against the future. He only hoped Ishumi was truly resigned to the fact that her son would never help her fulfill her ambitions. Decian had about as much desire to sit on the Alyrion throne as Caius had to climb on a ship for four solid days of travel by sea.

Conversation continued in fits and starts as the cart rattled down cobblestone roads toward the docks. The smell of brine and rotting fish filled the air — the same stench that had alerted Tertia to the location of the warehouse where Proclus' men had taken her and her daughters after abducting them.

Today, peace reigned in the streets after the long weeks of rioting. It was a still a fragile peace, to be sure... and yet, it was holding. Tradesmen and passersby bustled about their business. Caius could almost convince himself that this would once more become the normal state of affairs for his beloved empire.

"Here we are, Ma'am," said the driver.

They'd arrived in the busy port, at the edge of the docks. Caius could sympathize with the driver's reluctance to enter the crush of goods wagons ferrying crates and barrels to the individual ships.

"Thank you," he said, pulling the strap of his bag over his shoulder and swinging down from the vehicle. "We can get the rest of the way on foot."

"I'll walk with you," Ishumi said. "That way I can see you off properly."

Decian handed her down and hopped nimbly to the ground after her, slinging his own bag casually over a shoulder. "I think I've spent more time on boats and ships in the last month than I did in the previous twenty-six years combined," he said.

Caius looked around to get his bearings, mapping their surroundings against the description of the pier where their ship was supposed to be docked. "This way," he said, pointing toward a distinctively painted warehouse.

Ishumi walked arm-in-arm with Decian, her headscarf a bright splash of color among the drab clothing of the dockworkers. "When you get to the village, find out if old Indrii is still around. If he is, tell him from me that he was a terrible person for sending me away as Constanzus' trophy. And that he should treat you and Caius very well indeed to make up for it."

"I'll tell him that much, and probably a few more things, besides," Decian promised.

Ishumi shrugged. "Eh. I imagine he's dead by now anyway. Find my sisters. They'll make certain you're taken care of."

They passed the ochre-painted warehouse. Several men loitered by the wall, passing a pipe of something noxious-smelling back and forth. Some distance beyond the huge building, the sleek ship that would take them down the coast was moored. While far smaller than the repurposed fishing vessel where Ishumi had been hiding at sea — or the massive naval ship that had transported Caius to Eburos as a young man — it still looked like there would be plenty of room for two travelers along with whatever cargo it was carrying.

"Is that it?" Decian asked.

"Yes, that's the one," Caius said.

They crossed the open expanse of weathered wood, heading for the pier. The bustle of other parts of the dock was largely absent here. The cargo was already stowed, and the ship awaited only their arrival.

Something prickled at the back of Caius' neck — a sense of enemy eyes on him, honed by decades spent on battlefields. He turned sharply. Decian caught the movement and turned as well, frowning.

"What is it?" he asked.

Before Caius could answer, Decian grunted and staggered, clutching at a crossbow bolt protruding from the side of his chest.

TWENTY-ONE

"No!" Ishumi screamed, even as Caius flung himself at the pair. They were in the open, they had to move, before—

More arrows whizzed past, one of them burying itself in the leather bag at Caius' hip even as he dragged Decian and Ishumi sideways. He couldn't let Decian go down, had to keep him moving, had to keep him *alive*. Caius *would not* lose him now, not when they were so close to safety.

The attackers—and it had to have been the men he'd seen loitering by the warehouse—must be reloading after their first volley. Instinct propelled Caius to turn and draw steel… to try and take them down before they could fire again. But there had been at least half a dozen in the disreputable looking group, and there would be no rhitsaaru charging to his rescue now.

"*Thieves!*" Caius bellowed at the top of his lungs. "*Help!* Come quickly—they're stealing the cargo!"

He dragged the others toward the ship, praying to a god he didn't believe in with every step. *Please don't let Decian collapse, please let the bolt have missed anything vital!* Decian's staggering gait meant they were zigzagging crazily—useful whenever the attackers succeeded in reloading their crossbows, but less useful when it came to reaching the ship *quickly*.

Caius did his best to keep his body between Decian and Ishumi and their attackers, knowing he was failing.

"*Thieves!*" he thundered again for good measure, and was rewarded by the sound of shouting behind them. He chanced a lightning-quick glance over his shoulder, and saw men spilling out from the warehouse, milling around in confusion and blocking his line of sight to the assassins.

"Hurry!" he urged. "Ishumi—run ahead, tell the captain to get ready to cast off the moorings. Tell him we have gold, we'll pay extra."

"But, Decian—" Ishumi cried. "My son!"

"I have him," Caius told her. "Now, go! *Go!*"

Ishumi shot her son an anguished look before haring off across the expanse of dock still separating them from the pier. Caius hoisted Decian's arm on his uninjured side across his shoulders and dragged him stumbling after her.

"Stay with me," he begged. "Decian, *stay with me*—we have to get to the ship."

"*Kaeto,*" Decian grunted, leaning on him heavily.

Caius felt a rush of relief that he had enough breath to speak. "It has to be," he said. "He could have had our trunks followed to find out which ship we'd booked passage on. Come on; keep moving. We're so close. Just a few more steps…"

Behind them, the sound of angry shouting grew louder as more longshoremen joined the crowd coming to see what was happening. Ahead of them, Ishumi appeared on the gangplank, gesturing at them wildly.

"Hurry!" she called.

The sense of wearing a fat target on his back didn't dissipate until he'd dragged Decian aboard the ship and lowered him down to sit on the deck, the wood of the hull blocking them from the view of their attackers.

A man dressed for sailing with the bearing of a natural leader strode over to them, looking down at Decian in shock. "What in the One God's name?"

He had the accent of someone from the eastern reaches of the empire, and the bearing of someone who'd seen military service.

"We were attacked by bandits," Caius temporized. "They must have known we were carrying gold. Please— we'll pay. But we need passage for a third person, and we need to cast off *now.*"

Ishumi looked at him in shock. "*What?* No!"

Caius held her dark eyes. "Leave this ship, and you'll be dead by morning." Then he played his best card. "Ishumi—your son needs you."

The captain looked skeptical. "This was not part of the contract."

Caius delved a hand inside his jerkin and pulled out a small ring of keys. "Believe me, it's not how we'd intended to spend our morning, either. But I have to point out that the gold these men are after is in your hold now, captain." He handed the keys to Ishumi. "Please take the captain to the hold and pay him whatever seems reasonable for the extra trouble. Our trunks are the ones made of ironwood with maker's marks in the shape of an eagle in flight. Also, do you have someone aboard who acts as a physician or medic?"

"No one qualified to deal with anything like this," the captain said. "I'll send our herbalist."

"Thank you," Caius said, his hand still clasped on Decian's shoulder in an attempt to ground him. "But please, get this ship moving before anything else."

The captain scowled, giving a reluctant nod. "Come along, Madame."

Only when they'd left, and the sound of barked orders flying back and forth across the deck reached him, did Caius let himself dismiss the crisis of the assassins in favor of the crisis of Decian's injury. He grabbed a dagger from his belt and started cutting his lover's tunic away.

"Can you breathe?" he asked, knowing that a punctured lung was still the greatest threat after Caius had forced him to run to get to the ship.

Decian gave a tight, affirmative nod. His face was pasty beneath his dusky complexion, but his lips weren't turning blue. Caius reminded his own lungs to breathe, and lifted a hand to cup Decian's cheek for a moment.

"Good," he said. "That's good. Don't try to speak. Stay still and try not to move your arm at all."

The deck shifted subtly under him, sending Caius' stomach into an unwelcome flip and roll as the ship moved away from the pier. Sailors called back and forth, hauling on the rigging until the sails billowed out, catching the wind. And it was no good—Caius lunged for the railing and expelled his paltry stomach contents over the edge and into the sea below. He retched until there was nothing left, and then spat twice and slithered down to kneel next to Decian again.

"Fuck," he rasped, and went back to removing Decian's torn tunic so he could see the extent of the damage.

The crossbow bolt had entered through Decian's left pectoral, but when Caius carefully lifted his arm, he could make out the bulge of the metal tip beneath the skin, just below his armpit.

"I think the bolt hit one of your ribs and slid along it," he said, still supporting the arm to keep its weight off the protruding arrow tip. "It's bleeding, but not gushing. I don't dare try to pull it out, though, or that could change."

"Want... to... shift..." Decian forced out between gritted teeth.

Alarm clawed at Caius. "*No.*" He grasped Decian's other shoulder and squeezed. "Decian, you mustn't. The rhitsaaru is shaped differently—if you try it, the pressure of your shoulder blade could push this bolt right into your lung. Also, we're on an Alyrion-crewed ship. The captain swore on the One God. They can't learn what you are."

The look Decian gave him was helpless with agony, but he nodded. Caius let out the breath he was holding.

"We're going to bandage this up tight and get you something for the pain," he said. "These things are designed to do more damage coming out than going in. The first port we come to, we'll find a surgeon. They'll probably want to push it the rest of the way through rather than pulling it out backwards."

"Bloody... butchers..." Decian rasped, rather pointedly—recalling Caius' usual description of physicians and surgeons.

"Normally I'd agree," Caius told him. "But this should make a nice, clean wound if we can keep it stable until then. You'll heal, Decian. You're young and strong, and for a torso shot, this isn't positioned badly. Give it a year, and you'll barely know it ever happened."

He was on the cusp of babbling, weak with reaction and relief that at least it hadn't been worse. They'd managed to get away — if not cleanly, then at least without assassins storming onto the ship with them.

Ishumi returned, accompanied by a slender, stoop-shouldered man with dark hair and darting eyes. He was carrying a box, and his eyes landed immediately on the protruding crossbow bolt.

"Please tell me you have bandages in there," Caius said.

The man nodded. "We should bind that and move him to a bunk. Whatever you do, don't try to remove it."

"I know," Caius told him. "I have more experience than I'd like with battlefield medicine. For what it's worth, it hasn't hit his lung. I think it slid along a rib. Do you have anything for the pain?"

The sailor nodded. "For your stomach, too, if you want it. I recognize that look you're wearing."

"Only if it won't also put me to sleep," Caius said.

"It would, sorry to say. Here, support him for me so I can bandage him up."

Between the three of them, they got Decian's wound stabilized as best they could, and carefully levered him to his feet. He could still walk, much to Caius' relief, so they led him slowly across the deck and down into the ship's belly. The passenger quarters were nothing like the pleasant cabin where Ishumi had been staying, on the ship anchored off the coast of Osca. But there were bunks, and they didn't appear to be sharing the space with a large rat population.

The herbalist, whose name was Pieter, fed Decian a concoction that put him out like a snuffed candle within fifteen minutes. He left them with instructions to watch Decian closely and make sure he didn't move too much in his sleep. Once they were alone, Ishumi sank to the deck with her face in her hands.

"He should recover," Caius offered, perching on the edge of the bunk and taking Decian's hand. "A decent physician will be able to get that bolt out of him without doing further damage. It could have been worse."

Ishumi looked up. Her cheeks were wet.

"*Kaeto*. That snake," she hissed. "That fork-tongued, poisonous *viper*."

"It's my fault for having trusted him a step too far," Caius said tiredly. The ship rolled over a larger than average wave, and his treacherous stomach lurched. He swallowed, trying to keep everything down.

"No," Ishumi said. "It's my fault."

Caius shook his head. "If you hadn't marched on the capital, Proclus would still be in power. Pagans would still be dying. There would have been civil war."

"What if Kaeto lied about protecting the pagans, too?" Ishumi asked bitterly.

Caius considered that for a moment, but dismissed it. "No. Eliminating you and Decian was in his best interest. But quelling the unrest caused by the pagan persecution is also in his best interest. Unlike Proclus, Kaeto is too wily to want to rule over ashes and graves."

She sighed heavily. "I hope you're right."

"Come with us to your village," Caius told her. "We'll regroup and let Decian recover. You can always decide later what you want to do from there."

Caius had been giving a lot of thought lately to his dreams of an idyllic country life with Decian. He didn't know if the sort of place he was picturing even existed in Kulawi... but at least there, they could be together openly, without fear of violence or persecution. It was enough. He was done with war... with politics and scheming.

No more.

"Yes," Ishumi said wistfully. "My village."

"Look at it this way," he said, rubbing his thumb absently over Decian's knuckles. "At least if Indrii's still alive, you'll be able to shout at him in person."

She huffed—the barest breath of laughter. "Yes. I suppose there's that."

They sat with Decian, the hours passing in restless monotony. He was still resting more or less comfortably, thanks to whatever concoction Pieter had provided, and his bleeding had slowed to almost nothing.

The sound of boots against wood roused Caius from his fugue state, and he straightened as the captain appeared in the passenger quarters, looking thunderous. Caius rose to meet him, the sinking feeling in his gut having little to do with his seasickness.

"What is it, Captain?" he asked, dreading the answer.

"There is another vessel," the captain snapped, biting off each word. "*Following us.* It is time for you to tell me the truth of what is happening. You've put my ship and my crew at risk, and I *will* know why."

TWENTY-TWO

Caius let out a slow breath. Ishumi looked at him, wide-eyed. He'd refused to devote as much mental energy to this possibility as he should have, foolishly assuming Kaeto would have given up once his assassination attempt had failed to do more than wound Decian.

He'd already lied to the captain, relying on a story of bandits and the promise of generous payment to keep him from throwing the three of them summarily off his ship. He could continue to prevaricate, spinning a tale of pirates or some such, but the prospect suddenly felt like wading deeper into quicksand.

If the captain thought pirates were chasing his ship, the obvious thing to do would be to make for the nearest port with all speed. They'd been planning on doing that anyway, so they could find a physician for Decian — but it would, by definition, be an Alyrion port. And if Kaeto was truly this serious about seeing them dead, docking at an Alyrion port would be suicide.

He closed his eyes, opening them again a moment later to meet the captain's angry gaze.

"What flag is the pursuing ship flying?" Caius asked.

"The imperial flag of Alyrios," the captain replied. "No more deflection. Tell me what is going on, and explain to me why I shouldn't throw the three of you overboard right now."

The man's gray eyes snapped with barely controlled rage, and the worst part was, Caius couldn't blame him.

He gestured at Ishumi and Decian. "You're looking at the true empress of Alyrios, along with Constanzus' eldest and only legitimate son — the rightful heir to the empire," Caius said tiredly.

"I *beg* your pardon?" the captain snapped.

"It's true," Caius told him. "Before he wed the Lady Stasia, Emperor Constanzus wed a fifteen-year-old Kulawi girl as part of an agreement meant to stave off the prospect of Alyrios rolling right over Kulawi, as it had done to so many other nations. He brought her back to the capital, but the court wouldn't countenance the marriage. Constanzus was still young himself at the time, and his advisors managed to bully him into expelling her from Amarius and pretending the whole thing never happened."

The captain stared between the three of them, openly gaping. "You expect me to believe this fantastical tale?"

"I can't force you to believe it," Caius told him. "But even back then, Constanzus was a fool. He'd given Ishumi an imperial signet ring bearing a seal of their union, and no one got it back from her before she was driven out. She was already pregnant by then."

He reached over and eased the chain from around Decian's neck. The younger man didn't even stir. Caius lifted the ring, presenting it to the captain while Ishumi looked on warily. The man took it, frowning over the embossed lion and hound.

"Decian wasn't raised to rule," Caius continued. "He has no desire for the throne. When Kaeto deposed his older brother, we made a bargain with him—Decian would disappear and never become a problem. In exchange, he would agree to let Ishumi stay at court as an advisor, and enact moderate policies designed to keep the peace within the empire's borders."

"And, of course, he also agreed to allow Decian safe passage back to my homeland," Ishumi added in a venomous tone.

Caius scrubbed a hand over his face and met the captain's eyes again. "Quite honestly, the smartest thing you could do is kill all three of us and hand our bodies over to the men chasing us. There's a possibility they might still kill you and your crew as a precaution against future rumormongering, but there's a possibility they wouldn't. I'd try to stop you, of course—but I'm only one man."

The captain was silent and still for a long moment. Then, very deliberately, he handed the ring to Ishumi, who closed her hand around it and pressed it to her heart.

"God help me, what a tale," the captain murmured.

Caius remained silent.

The man's shoulders rose and fell on a deep breath. "Perhaps it's telling that I can't even drum up much skepticism about your story. This empire has been sliding into corruption for years. I saw it when I was in the navy, and I've seen it as a merchantman, as well."

"We've all seen it," Caius said, the weight of his own complicity over the years resting heavily on his shoulders.

The captain gave a slow nod. "Very well. The ship chasing us is faster than we are, so I'm probably signing all of our death warrants by doing this. But I will attempt to get an innocent woman and her son to safety, because it's the right thing to do. I assume Alyrion ports are out of the question?"

Gratitude clogged Caius' throat for a moment. He coughed to clear it. "I expect so, yes. And I assume we'll never make it to Kulawi before they catch up to us. Which is closer, Utrea or Eburos?"

"With these winds? Eburos, by perhaps half a day," the captain replied. "The port of Rhyth sits at the southernmost point of the island, and Eburos as a whole isn't well disposed toward the empire. They'd probably accept you as political asylum seekers."

"Thank you," Ishumi said. She was weeping.

"Don't thank me," the captain told her. "I have serious doubts about our ability to get you there before we're caught."

"It's conceivable the emperor's ship will abandon the chase if we can make it to Eburosi waters," Caius said. Privately, he wouldn't have put money on that—but it was still a possibility.

"I suppose it depends on how motivated our new emperor is to see you dead," the captain replied. "Unfortunately, from where I'm standing, he seems *very* motivated. Stay here. I'll see to the course change and inform you when there's anything worth passing on."

Once he'd left, Ishumi turned to Caius. She was still clutching the ring. Salty tracks dampened her cheeks, but not a hint of tears could be heard in the steel of her voice when she spoke.

"I will not allow Kaeto to have me," she said. "I was traded once to an emperor already, as though I were a sack of goods and my body was not my own property. It will not happen again. If they catch us, I will slit my wrists and throw myself into the ocean before I allow that bastard the satisfaction of executing me. I rely on you to ensure Decian doesn't end up in his treacherous half-brother's hands either."

Caius didn't allow himself to think too closely about exactly what she was asking of him. "I don't think capturing us is the goal, for what it's worth. However, Decian makes his own choices. He should be awake to make them, though. No more painkillers strong enough to knock him out. I'll find the herbalist and see if he has something milder."

Ishumi hesitated for a long moment before nodding. "Agreed."

The slight, disconcerting shift to his balance that signaled the ship altering course sent Caius' stomach roiling with fresh nausea. He gulped, and Ishumi handed him a bucket without comment. Caius heaved a couple of times, but nothing came up. Flopping down on the edge of the bunk again, he leaned his elbows on his knees and curled forward.

"Fucking Eburos," he muttered, before reminding himself it was far more likely they'd all end up dying at sea.

TWENTY-THREE

Decian gritted his teeth and accepted Caius' help to swing up into a sitting position on the narrow ship's bunk. The gentle rocking that had been a source of hazy comfort when he was drugged out of his mind was growing into an unpleasant pitching and rolling sensation. It wasn't doing wonders for his already fragile equilibrium, to put it mildly.

"What's wrong with the sea?" he slurred, wincing as the crossbow bolt stuck in the side of his chest shifted painfully.

Caius steadied him, while his mother knelt at his feet and placed a hand on his thigh.

"We have a number of new problems," Caius said, using an extremely even tone of voice that meant things were about to go to shit.

Decian closed his eyes, only to open them again when it made the vertigo worse. "Tell me," he muttered.

"That snake Kaeto has sent a ship after us," his mother said. "We've changed course for Eburos, because it's closer. But the other vessel is still closing on us quickly."

The last dregs of fragile hope Decian had been holding onto circled the drain and disappeared. "Oh." He blinked a few times, trying to get his wits in some sort of working order. "What's that got to do with the boat rocking?"

"There's a storm ahead," Caius told him. "The ship's captain seems to think our best chance is to sail straight into it, and hope we fare better than the other ship."

Decian digested this for several moments. "That sounds like a shit strategy. Are you and this captain related, by any chance?"

"Not to my knowledge," Caius said. "He seems like a good sort, though. Honorable."

"I hate him already." Decian lifted a hand to the tightly wrapped bandages circling his chest and shoulder. At least the blood staining them seemed to be dry, rather than fresh. "So, what's our plan?"

His head was admittedly still pretty muzzy, but the look Caius and his mother exchanged seemed awfully loaded, somehow.

"I'm sorry, Decian," Caius said, "but I think we're in the captain and crew's hands now. Either Kaeto's ship will catch us, or it won't. Either we'll capsize in the storm, or we won't."

Decian looked at him for a long moment, then turned his gaze to his mother. "Maaytú?"

She held his eyes with her wide, dark ones. In the low light of the ship's hold, her irises and pupils blended into an undifferentiated ocean of blackness. "My son... I won't allow Kaeto's men to capture me." She hesitated. "And you shouldn't either."

It took him a moment to parse her meaning. When he did, the cold, dead feeling swelling inside him grew larger. "Caius?" he asked. "Are you telling me if the other ship catches us, you won't fight until you drop? Because if so, I don't believe you."

"No." Caius shook his head and cupped Decian's cheek with a warm, callused hand. "I will fight for you both with my last breath. But this time, it's likely that I'll fail."

Decian leaned into the contact, staring unblinkingly at Caius' hazel eyes as his mind went abruptly and utterly blank. They were both asking, without asking, for him to make a decision about something that no one should ever have to decide ahead of time.

He thought of every time in his life that he'd believed he was about to die, and swallowed.

"You say shifting form might kill me," he said slowly. "If they come for us and you have to fight, I'll shift anyway. If it kills me, it kills me. And if it doesn't, I'll fight by your side, win or lose."

The dampness shining in his lover's eyes was something Decian had never thought to see. Caius blinked it away and nodded.

"Together, then," he said, before tearing his gaze away to look down at Decian's mother. "Ishumi, I can't force you. But as your son's lover, I'm asking you. Please don't make him watch you die by your own hand."

His mother was crying, her eyes red-rimmed and bloodshot. She clutched Decian's leg as though it was her only tether to reality. "Only if they are right in front of me, ready to take me away, and you are already dead, my son," she promised.

Decian wanted to weep with her, but it wouldn't help, and he could only imagine how painful it would be with the arrow stuck in his flesh. The moment was broken by the muffled sounds of shouting and pounding footsteps above their heads. All three of them froze, waiting to see what would happen next.

A young boy ran into the passenger berths. He was barely older than Pip and soaked from head to foot, panting like he'd just run a footrace.

"Cap'n says the enemy ship is throwing grappling hooks!" he said in a rush. "He says you should hide in the cargo hold!"

The lad turned and sprinted back the way he'd come without waiting for an answer. Caius dipped his head as though gathering himself. Decian leaned forward and kissed him. Taken by surprise, Caius made a startled noise into the kiss before responding, taking control and plundering Decian's lips for far too short a time.

When he pulled back, Decian grasped the nape of his neck. "I love you, you horrible, foul-tempered old arsehole."

Caius caught his breath. "You brought me back to life, Decian." The words were a hoarse rasp.

Decian swallowed back the sob that wanted to escape, forcing himself to focus on practicalities. "We need to be topside," he managed to choke out. "How's your seasickness?"

Caius cleared his throat. "Better than it was when the sea was calm, perversely enough."

Decian nodded, and turned to his mother. It hurt to look at her. "Maaytú? I love you. I'm so glad we found each other again."

She clasped his hand in both of hers. "I love you, my son. I'm so sorry. This is all my fault."

"No. This is Constanzus' fault," Decian told her. "And Proclus', and Kaeto's. Never yours, Maaytú."

The sound of thumping came from above. The ship lurched, its hull groaning.

"Time to go," Caius said. He rose, checking his sword belt, and leaned down to pull Decian's good arm over his shoulder.

The crossbow bolt was hot, throbbing agony when he moved, but it wasn't the worst pain he'd ever suffered. That honor went to a mangled back crisscrossed with open wounds from a vicious flogging. For now, his legs still worked—though they might have worked better if the deck wasn't moving beneath them like a bucking horse.

Caius supported him up the narrow steps leading to the main deck, his mother following behind with a hand on his back to steady him. Torrential rain soaked them as soon as they reached the opening cut from the deck. It was chilly, and the droplets stung like needles. Up here, the pitching seas made things even more disorienting. The wood beneath Decian's boots was slippery. Crewmen hurried to and fro, shouting orders and responses.

Ignoring the pain in his chest, Decian craned around, trying to peer through the sheeting rain. Then he saw the other ship.

It was close. Way, way too close.

Caius must have seen it, too. "We should stay out of the crew's way!" he called over the din.

Squinting, Decian made out several sailors huddled around an iron hook caught on the railing. They were sawing away at the rope attached to it with wickedly curved blades.

"Is that a grappling hook?" he called, shuddering when his injury protested the force behind the shout.

Caius and his mother half-dragged him to the far side of the ship.

"Yes!" his mother said. "They'll try to hook the railings and rigging, and use them to draw us close enough for boarding!"

As they watched, a second four-pronged hook came winging through the air during a lull in the sheeting rain, snagging high up in the web of heavy ropes attached to the mast. The ship slewed, and Decian grunted with pain as he staggered against Caius' sturdy bulk. Next to them, his mother grasped the railing with a white-knuckled grip.

The ship was being reeled in like a fish on a line. The other vessel grew huge in Decian's view, even as the wind and rain picked up, howling around them. It dripped in Decian's eyes faster than he could blink it away. His body felt like ice.

We're going to die like this, he thought.

"*Wave!*" cried a voice from farther down the deck, bellowing loud enough to be heard over the storm and the groan of the ship's bones. "*Brace!*"

Caius cursed sharply and bore Decian to the deck, grabbing at a coil of rope lying next to them and wrapping it around his arm. His other arm circled Decian's waist in a death grip. "Ishumi!" he yelled, and Decian's mother fell to the deck, grabbing Caius from the other side.

The arrow wound throbbed at the sudden jostling, taking Decian's breath away. Beneath them, the deck seemed to rise and rise, as though the entire ship was poised to leave the ocean behind and take flight into the sky. If not for Caius' arm tangled with the rope, all three of them would have slid down the deck like children sliding down an icy hill in winter.

The heaving deck started its sickening journey downward, leaving Decian's stomach somewhere in the sky above. A deafening boom shuddered through the hull, and half of the ocean arced over the deck railing and crashed onto them. Decian would have flailed and panicked if not for the arm circling him like a steel band. It felt like drowning, but it was probably only seconds before the wave broke, pouring across the deck and leaving them sopping and coughing.

"All right?" Caius choked out.

"Alive," his mother croaked. "Decian?"

Decian couldn't speak around the pain caused by coughing, but he nodded. The fickle rain lightened again. Decian's eyes widened as he took in the other ship's mast—tipping and tipping, falling toward their ship's deck like a felled tree.

"Great goddess!" his mother cried.

The huge wooden pole with its tangled sails and rigging crashed into the railing, shattering it. The ship heaved under the sudden weight of the fallen mast, tipping sharply before righting itself more slowly. Beside Decian, Caius went very, very still.

He turned and met Decian's eyes.

"It's a bridge. I'm going across while they're distracted," he said.

Decian's heart stuttered and skipped as he realized what Caius intended. "What? No!" he cried, heedless of the way the arrow shifted and tore inside his flesh.

But Caius was already untangling his arm from the rope, wrapping it around Decian's good arm and handing the end to his mother so she could do the same.

Caius climbed to his feet on the swaying deck and paused, looking down at Decian with an expression of agonized affection on his craggy face.

"I love you," he said simply... and then he was jogging across the treacherous wooden expanse of planks toward the collapsed mast, skidding and staggering.

Decian couldn't breathe. He struggled with the heavy loops of rope, heedless of his injury as he tried to jerk his arm free.

"Decian!" his mother cried, tugging at him—trying to keep him from following.

He jerked away from her, finally succeeding in getting free from the entangling rope. Staggering upright, he lurched forward, having to catch himself repeatedly with his good arm as he stumbled after Caius. But his lover was already over the destroyed railing, crab-crawling along the heavy wooden beam connecting the two ships, pausing to clutch at it whenever a wave sent the precarious bridge swaying.

It was like being trapped in one of those nightmares where his feet were stuck in invisible mud, holding him back as he tried to run. Through the dancing spots in his vision, Decian could see the confusion on the other ship. A handful of bodies lay on the deck, rolling limply back and forth as the ship swayed. Others were frantically hacking at ropes and fallen sails, the grappling hooks forgotten.

Caius reached the far end of the mast and leaped onto the deck, sword drawn. Several crewmen cried out when they noticed him, but he was already hacking at the ropes attached to the grappling hooks. The first one snapped, the line attached to the hook tangled in their boat's rigging falling loose. He was working on the second one when the first two men converged on him, also wielding swords.

Decian stared in despair at the fallen mast, knowing he had no chance of negotiating it in his human form. Not now, not like this—with an arrow sticking out of him and his chest pulsing with fresh blood. He turned his fractured focus inward, reaching for the shift, and collapsed to the deck, gasping in excruciating pain. His body twisted back into its normal form, leaving him so lightheaded he could barely see.

"My son!" his mother slid to her knees at his side, her hands hovering over his bandages.

"Help me up!" he tried to gasp, but it was only the shape of words.

Slender hands tugged at him, and he managed to get to his knees, vision wavering dangerously before it settled. The rain was picking up again, and the wind as well—but Decian peered beyond the crushed railing in time to see Caius hack at the rope of the second grappling hook as several more men converged on him.

The captain ran up to the damaged section of railing next to them. "He's cut us free of the hooks!" he bellowed. "Full sail! Pull away from the downed mast!"

No, Decian thought, as driving rain obscured his view of the figures descending on Caius. *No, no, no...*

The ship's structure groaned as though it was being pulled apart at the seams. The huge wooden beam scraped along the deck, tearing at the planks as it went. His mother pulled at Decian's arm with her full strength, dragging him away from the crushed and mangled area.

Under the force of the heavy winds, their speed picked up by increments, more and more of the fallen mast disappearing through the gap it had made with a terrible shriek of protest, until the end slid free and the whole thing crashed into the sea. The ship heaved and bobbed beneath them, buffeted by wind and wave.

"Caius," Decian whispered, straining against his mother's desperate hold on his arm. His wound screamed in agony, warm blood soaking the bandages already sopping with cold rainwater. He fell to his knees, staring at an imperial attack ship he could no longer see through the downpour. Heedless of the crossbow bolt tearing at his insides, his voice rose to a hoarse cry, and then a full-throated howl.

"Caius! *Caius!*"

TWENTY-FOUR

It was daylight again—the second time sunlight had stabbed through his closed eyelids since this ordeal had begun, he was fairly certain. Caius' lips were cracked, and something was badly wrong with his left shoulder. Something *new* was wrong with it, to be clear. The hard surface beneath him rocked gently, and it was just as well he didn't have a single spare ounce of liquid left in his body, or he might have been tempted to throw up.

He lay tangled in heavy rope, one loop of which was uncomfortably close to choking him. If it would do the job properly, that would be a blessing at this point. But it was just tight enough to give him the panicky feeling of strangulation, without actually accomplishing the task of putting him out of his misery.

An unwelcome thought intruded, sending his pulse thundering. The other ship. He needed to get up and look… see if Decian and his mother had escaped…

His muscles jerked weakly, without the faintest hint of coordination. The pain in his shoulder flared. Dislocated? It was probably dislocated. There was no barbarian axe lodged in the bone this time. That had been before.

His head ached. He needed to get up and check whether Decian got away safely… if only it weren't so hot. Hadn't he been cold before?

It had been raining.

A storm.

That was why he'd tangled himself in this bloody be-damned rope. No mast. No way to control the ship. And everyone on board was dead anyway. He'd killed some of them himself. The storm got the rest of them, he assumed, or else someone would have showed up to finish him off by now.

That would have been helpful, actually.

But right now, he really needed to get up and make sure Decian had made it away safely. Hadn't he meant to do that before? He blinked sandpaper eyelids open, only to be dazzled by the sun. He was certain he'd meant to check earlier. Decian's wound had started bleeding again. They shouldn't have moved him from belowdecks. Caius needed to check on him...

Something large passed overhead, momentarily blotting out the sun. Caius tried to get his eyes working, but to no avail. A few moments later, it happened again. A screech like an angry, giant bird of prey pierced his ears, chasing away the rhythmic *shush-shush* of his own heartbeat. Strong wind buffeted his body, right before a heavy thud reverberated through the deck planks. The ship swayed alarmingly, sending his stomach rolling again before it gradually settled.

Maybe something from the pagan afterlife had come to take his soul away. If rhitsaaru dragged you to the endless void of the underworld, was there something else that came down from the sky to take you to a better place after death? If so, that was a surprise. He wouldn't have thought his soul would qualify for something like that.

Thoughts of the rhitsaaru inevitably led to thoughts of Decian. It occurred to him that even if he had enough strength to get up and check for the other ship, whether it was there or not, Caius would never see Decian alive again. If Caius had failed to free Decian's ship, he'd almost certainly be dead by now. If he'd escaped, that meant he was already gone—and it seemed obvious enough that Caius would die soon.

The last time he'd seen Decian was the last time he would ever see Decian. The realization brought tears to his eyes. Trying to blink them away finally succeeded in clearing his vision enough to see more than dazzling light and vague shadows surrounding him.

There was a dragon crouched on the deck.

He blinked several more times in rapid succession.

There was still a dragon on the deck.

It was a massive beast, with scales like glittering amethyst. It was wearing... a saddle? And it was looking back at him, with almond-shaped eyes the same blue-violet shade as fine, polished iolite.

So focused was he on the dragon, he completely missed the presence of the woman until she crouched in front of him, blocking his line of sight. She had dark hair pulled back in tight braids, though wisps had escaped, leaving her looking windblown. Her eyes were an unusual light brown that almost seemed lit from within by flecks of gold. She was dressed in scout's leathers, and she pulled a gleaming bronze dagger from a sheath at her belt as he looked on, slack-jawed and witless.

"You speak Alyrion?" she asked, in a passable accent.

Caius nodded dumbly.

She started sawing at the ropes tangling him, and in a few minutes, he was free. Sheathing the knife, she unslung a waterskin from her shoulder and raised the spout to his lips. Caius drank greedily, rivulets escaping to slide through the crust of salt covering his skin. After a few moments, she pulled it away.

"That's enough for now," she said. "What's your name, soldier?"

"C—" he tried, only to descend into coughing. "C—Cai—"

More coughing, and this time the pain from his dislocated shoulder nearly made him pass out.

"Caius Oppita?" the woman offered. "You match the physical description, anyway. Well, Caius, it appears you're quite a lucky man. There are people waiting for you in Rhyth. Let's get that shoulder in its socket where it belongs, and we'll get you back to them."

He couldn't reply… couldn't do anything except lie slumped against the hull as she grasped his left arm and started applying traction to the shoulder joint. And then he really *did* pass out.

A heavy lurch brought him back to himself some unknown amount of time later. He was lying on his stomach, draped across scaly shoulders like a sack of grain. The world was moving crazily around him, wind rushing past his ears as the deck of the ship fell away from beneath him. The sound of great wings slicing through the air filled his hearing.

He got a dizzying view of the ocean sliding past, followed by a view of blue sky as the beast banked sharply. The damaged ship appeared in his field of vision, and he noted with relief that it floated alone in the choppy sea. There was no sign of Decian and Ishumi's ship.

The dragon dove toward the mastless wreck, and a spout of fire strafed it, setting the torn sails alight. A second pass had the deck burning as well. Distantly, Caius wondered if Proclus would have been in such a hurry to turn outward to conquest, if he'd seen what Caius had just seen. What could a group of beasts like this do to a navy?

The dragon abandoned the burning ship and its dead crew to their watery fate, its vast wings cutting through the air. The frothy waves below passed by faster and faster, making Caius so dizzy he eventually had to close his eyes. This time, he didn't open them again.

⤛⋙⤜

The next time he regained consciousness, he was on the ground and it wasn't swaying beneath him. His shoulder felt like someone had hit it repeatedly with a heavy iron bar, but it wasn't on fire the way it had been before.

Fire.

His eyes flew open. Had that been… real?

He definitely wasn't on the ship anymore. He was lying on a bed, with a proper pillow and a proper mattress. The room was lit with the warm glow of firelight, the shadows too deep for him to make out much more in the way of details.

"*Wha—?*" he tried to ask.

The sound of chair legs scraping against stone preceded a strangled cry of "*Caius?*" And then Decian was there, leaning over him. His upper body was swathed in bandages, but there was no sign of a protruding crossbow bolt. Ishumi appeared next to him, but Caius couldn't tear his eyes away from the man he'd feared he'd never see again—at least in this life.

"Decian," he rasped, a bare exhalation.

With a choked cry, Decian folded forward against Caius' chest, clutching at him with the arm that wasn't bound tightly to his side with bandaging.

"It's all right," Decian managed around hitching sobs, burying his face against Caius' uninjured shoulder. "We're in Rhyth, on Eburos. We're safe. Oh, gods, Caius. It's finally going to be all right now."

Caius lifted a heavy arm to wrap around his lover's shoulders, closed his eyes, and held on tight.

EPILOGUE

One Year Later

Caius lay on the bed he shared with Decian, listening to the birds chirping in the trees beyond the window of the squat, tile-roofed farmhouse. Dawn hadn't yet begun to paint the eastern edge of the sky with pink and blue, which meant there was no reason for either of them to be up quite yet.

Decian yawned and stretched, his lithe body sliding against Caius' battle-scarred one. Not that Decian didn't have his own scars—the ones on his back now joined by a puckered indentation near the edge of his chest, where an Eburosi healer had pulled out an Alyrion crossbow bolt. It had healed well, for what it was. One of the many benefits of youth, Caius supposed.

For his part, Caius' bad shoulder hadn't been improved by also being dislocated a year ago, but he supposed it was moderately useful in his new life to have a reliable predictor of rain and cold weather.

"'S it time to get up now?" Decian mumbled into the side of Caius' neck, sending a pleasant shiver of gooseflesh across the sensitive skin.

"Not yet," Caius told him, letting his right hand stroke up and down the length of Decian's flank. Decian hummed in appreciation and rolled his hips, rutting gently against Caius' body.

Soon, they would need to rise and see to the day. The sprawling farm lay a short distance outside the city of Rhyth, nominal capital of southern Eburos. It was owned by an absentee landlord—a man who'd struggled to keep up with the changing times on the island, after slave labor had been outlawed some twenty years previously. Not long after Decian, Ishumi, and Caius' request for permanent asylum had been granted, the Rhytheeri ruling council had helped facilitate Decian and Caius' employment as managers on the property.

Neither of them had agricultural experience—not beyond growing up in the country, and, in Decian's case, a brief stint as houndsman of a royal kennel. But Caius understood organization, and Decian was utterly tireless now that he'd finally achieved his dream of honest work, enough food, a roof over his head, and no one trying to kill him.

Between them, they'd instituted a sharecropping system with the locals to ensure the cropland was utilized to its best benefit, in addition to starting a sideline in breeding and training hunting dogs. The stables had been in a shambles, but as they were repaired and upgraded, Caius had begun to acquire a few mares. He was currently in negotiations for a yearling colt that, in his opinion, had good prospects as a breeding stallion.

"Nope," Decian said, stretching again and rolling up to straddle Caius' hips. "It's no good. I can't sleep. You're too distracting."

Caius raised an eyebrow in the dark, grasping Decian's hips to hold him in place. "*I'm* distracting?"

"Mm-hmm," Decian said, curling his hips until his cock brushed against Caius' morning erection.

Caius reached up with his right hand and guided Decian's lips down to his. Ignoring the fact that both of them had morning breath, he teased his way into Decian's mouth and began to plunder it with ruthless efficiency. Decian groaned and went pliant in his arms, their pricks trapped and rubbing against their bellies.

"You're too good at that," Decian said breathlessly, after breaking away from Caius' sustained assault. "There should be a law."

"There might be," Caius said. "I suppose we should probably find out, at some point."

From what Caius had been able to gather, up until the last generation or so, Eburos hadn't been any more welcoming to inverts than Alyrios was. That had begun to change after several people high in the ruling class had engaged in very public relationships with people of the same gender—most notably, the infamous Wolf-Priest of Draebard, whose four-legged army had come uncomfortably close to ending Caius' life on a beach not so very far from here.

Whatever the case, while Caius and Decian didn't publicly flaunt their relationship, no one in this part of the world was going to come pounding down their door in the night to examine their sleeping arrangements.

This was just as well, since Decian had risen to his knees again in the faint glow from the embers of the banked fire. He took both of their hard pricks in his hand, fisting them up and down with lazy movements. Caius let his eyes slide shut, focusing on the slow build of pleasure in his gut.

"Mm, that's good," he murmured, thrusting up in counterpoint to feel his stiff, sensitive flesh sliding against Decian's.

"So good," Decian agreed.

The day still lay ahead of them, and their lazy lovemaking couldn't last forever. When Decian spilled slick seed over his hand, turning the slide of Caius' cock hot and silky, Caius followed him, pulsing and jerking through a languid, full-body release.

Decian flopped down next to him with a heartfelt moan, and reached for the clean rag they kept on the bedside table to clean them up.

"Do you have to go into the city for training this morning?" he asked.

Not long after Caius had awoken from his ordeal on the Alyrion vessel, the young dragonrider who'd been sent to find him at sea had showed up at his bedside.

Judging by the number of dead bodies on that ship, she'd said, *you must really know your way around a sword. Want to come train recruits part-time?*

He'd agreed without even thinking.

"Not until midday," he told Decian. "The recruits are out on a two-day hike. They won't be back until after dawn, and the commanders will let them have a few hours of sleep before training."

"What," Decian teased, "you mean you didn't offer to go out and camp with them in the wilderness?"

"Absolutely not," Caius said. "That kind of thing is above my pay grade."

With a snort of laughter, Decian rolled into a sitting position and scrubbed his hands through his short, dark hair. "S'pose I should go gather eggs and take care of the dogs and horses. Not all of us have the morning off."

"I'll work on the accounts for a bit, and have breakfast ready when you're done," Caius said, carefully working the kinks out of his shoulder. "Check the sorrel mare for me, will you? Her off hind fetlock was swollen yesterday."

Decian grunted acknowledgement and rose to dress. Caius waited until he was finished and did the same. The morning passed pleasantly enough. It was an unseasonably warm day, so he threw open the shutters to let in some light and air while he was working on the accounts.

He and Decian were seated at the table with the mid-morning sun slanting in, eating porridge, day-old bread, and fried eggs, when a knock sounded at the door.

Caius went to answer it, only to find Decian's mother on the doorstep. "Hello, Ishumi," he said. "This is a pleasant surprise. To what do we owe the visit?"

Ishumi smiled brightly at him, the expression warming further when Decian appeared in the entryway.

"Maaytú," he said, coming forward to catch her up in a hug. "We weren't expecting you today. You must have left early to get here. Has something happened?"

She hugged him in return—rubbing his shoulders before pulling back, her smile as bright as ever. "In a manner of speaking," she said. "I have a surprise for you."

Two more figures appeared behind her in the doorway, and Caius had to blink before he could be certain his eyes weren't playing tricks. The tall, gray-eyed woman and the shorter, dark-skinned one peered past Ishumi, taking in the little farmhouse with interest.

"Hello, you two," said Saleene. "Fancy meeting you here."

Caius sliced more bread, fried more eggs, and brought out some cheese. The five of them sat around the kitchen table, passing food back and forth.

"How on earth did you find us here?" Decian asked. "As far as you knew, we were going to Kulawi."

"I sent them a message, of course," Ishumi said, with a serene smile. "It cost a fair bit to get it there, but the Rhytheeri Council is keen to open informal talks with the pagans in Alyrios. It's all under the table for now, but I thought, who better?"

Ishumi had, in fairly short order, gained a place within the government of Rhyth in an advisory capacity. To say that relations between Eburos and Alyrios were tense was an understatement. The ruling council was thrilled beyond belief to have access to someone who'd successfully raised an army under the empire's nose and used it to alter the imperial succession.

Caius turned to Saleene and Zuri, his eyebrows climbing. "Pagan representatives? Don't tell me you've turned respectable. I won't believe it for a minute."

Zuri snorted. "Respectable brothel owners, anyway."

"You were able to reopen, then?" Decian asked. "You haven't had any trouble from the palace?"

"Yes, we reopened not long after you left, and no, there's been no trouble so far," Saleene said. "Aside from the small matter of trying to have you murdered—*yet again*—Kaeto seems to be behaving himself. It hasn't been an entirely smooth road, but the protections he put in place are still there."

"And still being enforced," Zuri said. "Rather ruthlessly, in fact."

Ishumi nodded in satisfaction. "So now, we pagans are reaching across borders. It makes no sense for us to remain in isolation when we are stronger together. And that leads to the question we have for the two of you."

"Here it comes," Saleene muttered. "As if the poor sods haven't already had trouble enough for a lifetime or three."

The others ignored her.

"Caius. Decian," Zuri said. "We'd like you to join the group seeking to build ties between the Eburosi and Alyrion pagans. Shapeshifters are rare—but here, they're revered. And Caius—who better to advise on matters pertaining to Alyrios than a former imperial advisor?"

"Your talents are wasted here, raising animals and working the land," Ishumi added. "And, yes, I know you're helping with the army recruits, Caius—but come help on the political side, too. We can still change the world, even if it's not exactly how we'd originally expected to do it."

Caius looked around their cozy little farmhouse, letting the sounds of the idyllic countryside beyond the open window settle over him like a comforting cloak. He met Decian's eyes, knowing his expression conveyed his answer just as clearly as Decian's did.

"I love you dearly, Maaytú," Decian said. "And believe me, we're flattered you'd ask. But the answer is no. Not a chance in hell."

finis

The Eburosi Chronicles will continue in
Mistress of War: Book 1.

For more books by this author, visit www.rasteffan.com